MORE PRAISE 1

"*Scout's Honor* is a gripping tale of a man tricked into smuggling drugs followed by his betrayal and violence. Yet, it is also a story of the ability to rise above one's past to carve a path of honor and selflessness, a testament to the indomitable human spirit and the power of redemption. A must-read for those seeking an enthralling narrative that explores the depths of human experience."

—James Doty, *New York Times* and international bestselling author of *Into the Magic Shop: A Neurosurgeon's Quest to Discover the Mysteries of the Brain and the Secrets of the Heart*

"*Scout's Honor* is the thrilling tale of a New York real estate developer haunted by his criminal youth. The galloping narrative contrasts the protagonist's wild success with his eternal struggle to keep his crimes hidden, exploring themes of redemption, identity, and the power of secrets. Set against the competitive backdrop of Manhattan's real estate scene, the novel dives deep into the protagonist's dual life, filled with tension, moral dilemmas, and the relentless pursuit of a legacy untainted by his past. McNellis's vivid portrayal of the city and its cutthroat industry, alongside his hero's complex and admittedly flawed character, make the compelling case that no one can truly escape his past."

—Vladimir Bosanac, Co-founder & Publisher, THEREGISTRY

"A fascinating character study of a man who changes in nearly every respect except for his drive to succeed and his capacity for love. *Scout's Honor* is a compelling page turner with twists you will never expect."

—Hannah Wood, author of *Gary the Lion*

SCOUT'S HONOR

JOHN MCNELLIS

Published by: Hubbard House

Paperback ISBN-13: 978-1-7363525-4-0

Ebook ISBN-13: 978-1-7363525-5-7

For information on distribution and reprint rights, please visit www.johnmcnellis.com or email john@johnmcnellis.com.

DEDICATION

For Jamie, Jenny and Courtney

CHAPTER 1

SUMMER OF '69

EDDIE KAWADSKY GRIPPED HIS VW van's wheel as if it meant his life. Spying Roy's Marlboros, he jerked one from the crumpled pack, tried to light it as he drove north in the battered van toward Tijuana, fifty kilograms of cocaine beneath the surfboards in back. His hands shook. He tried again, and again, but his trembling fingers failed him. He somehow lit the fourth match, burning his forefinger. Then he remembered the van's cigarette lighter and jabbed the knob. Only nineteen, he'd never had a cigarette in his life. He coughed hard, struggling to hold the smoke down, inhaling again, coughing more, ransacking his memory for someone he could trust, prayer on the edge of his scattered thoughts. In his rising panic, he was blind to the yellowing brown hills soft in the late afternoon light, the wretched trailer parks scarring Mexico's coastline, and the roadside taco stands.

As his coughing subsided, he felt dizzy, but calmer. Once more, he struggled to bottle his despair and plan his way out. He punched the dashboard and swore. How had he ever let Roy Cross talk him into smuggling marijuana across the Mexican border? He had known all along the idiot's foolproof plan was worm-riddled. Yet Eddie hadn't known until that afternoon—while the pair lolled at the beach called K-39—that Roy was smuggling a fortune in cocaine, not a couple pounds of pot. And what doomsayer could have foretold the half-wit Roy's arrest in Rosarito hours before their return, leaving Eddie alone, holding the cocaine in his van? He couldn't stay in Mexico. No American car was ever safe there. And, if the shipment were stolen, he was dead.

He had to follow Roy's plan, cross the border at the appointed hour, pray Roy's bribed customs inspector was in the right line, and that the secondary inspection unit would ignore him. Even if he made it across, what next? Eddie had no idea who Roy's customers were, no way of contacting them or an inkling as to where to deliver the shipment. No matter their identity, Eddie knew what happened to those who disappointed drug lords. He had to cross the border, stash the drugs, race back to Rosarito, bail out Roy, then pray the narcotraficantes wouldn't blame him for the delay. His head swam from the nicotine, his stomach roiled from his anxiety. He pounded the plastic steering wheel.

Eddie played out scenarios—all bad—as he approached Tijuana in the humble VW van that had doubled as his home since he finished high school. He stopped outside a tumbledown tienda a half-mile from the border, locked the van, sprang inside the small shop that reeked of fried corn oil, bought a Coke, and hustled back. Forced to await his crossing's appointed hour, he frittered, opening the van's sliding door and rearranging his scant belongings: foam pad, sleeping bag, clothing, toiletries, and his books. He jammed the duffel bags further beneath the patched surfboards. He set his hamper—his father's canvas flight bag—on top, the stenciled "Lt. Commander Paul J. Kawadsky US Navy" facing the door.

Eddie relocked the van, lit another Marlboro, and stood outside, guarding it, straining to appear nonchalant, watching the cart-pushers stream by peddling everything from sombreros to fireworks to pharmaceuticals of questionable provenance. When his chaotic thoughts flashed by his father, Eddie was almost glad he'd been killed in Vietnam, certain the hard man's disgust over his son's drug-running would have been unbearable. The commander would have dismissed Eddie's need for college money with his favorite word: bullshit. Checking his nerves, he failed his father's test, his outstretched hand trembling. He tried pushing his plight from his mind, filling it with happier memories.

He found one: the warm Saturday his father took him to Edwards Air Force Base to get a peek at Lockheed's secret SR-71. When they were turned away at the gate, they drove to the Antelope Valley Soaring Club, his father rented a two-seater Schweizer sailplane, and thrilled Eddie with an hour of soaring—gliding in primordial silence—wheeling above El Mirage, seeking thermals on which to rise like gods. The overwhelmed fourteen-year-old was hooked within moments after his father let him take the stick, knowing he too would become a Navy pilot. The boy had never wanted anything so much in his life.

A toothless Indian woman selling chewing gum interrupted his reverie with a beseeching por favor. He fished in his pocket, gave her a dollar for luck, then another, but waved off the gum. A gold-toothed cab driver ghosted by, pimping the beauty of his señoritas. Eddie shook his head, but the thought of sex briefly snagged him. Then he prayed Tommy Mahoney, the crooked inspector, would be in the promised lane. Please God, let him be in Lane 7.

The fading light was smog-dust orange when he turned the ignition. Within minutes, traffic merged into a clogged artery pulsing slowly toward the border. Eddie had donned his NAVY sweatshirt and stuffed his long hair inside a baseball cap that read "Fightertown USA". He eased the van a few lanes to the left to align himself with 7, the lane Roy's foolproof plan had Tommy Mahoney in starting at 8 p.m. Six cars back he saw a middle-aged man peer out of its booth. No Tommy. "Oh, shit, shit, shit," he shouted, drawing a puzzled look from a Mexican in a rattling Plymouth across from him. "I'm so fucked."

CHAPTER 2

TWO WEEKS EARLIER

"Edward, look at you. Go wash up. We're leaving in two minutes," said beautiful Jonnie Collins, stepping from the front door of the Riviera Inn, shaking her head. Eddie had delivered on his promise to change her new Cadillac's tire in ten minutes flat. Grinning, he held the tire iron aloft—pumping it like a trophy—then dashed toward the lobby's restrooms, gleeful in his triumph.

Awaiting his return, Jonnie winced at her crumbling parking lot and the sparse desert landscaping. She ran the Riviera Inn—a weight-reducing spa on San Diego's Coronado Island that she'd founded with her husband ten years earlier—but seldom ventured outside its buildings. Her two assistants handled the small resort's day-to-day operations, while Jonnie comforted the heavyset women who struggled against its draconian diet plan. She tried her best to leaven her guests' stays with fun, teaching the resort staff—her boys—the art of pretending the Inn itself was fun, their special clubhouse. She showed her more talented boys how to clown just so during the aquatics classes, the jazzercise, the announcements, and the sing-alongs after the so-called dinner. Eddie Kawadsky was her brightest star—the tall, lanky, nineteen-year-old she envisioned running the Inn one day, knowing he had a head for figures and a riptide of ambition. She could have driven herself to her appointment with this new psychiatrist in Newport Beach, but she had a better use of her time: she could tutor her pupil.

"Let me give you some advice, Edward. Never do it again." Jonnie flicked out a fresh Kool as he eased the sapphire blue Cadillac onto northbound Highway 5.

"Do what?" Eddie glanced at her, taking in her blonde bouffant hairdo, lingering over her tanned arms and coltish legs. At forty-two, Jonnie looked like a mature fashion model. He swallowed dry, thinking her stunning. He had never admitted—even to himself—how smitten he was.

"Tires. Don't change tires or unclog sinks or toilets. You need a handyman, hire one. Do you think a millionaire knows a screwdriver from a flyswatter? No. He works with people, with ideas. Never work with your hands."

"OK." Chortling, Eddie pressed his left thigh up against the blue steering wheel and let go with his hands.

"What the hell are you doing?" she cried.

"You said not to work with my hands." He laughed. Fresh from his triumph over the flat tire, thrilled by Jonnie's undivided attention, he was happier than he'd been in weeks.

"Grab that goddamn wheel. Don't be a wiseass, young man."

Eddie drove north, along Southern California's sprawling beach towns, occasionally nodding at Jonnie's anecdote-larded lecture, leaning away from her cigarette smoke. He'd heard about her older brother—gifted with his hands, but flat broke—often enough that her epistle required little attention, especially because he knew she was wrong. Real men worked with their hands. Yet forgiving the enchanting Jonnie her mistakes was easy.

"But don't try to become a millionaire, either—they're all crooked," she persisted. "Every other one is a criminal."

"OK, got it. Work smart and get rich, but not too rich. The not-too-rich part should be a piece of cake," he joked. "Is that the building past this signal?"

"Right in here." She checked her makeup in the rear-view mirror for a third time and re-perfumed herself with Youth Dew. She waited a moment, then sighing theatrically, turned an inquiring gaze to Eddie.

"Oh, right, sorry." He scrambled out of the car and opened her door with an exaggerated bow.

"What did I say about being a smart-ass?" With a nod toward the books in the backseat, she said, "You going to study all that?"

"Yes, it's my calculus homework."

"Books are fine, Edward, but they'll only get you so far. To learn life, you have to live it. You need to live a little more, kiddo. Have some fun."

Eddie watched her disappear inside the garden-style medical building, wondering why she had to visit a psychiatrist—she was totally normal, practically perfect—and what she could possibly talk about for a whole hour? He thought Jonnie beautiful, exciting, and sometimes outrageous. He knew she liked to shock people with her wild commentary, and could usually tell when she was serious and when she expected nothing but laughter in response, yet this morning's lecture had hit home. She had to be wrong. But his father would be alive if he'd been in procurement instead of a fighter pilot. Would his grandfather be enjoying his old age if he hadn't worn himself out fixing toilets? Eddie opened his book and tried to concentrate, but drifted away from the equations, pulled by her words. No, she was wrong. If no one ever checked the oil, the world would literally grind to a halt. At length, he abandoned the universe of small numbers, switched on the engine, popped the hood, and slid out the dipstick with a practiced hand.

Her laugh spun him around.

"If I wanted to be ignored, I could have talked to my own children." Jonnie's wig was slightly bent, her eyes happy, gleaming. The appointment had gone better than she'd hoped.

"No, ma'am, I just wanted to—"

She smiled, shook her head, cigarette smoke trailing her, and walked to the passenger side. He hurried to her door and opened it, again with an awkward courtier's flair.

Jonnie's thoughts danced from her marvelous session with the doctor to the young man behind the wheel, examining him with sly sidelong glances. If she squinted, he was almost handsome. She was struck by his eyes, the bright, comprehending eyes of a gifted child wanting to please. She wished she knew more about his background. She knew he'd found himself alone on the streets at sixteen, and fretted again over how that scarred him. She had to help him. "Guess how many of our guests have had nose jobs."

"The good-looking ones?" he asked, chuckling.

"Oy, all of them." She laughed. The daughter of a pious Methodist minister, Jonnie had cheerfully stolen the slang, phrasings, and intonations of her largely Jewish clientele. "Anyway, do I know from great plastic surgeons or what? And your poor nose. Come on, don't look at me like that. Whoever broke it should be in jail. Fixing it would make you so gorgeous."

"No, I don't want to talk about that again. I need to save money for college."

"College is where the bright kids go to have the fun the dumb ones had in high school. The bigshots—the millionaires—they never went to college. You learn how to run a business on the job, not from some book. Hell, you already know almost enough to run the Inn."

"I don't know about that," Eddie said, swelling at the high praise, cocking his head to the side. But he did know how to handle the guests.

"You do need a little fun… but not with any of the girls at the Inn." She cackled. "The last thing I need is you schtupping someone's daughter."

He reddened, concentrating on the wing mirror. The last thing he would ever admit to Jonnie was how badly he wanted to schtupp someone's daughter. Deflecting her, he asked what she thought of a career as a pilot.

"I'd rather be a bus driver. They go home at night."

"What? But flying in the Navy? That's a good idea, isn't it? I have to go to Vietnam anyway. That's not bus driving." Eddie had been raised on air shows and pilot swagger. Standing at his father's side, he saw—no, felt—the awed deference lavished on the Navy's warriors. He knew second-hand the terrifying thrill of landing an F-4 on a night-blackened roiling carrier deck, the intoxicating smell of jet fuel. Nothing could touch being a Navy flyer. Nothing could touch being a hero.

"It's worse. It's driving a hell-bound bus while people are trying to kill you. Edward, you *don't* have to go to Vietnam. I can get you in the National Guard. Look what I wangled for Jerry—two years of caddying for generals in San Antonio."

Eddie nodded without assent. "What percentage of our guests come from Beverly Hills?"

"All of them," Jonnie crowed.

"Half?" He pressed.

"Probably more, why?"

"Because it's a pain driving just to Newport and—what?—another hour to Beverly Hills?"

"So?"

"So, in the off-season, we should run a weekly shuttle to Beverly Hills, offering a free pickup and return as part of a holiday package. Maybe meet them at the Century Plaza. If we take the drive out of it, I bet we could fill an extra ten rooms."

Jonnie laughed in delight. "Hell, we have the van—half my boys hide all afternoon anyway—it would cost us nothing but gas." She leaned over and kissed his cheek. "You're so clever."

He blushed and touched his cheek, her red lipstick coloring his fingertips. She leaned back, and their conversation faded as they drove south, allowing him to reflect. He trampled Jonnie's seedling doubts and mulled his destiny as a Navy pilot. Money was the issue: to be an officer—to fly—he needed to finish college, and to attend full-time.

He'd banked nearly $3,000 after eighteen months of sleeping in his van and cadging food (such as it was) from the Inn's kitchen staff. He was inching closer; he'd work another year, take night classes, and then apply to the university.

CHAPTER 3

THE FALL GUY

ROY CROSS SAUNTERED INTO THE Denny's, nodding at the tired restaurant as if he owned the place. He cooed *"hey baby"* to the frowzy hostess twice his age and chucked her under the chin when she giggled her delight. He spied Tommy Mahoney in the far booth, head down on the table like a napping kindergartner. Strolling back, Roy eased himself onto the warped plastic banquette, flipped up his Ray-Bans, and shook his shoulder-length hair into place. He lit a Marlboro with a gold lighter. A pretty teenage waitress appeared at his side before his first smoke ring drifted away. Pointing at his sleeping friend, Roy shushed her with a finger to his lips, mouthing the word *"coffee."* The teenager gawked at him, then fluttered off to make a fresh pot.

The cigarette dangling from his lips, he leaned back, clasping his bare arms behind his head. He knew why Tommy had demanded the meeting. A month ago, Roy would have been desperate at the thought of his partner bailing on him, but now the score of a lifetime was a mere handhold away. He only needed a little more time. Juan Sierra was on the verge of entrusting him with serious weight, the crooked cop Schmidt was circling the bait, and he'd figured out the perfect fall guy. Someone he hadn't seen in years, someone he couldn't be connected with, someone few would miss.

A few more smoke rings lazed upward before Roy softly patted Tommy's shoulder.

"What?" Tommy whimpered in his sleep. Groggy, the pudgy twenty-four-year-old sat up blinking. He groped for his thick glasses, shook himself awake, but couldn't shake his firing squad nightmare. Awake, his terrifying visions were more realistic: Roy fingering him as the genius behind their drug smuggling, a federal judge decreeing that Tommy had betrayed his sacred trust as a U.S. Customs inspector.

"Music Man, what's with the siesta?" Roy asked.

"I can't sleep any more. You're late, Roy, you're always late. How did they even let you in here without a shirt?" Tommy snapped, pointing at the black leather vest that covered little of Roy's lithe chest and muscle-rippled stomach. "Jesus, you get away with *everything*."

Roy chuckled, nodding in apparent agreement. "T, you know the difference between lunch and a blow job?"

"For Christ's sake. No."

"Great, meet me here tomorrow at noon." Roy laughed. The short-skirted waitress hustled back with coffee and a half dozen tiny plastic creamers, gushing to Roy about his boots. Tommy hesitated, looked under the table, and rolled his eyes. Roy was wearing skin-tight black leather pants and black cowboy boots. The pants' seams were adorned with silver conches and the boots with anklets of silver stars. Tommy blanched.

"OK, dude," said Roy, slurping the coffee. "You called this meeting, what's so important you had to get me up at, like, the crack of dawn? Hey, maybe I'd get it up for Dawn's crack."

"I quit," he said, ignoring the meager jest. Tommy had long since realized that Roy used humor like a safecracker's tools, a way to break in.

"What?" cried Roy, his surprise feigned.

"You heard me, I quit my job. We're done. No more runs. Finito." Tommy was so determined to get out, to flee San Diego—to hide somewhere Roy could never find him—he'd walked into the chief inspector's office and resigned, declaring that the border traffic's endless exhaust was fueling his asthma, killing him. He'd added that he'd been accepted at some East Coast music school he'd seen an ad for in *Guitar Player* magazine. "I mean it. I'm done." Tommy ran his fingers through his unruly copper-colored hair and thrust out his soft chin, working on his defiance, wishing he'd defied Roy from the start, wishing he'd never met him.

"You, like, quit already?"

"I had to give two weeks' notice. Dolores and I are out of here the Friday after next. The moment I get off work."

"Dude, think of all that dinero you'll be losing."

"I'd leave tonight if I could, King." Tommy held a trembling thumb and forefinger a dime's width apart. "You and I are *this close* to getting caught." "How many more times do I wave you through before Secondary stops you and fries us both?" He'd met Roy at a party a couple years earlier. Roy and a handful of his friends—two had actually finished high school—had thrown a wild class of '67 graduation party. The cops were called three times. Tommy's garage band was the entertainment, everyone was high, and Roy's extravagant praise of his wicked guitar had Tommy insisting he wasn't a rock star, just a customs inspector at the Tijuana border. Almost overnight, Roy was winking at him as he rolled across the border with sacks of marijuana. The more runs he made—the more he pocketed—the more outlandish his dress, his muscle cars, and his behavior had become. Now Roy stood out like a peacock on a turkey farm, begging to be slaughtered. Was he ever sober? Tommy knew his imperfect system for knowing his line assignment in advance—the trick to Roy's smuggling—only had to fail once for them to be imprisoned.

"OK," Roy said. Grinning, he banged out a drum roll on the table, and shot Tommy with a finger pistol. "OK."

"OK? OK what? You're really cool with that?" Tommy asked, incredulous. Having steeled himself for battle, Roy's indifference was astonishing.

"OK, T. I get it. We're cool. You're not cut out for a life of crime." He laughed so hard the waitress giggled from behind the pick-up counter. A blue-haired pair looked up from their waffles.

"Roy, please. Everyone can hear us," Tommy begged.

Roy raised his hands in a papal gesture and smiled, the picture of benevolence. He'd been expecting the breakup for months, since he'd first noticed his chubby partner losing weight. But he thought he'd have more time to polish his scheme—the last run where he'd rip off the Colombians. If it worked, Roy's beach party would be endless; the twenty-one-year-old's life would be one wave, one high, and one girl after another.

"Tranquilo, T," Roy said, chuckling. He set his cigarette on the table and again folded his arms behind his head, contemplating his useful friend. He was glad Tommy was leaving town. Not that he really cared about him—or anyone for that matter—but the music man had made him a boatload of money (if only he hadn't pissed it all away) and had been true to his word. His plan was foolproof, but nothing wrong with Tommy out of harm's way.

Roy remembered he was hungry. The joint he'd smoked on the drive over had him craving something sweet. "Let's celebrate. Let's get some pie. Yeah, baby, some banana cream pie. Then let's talk about one last run... for old time's sake. I've got a dude I want you to meet," Roy crooned, reflecting on his fall guy. "I guarantee he'll take all the worry out of it for you. The guy's such a wuss he washes his cock *before* he takes a piss."

He beckoned the waitress with a smile, and the eager teenager trotted over with her pad and pencil in hand. She stood close to him, pressing against the table. Roy leaned forward, dragged on his cigarette, insisting Tommy try the apple pie. Meanwhile, he trailed his free hand up the back of the girl's thigh, stroking it. She sucked in her breath as he toyed with her panties' elastic band. He laughed, softly this time.

CHAPTER 4

THE CATCH

The afternoon was warm: golden on the beach and lazy in the coffee shop where the Riviera Inn's guests played bridge, swapping diets like recipes, smoking, reminiscing of foods past, gossiping. But for the professional scale against the back wall, the restaurant contained little to suggest a weight-reducing spa, furnished as it was with holdover Polynesian decorations from the Inn's prior life as the Tiki-Palms Lodge. The picture-windows looked onto the pool where an ill-attended aquacise class was underway. A large woman was weighing herself for the fifth time that day, while a girl of perhaps nineteen sat cross-legged at a booth writing a letter, aloof from the tables of bridge players, pretending not to devour their bawdy conversations.

The talk ceased when a stunning young man entered, promenaded to the nearest table, and, with an easy smile, asked if Eddie Kawadsky were around. Eight players and one kibitzer answered at once, contradicting and dismissing each other.

Roy Cross flashed a perfect smile. "Is this, like, a multiple-choice quiz?"

"His van's parked behind the kitchen," the letter-writing girl said. "You might find him there."

Eddie heard rock blasting from the parking lot. Striding through the breezeway between the coffee shop and the indoor pool, he saw his boyhood hero Roy Cross preening against the hood of a new Malibu convertible—top down, its car wax glistening circular in the slanting afternoon sunlight. Roy sang along with the Doors, seemingly unaware his singing voice suggested strep throat. Eddie walked around the convertible, admiring the chromed racing wheels, tracing a finger against the fat tires. "Jesus, Roy, you must be dealing a ton to afford this."

"*King*. Roy is French for King. Everyone calls me King now."

"King's a dog's name," Eddie said, stifling a laugh. Delighted as he was with his one-time idol's visit, his guard was up. He'd instantly—irrationally—hoped Roy missed him, but knew better. The young men hadn't been close for years, ever since Roy began his reign as the dope-smoking clown prince of junior high. Living three doors apart, the boys had been inseparable when Eddie was six and Roy eight, but their paths had branched far from one another. As the years passed, Roy had come to view Eddie as a playmate of last resort, almost never seeking him out. Eddie had been saddened by the loss, but understood he had no place in Roy's sybaritic beach life.

"Good to see you, dude." Sliding off the hood, Roy frowned. "Whoa, I used to be way taller than you. What are you? 6'2?"

"6'3.". What are you doing here, *King*?"

"Did you hear the one about the dumb priest who goes to the head nun, 'Sister, what's a blow job?' She goes, 'Ten bucks, same as downtown.'"

Eddie shook his head at the old joke, chuckled at Roy's full-throated laughter, warming despite himself to his old friend's vulgar charm.

"You want to catch some waves?" Roy asked. "Come on."

"No, I've got to study." But Jonnie's words tugged at him. He should have more fun.

"Come on, Wad, you know you want to," said Roy, using the nickname he'd saddled Eddie with years earlier.

Eddie had an hour before he had to set up the Sea Grotto bar for the nightly cocktail hour, the hour he served sliced vegetables and diet drinks to the ravenous guests. He grinned and said OK. He stepped behind his van, snapped off his tie, pulled his shirt over his head, dropped his slacks, and slipped on his trunks. He grabbed his fins and a tattered Inn towel.

They picked their way through the dunes onto the apron of gray-speckled sand. The beach was alive with vacationers, locals with night jobs, ankle-deep parents watching their toddlers play tag with the tide, soaked children shrieking with delight, teenagers entwined on blankets. Smells of mustard, chili dogs, and Coppertone carried on the breezes as the gently rumbling surf muffled sounds of ball games and rock and roll. A pack of boys played touch football amid a volley of Frisbees.

"What's doing with you, Wad? You must be getting it night and day with all those lonely, starving chicks moping around. You just go, 'Whoa, babe, this sausage ain't fattening.'"

"I'm working full time, going to school at night," Eddie said glumly, knowing he was the ant to Roy's grasshopper in Aesop's fable, perhaps wishing the industrious ant wasn't such a stiff.

Roy took off running at the water's edge, seeking to reestablish his dominance over the neighborhood boy he'd always envied. Each time Roy's father told him he should be more like Eddie—more respectful and hardworking—his resentment hardened. The father who'd never loved him thought the world of Eddie Kawadsky.

"Want to get high?" Roy asked.

"No, I have to be back at work in an hour."

"Then let's hit the waves."

An excellent swimmer, Eddie loved bodysurfing. He had been an all-conference water polo player, and had his world not imploded at the beginning of his senior year, he might have been offered a scholarship to a lesser university. He powered through the small swells like a cormorant chasing fish. With a gap-toothed grin, he jumped a wave, raced ahead of its break, and—popping up in the foam—shook his long, curly brown hair and looked about for Roy. Eddie saw the back of his head, hidden at first behind the following swell, about thirty yards out—beyond the break—and swam to him. Just as he reached him, Roy spun around and blew a cloud of smoke in his face.

"Want a hit, man?"

Startled, Eddie took the joint, if only to keep it dry. "How did you do it?"

"Toke first. Talk later."

Laughing at Roy's trick, Eddie took a hit, but didn't inhale. He handed the joint back, treading water effortlessly. Roy sucked down a monster hit and insisted he take another. Inhaling for real, Eddie fumbled the joint on his hand-off.

"Sorry, Roy, I mean, your *Highness*." Eddie laughed, his thoughts loosening. "Get it, King? Highness? Tell me how you did it? How you kept it dry?"

Roy fished his hand below the surface and brought forth a thumb-sized steel cylinder, a waterproof match container. "Thought you were the only Boy Scout, dude? Be prepared. Always keep it in my suit—makes my dick look bigger."

Twenty minutes later, the two lay on the warm sand, Eddie unraveled by the pot, lost in a daydream.

"This is a blast, man. Just like old times, Wad, old times," Roy gushed, as he sat up to brush out his blond hair. He had to sell Eddie fast. "We should do this again soon. Hey, I have an idea. We go down to Mexico, do some real waves, not this chickenshit soup. 39 has the righteous waves. Yeah? That'd be cool. If we take your van, we camp right there. A little bonfire, fish tacos, some smoke, and the Mexican stars are like a light show. I'll score a couple señoritas for us. Cool, huh? You listening, Wad?"

Eddie was wiggling his toes in the sand—thinking the unthinkable—dreaming about screwing a woman his mother's age, the youth of no experience aching to touch her long limbs. Roy's purring was distant, indistinguishable, another instrument in the shoreline's symphony.

"You know what sucks?" Roy asked, pressing a little harder. He knew his pitch was perfect, but Eddie wasn't catching. "Some Mex charges a buck and half if you leave your car at 39 overnight. Does that suck or what? Let's do it, bud. I'll pop for the buck fifty."

Eddie lay scrunched down, face on the towel, hands shaping and cupping warm sand breasts, the leggy Jonnie panting beneath him. He heard Roy from far away.

"Are you listening, man? What do you say? Mexico—let's do it. You and me, the dynamic duo together again." Irritated, unaccustomed to being ignored, Roy shifted his position, reminding himself to work his tan. Eddie had to come to Mexico—everything depended on it—but now the dick was too cool to answer him. Roy nursed his useful resentment: Eddie was now taller, better muscled, and on his way. Frowning, Roy slunk to the water's edge, needing to think. He had spent his life on the beach, from sunrise to sundown, waxing his board, acting older to fit in. He'd been prized first as a mascot, then as a leader, smoking cigarettes, dope, taking pills, drinking beer, wine, anything wet. And always surfing, always partying. The beach party would be endless if he saw his plan through. In his dreams, Roy acquired wealth with ease, winning big in Vegas or tripping over an egg-sized diamond. He scuffed at the packed, wet sand. Something was off. The score of a lifetime was only days away, yet his stomach ached. Was it the backwash of happy memories, simple times playing together as kids? Could he really set up Wad to take the fall? He consoled himself with the thought that the Eagle Scout with his unblemished record wouldn't do more than a couple years of hard time. Despite the day's warmth, Roy shivered, flicked his golden hair, and padded up the beach.

"C'mon, Wad," he said, returning to Eddie. "My dope's not *that* good. Don't you have to be back at Fat City?"

"What? What time is it? Oh, shit. I'm late." Eddie staggered to his feet and sprinted toward the public showers with Roy chasing after him. He stood beneath the corroded shower tree's miserable trickle, wiping away the sand with one hand while holding the shower chain down with the other. He pulled his trunks from his flat stomach to let the water run down his crotch, flushing out the sand.

"Are you in? Two days of K-39, no ties, no fat chicks, just righteous times. Let's do it, man."

"I can't."

"OK, Wad, time to pull out the big guns: You owe me. Where'd you stay after you ended up on the street? Whose mother fed you and did your laundry? She even nursed you through the flu."

"I owe your mom, not you," said Eddie. He did owe him, he thought, even if Roy had barely acknowledged him during the two months he'd lived in the Crosses' spare bedroom. Contemplating their shared past and his debt, he sighed. "What's the catch?"

"No catch, man."

"My ass," Eddie called, laughing over his shoulder. There was always a catch with Roy. He still shuddered over the time when, as a ten-year-old, he'd been caught shoplifting a couple candy bars at the Thrifty Drug Store, a crime he'd committed at Roy's urging.

"OK. OK. The catch is we take your van. The Malibu would be toast if we took it. Fucking Mexicans. Besides, it's easier to pop the boards in this old dude." He patted the van like a dog.

"Tell me the truth, Roy. I'm not running any dope. No bullshit."

"It's *King*. OK, no bullshit. Absolutely no risk and you get, like..." He paused to consider pricing. "... a grand for surfing. A thousand bucks for driving—"

"No way. Oh, shit, shit, shit," Eddie said, strapping on his Timex. "Jonnie will kill me."

"What's wrong?" Roy asked, telling himself to stay cool. Wad would buy in.

"What's wrong is doing some crazy dope deal with you." Eddie clipped on his polyester tie.

"But this is two hundred percent safe." Roy explained that his partner Tommy Mahoney was a customs inspector who checked cars coming in from Tijuana and how Roy sailed right past him every time with a load. Now Tommy was getting weird—turning into an old lady—thinking Roy too flashy and his cars too wild, so he needed a new driver. "The dude is paranoid, man, but he calls the shots. I've got to use his lane. His freaking out is your gain."

"It can't be that easy." Eddie remembered the border's long lines, the exhaust-fueled smog, the stooped peddlers wandering among the cars with their serapes and velvet-painted bullfight scenes.

"Promise you won't tell anybody, ever. Promise?" Roy urged. He could sell crows to a farmer.

"Yeah," said Eddie.

"These guards rotate all day long, every hour, and it's supposed to be anonymous, but Tommy broke the code and he can figure out which lanes he'll get. Don't trust me, don't believe one word, just meet Tommy. OK? We'll go to the A&W tomorrow? If you just meet Tommy, you don't owe me a thing. We'd be totally cool. Deal?"

"And you'll never ask me another favor?"

"Swear to god." Roy hesitated a moment, flashed his shark smile, and pulled a roll of bills from a blue Maxwell House coffee can under the driver's seat. "Do me this favor—take an advance."

"No. Put that away. I'm not doing it."

"Come on, you know you want it." He twisted a rubber band off the roll and peeled off bills. "If you don't go, you can pay me back when you feel like it. This can's jammed anyway." Roy savored this fleeting self-image, giving money outright, his generosity softening the torment that had seized him on the beach.

Eddie grabbed his hand. "Put that goddamn money away."

"Cool, no problemo. But you can at least do this for me… for old time's sake."

"What?" Eddie shoved his hands deep into his pockets, as if that could thwart temptation.

"Take the Malibu." He tossed the keys. "I got to look at a car I might buy. Maybe have to drive it home. Tommy can bring me tomorrow. It'd be a big favor."

Eddie rolled the keys in his hand. "OK, but I won't drive it. I mean, I'll drive it to meet you, but that's it."

"Whatever, dude. Take it to Frisco or let it rust. Later." With a flip of his hair, Roy turned toward Orange Avenue, swinging the Maxwell can, wondering whether he really should buy another car. He assumed a hitchhiker's stance at the curb, yet left his thumbs hooked through his belt loops, a study in surfer nonchalance. He remembered he had to talk to the crooked cop Schmidt, shivering at the thought. He still had plenty of time—tomorrow would be better. He'd have to get really high first, dealing with that dick was such a bummer. A Ford Fairlane braked a few yards past him. Roy nodded and sauntered toward it.

CHAPTER 5

PIECE OF CAKE

B<small>EHIND THE WHEEL OF</small> R<small>OY'S</small> tricked-out Malibu, Eddie pulled into the A&W the next day, thinking—hoping—he looked pretty cool for once. The burger joint was mobbed, cars circling the lot for a parking spot beneath its sagging orange canopy. Teenagers slouched across the picnic tables near the front door, catching the last of the July sun. A couple twelve-year-olds rode past Eddie on their Schwinns, popping acrobatic wheelies no one noticed. He looked for a salt-rusted, red Toyota, and was relieved when he failed to see it. Maybe the deal was off. Maybe he was truly done with Roy Cross. Eddie turned up the car radio, jamming his misgivings about running marijuana. A moment later, he spied the tattered Toyota behind a camper, eased into a tight spot, and waved the pair toward him, curious about the Customs guy.

"There he is, Music Man," Roy said. "Does he look normal or what? Now you can decide for yourself about the easiest ten grand you'll ever make." Barbiturate calm from a red, he'd been selling Eddie Kawadsky to the dubious Tommy for the better part of an hour, retailing his boy-hood friend as another Tommy: someone so bland, so banal no inspec-tor would ever look twice at him. Roy lit a cigarette with his Dunhill lighter, grabbed a greasy white paper bag, stepped out of the sedan and stretched. He put his arm around Tommy's shoulder. "You know, T, what if we not even call it *coke* when we talk to Eddie or maybe just call it the *shit*? In case somebody's trying to overlook our conversation."

"Sure, that's a good idea," Tommy said, as shocked as he was pleased by Roy's newfound caution.

"Yo, Wad," Roy called from a couple cars away, pulling a joint from behind his ear. "Let's toke up. It'll make this shit taste delicious." He waved the paper bag.

"Damn it, Roy." Tommy pleaded. "Hide that. There's like a hundred people here. Come on."

"It's cool." Roy shrugged. "I got you a cheeseburger and a root beer float, Wad. What'd you think about the ride?"

"Whoa, it's like flying. I ran it up to La Jolla in nothing flat. My van's a wagon compared to this rocket." Eddie caught himself before claiming it was better than sex, certain he wore his virginity like a merit badge. He raved about the car, the looks it drew, the way it cornered, the chromed rims—everything down to the 8-track tape deck—until he realized that Roy, intent on selling him, would let him prattle on forever. He sighed. Changing gears, he glanced about, appraising the A&W. "This place could double its business if they paved that dirt lot. They could add twenty parking spots."

"Dude, what about our business? Let's double that," Roy said.

"Tell me about your setup."

"It's pretty simple," said Tommy. "There's nineteen lines—you say lanes, we say lines— at the border. Each day, the shift supervisor has to figure out a random schedule for us so…," he paused, glanced at his ragged sneakers, sighed. "So we can't collude with, you know, smugglers. So we start in a random booth, then each hour we move to the next one, the guy who starts in Line 1 moves to Line 2, then to 3 and so on. Simple rotation. With me?"

"Yep. The boss picks the opening slots out of a hat and after that everyone goes in order."

"Bingo." Tommy was surprised again, this time that Roy could have a friend so quick. Maybe one last deal—ten thousand was a fortune. "Except our bosses don't use hats and some of them have been doing it so long their random isn't that random. I figured out one old guy's system, uses the first letters of his family's names for line numbers. So we make sure he's on when King comes through with the *stuff.*"

"What if he's not on duty?" Eddie's thoughts sprinted from picking the plan apart to wondering whether marijuana should even be illegal to Roy's proven unreliability and then to the money. The money. The money that would allow him to attend the university full-time and be flying years sooner. Everyone smoked pot. Everyone knew it was better for you than alcohol and that it'd been the liquor industry alone that had it outlawed. Yes, it made you stupid and hungry, but where was the harm in that? Was sneaking an innocuous drug across the border really a sin? How risky was it? Roy wasn't a total moron and he'd been running pot for years. And the money would free him. Instead of coddling the Inn's neurotic rich, he could be his own man.

"We only plan it for shifts he's working. Like Monday night."

"But what if he gets sick or forgets his own system, or traffic's too heavy and you have to switch lines or go on break before we get there? It's not guaranteed, is it?" Eddie quizzed, watching Tommy's reaction, ignoring Roy. The greasy burger dripping in his hands was the only free lunch he'd ever get from Roy Cross.

"There's always a traffic jam, always some wait," Tommy said, improvising. "While you're sitting there idling, you can hop out, walk over to the pedestrian Customs, you know, on the right-hand side, and get close enough to see if I'm in the booth. If I'm there, go back to the car. If not, make Roy drive through alone and bus it home."

"Way to go, T," Roy hooted. "Wad, you see Tommy, you drive home; if you don't, you take the 'Hound.'"

Eddie bit off a chunk of burger and chewed slowly, giving himself a chance to think. This was way too good to be true. "What about my van? If Roy gets arrested, they'll keep it, won't they?"

"Yeah, they'd impound it."

"Whoa, whoa, whoa." Roy slammed the dashboard. "The King goes down and you're worried about that piece of crap? Fuck it, make it two grand. Deal?"

"How much, how many pounds of—"

"You don't want to know, man," Roy snapped. "You know what you want to know? *Nothing.* More insurance. Anyone ever asks you, you don't have clue one. You're clean." Roy's fingers trembled. He regretted not taking the other red. He lit a fresh cigarette, sucking the smoke deep, fearing the deal might blow, wondering whether to throw more money at Eddie.

"Two thousand in cash before we leave the Riviera and if I don't see Tom in the right line, I walk to the bus station? That's your offer?"

"I'm shaking on it," Roy said, extending his hand.

"I don't get it." Eddie was struggling against his judgment. Something must be wrong. Roy was offering too much. But he'd begun aching for it, the money that would launch him off the carrier deck. "If it works like you said, you don't need me. Why pay me so much?"

"I wouldn't pay anyone else that much," Roy said, "but we're old buds and I kind of, like, owe you for before—"

"That's bullshit," Tommy interrupted. "I'm making him do it. Look at him, all this stupid leather—this ridiculous vest—he looks like a pimp. Or this crazy car. How many times does a guy dressed like Mick Jagger bomb through in a hot convertible before Secondary pulls him over behind me? The surfing, your van with the boards, and all your stuff is a perfect cover. With you—a normal guy—and your VW, it's a piece of cake."

"I don't know." Eddie chomped into the burger, chewing deliberately. Tommy seemed sensible. "I need to think it over."

"Look, Eddie," Tommy began. "I'd feel the same way in your shoes, but a week from Friday is my last day. Monday's the only day my schedule matches with that old supervisor's. It's now or never."

"Why did you quit?" Eddie asked.

Tommy looked toward the pick-up window, seemingly distracted by the spirited kids on their bikes. After a moment, he said, "We've made so much doing this I can take a year off. Travel with my wife Dolores and our kids."

Eddie swallowed, contemplating what he could accomplish with a couple years off, imagining himself supersonic in an F-4. He glanced from Tommy to Roy, weighing the two, half-convinced by Tommy, certain Roy was trouble. A natural businessman, Eddie had yet to learn that the thrill of the chase—of cutting a brilliant deal—could veneer the merits off the prize. He countered. "Three thousand and I'll *consider* it."

"Three thou? No way. Kiss my ass."

"Three thousand and kiss your own ass," said Eddie.

"You're fucking me. Hey, there's a cop," Roy said, as a squad car swung into the drive-in. Roy jumped up onto his seat in the open Malibu and yelled at the patrolman. "Officer, officer, help. This guy's trying to rob me."

"Would you cool it?" Tommy grabbed his wrist, tugging him down, his eyes wild with fear. "*Please.* Take it out of my share."

"No way, T. You got kids. The King will pay this dick three large, but if he asks for another goddamn dime, I'm…" he paused, and then adopting a credible Donald Duck voice, added, "I'm going to have my big brothers beat you up, you big bully."

Their laughter eased the tension.

Tommy sagged with relief and glanced up at the blue sky, allowing himself a vision of driving his small family through forgiving forests on their way north. Maybe Seattle. "Got to go, guys. See you Monday."

Roy drove Eddie back to the Inn, his forefinger steering from the bottom of the wheel, singing with the radio, his free hand failing to keep time. He pulled a paper from his leather pants and read off a list, his lips moving. "You still got your old man's gun?"

"So?"

"Don't bring it Monday."

"Why not?"

"Think about it, dude. If that million-to-one screw-up happens and you walk across the border while the King goes down, the gun adds years. Cool? No guns."

Eddie often worried about the .45, his second-most prized possession. His van was as easy to break into as it was to unlock, and the thought of losing his father's Colt distressed him. He weighed stashing it in the bushes, but then remembered the gardeners, the moisture, and salt air.

"So you're in?" Roy nodded, checking the gun off his list, ignoring Eddie's failure to respond.

"I'll let you know."

Watching him drive off, Eddie decided to walk away. He had little fear of getting caught, thinking he could parry a border inspector even if he ended up in the wrong lane. He thought he could handle pressure. When a Tenderfoot had drowned years before, he alone among the panicked Scouts had scrambled down the bluff, fished the bluish body from the stream, and calmed the troop until the drunken Scoutmaster returned. Eddie knew thousands of cars pulsed across the border daily, only a handful searched, and guessed he could ingratiate himself with any inspector, using the charm he'd honed at the Inn. It was neither the risk nor the morality—marijuana was a waste of time, nothing worse—but dishonoring his father that had him saying no.

CHAPTER 6

JONNIE

His dinner shift over, Eddie strode to the VW beneath the stand of wind-twisted Monterey pine in the Inn's employee lot. Troubled—and tempted—as he was by Roy's offer, he knew sleep would only come through exhaustion. He slid open the van's side door, whipped off his work shirt and slacks, and donned his baggies. He would swim hard until the twilight failed. He considered his body. His shoulders were broad and muscled, his waist narrow, almost hipless, his frame whippet-lean from a lifetime of swimming and indifferent eating. He flexed a bicep and nodded, knowing that, if not handsome, he was fit. Trotting to the darkling ocean, he waded through the shore break, diving into a wave when the water deepened. He swam straight out, twenty yards beyond the small breakers, and then turned toward Naval Air Station North Island, shaking off the sea chill. He swam parallel with the shore, trying to concentrate on his stroke, but the money had commandeered his thoughts. He saw himself attending a quality university instead of kowtowing to irritable dieters, standing on a carrier's flight deck rather than hustling for dollar tips. The money would change his life: he could live in a college dorm rather than a VW, eat in a warm cafeteria instead of scrounging scraps from the Inn's kitchen. He would be a man instead of a servant. Visualizing the smuggling's bounty was easy, but no easier than foretelling a tiny slipup, a flat tire, an inquisitive highway patrolman.

He swam on.

With the light gone and his shoulders aching, Eddie clambered from the sea, showered—as he often did—at the beach's public shower tree, and returned to his van, thinking calculus homework the key to sleeping. It worked. He dozed, but awoke hungry a couple hours later, and checked his Timex. The coffee shop would be locked, but the night man didn't finish until midnight, the kitchen's salt-rusted back door would be open. With luck, Eddie could find a piece of cold chicken in the walk-in cooler. He slipped on a worn polo shirt, returned to his dilemma, deciding the candle wasn't worth the game. He would tell Roy he was out.

He stepped into the back kitchen, said hi to the stoned dishwasher, and cast about for something to eat, finding the tinfoil-wrapped leftover steak the kindly chef had set aside for him. He heard glass shattering in the coffee shop, pushed open the kitchen's swinging door, and saw Jonnie's husband Dr. Collins wringing his soft hands, staring at a kaleidoscope of glass shards and puddled milk on the freshly mopped floor.

"Are you OK, Doctor Collins?" asked Eddie.

The myopic doctor peered at the youth. Despite the late hour, he wore his uniform: a bowtie and a white lab coat with a stethoscope draped over his narrow shoulders. In his mid-forties, the doctor had a kindly, soft-spoken, professorial manner and had perfected the knack of appearing to carefully consider his patients' complaints. He thus inspired boundless confidence in his quackery, assuring the hopeful that starving themselves for a week—better, for two—would change their lives. He took off his thick glasses, rubbed the bridge of his nose, distracted. "It's Edward, isn't it?"

"Yes, sir."

"I seem to have lost my grip," said the doctor, chuckling. Despite the flaccid joke, he seemed upset, his face flushed, perhaps with anger. "I'm sorry to put you out, Edward, but would you please take care of this for me. I must… I have an appointment." The doctor hurried out.

Eddie fetched a broom, a dustpan, and a mop from the back. Returning, he heard a sob from inside the bar, a narrow twilit room that, despite offering nothing more intoxicating than Fresca, looked every inch the beachside Tiki lounge. "Jonnie, what are you doing here? What's wrong?"

"You got a lifetime, kiddo? I'll tell you what's wrong. Sit, sit here," she patted the leather banquette next to her, daubing at her tear-streaked mascara. The Inn's books, its last quarter's operating statements, lay before her on the table. "Wait, first, go behind the bar. There's a plastic jug labeled cleaning fluid under the larger sink. Way in the back. Bring it to me with a glass of ice. Hell, grab a glass for yourself. Hurry." Jonnie retrieved her compact mirror, pouted at her ruffled image, sighed, and reapplied her lipstick.

She filled the glass with the cleaning fluid, draining a third of it in a long gulp. Smiling sadly at her protégé's amazement, "It's vodka, Edward. How do you think I put up with these tiresome bitches every day? Pour yourself a little." She clinked his glass, said cheers and they both drank.

She'd met the good doctor when he was in college and she in high school. Pregnant by their fourth date, they'd married, she'd put him through medical school by waitressing, her mother watching over their babies. He had the dreams and she the drive. With his "guaranteed weight-loss program," Dr. Collins would win the Nobel Prize and they would become rich. But Jonnie knew within months of the Inn's grand opening that her husband's "medically supervised" program was farcical—if not criminal—that their patients regained their weight as quickly as they lost it. But with neither interest in nor aptitude for numbers, she was years before realizing her doctor was a terrible businessman. To invest in schemes even more fanciful than his own, he'd bled the Inn white.

"We're this close to broke, Edward," said Jonnie, gapping her thumb and forefinger. She stubbed out her Kool. "Forget this business. How many employees do I have?"

"About fifty," said Eddie.

"And do you know how many headaches I have? *Fifty*. No," she caught herself, smiled. "Forty-nine. You've never been a headache, not for a moment." She rested her hand on his forearm, sipped her drink, holding his gaze. She of course knew the youth had a crush on her— she'd seen his longing expressions, forbade her catty assistants from laughing over his mooning. "You're my treasure."

"Wow, thanks, Jonnie." Eddie's face glowed.

Reverting to her habitual breezy tone, she added, "And is every guest a total pain in the ass or what? I should work sixty hours a week so my idiot husband can invest in Arizona chinchilla farms?"

"I'm sorry."

"Don't be sorry, learn from my mistakes. Forget the Inn and get into real estate." With the vodka slowly gauzing her, she spoke expansively, tapping his arm to emphasize her life lessons.

"Real estate?" asked Eddie.

"Half the money in Beverly Hills comes from real estate. The other half... real crime," she said, laughing.

"But how do you buy a hotel?"

"You don't. You buy a rundown house cheap, paint it, throw some petunias in front, and sell it. Desperate sellers will give them up for almost nothing down. How do you think we bought the Inn? I went from fixing up houses to a sixty-four-unit apartment building that we traded into this dump," said Jonnie, her words running together. She snapped open her rhinestone cigarette case and frowned. She squeezed his arm, smiled into his eyes, and said, "Be a doll and get me another pack."

"Sure, Jonnie," said Eddie. He jumped up, feeling the vodka. He had poured himself a full glass and was the better part drunk. He stuck a quarter in the cigarette machine and pulled the knob for Kools, his mind stumbling from real estate to true love. He had long suspected Jonnie had no affection for the doctor, and now she'd proclaimed it. And how many times had she just touched his arm? Maybe, the vodka insinuated, maybe she loved him, too. Only one way to find out. His heart raced as he stuck his courage to the sticking place.

Trembling, he strode back into the bar, plopped down on the banquette, threw his right arm around her shoulder, drew her near and—without warning—kissed her hard, squeezing her long thigh.

"Edward," cried Jonnie, her shock writ large. "My God." She crossed her arms, leaned away, gulping open-mouthed. As with the unfolding of a terrible accident, the moment defied time, extending itself indelibly. But Jonnie grasped its tenderness—its humor—within seconds, giggled, then laughed out loud, shaking her blonde bouffant. "Oh, Edward, Edward, Edward, my poor boy."

"I love you, Jonnie, I really do," he swore, but her laughter, her fond motherly indulgence, had stubbed out his ardor. Mumbling sorry, sorry, sorry, he closed his eyes, dropped his head onto the table. "I thought…"

"You've had enough of this," she said, sliding the tumbler away from him. She laughed again, tousled his curly hair affectionately. "I could be arrested for child abuse. Hell, I'm old enough to be your…big sister."

"Oh, Jonnie, I'm so sorry," he muttered to the table. He had not felt this empty since his father's death. "Can you forgive me?"

"What's to forgive, boychik? I'm flattered. It's not every day a handsome young man makes a play for me. In fact, I'm so flustered I really need that cigarette," she said, comically waving her hands to cool herself.

With his forehead and broken nose resting on the cool table, he moaned. "I'm so sorry, I feel like an idiot… so terrible."

She lit the Kool, sat back, and exhaled toward the Polynesian thatched roof above the corner booth. "It's all my fault, I'm just too damn attractive," she joshed, toggling his shoulders when he failed to respond. "Come on, sit up, it's not the end of the world. Make this pitch when you're twenty-one, when I won't get arrested for statutory rape and… who knows? Maybe I'll get lucky."

But it was the end of the nineteen-year-old's world. Eddie had made the worst fool of himself, having misread her so completely. Knowing he was orphaned, had she simply appointed herself his mother's understudy? Beyond her maternal sympathy, had she ever had any affection for him? No. He was such an idiot. And now Jonnie was laughing at him. He knew how she loved spooning her delicious gossip to one and all. She would polish the tale of her lovesick boy until it was shiny bright and then delight her company with its telling over and again. Within a day or two, half of the guests—all of the regulars—would be cackling every time he walked into the coffee shop. How could he ever face her again? He had to get away. Roy had the ticket.

CHAPTER 7

DATE NIGHT

To seize the day, Roy Cross could say anything to anyone, occasionally even meaning it. While Eddie hung his head in mortification in the Tiki bar, Roy lay in a silk-sheeted bed one hundred and thirty miles to the north—in Juan Sierra's Hollywood pied-a-terre—nursing his raw pain with a cigarette, his body a pale blue in the moonlit bedroom. Juan squeezed his bare shoulder and asked, "Was it all right, mijo?"

"It was great, Juan," Roy said, his voice catching slightly. His sexuality may have been somewhat fluid—mouths and hands felt the same in the dark—but he recoiled at kissing men and his calculated submission to Juan had been anything but enjoyable, despite the mound of cocaine and two bottles of Dom Perignon. While he yearned for nothing more than to be alone with a Quaalude, he knew Ramirez would cancel his shipment if he and Juan parted on bad terms. "Really great."

"You do not like it, do you? Please tell me the truth, mijo," Juan Sierra pleaded, staring into his lover's faraway eyes. He gazed at his beautiful King as an art lover might, his eyes wide in near adoration. Juan had met Roy at a gay party given by a second-tier Hollywood producer a couple years before. After Roy had bragged of his drug dealing, Juan had been indiscreet about his own business, telling him he had distant relatives in a similar line of work. Desperate to have him, Juan had handed Roy an eight-ball of uncut cocaine and suggested he try it in the bathroom. He completed his seduction—or business arrangement, as Roy had preferred to see it—by promising to use his influence to let Roy buy from his relatives.

The Trujillo family, the most powerful of Colombia's narcotraficantes, had selected the polished thirty-eight-year-old Juan Sierra as its
distribution manager for Southern California only in part because he
could assume an unremarkable existence in Los Angeles. A stocky man
of middling height, Juan's face was rounder than he might wish and his
jaw beginning to jowl, yet he retained the dark good looks of his youth.
His eyes were striking, shining with intelligence, seldom flashing the
cruelty that had marked his early career.

After their first evening together, Juan had ordered his obese, smirk-
ing lieutenant Griego to supply Roy with a couple ounces on credit.
To the Colombians' surprise, the young man had proven reliable, with
Juan gradually increasing the weight for his border crossings. When
Roy had first announced Tommy Mahoney's system, Juan was pleased
with his ambition. And now his King wanted to bring over fifty kilos.
Roy's record had been flawless, he'd arrived on time for every pick-up
and delivery, paid every penny owed. Yet Juan was conflicted. His wispy
ruse—that he was but vaguely aware of his distant cousins' business—
prevented him from describing to Roy how thieves begged for death
once their torture began. Surely, he comforted himself, Roy had to
understand that stolen Trujillo cocaine was worthless; no dealer wishing to see the sun rise would touch merchandise stolen from the family.
Reasoning that Roy would have been careful to show up on time had
he intended to steal the cocaine—rather than two hours late—Juan
had concluded he could trust the youth.

"It was great," Roy insisted, smiling into Juan's liquid brown eyes,
selling what Juan desperately wanted to buy, shaking off his malaise.
"Let's party on." He spooned powder from a ring box onto the green
marble-topped nightstand and chopped it with a razor, lining up four
neat rows. Roy had in fact vowed to show up on time. He understood
the evening's importance, but his body rebelled, as it had every time
with Juan. And while he had no idea who would buy his fifty kilos, he

knew he would be set for life. He could break open a key, cut it with lactose and retail it at his endless parties. He idly wondered if Ramirez would blame Juan for introducing them, whether Juan might suffer afterward. He leaned over the nightstand and snuffed up two lines. "Juan, amigo, quit thinking so much. Let's play backgammon. I'll be red and you're white. Cool? I'll get the board and we'll play here. Party time."

Juan tried to smile, but hounded by his own sense of dignity, he found himself contemplating the world's view of a man in love with such a beautiful boy.

CHAPTER 8

K-39

EDDIE AND ROY STOOD NEXT to the van on a bluff overlooking a small, dingy beach. A faded signpost, *K-39*—the distance in kilometers from the California border—lay off to the side, knocked over by territorial surfers. Brown, muddy, and cobbled with stones, the beach was littered with bits of ancient, surf-polished plastic. The rusted hulk of a truck lay half buried above the high-tide line. They had been surfing until Roy wiped out a few minutes before, gashing his shoulder on a submerged rock. While he whined, Eddie daubed the inch-long cut with Merthiolate from his first aid kit, wondering why Roy, a dolphin in water, was surfing so poorly. It wasn't the joint Roy had smoked on the drive down—Roy was always high. Yet he seemed skittish. Was he that worried about their border crossing? Overselling, he'd called his plan foolproof so many times that, mocking him, Eddie had taken to labeling everything from his car radio to the impressive surf foolproof.

Roy tapped the gauze and winced. Lighting a cigarette, he reached for his brush, but cried out in pain attempting to stroke his shoulder-length hair. He switched to his left hand, bent over and slowly, methodically brushed his hair, counting his strokes.

Eddie stowed the kit, pulled a sheet from the van, wedged two corners into its doors, and tied the others to makeshift tent poles, creating a shaded porch. He spread a plastic drop cloth, unzipped his sleeping bag, and the boys sat, propped against the van, protecting themselves from its heating metal with their threadbare Inn towels. "You want to go out again?" asked Eddie. "The ocean's got to be less germy than half the girls you screw."

"No way. The salt would sting like hell. Not my day." Roy threw his head back and drained a beer in one impressive swallow and reached for another. "Cerveza?"

"Nah, I'm good." Eddie leaned back and looked up at the cotton sheet, the sun working through its worn fibers. He wondered if Roy's edginess was catching, and checked his hands for tremors. They were steady. He closed his eyes and after a time unmoored, drifting into thoughts of the next two years—at the university—paid for with one day's work. He saw himself treated as an equal, instead of as an overly clever servant, a dog that could stand on its hind legs. Away from Jonnie. His pleasant reverie meandered until, finishing his second beer, Roy asked, "You ever think about just disappearing? Leaving town, so no one can ever find you again?"

Amused, supposing his drug-dealing friend had ample reason to contemplate getaways, Eddie considered the question, unearthing a distant memory. "Once when I was a kid, I saw a headline in *True*—something like "50,000 men vanish each year." I thought it meant getting zapped by some Martian ray-gun so I opened the magazine. But the article was just about husbands taking off. Going out for a loaf of bread and never coming back."

"That's what I'm talking about. Never coming back." Roy pressed against the gauze pad on his shoulder. "But have you ever thought about it?"

"No," Eddie said, rueful, kicking at the sand with his sandal, thinking about what might have been. "Why would I? My life vanished on its own."

"Dude, cut the downer crap. C'mon. How about Montana?"

"No," said Eddie. "It'd have to be a big city, somewhere you could really hide."

"Like LA or maybe Frisco?"

"New York. They're always finding some Nazi hiding in New York. I'd disappear there, three thousand miles away." Turning away, he shut his eyes, hoping to revive his pleasant musing.

"New York…" Roy smoked while Eddie dozed, pondering what little he knew about Manhattan: Central Park, the Empire State Building, and what Juan Sierra had told him about Fire Island. Juan, he thought, scratching a nasty itch. Juan would be all right. No one could blame him for Roy's betrayal. How angry could Ramirez get, he wondered for perhaps the tenth time. Colombia produced tons of cocaine every day, smugglers lost shipments all the time to the border police. Ramirez would get over it. He rose, then trod down to the beach, distancing himself from his treachery. Roy pitied Eddie for a moment but swatted the thought away by assuring himself that Schmidt would change his mind; he would merely arrest him. A couple years in prison was no big deal. Holding his cigarette aloft, he dunked his head in the mottled soapy shore break, careful to keep his shoulder dry. He flicked his yellowed-straw hair back, stretched, and then trembled. Doubts had rushed in, slipping through the cracks of his near sobriety. The Colombians would figure it out, Eddie would get busted at the border, the crooked cop Schmidt would screw him. No, no, no. It would go according to his plan, he insisted, conjuring his magical island of turquoise waters, white sand, heavy-shouldered waves, beautiful girls, and drugs as plentiful as coconuts.

Time limped in the Mexican heat. At last, the dozing Eddie woke to the strike of a match.

"Here's the plan," Roy said, taking a hit from his third joint of the day. "You do some waves or just chill and I'll go pick up the shit in Rosarito. No risk for Wad. Cool?" High again—his hour in the Garden of Gethsemane past—Roy had consigned one and all to their separate fates and himself to paradise. "Toss me the keys."

An hour later, Roy was back. "Wad, I got a joke for you. What's the difference between dope and blow? I mean, cocaine."

"I don't know."

"Nothing. You get twenty years selling either one," Roy said.

"What?" Eddie asked, bewildered.

"The dope dudes gave me a way better offer and we can make some really big bucks."

"What the fuck," cried Eddie, catching on instantly. "You're talking about smuggling cocaine."

Roy slid open the van's door, yanked out a khaki duffel bag. "Check it out."

Eddie lifted the bag, unhooked the strap, and pulled out a kilogram of Trujillo cocaine. He turned the tannish block over in his hands. It was the size of a shallow shoe box, encased in resin, marked with an inlaid black eagle. He held it at arm's length, but with interest, a biologist with a viper.

"This is a kilo? How many did you get?" He noticed another duffel inside the van.

"Twenty-five."

"Do you ever tell the fucking truth, Roy?" Eddie snapped, his anger flaring. "This bag is heavier than fifty pounds, and that one looks full, too."

"I meant twenty-five in each bag. Why would I shit you when you can count them?" Roy pinched his cigarette between his lips, tucked his hands into his armpits and rocked back and forth, eyeing Eddie. "C'mon, Wad, it's no big deal."

"This why you've been so jumpy? The penalty for coke is way worse than pot? You lied to me again. Goddamn it."

"Twenty years is twenty years. But we're not getting caught."

"What's coke sell for in San Diego?" Examining the rigid kilo, he questioned the eagle's significance, guessing it was a brand. What little

Eddie knew about cocaine came in snippets from the Inn's fast set: it was the world's greatest party drug, Freud loved it, Sherlock Holmes used it to solve cases, and coke-fueled sex was amazing. It was the original *coca* in Coca-Cola, a simple pick-me-up that prohibitionist puritans had outlawed. No one spoke of its Shiva power to destroy.

"Doesn't matter, man, we're just bringing it across, you know, like mailmen. We drop it off tonight to los hombres malos."

"You bullshitted me again."

"Five thousand, muchacho." Roy held up a slender hand with five fingers extended. "Five big ones. The King's sorry for the surprise, but he'll make the pot right."

"How much is in your can?" Eddie demanded, Roy's money screaming at him, clouding his judgment, telling him this was his life-changing moment. He knew Roy's promises were worthless. Any payment had to be cash in hand.

"Count it, I don't know."

Eddie pulled out a plum from the Maxwell House can. A fat roll of hundreds. "I'll take it all."

"Fuck you, Wad, take it, take it all, I don't care," Roy said. "There's enough for everybody. I've got to get back to the hotel, call Tommy's wife to check on the lane number."

"Careful shifting into second this time."

"No, dude, I'll hitch. Can't cruise with the weight. You guard it." With that, Roy trudged toward the road. Out of Eddie's sight, he smiled big, relieved. Then he remembered what he was doing—and who would pay—and glanced back over his shoulder at his boyhood friend with what passed for regret. "Later, Wad."

CHAPTER 9

ROSARITO

SITTING ON THE RUBBLED BEACH awaiting Roy's overdue return, Eddie scowled at the jammed coffee can at his feet. How would he explain a staggering cash deposit to a skeptical bank teller? Would she press a hidden button for security? Swearing, Eddie suddenly understood why Roy kept his fortune in a can. He rose and, kicking at the packed sand, walked to the tide line, picked up a clutch of smooth stones and skimmed them seaward, occasionally glancing back at the wilting highway. He threw until his arm ached, perhaps twenty minutes, and then dove through the shore break to cool himself. Salt thirsty, he hiked up to the van for one of Roy's beers.

He tried reading but was distracted by Roy's lingering absence. After a time, a crumpled Ford Falcon wheezed onto the cliff, stopping near his van. A young, burly Mexican stepped out.

"Wad?" The Mexican asked.

"Yeah?"

The Mexican handed him a torn sheet of paper. *"Wad, I got busted. I'm stuck here in Rosareto. Tommy's ready at 9 in 7. Go thru, then get my car and bring it back so I can give it to these dudes to buy my way out of here. Sign this paper with your real name and give it to this dude so I know you got the messige. Double can for coming back. Hurry this place sucks. King."*

Cursing, Eddie read it again, then jotted his name on the note against the driver's door. "You speak English? Is Roy OK? What did he do?"

"OK. Smoking the mary-juana," the Mexican said, pantomiming smoking, then putting his wrists together in the universal sign of arrest.

He stepped toward his car, intent on collecting the other half of the hundred-dollar bill the gringo had torn to assure a round trip.

"Does he really have to bribe the federales with a new car? Isn't a couple hundred bucks enough?"

The Mexican shrugged, his Falcon coughing into life. He backed up the hill and drove off. Eddie cursed, then grabbed a rock and hurled it toward the beach. "That fucking idiot. Goddamn it."

He was in trouble.

Why hadn't he pressed Roy for details? If only he had a phone number, someone to call for advice, somewhere safe to drop the bags in Mexico. But there was nowhere safe in Mexico. "Like they don't know you and you don't know them. That's as good as it gets, Wad," Roy had assured him.

He knew Roy was gutless and would do anything—say anything— to get out of jail. He saw Roy squealing "Edward O'Hare Kawadsky" to his interrogators, switching their roles, claiming that he was the innocent friend along for the surfing. Was Roy stupid enough to tell the cops where to find Eddie and the van? To give him up to get out of jail? No, even Roy had to know that the hombres malos were his bigger problem. But could he take that chance? Eddie had to get out of Mexico. How would the hombres react when their delivery didn't show up? They would track Roy to the Rosarito jail in a heartbeat and then? Roy would cough up every detail he knew about Eddie to save his own hide, somehow even blaming him for his arrest. Within minutes, the narcotraficantes would know where to find Eddie, and then they would kill him… unless he had every kilo at hand. Even then Eddie knew he would be a loose end to men who dealt summarily with loose ends. He had to get the hell out, but it was hours until he could cross the border in Tommy's line.

Methodically, he began to repack the van. Almost without thought, he stashed the duffel bags beneath the foam rubber rectangle that served as his bed, then arranged his bedsheets, his father's canvas flight bag that served as his laundry bag, and finally the wax-laden surfboards on top. He had to drive the cocaine across the border, hide it somewhere, then hide himself until Roy had satisfied his dealers that their shipment was safe. He would call Mrs. Cross and ask her to have Roy leave a number where he could reach him. But where to hide?

He argued to the sun-whitened sky that drug dealers were businessmen, that they were reasonable, that they would listen as long as their shipment was safe. They wouldn't knife someone just because he was a witness to their crimes. But the indifferent sky mocked him.

He plopped down in the shade of the van, dropped his head in his hands, and cried.

CHAPTER 10

NOTHING TO DECLARE

On his way north to Tijuana, Eddie eased into Rosarito, squinting after a jail down each of the small streets off Calle Benito Juarez. The town was little more than a hotel and a few strips of huddled shops. He found it hard to believe it even had a jail. A couple streets were cobbled, but most were dirt. He saw a dust-yellow dog dead in the middle of one street and wondered how long it would lie there. He wrinkled his nose at the village's raw sewage oozing into the sea.

Farther north, an abandoned, half-built concrete house reminded him of crazy old Mrs. Doyle and her underground bomb shelter in Lemon Grove. He had been cutting her lawns for a few months before he chanced upon its entry hatch while trimming her bougainvillea. The rusted lock fell open, revealing spider webs and shallow pooled water inside the bare room. The house had stood vacant after her death, and he guessed the buyers never found the shelter. He could approach it from the hillside behind, slip over the back fence, and stash the drugs. No one could connect him with fifty kilos there.

He refined his plan as he idled along, deciding to stop first at the Inn and cram the duffel bags in Roy's trunk before heading to Lemon Grove. He could deny any knowledge of the car's contents if he were stopped by the police.

"I'm so fucked," cried Eddie again, six cars out from crossing lane seven, as he spied the middle-aged inspector leaning from the booth.

With madly darting eyes, he realized Tommy was neither in Lane 6 or 8. Even if he was, it was too late to jump lanes without drawing suspicion. His heart hammering, Eddie reached for another Marlboro, took a half-dozen quick drags, thought he glimpsed Tommy in Lane 11 and swore anew. Reasoning that border guards were likely suspicious of nerve-calming tobacco, he hit the cigarette one last time, then tossed the butt. If only he were that red-tailed hawk he'd imagined himself in Antelope Valley, if only he could soar to Coronado. Then he remembered the panic he'd felt that day when the glider nosedived after his father had dropped the stick, barking at Eddie to fly it himself, to tough it out. He'd lost a couple thousand feet of altitude and stalled it just once before realizing he could level the plane if he just stayed calm, if he was gentle with the damn stick. Now, he inhaled deep, held his breath for a sixty-count, telling—no, *begging*—his heart to slow.

"You a California resident, son?" The lean inspector had noticed the crumpled hippie van when it was five cars out, thinking it held more promise than the sedans and pick-ups. He looked ex-Army, a retired sergeant in his early forties working on a second government pension. Suspicion came to him naturally.

"Yes sir."

"You really in the Navy?" Dubious.

"Not yet, sir. I'm enlisting as soon as I finish school. This was Dad's." He touched the brim of his Fightertown USA hat in a near salute. "He was a Navy pilot."

"You have anything to declare?"

"No sir, nothing to declare."

"What were you doing in Mexico?" He glanced past Eddie toward the back of the van.

"I was surfing, sir, with my buddy from Pendleton. He got lucky with some girl on the beach, and I'm stuck coming home alone."

"What's all that back there, son?" The inspector nodded toward the rear, but kept his hard gaze on Eddie.

"Sir, after Dad got shot down in Vietnam, my mother… she passed too, and I've been living in my van to save money for school. I work at the Riviera Inn in—"

"Your daddy got killed flying in Vietnam?"

"Yes, sir. He was awarded a posthumous Distinguished Flying Cross. Would you like to see it?" Eddie pulled the small box from his glove compartment. To this point he was rehearsed, but as he handed over the red, white, and blue ribboned medal, tears welled up. He wiped his cheek, he said, "I'm sorry, sir. He was a great man."

"That's all right, son." After admiring it, the inspector handed the medal back to Eddie. "You just get in the Navy and do right by your country. Sorry about your folks," the tough inspector added in a kindly voice that would have shocked his co-workers. "Take care in that war, boy."

"Thank you, sir." Eddie slipped the long stick shift into gear and drove off, keeping his eyes straight ahead as he passed the secondary area. He stroked the medal box as if for luck, then tucked it inside his sweatshirt.

CHAPTER 11

A RIDE DOWNTOWN

Sergeant Rudy Schmidt drove into the Riviera Inn and parked his wife's Chevy wagon within sight of Roy's convertible. He settled himself in for the wait, squeezing his grip-strengthener as he listened to the Dodgers on the radio.

A law school dropout, Schmidt had made sergeant in five years and earned a medal of valor for pulling a child from a burning duplex in southeast San Diego. Balding and barrel-chested, the thirty-five-year-old seldom smiled at anyone other than his superiors, small children, or the rare woman who chose to flirt with him. Divorced and remarried, he had two young households to support and a grudge against the fates—police work was beneath him.

Roy Cross had found Schmidt by quizzing his father about corruption in the San Diego PD. A retired sergeant who'd spent his career in personnel, his alcoholic father had sworn the department was the cleanest in the country, but finally threw out some second-hand, unreliable gossip about Schmidt to rid himself of his annoying, good-for-nothing son. Motivated, Roy had wasted little time in finding Schmidt and offering him the bust of a lifetime. Roy said he knew a major dealer who brought truckloads of cocaine across the border. Schmidt could lie in wait and arrest him when he arrived at a transfer point, report a couple kilos, and deliver the rest to Roy in exchange for a small fortune.

"How many kilos are you talking about?" Schmidt asked.

"Big-time, man," said Roy. "Twenty, thirty, maybe more. That's why you could do the deal with me and still have this monster bust. Five or six kilos of blow—cocaine—and you'd be on the evening news… and you'd be rich."

Schmidt had listened—listened hard—telling himself he would go along with the kid's scheme, then arrest the dealer, report the whole load, and put the punk away for attempted bribery. Yet in the ensuing days, he'd entertained himself noodling out details for a workable scenario, shaking his head at the kid's half-assed plan. A week later, the pair had met on the wide beach in front of the Del Coronado hotel, Roy insisting they go shirtless to eliminate the possibility of a wire. Still intent on a clean bust, Schmidt nevertheless took perverse pride in explaining a workable plan. One man couldn't do it. An on-duty patrolman couldn't hide out while making rounds and responding to calls from his dispatcher. Two officers could. One off-duty to force the dealer at gunpoint to a remote stretch within the on-duty's beat. The perp would be forced to sit while the off-duty, using a street pistol, shot the patrol car full of holes. The on-duty officer would return the fire, killing the suspect, while his partner sped off in a getaway car with the bulk of the cocaine before backup could arrive. The crime scene investigators would buy a Wild West shootout.

"Whoa, whoa, whoa." Roy was shocked. "You talking about—about…?" He made a shooting gesture with his thumb and forefinger. "That's way too heavy, man. No can do, muchacho."

Schmidt turned hard. "Your perp would be looking at twenty years for that much weight. He wouldn't stop talking till they slab him."

"Like no way." Roy had never connected murder with his scheme, supposing his fall guy would just do a couple years.

"Good luck with your nickel-and-dime dealing, kid. See you at the lineup." Schmidt put on his shirt and stalked off. Roy caught up him five minutes later in the public parking lot off Orange.

"OK," Roy said, his voice small, forlorn. He lit a joint as he watched Schmidt drive away. Because of Tommy's desperation, Roy was out of time and Schmidt his only hope. He held his breath, holding the smoke deep, and was soon pleasing himself, imagining the conversation in which he'd talk Schmidt out of murder.

EDDIE CHUGGED HIS VAN INTO the parking spot under the dusty Monterey pine, shut off the motor and gathered his clothes on the passenger seat. He was rolling up the window when it struck metal. He froze, facing a pistol barrel.

Schmidt jammed the gun and his badge through the window. "Edward Kawadsky. You're under arrest for transporting narcotics. Put your hands on the steering wheel and don't make a goddamn sound."

Stunned, Eddie felt his heart stop, then pound as if exploding from his chest. He watched in horror—in slow motion—as the burly gun-wielding cop sidled around the front of the van, opened the passenger door, and climbed in. A lightning storm of wordless images—from handcuffs to prison to a weeping Jonnie—bolted through Eddie's consciousness. Knowing his life was over, he made no effort to stem his tears.

"Not a fucking sound." Schmidt pressed his pistol against Eddie's temple, the gun sight nicking him, drawing blood. He slapped the youth's sides and ran a professional hand down his legs, squeezing his crotch, feeling for weapons. "We're going for a ride. Back out slow." Jamming the throwaway .38 against Eddie's ribs, he reached back for the nearer duffel bag, unhooked the strap and fished out a kilo, another spilling onto the floor. "How many you got?"

"Fifty, officer. But they're not mi—"

"Shut up."

"I've never been arrested before," Eddie pleaded, racking his brain, but coming up empty. With no bigger fish to give up, no one to help the police arrest, Eddie realized he was the end of the line—the only prize at the county fair. With the truth useless, all he could do was beg. "Honest. They're not mine. I was just helping out a—"

"Shut the fuck up." Schmidt looked away from the crying kid and swore over Roy's lies; this kid was no criminal, no big-time dealer.

"I've never done this before."

"Don't talk to me. Not a goddamn word. Keep your eyes on the road." The cop eyed the trembling bill of the boy's baseball cap.

Eddie raised a hand to wipe his cheek.

"Your hand leaves that wheel again, you get a third eye." Schmidt shook his head, dismissing Roy's lies and ticked through the remaining steps of his plan. If he regretted the need to murder an innocent kid rather than a hardened dealer, his remorse was fleeting. Killing Kawadsky was only business, the cost of winning the criminal lottery. Schmidt was tough. He knew he could shoot the kid, go home, screw his wife, and then sleep sounder than his four-year-old. In fact, he half-wished he could do the shooting himself—that would be something—but the on-duty, Delagarza, had to do it.

"Which way now?"

"We're going downtown." No one would miss the sniveling punk.

CHAPTER 12

BANG, BANG, BANG, BOOM

EDDIE'S MIND RACED, DANCING FROM his empty future to his moves at the police station, how he would get a lawyer, whom he should call, what Jonnie would say, whether she would hire him back when he was released from prison, whether convicted felons were permitted to attend college, how Roy's dealers would react to the loss. Were felons even allowed real jobs? How much did criminal lawyers cost?

And then it occurred to him. Why was he driving instead of hand-cuffed inside a squad car? And why was the cop wearing gloves? Wait. The cop had said Edward Kawadsky. How the hell did he know his name?

"Isn't the police station on Market Street?" Eddie demanded. What was happening?

"I'll tell you when the hell to turn. Shut the fuck up."

Schmidt scanned for his on-duty partner as they approached Pill Hill, Delagarza's beat around the hospital. His plan was simple. Delagarza would radio in for his meal break and follow the van toward the airport, parking at an air cargo lot beneath the rumbling freeway. Delagarza would report that he'd observed a vehicle with a broken headlight pull into the lot on his way to dinner. Suspicious, he'd followed, noticing a meet-up with another vehicle for an apparent narcotics exchange. The officer had approached with caution and suspect number one had opened fire. The officer had immediately called for backup. Suspect number two had sped off in a late-model sedan as the officer returned fire, terminating suspect number one.

"Officer, what are we doing here?" asked Eddie.

"You're getting arrested."

"Why aren't we going to the station? This isn't right."

"Shut up. Stop near that wagon, not too close." The last thing Schmidt needed was a bullet hole in his brother-in-law's car.

Delagarza braked behind them, and sprinted over to the van, asking, "How come you're not driving?"

"How the fuck would you explain handcuff burns on his wrists? I frisked him—he's clean. Keep your piece on him while I move the stuff." Schmidt threw the two duffel bags in the station wagon, started it and, leaving the engine running, ran back to the van with a pound of marijuana in a paper bag.

"Ready?" Delagarza asked, grinning. Delagarza was more than ready. A first generation Mexican-American who'd endured thousands of racial slurs—wetback least among them—and institutional, if not universal discrimination, the thought of getting away with murdering a white dealer was nearly irresistible.

"Break a headlight on your way back and get the hell away from your vehicle. You don't want to catch a ricochet. Remember, I fire three shots into your cruiser, jump out of the van, and then it's your turn." Schmidt waved the pistol at Eddie and barked, "Get in the passenger seat." He climbed into van, tossed the marijuana in back, and wiped his forehead on his sleeve. He shouted at Delagarza. "Get farther over there, stay down, but keep your piece on the perp."

Eddie's heart hammered, his mind caroming in the terrifying moment's eternity. How did they know his name? How did they know about the Inn? Roy. Only goddamned Roy could have told them, but when? He was locked up in Rosarito. Or was he? Had Roy set him up? But why? The only thing he had no need to guess about was his own murder. He'd witnessed their theft of the cocaine, the elaborate tableau they were constructing. "How the fuck would you explain hand-cuff burns on his wrists?" the gloved cop had said. The gloves spoke chapter and verse. Eddie knew they would murder him in a matter of moments. Besieged by images of blood and death, he cast about wildly for some way out. He was dead either way—if he ran, they'd shoot him in the back; if he stayed, in the head.

"Not a fucking move, kid." Schmidt fixed the youth with a fierce stare. His shots into the patrol car had to be at the right angle for the forensics team. He turned away from Eddie, twisted from the waist and stuck his head and arm out of the window, craning toward his target.

Eddie's murder was next. His heart pounding in his ears, an image of his father's gun flashed by like a card in a shuffling deck. He snaked his hand toward the floor, groping beneath the seat, brushing the coffee can. Frantic, he scrunched down, reaching further, finally fingering the big Colt. Gripping it, he raised the black pistol soundlessly, cocking it just as the cop fired his gun.

Despite his hurry, Schmidt wanted to hit the squad car's windshield at least once. He fired high and cursed the worthless .38 and then his partner for parking too close behind the van. He waited for a jet's roar to cover his shot, then squeezed the trigger. Swearing, he dropped his aim and fired again, the bang answered by the crackling of safety glass. He fired a third time, shattering glass.

Boom! The last shot was much louder. Delagarza jumped up from his crouching position fifteen yards from his patrol car, his gun at the ready. "Let's go, Sarge, hustle up. I've got to call for backup."

Schmidt was going nowhere. Blown off by a .45 slug to the base of his skull, his cranium had exploded in splinters of bone, arcing across the parking lot.

"Sarge, c'mon," the patrolman yelled.

Peering over the dead sergeant, Eddie fired again, his shot was high, but it froze Delagarza. Eddie gripped the gun with both hands, the way his father had taught him, resting it against Schmidt's slumped shoulder, and fired. The bullet ripped into Delagarza's chest, slamming him backward, his hat rolling off as his head thudded against the pavement. Eddie looked at the body beneath him, half out his window, fouling itself, and the other jerking on the asphalt, and he lost it, gagging as he pushed open the door.

He heard the station wagon's running engine when he glanced up, wiping his mouth on his sweatshirt. A moment later, he was scrambling out, only remembering the coffee can because he had just touched it. He sprinted toward the idling car, threw it into reverse by mistake, smashed a pair of bollards, put it in drive and stepped on the gas. He screeched out into the night as an unseen jet rumbled down the nearby runway.

"CHIEF?" SGT. WILLIAM POWERS REPEATED his one-note question, weighting on one foot, then the other. The gathered squad cars' flashing light bars lent a false dawn to the midnight crime scene. It smelled of blood. Patrolmen stood around, doing nothing, murmuring among themselves, watching the crime scene investigators' methodical process. Something about the chief looked wrong the moment he'd stepped from his wife's Buick. At first Powers thought it was his surprise at seeing the great man out of uniform. Then he realized the chief had forgotten his hairpiece.

"Ah, Chief, would you happen to have a cap in your car?" The sergeant rubbed his head.

"What?" Following his gaze, Chief Ross felt his bare head, swore, and fetched a Padres baseball cap. He'd been on the radio while he raced to the scene. Even without the watch commander's sketchy details, the chief would have taken it in at a glance. Schmidt was wearing gloves.

"You're Peters?"

"Powers, sir."

"Right. You knew Rudy Schmidt?"

"I worked with him a bit at the Seniors' League, poor soul."

"Good man. I can't believe this, this, this—I just can't believe it. You know our patrolman?"

"No, sir. Well, of course I seen him around, but I—"

"You think this was his idea? Maybe relatives in Tijuana? Brothers or cousins dealing drugs?" A tall man who jogged to keep his weight in check, the chief straightened his slouch as he did before addressing audiences. His handsome, lined face was haggard, ghostly in the gloaming. "What do we have so far?"

"The slugs in our vehicle are .38's, probably from the gun in Schmidt's hand. The lads were both killed with something bigger, a 9mm maybe, maybe a .44. We haven't found any other weapons."

"The van?"

"Registered to an Edward Kawadsky. Teenager. No rap on him. He's clean as far as we know. We're getting an APB out, but the van might be hot." Enjoying his first one-on-one with the chief, Powers went over their preliminary findings in detail—the throwaway pistol, the powder burns on Schmidt's gloves, the marijuana, the two kilograms of cocaine with eagle markings. He detailed everything but their fallen comrades' complicity.

Chief Ross's attention wandered from the damning gloves to the press conference he would call in the morning, how he would announce a full-scale investigation into departmental corruption. The mayor would showboat as usual, insisting on head-rolling even if they proved this was an isolated incident. "What'd you just say?"

"I said maybe contacting the FBI—"

"This is our mess, and we'll clean it up ourselves. But, gentlemen," he barked at the officers working the scene. "Do you hear me? We're not resting until these perps are caught, tried, and convicted. We're not pulling any punches because of this... this involvement. This investigation will go all the way."

CHAPTER 13

LAS TUMBAS

A FEW BLOCKS NORTH OF the hotel, Rosarito's police station squatted on a dirt road next to a used-car lot. The station was on the ground floor of a white-plastered, two-story building that still looked like a medical clinic. The cars in the lot, junkers to Chryslers, were the bail Americans posted for their freedom. Few were ever reclaimed.

Manuel Chávez strode into the station's waiting room. Ignoring the filth, the fading advertisements, and the beaten-down supplicants, he rapped on the sliding glass window that protected the clerk from the outside world. Although Chávez was a slight man, his stature increased the moment he spoke. His voice was deep, scented with education. He chose his words with care and had developed the habit of making the world strain to hear him.

Señor Chávez confirmed the prisoner's presence with the clerk and asked to speak with the station's commanding officer. When the officer appeared, Chávez explained how impossible it would be to conduct his client interview in the station. With a wave of his hand, a whisper of his silk suit, he offered to pay for an officer's time to accompany attorney and client to the hotel's bar. The officer said he would bring the prisoner himself, promising to have him there in ten minutes. Chávez strolled out.

"Now, Mr. Cross. Please tell me again how it came to happen you were smoking a marijuana cigarette in front of this hotel." With a flick of his thumb, Chávez opened his silver lighter, lit a cigar that dwarfed his small, manicured hand, and glanced around the blue-tiled, white-washed bar. Chávez was puzzled and thus interested.

Roy tossed his hair from side to side. "I told you, man. I just forgot about it being a big deal. Didn't see any federales hanging around. That's cool."

"But if you did not think it was the big deal, why did you first assure yourself of the authorities' absence?" Chávez, sipping his gin and tonic, nodded in the direction of the patient officer three tables away, tried to make eye contact with a pair of women sitting at the bar.

"I was just being careful." Roy followed the lawyer's gaze, appraised the women in a glance, and grinned. "Not so malo, man."

"So careful you smoked not one but two marijuana cigarettes at Rosarito's most busy place?"

"Why don't you just bail me out and take me to Ramirez? He's cool."

"Let us talk first of the shipment," said the lawyer.

"Can I get another rum and coke?"

"Where is it now?"

"Like I told you, Mr. Lawyer Man, I don't know where it is right now. Hey, por favor, another bebida."

"You must tell me where the shipment is, Mr. Cross. Otherwise, I cannot help you." Chávez wondered about Cross's apparent indifference to his plight. Was this golden boy an idiot?

"Somewhere in San Diego. Eddie, my friend, has it in his van. Want me to, like, describe him again?" Roy had hoped to give Ramirez enough details to identify Eddie and his van, but not before Schmidt could get to him. A miscalculation. He had planned on hours before help arrived, but Chávez's quick appearance and polite questioning was unnerving him.

"Now, it is in San Diego? Please forgive me, but I thought you said it was still in Mexico."

"Look, man, I don't know whether it's here or there, because I'm stuck here talking to you. Bail me out and we'll meet Eddie at midnight at the hotel in Coronado. He'll have the shit and everybody goes home happy."

"Describe the auto again for me please." Chávez admired a rich-look-ing American whose bikini was covered with a flimsy wrap.

"Dude, I told you. It's a beat-to-shit, blue and white VW van; license plate number D-A-B-2-6-4." He stared at the lazy ceiling fan, telling himself to stay cool, be helpful.

"Most impressive." Chávez scanned his monogrammed black leather notebook to check the number against the first one Roy had given him. "I am sorry, but my handwriting is deplorable; you said your own license number was?"

"Let's see. B, A—no, R—yeah, R, G, and the numbers are 0-6-9."

He jotted the number down. "I am curious, Mr. Cross. If you were home in San Diego, would you smoke the marijuana on a busy street?"

"Dude, I'm always high, I smoke wherever I'm at. No big deal."

Perhaps the story was truly one of a dull boy whose need for mari-juana overcame the most elementary caution, but Manuel Chávez had become wealthy by discounting nearly everything he was told, espe-cially from clients. He stood and politely excused himself. He called Juan Sierra's chief lieutenant in Los Angeles. In recounting the arrest and Cross's casual explanation, the lawyer opined to Héctor Griego how peculiar it was for a young smuggler to almost seek arrest. When one contrasted the youth's evasions with his specific information about Kawadsky—particularly, his friend's license plate number—one had to conclude Cross was lying. His small doubt sprang from the young man's vulgar insouciance.

"What do you think, Counselor?" An obese man whose weight caused most to underestimate him, Héctor Griego disguised his ela-tion over the arrest with plodding questions, as if fearing the phone in his garden supplies warehouse were tapped. Griego had longed for Juan Sierra's job from the moment he arrived in California, and now it might be his. The maricón had foolishly—fatally?—entrusted the family's cocaína to his pretty chico.

"Perhaps I am too cynical for forty-five years of good fortune on this earth, but I wager this boy has a far more entertaining story than the one he told me. If he were merely a pendejo, why would he describe his friend in such detail?"

"Will the pendejo be safe in Rosarito?" Griego asked, rubbing a hand through short-cropped black hair. His rubber-topped steel desk was as sloppy as he was, littered with reminders, files, and the remnants of a prodigious lunch.

"They will not keep him here long, Señor. Even the Americans are transferred to La Mesa. You do not need to worry about his escaping, if that is what you mean by safe. But if you are concerned about his welfare, I would advise you to keep him out of La Mesa."

Griego bit down on his fat thumb, imagining Sierra's murderous rampage if it happened that his beloved were guilty only of smoking marijuana, but shipped off to La Mesa with Griego's acquiescence. He asked Chávez if he could arrange to have the boy watched at Rosarito.

Returning to the bar, Chávez observed Cross with keener interest, wondering why Griego was protective. In his soft voice, Chávez explained to the officer how important this boy was to his most influential client. He opened his leather briefcase and, withdrawing a newspaper, set it on the table, suggesting the officer read the financial section. Chávez said no fortune the boy might promise would be worth the consequences certain to arise from his release, escape, or even minor injury. Tapping the bulging newspaper, he said, "My clients are generous to their friends, Señor, but they are simple men who live by an ancient code. They see everything in black and white, and nothing could be blacker than the boy's disappearance."

With his right hand on the paper as if it were a courtroom bible, the officer pledged he and his brother would guard the prisoner round the clock.

Roy fumed when Chávez told him that he would remain in Rosarito pending the midnight delivery. He chased after Chávez into the dirt parking lot, the smiling officer trailing at a distance, clutching his newspaper to his chest.

"Does Juan Sierra know I'm here?" he demanded.

"Who?" Chávez almost masked his surprise. How could this boy possibly know Juan Sierra? Chavez himself had exchanged no more than the most skeletal of pleasantries with the infamous head of the Trujillo family.

"Juan Sierra. He's a really good friend of mine. A guy he knows is buds with Ramirez. Juan can do a number with his buds and they can trip with Ramirez. He'll spring me then. Cool? Can you call Juan?"

"If you truly know Mr. Sierra, you know that is impossible." Chávez was flustered by the boy's request and his incomprehensible slang and, puffing on his cigar, coughed when he accidentally inhaled.

"Why not? I have the number."

"I have no more time for your games, young man." Chávez frowned at the dust on his car. "Your Ramirez and all of his bosses do not sleep until Mr. Sierra says good night, and lawyers lose not only their clients but their heads when they disturb him." He yanked his door shut, disappeared behind its black-tinted window, and spun off in a spray of dust, powdering an open-mouthed Roy and the officer.

"Fucking lawyers think they know everything." Roy held a finger to the sky, vowing to spend no more than one night in jail. With the bills he'd stashed beneath his soles, all hundreds, he could walk out in five minutes.

He had it covered.

JUAN SIERRA'S JAW ACHED FROM his root canal. He swallowed four aspirin with vodka in his favorite restaurant, a quiet place in Westwood with brick walls, deep, red leather booths, white tablecloths, and respectful waiters. His King must have done it, he told himself. Whatever doubt their clever lawyer had would have vanished had he known this shipment was worth a dozen times his standard delivery.

"George, please. Another bloody Mary. A double. The celery is not essential." He nodded at the two stalks in front of him. "Perhaps a cup of bouillon, yes?"

"Of course, sir."

He mulled Roy's tale of going to the hotel to call Tommy Mahoney, of his uneasiness, of his wanting to get high before hitchhiking back to the shipment, of looking up and down the street for police and then deciding a quick cigarette was safe. Juan knew how much he smoked, how little caution he displayed. His fury with the boy was tinged with guilt. He'd intended only one stiff drink after the dentist, a soothing vodka to make sense of his numb lip, but the bar afforded other possibilities. His pimpled trick had left him not only depressed but questioning why he had been faithful to Roy, why the act without the youth released only sadness. Denying he might love him, Juan insisted his fidelity was merely the result of a busy schedule.

He sipped his drink and scanned the expensive, crowded restaurant. Griego had been optimistic about recovering the shipment, perhaps even before midnight. Assuming he succeeded, Juan wavered over letting Roy escape with a minor beating, one that would require a mere overnight hospital stay instead of six months in a wheelchair.

Griego approached Juan's booth with somber eyes but a step remarkably light for a man of his girth.

"What news? Sit, please sit."

"They found the van." Griego closed his porcine eyes as if in prayer. "Empty."

"They are certain?"

"Yes, Padrino. It matches Cross's description. The license plate number is the one he gave us, and two of our kilos were found on the floor."

"Goddamn him to hell." Juan ground his fists into the tablecloth. "Goddamn him to hell. He dies the moment we recover our shipment. You promised me we would get that shipment back tonight."

"We will, we will. Let me explain. I—"

"Explain on the way to the airport." Juan rose. "Call Pedro to ready the plane and file a flight plan to San Diego." In a fury, he ordered Griego to repeat the details about the dead policemen and the empty van. "This parking lot where the shooting occurred? Where is it?"

"Pacific Coast Highway. Near the airport."

The aching from his tooth worsened. "Could this one boy have killed two policemen by himself?" asked Juan. "No. And we know he didn't walk away with fifty kilos. Someone was waiting in that parking lot. The police must have followed him there, and the shooting happened when they interrupted their exchange."

"We only know what Valiente heard from his source," said Griego. Noticing his boss's grimace, he remembered his root canal and added, "Juan, you are in pain, no? May I offer you a codeine tablet? I take them for my chest pains."

"No, gracias." When had Griego last bathed? Juan rolled his window down halfway and leaned his aching jaw against it, blessing the breeze. "This Kawadsky could not have been part of the plan. Cross would never have described him to us if he were."

"I think the Mexicans must be involved."

Juan clenched his jaw at Roy's deceit and winced, his eyes watering. "Hand me that small bottle in the side pocket. Now." He shook three pills onto his tongue, swallowed them dry. "He will die slowly, but first he will tell me where my cocaína is."

"Could it be a remote possibility? No—I suppose not." Certain the maricón would indeed tell Juan everything within minutes of even anticipating pain, Griego had to buy time. If Juan dealt with the boy swiftly and recovered the cocaína, Griego would have no story to tell Medellín, no sure path to a field promotion. He eased off the gas. "May I say something? As a friend, not as a business associate?"

Juan waved a tired hand.

"I know you better than anyone. Yes. You are harder on yourself than anyone else." He paused, expecting a denial. "You are. I know you have a good friendship with this boy and maybe you identify yourself too much with his mistakes. I am not clever and cannot explain this well, but could you be too hard on him because you like him so much? The boy could be innocent and yet you are planning his death."

"Innocent? Hah." But he considered Griego carefully. Because his secret life rendered compliments meaningless, Juan was impervious to flattery, even heartfelt praise. His weakness lay in his children. On his knees he would pray for his sons' perfection—to be worlds apart from him—and Roy was more than a son to him. Now, in his first conversation ever about Roy, a respected lieutenant was defending him.

"The boy is sitting in jail, two policemen are dead, and he did not—at least personally—steal our shipment. That we know. The rest we must guess, and Chávez said he was so calm he might be telling the truth." They were nearing the Burbank airport. "What if the other boy saw his opportunity when Cross was arrested and made his own arrangements? Or Cross has been bragging about his business and someone told crooked cops who tried to take the cocaína from this other boy. Maybe this Zawadsky will show up tonight at the hotel with the rest of the shipment. Maybe Cross is innocent. If he is interrogated tonight, he will be hurt badly. See him in a few days when you are no longer so angry. Would you like to hear my plan?"

Another languid hand wave.

"We have him sent to La Mesa and have Ramirez take care of his cousin Mahoney, the border guard."

"I wonder if they even are cousins," Juan mused, distracted. "Perhaps it was all part of a lie to make me entrust our shipments with him. The boy is clever; he knows how we value family."

"Cousin or not, we deliver his cojones to Cross in a jar. That and a few days in a real prison will have him begging to talk to us."

"La Mesa." Juan knew its reputation as the worst prison in North America, doubting his lovely güero would survive even a few days there. Then he laughed aloud, laughing at himself for fretting over his King's safety while knowing he would strangle the boy himself.

Griego twisted his ragged knife. "The problem is unless we protect him, we will have nothing to interrogate in a few days. You have heard of Las Tumbas?" All new prisoners started life in the Tombs, he explained, where they slept a dozen to the cell, where the murderers and gang members would assume Roy had money. They would beat him long after he lost consciousness.

"We should keep him out of Las Tumbas, yes?" If Griego could extract a request to protect the boy, he would buy a carraca within the prison, hire a bodyguard, and then inform Medellín how he had been forced to baby Juan's lover when the maricón should have been sliced open like a spring melon. That would seal Juan Sierra's death warrant and his own promotion.

"He would be killed?"

"Let me take you home, Padrino. You need to rest—your tooth is troubling you too much. I will assure his safety and find this friend and the cousin, and I will visit La Mesa to make sure the boy is treated well. But you will personally conduct the interrogation. Yes?"

Juan heard the words as if from a distance. This prison would be a purgatory in the boy's descent to hell.

"Yes?"

"Yes, all right." He rolled down the window again to breathe in the night air as triumph stole across Griego's pendulous cheeks.

CHAPTER 14

THE PINTO

EDDIE'S LEG WAS ASLEEP. TINGLING—NUMB from the hip down—it had pressed too long against the coils of rope and folded canvas in the semi's cab. He raised himself from the cracked seat and shook his unfeeling leg, massaging it. He glanced at the garrulous trucker, a wiry man with sideburns that razored along his jaw line. Peering ahead into the black desert night, the trucker was pushing his eighteen-wheeler hard.

"That's Elko up there. Remember I told you I got me a gal at the Pinto? Ain't just a customer to her neither. Said I was special. Shit, probably wants me to spend the night, give me a long-haul rate. Maybe you ought to get one." The trucker bathed himself in after-shave, stuck a flattened tube of toothpaste in his mouth, and, unscrewing the cap between his teeth, sucked on it. "You ain't much company, kid."

The Pinto Club was a wind-bent trailer park clustered behind a wood-framed house that faced the highway. The red lights alone suggested the club's raison d'etre. From experience, the trucker slowed some distance from the brothel and turned his rig around in the graveled lot, parking it head out nearest the exit.

"This way we ain't eating everybody's dust. Lock the door."

Eddie's leg buckled when he hopped from the cab and he collapsed onto the hard gravel, catching himself with his hand, grunting his pain. He sat up and examined his palm, sharp pebbles embedded in the skin, the sting cutting through his catatonia. In the forty-eight hours since he'd fled San Diego, he'd been more numb than his leg, his every action instinctual, unthinking. A quarry in flight.

"Hey, kid. Where'd you go? Lock that door—Miller ain't leaving his rig unlocked in front of a whorehouse."

"Down here, I just—"

"I'll lock the goddamn door myself." The trucker strutted around the pinging motor. "Give some asshole a ride and he won't even—oh. You, OK? You fall or what?"

"I'm OK, sir. Just need to wash my hand." Eddie rose to his feet, shook his tingling leg, and grabbed his knapsack. He locked the truck's door, taking care not to slam it. Unconsciously, he scanned the parking lot for squad cars. "Thanks for the ride."

"Told you not to call me sir," the trucker said, looking pleased, if uncomfortable with the title. He swept his greasy, curly dark hair back with his fingers, then wiped his hands on his jeans. He wore his keys on his belt loop and his jeans a couple inches above his crotch. "You can wash up inside. One thing they got is plenty of soap. Where'd you say you was heading?"

"East."

"A lot of east that way." The trucker thumbed across Nevada. "Whole damn country. Come on, Honey'll let you wash up. Hell, she'll probably wash it for you."

Eddie followed the trucker into the Pinto and scrutinized the dark, scented room, wary of lurking police. The living room's ceiling was low, its peeling red wallpaper flocked, and its windows blacked out with aluminum foil. Two candelabras graced a flimsy bar that ran along the back wall. The middle of the forlorn room was open, as if for dancing. Two women were playing cards on a plastic-covered couch. They were as remarkable for their nonchalance as their undress. The older woman wore white panties, a lacy black bra, and red high heels. The younger, a platinum blonde lost in her twenties, wore a fraying bikini and a palette of makeup.

"You boys ain't looking for virgins, are you?" The older woman cackled, pulling her cards to her impressive bosom. A worn John Coltrane album played on the record player, competing with the swamp cooler's whooshing.

"Hell no, Honey. I'm here for Dee Dee, she knows I was coming."

"I remember you, handsome. She'll be free—" Honey caught herself, laughed, fluffed her jet-black hair. "I mean she'll be *through* in a few minutes. Sit down and keep a hold of it. How about you, cutie? You got a reservation too?"

"No, ma'am. I just need to wash my hand. I fell outside," said Eddie.

"You don't want a date?" She arched a painted eyebrow at him.

"No. Just my hand." He showed her his bloody palm.

"So you just want a hand job?" Throwing her head back, she laughed as if she were on stage, roiling her ample stomach. "'Oh, no, Mama, I just went in to get my hand washed.' Soldier-boy, I can die happy, I've heard them all now."

"I'll go. I'm sorry." Eddie was out the door and halfway across the gravel parking lot before thinking about finding a hose to rinse his hand. Glancing about, he shook his shoulders against his growing fatigue. Beyond the gibbous moon, the stars were bright, far brighter than those at home, and he searched for Orion. He craved a familiar landmark, something untainted by Mexico. Something clean.

"Hey soldier," the younger woman called from the door. She had slipped on a white cotton bathrobe. "You can wash inside. Honey didn't mean nothing, just we ain't never seen soldiers in here only wanting water. Let me see your hand. Come here, I won't bite you." Her sweet voice suggested she was neither as hard nor as old as she looked.

"Do you have any Merthiolate?"

"Hell, we got our own doctor, comes every Thursday, but I don't know if he's any good. Let me see it. Been a while since I helped a man above the waist." She giggled. "Give it to me." She cupped his hand with hers and inspected it. "Need to see it in the light. I was supposed to be a nurse. Come on."

He followed her through the living room, past Honey and the grinning trucker, and down a red-bulb-lit, low-ceilinged hallway. Her clean, spare room had few decorations: a window blacked out with foil, a double bed with its spread folded over a trunk at its foot, a sink in the corner. A warped plywood shelf sagged above the sink, weighted with bottles, powders, creams, oils, and polishes. Above the clutter, a gilt-framed mirror hung loose off the wall like a painting.

"You didn't bump your head, did you?" She patted his crewcut. "Bring that stool over here and sit down." She turned on the water, letting it warm to her touch, and then she was asking about his life, but he was quiet so she talked about hers instead, telling him her name was Eden.

"Really, it's Karen, but we got stage names, you know, like actresses. We're entertainers, too. Fact, soon as I save up enough, I'm moving to Reno and taking dancing lessons to be a showgirl. Hold your hand still." Plucking the pebbles with eyebrow tweezers, she studied Eddie's closed face and recognized another lost soul. Another runner. Did his father beat him, too? "The real reason we have these silly names is so no weirdos can get after us. But Eden sounds nice, don't it? Garden of Eden, Adam and Eve, but I don't like snakes. Besides, who ever heard of a party gal named Karen?"

She worked with pleasure, saying whatever occurred to her, expecting nothing from the hurting boy who she'd decided was AWOL. Concentrating on her work, humming, murmuring, she felt the soldier gradually drift off and relax his hand in hers. After a while, she coaxed him into removing his horn-rim glasses, hoping he would think her prettier if she were out of focus, and then she remembered staring back at herself from a scratched gas station mirror the night her alcoholic mother had locked her out.

Eddie heard the girl as if she were visiting someone else in a shared hospital room while he was delirious, slipping in and out of consciousness. A tear welled up in his eye, but he blinked it away. He had killed two policemen while breaking the law, while smuggling cocaine. He was guilty and they would catch him and drive him straight to the gas chamber. It was hopeless—the police, the FBI, the dealers, someone would seize him any minute.

"I don't care if you're baptizing that boy in there, Eden, long as you're getting paid," Honey cawed from the hall.

"He's paying, course he's paying," she said, raising a middle finger at her boss through the closed door. "Honey, since it's so slow, could I give him a special for an all-nighter?"

Honey scratched a wide thigh and smiled, flicking her tongue over a missing tooth. "Two hundred."

Shushing Eddie with a finger to her lips, she replied, "He says he ain't got two hundred, but can go a hundred. I'm doing it."

"You get that money now, hear me?" Pleased with the uptick in the evening's fortunes, Honey swayed on her high heels down the hall to listen to the trucker's duet with Dee Dee.

"Don't worry about it, sugar," Eden said to Eddie. "I got the money. I got four hundred sixty-seven dollars saved up."

"No. I mean, I can't. Got to go."

"Be still, I ain't finished yet. If you think you're hitching a ride in front of the Pinto this time of night, you're a lot dumber than you look. Sides, we ain't doing nothing." She straightened her shoulders, envious of her soldier's posture. "I only do it for pay. So don't get your motor running."

"Why would you do that for me?"

She thought about answering, about telling him they were two of a kind, but her guard had been up for so long. "You got a name?"

He looked her in the eyes for the first time and shook his head.

"You can make one up, don't matter, already figured you're running. You AWOL? Sorry, I didn't mean to ask nothing." Vietnam casualty counts competed on the nightly news with stories of frightened boys racing to Canada.

"Joe," said Eddie.

"You ought to pick a better name than *Joe*. There, I'll tape it up in the morning, let it air out tonight. You're staying." Her rising inflection betrayed her hope. "I'll give you a ride to the bus station in the morning. If you need mone—"

"I don't need any money."

Eden put away her tweezers and the sewing needle, zipping them into a pink plastic manicure kit. "You need a back rub, Joe. Yeah. Take your shirt and jeans off and get on the bed. You can leave your skivvies on, we ain't doing nothing. Don't look, I'm changing. I hate this damn bikini." With occupational indifference to nudity, she slipped out of her bikini, pausing to let him disobey her, sulking when he didn't. She shimmied into her favorite nightgown—the winter flannel she wore when she wasn't entertaining.

"I seen clocks wound looser than you." He lay face down and she straddled him. She worked on his broad shoulders, stretching her arms the length of his back, pressing her fingers against hard knots. "Could do better if I didn't have these nails." She kneaded his neck with her palms, cooing about her dreams, about dancing in Las Vegas, about being admired for her talents outside the bedroom.

Exhausted, Eddie drifted away from his last forty-eight hours. He had driven blindly from the horrific killings until he remembered Mrs. Doyle's bomb shelter. He'd found it hidden beneath the bougainvillea, pleaded with God to watch over the cache, praying he could trade it for his life. Then he'd raced downtown, to where lost men drank from paper bags. He'd rolled the windows down, left the keys in the car. Carrying only the coffee can and the .45, he'd forced himself to walk— not run—to the rail yards, arriving as a freight train coughed to life. He had scrambled onto an empty boxcar, had no luck shutting its metal door, then smalled himself into a corner and hugged his knees, swearing he would not sleep. He'd awoken the next morning in Sacramento and thrown the gun from the Tower Bridge into the willow-green river.

Eden giggled and raised her nightgown so her flesh pressed against his as she straddled him. Cat-like, she rolled her arched back forward, grinding her pelvis against him. "Joe… Joe?" She shook her head when she realized he was asleep, mumbled, "Shoot, if all they ever got was back rubs, the job would be OK."

He awoke in the blackness, a stream of sunlight beaming through a pinhole in the window foil. She lay sleeping on her side. He eased the sheet up and beheld her lush guitar-shaped figure, the warmth of her body causing him to bulge. He sighed, thinking her angelic without makeup. His crotch ached at the sight of her breasts and the curve of her hips, and he shut his eyes, telling himself he had to go. A moment later, they popped open when she stroked his underwear. "Not letting that go to waste," she murmured, tugging at him, taking charge.

She fell back asleep when their cloudburst passed. He dressed in silence, pulled a hundred-dollar bill from a hidden pocket and set it atop the shelf. Then, pitying her more than himself, he dropped five more hundreds on the rumpled bed. He'd eased open her door before realizing he'd forgotten the drug store eyeglasses that, along with his crewcut, constituted his thin disguise.

He'd walked a mile into the rising sun, turning to face each car with an outstretched thumb, when a dilapidated Peugeot with a clothes hanger for an antenna pulled over. The driver studied him as he approached, ready to speed off if her impression were wrong. In her mid-thirties, the earthy woman wore a tank top over patched jeans, her frizzed hair tied off with a red bandanna.

"Where you heading, ma'am?" asked Eddie.

"Ma'am? Far out. What's your sign?" She peered over the top of her round sunglasses.

"What?"

"Your astrological sign, like, your constellation," she said.

"Aquarius." He stood a respectful yard from her car door, his hands clasped, recalling Inn conversations that revolved around the stars at the hour of his birth. Conversations in which he'd kept his opinions to himself.

"Bummer. I flashed on you as Capricorn all the way. What's your birthday?"

"January 22nd, ma'am."

"Well, far out, I only missed it by a day. I'm going to Salt Lake to pick up my old man and then we're tripping to Chicago. Where's your head?"

"You mean where am I going? Back east."

"Climb in. You a soldier?"

CHAPTER 15

ZAPATOS

THOUGH LESS THAN AN HOUR'S drive from their hometown of Lemon Grove, Roy's trip was longer than Eddie's cross-country flight. His was to the nether world. It had begun in Rosarito the moment the police-man laughed at his fistful of hundreds, shaking his head, telling him to save it for La Penitenciaría de La Mesa. Upon arrival at the feared prison, a manacled, frightened Roy was met within the hour by the warden himself. Having been apprised by Griego of the boy's value to the Trujillo family, Comandante García had his shackles removed and offered him a glass of water.

"I mean it, man, ah, Generalissimo. You name it, I'll pay it. I just have to get the hell out of here. It was only one joint, dude. One cigarette, comprendo?" Roy spoke loudly, thinking it would ease understanding.

"This is not America. You cannot buy justice in Mexico, we are a country of laws," the comandante said, amused with his own irony. He scratched the head of a large dog sleeping at his side. "You could be here seven years, even ten if the judge decides you are a traficante."

"I had one joint. Take the money, feel it. I've got lots more. Here." His voice cracking with fear, Roy dropped his hundreds on the scarred wooden table between them.

"Ramos, count his money," the comandante said to his lieutenant. "You do not appreciate how happy you are, young man, that I meet you here in person on your arrival, that I will place you in a private cell. Otherwise, my lovely prisoners will take everything you have— not only this money, but your shirt, your cigarettes, even your zapatos. We give your money to the American Consulate. They are the bank for our American nuevos. Your money will help you here, but never to free you."

"A hundred bucks for one phone call, please, man, please."

"Perhaps tomorrow after we meet your visitor."

Héctor Griego arrived at La Mesa the next day with a briefcase, a small shopping bag, and a salsa stain on his white shirt. Like a visiting dignitary, he was escorted with a measure of pomp into Comandante García's inner office. The comandante smiled at his guest, flashing yellow teeth framed by gold caps, delighted to see Griego was even heavier than he.

Griego set his two items on the comandante's elaborate, hand-carved desk, next to pictures of a smiling wife, five smiling children and an amateurish portrait of a German shepherd, also smiling. He clicked open his briefcase, waited for his host to appraise its contents, and complimented the office and its ornate furniture.

The comandante froze at the fortune before him, barely managing to stifle a gasp. Recovering, he said, "I am at your service, Don Héctor. How may I be of help to you?"

Griego had made a mistake. Between his great haste and need to handle all details himself, he had failed to inquire about the going rate for bribes, what bodyguards and carracas should cost. He'd overestimated both by a factor of ten, his mistake an unintended consequence of running a business that weighed rather than counted its cash. He had erred on the side of caution, knowing that if Juan Sierra received unexpected sympathy in Medellín and returned, Griego's survival lay in preserving the boy. By happy coincidence, he also knew that little would enrage Medellín more than learning that Juan had arranged for Roy to be treated like royalty in La Mesa, given a fine carraca, round-the-clock bodyguards, and open visitation rights.

"This güero is extremely important to us. We must know he will be protected—"

"Yes, Don Héctor. All my guards will be informed of this duty, and we will select the prison's most feared killer to be his personal bodyguard."

"And he will be given the finest apartment in the prison?"

"Yes, the very finest carraca. Two stories, two bedrooms, fully furnished, hot and cold running water, a real kitchen, a television—two if you like—a solid door, not plywood, with locks that work. He can have it tonight." García laced his hands across his stomach, praying the fortune in the briefcase was for him. The moment he glimpsed the rows of stacked hundreds, he had reassigned Roy the best carraca, mentally issuing an immediate pardon for its owner.

"You will take personal responsibility for his security? I cannot overstress the importance of his continuing good health. It would offend us gravely if something happened to the boy." Griego lifted a cardboard box from the shopping bag. "Two nights ago, a young man offended us. Open this."

The comandante pulled back the lid, removed a jar and, holding it to his poor eyes, squinted at the object floating in water. "Madre dios." The glass jar slipped from his soft fingers. Anticipating the reaction, Griego caught it. The comandante panted for air, the empty box fluttering in his hand.

"This was your prisoner's business partner. Mr. Cross must be reminded of how our family reacts when offended. Because you have no need of childish lessons, I will speak with him alone. *Now.*" He sat on a worn leather chair that smelled of dog and dropped his wallowing chin onto his chest.

García swiftly returned with his prisoner and sidled out backwards, pulling the ancient shepherd along, his eyes fixed on Griego.

"Who're you?" asked Roy. He had spent the night awake in an empty cell, and appeared worn, hunted. The taunts he'd heard half the night from the adjoining cells had not taxed his rudimentary Spanish.

"Ramirez works for me,' said Griego, shifting his mass in a vain search for comfort. "You worked for me."

"OK if I smoke?"

"Where is our shipment?" Griego asked, neither expecting nor desiring the truth. He shook his fleshy head, not understanding why, when the world was awash with pretty girls, maricóns fell for beardless boys.

Roy blew out a match, pushing himself to adopt an attitude. "If Ramirez works for you, how did I meet him?"

"Through my unfortunate friend, Juan Sierra, pendejo. I will ask the questions. Where is—"

"You know Juan? Far out. Then get me out of here because we have business to do, you owe me for the fifty keys. I have to pay Wad."

"Your friend is missing, probably dead. The cocaine is also missing, and you know where it is."

"No way, man," Roy cried. "Wad dead? I don't fucking believe it. Fuck no. C'mon—"

"Silence. You stole our cocaine. Save your story for, for…" Griego paused and then smiled, his hooded eyes without emotion.

"I didn't steal anything. Hello? I'm in jail, they frisked me. No drugs."

"Read." Griego handed him a copy of that day's *San Diego Evening Tribune.* The story about crooked police murdered in a drug deal dominated the front page. Roy read with effort, one word at a time. He blanched. Schmidt was dead? His partner killed by unknown drug dealers in a shootout? And the police were looking for a person of interest, one Edward Kawadsky, perhaps the victim of foul play.

"Now. The names and addresses of your partners, the men who killed the police, and where we may find them." Griego kept his voice soft, even mild; he had to report an inconclusive interrogation to Medellín. He would remind his superiors of Juan's legendary capacity for violence and how reckless ignoring his instructions for the handling of his young lover would have been.

"What partners? I don't have any partners." Roy dropped onto a chair, sniffling, wiping tears from his cheeks. "Juan?"

"Juan Sierra is on his way to Colombia. Better to ask me about your friend Mahoney. He is not gone. He is right here." He removed the Mason jar from its box. "Perhaps you have inspected this closely before?" Roy stared uncomprehending at the ragged-cut object with its floating jellyfish-like tendrils and hairs, until Griego turned the penis toward him.

Roy's screams carried far beyond the comandante's office wing.

HIS RAPE WITHIN THE HOUR after Griego's departure and the near instant execution of not only his three rapists but his negligent bodyguard all but confirmed the rumors flying around the gossipy prison: The güero, the blonde, was a Trujillo, the bastard offspring of a Hollywood star and the great drug lord himself, and he had purchased the most magnificent carraca with cash he carried in a golden briefcase. Even the nuevos gloated over how he had demanded an audience with the comandante, how every guard was at his disposal, how he would escape by helicopter the next week. Outrage over his rape was universal. Old hands dismissed the rapists' fate, instead dwelling on the bodyguard, whether he had deserved the death penalty for mere negligence. They all knew the facts. While awaiting the prince in the administration building, the bodyguard had stepped outside to stretch his legs. Panicked for reasons unknown, the prince had raced out into the main yard where the prisoners smoked, walked, and played basketball, getting no more than forty paces before the foul dogs seized him by knifepoint, bending him over the laundry sinks.

Comandante García was terrified, knowing he too would be preserved in formaldehyde if news of the boy's dishonor reached Griego.

With no Colombians among his inmates, there was a slim chance it wouldn't. God willing. But his petty traficantes? One of them must have some connection to the family. Someone would talk. García shrank in his office—petting his cranky dog—drowning the floating scrotum nightmare with whiskey. Before him lay his hurried notes, his outline for his last will and testament, and a half-empty bottle of Jim Beam. He had scrawled his defense on a separate sheet of paper, how he had responded to the heinous crime, how his personal physician had tended the boy and assured him of his full recovery, ideas for favors and gifts he might lavish on the güero for his silence, where he might flee, who might look after his wife and aged mother. On into the long night the comandante drank, his fears growing larger, his thoughts smaller.

CHAPTER 16

TERMINAL

The LAX international terminal was crowded, bustling, its check-in lines long, with unshaven arrivals embracing their excited families, while embarking passengers bid teary farewells. A stylish handsome man dressed in a blue tailored suit stood talking to a remarkably fat man eating fistfuls of popcorn. The stylish man was smiling, in his happiness gesturing with fluid movements most men avoided. His companion nodded as he chewed, glancing about the terminal, his mouth set in a smile.

"How can I leave you in charge of the entire West Coast when you cannot tie your own shoes?" said Juan, laughing, his face aglow. Medellín had called two days before, asking him to take over distribution in New York, requesting he fly home to meet with his counterpart to discuss the territory. Relieved, Juan could explain the missing cocaine in person, how he would recover it, and how, if unsuccessful, he would personally reimburse the family for its loss. "Héctor, it is bad manners to forget one's employer while standing in his presence."

"I'm sorry, I have been so preoccupied with the problem I am bad company," said Griego. Thrown off guard by Medellin's ploy for ensuring Juan's return, Héctor Griego was unprepared for his superior's flood of goodwill. He rolled his sloping shoulders, worried over his nagging chest pain, telling himself it would disappear once Juan stepped onboard his flight.

"But perhaps you are working too hard on it," Juan said. "You look tired. Are you getting enough rest?" He was grateful to Griego for talking him out of garroting Roy the first evening. His King must still die, but the passage of a week would remove the last scintilla of doubt. When he returned from Colombia, he would drive to Tijuana alone, arrange Roy's release and then gently quiz him like an errant schoolboy on the drive back to Los Angeles. His King would enjoy a final sunset overlooking his beloved surf.

"Yes, I'm fine, but shouldn't you be boarding?" Griego asked.

"The pendejo—no possibility of escape?"

"No, of course not." Griego hid a smile behind the greasy popcorn box. "He cannot escape, I took care of it myself. He is safe, but madre dios is he scared. The comandante—a strange man—told me the pendejo screamed all night after he saw our little present. His partner's cojones were never so useful."

"He is all right?" asked Juan. He couldn't help it, he loved the boy so.

"He is fine, just badly frightened. By the time you return, he will be begging to tell us everything. And now you must go. Vaya con dios."

Griego was determined no one from the family would ever speak to the boy again. His quandary was when to have him killed. Juan had to be dead first of course, but even then, his revenge-minded clan might challenge Griego's tale of Juan's all-consuming homosexuality. Cross openly coddled in La Mesa's finest carraca was the insurance policy Griego needed. The proof that Juan had placed his young lover's care above the family's needs. As Griego shuffled toward the exit in shoes he could neither reach nor tie, he thought he'd give it a year, possibly two, before he had Cross knifed in a La Mesa brawl. He might have done it sooner out of sheer anger had he learned that his Mexican assassin—unable to find the long-gone Tommy Mahoney—chose the simple expedient of disemboweling another border officer.

As it happened, Griego outlived Juan by less than six months, his heart more victim to his elephantine girth than the stress of his criminality. Despite these personnel losses, the Trujillos' tons of cocaine rolled ever northward and Roy Cross was soon a footnote, then forgotten altogether, save by the terrified Comandante García who would keep the güero alive, well, and under lock-and-key until the murderous Colombian returned one day to claim him.

CHAPTER 17

PENNSYLVANIA

"Austen," called the matronly clerk. "Richard Phillip Austen Jr."

The small gathering of supplicants looked about the dreary DMV's institutional waiting room, impatient for their turn at the window.

"Austen? Richard Austen?" she asked again, louder.

"Here," Eddie said, jumping from the plastic chair, surprised at hearing the name said aloud. He hurried to the counter. "I'm sorry, ma'am. I must have been daydreaming."

"That's all right. You weren't daydreaming when you took the test. You scored one hundred percent. I have a question for you, though. Are you sure you want to drop the "junior" from your license?"

"Yes please, ma'am. My father died when I was a boy, I've never used it."

"I suppose we can do that."

"And, if it's OK with Pennsylvania, I would just as soon drop my middle name too. I never use it either."

"So, just plain Richard Austen?"

"Yes, ma'am."

"All right then. Are your people from Harrisburg?"

"No. Wilkes-Barre," said Eddie, remembering the graveyard where he'd found the elfin tombstone commemorating Richard Austen's brief life. He had taken that information, along with the knowledge that birth and death records were not cross-referenced by the Pennsylvania Department of Health, to obtain a copy of Austen's birth certificate. He hoped dropping the middle name and the junior would scatter leaves across his trail.

"Coal country? You don't sound like you're from Luzerne," she chuckled.

Eddie had thought of that. "My mom moved away, out west, when I was young, after my dad died in the mine. Didn't like it much and we came back a couple years ago. May I please ask one last favor, ma'am?"

"Well, you certainly are my politest customer of the day," she said, smiling at the clean-cut youth.

"I'm about to enlist in the Marines, and I'm not sure exactly where I'll be in the next couple weeks. Is it possible to pick my license up here when it's ready?"

"You come back in two weeks, Richard. Ask for me, Mrs. Hubbard. I'll have it for you."

AUSTEN HAD BEEN SITTING, SOMETIMES kneeling, for the better part of an hour in the Cathedral Basilica of Saints Peter and Paul. Alone in a brightly polished wooden pew, he bowed his head beneath the Basilica's great copper-clad dome—not in prayer—but debate. He'd picked Philadelphia's biggest church, reasoning he could melt into its throngs of worshippers should his confessor become overly curious. But should he even confess? Had he committed any sins? If intention were everything, was he guilty of anything beyond intending to smuggle marijuana? What help could a priest be? Austen's internal debate had so consumed him that he'd noticed neither the cathedral's imposing Roman-Corinthian brownstone exterior upon entering nor its awe-inspiring nave. He had to decide soon, confession ended at five. He rose, adjusted his awkward horn-rimmed glasses, pulled his baseball cap from his pocket, and joined the short line outside the confessionals. When his turn arrived, he donned the cap as he entered the closet-like booth as a test, knowing that if the priest ordered him to remove it, the small latticed window between them offered too little anonymity.

"Yes?" said the priest after a pause.

"Bless me, Father, for I have sinned, it's been six years since my last confession," said Austen. He had forsaken confession—and ultimately the Church itself—within a year of reaching puberty, when he realized the Church would forever condemn him over his simple urges for which he felt neither guilt nor remorse. "May I ask a question?"

"Yes."

"You know how sins and crimes don't always overlap?" said Austen. "Like, it's not a sin to jaywalk or a crime to swear… Is it a sin to smuggle an illegal drug?"

"Endangering God's precious gift of physical health with drugs, whether in yourself or others, is a grave sin. What alienates us from Our Lord or our neighbors is a sin," said the old man, his rote reply suggesting he'd heard innumerable versions of this question in the past.

Austen shook his head, more in self-preservation than denial, hoping the priest wrong. Alcohol was a drug, too, far worse than cocaine according to the Inn's fast set. If the old man were right, every liquor store owner in the country was hell bound. He persisted. "But what if the drug is harmless?"

"My son, would you be here this afternoon if you weren't already heartsick over these sins?" asked the priest. He drew his cassock sleeve back, glanced at his wristwatch, a practiced gesture meant to prod meandering penitents. "Are you ready to confess?"

"I know the bible says killing in self-defense isn't a sin," said Austen, upping the ante. He paused a moment in vain for his confessor to agree. "But what if—hypothetically—that self-defense happens while committing a crime? It's still not a sin, right?"

"Killing?" cried the priest, peering hard at Austen through the latticed window. "Is this your sin?"

"No, no, no," snapped Austen. "I was only asking hypothetically."

The old man straightened in his chair, leaned into the window, his voice hardened. "Hypothetically then: Until you confess your crimes to the police and your sins to our mother Church, your soul will not rest, and your righteousness—your honor—will be lost. Do you hear me?" he demanded.

"Yes, Father."

"Now, do you have any sins that you *do* wish to confess?"

Stung by the old fool's wrong answers, Austen replied, "I had sex with a girl… but that's not a sin either. Tell you what, father, just for the hell of it, I'll say five Hail Marys anyway." He jammed his cap lower and sprang out of the booth, half-running for the exit beneath the Basilica's great pipe organ.

Goddamn worthless Church.

CHAPTER 18

WHERE THE DIFFERENCE BEGAN

Nestled between the mouths of the Broad and Beaufort Rivers in South Carolina, Parris Island is a sand spit a few miles across, its salt marshes held together by water oaks, palm trees, and sawgrass, home to alligators, shore birds, mosquitoes, and Marines. While Vietnam burned, Parris Island hummed with thousands of boys on their way to Southeast Asia.

One steamy afternoon, the sixty-six members of Platoon 198 of the 1st Recruit Training Battalion stood at parade rest while a water-survival instructor lectured them. "If y'all can't swim, you're gonna die," the lance corporal drawled, opening his talk about stroke technique while weighted down with utilities and boots. Each recruit had to jump from the ten-foot tower into the deep pool and then swim twenty-five yards while in field dress.

Soaked through with sweat, Private Parson Shoer was eager to jump. The platoon's best athlete, he was so light-skinned that a spindly kid from Detroit named Malik Harris teased him relentlessly about his open-minded grandmothers. That Shoer could laugh at himself and shrug it off charmed his fellow recruits. He'd cemented his popularity the second week in camp when, after lights-out, Harris stage-whispered, "Who this? 'Mother, please pass the cream. I desire some for my oatmeal.'" Recognizing the stuffy white voice as his own, Shoer laughed harder than anyone else, emboldening the comedian Harris to add, "I seen polar bears, hell, I seen snow blacker than Private *O-reo*." Overnight, the platoon called Shoer nothing but O.

Shoer felt rather than saw gunnery sergeant Phil Dorland tiptoeing through the ranks behind him and knew the drill instructor was
searching for daydreaming, butt scratching, and other acts of mutiny.

"Four-eyes," 198's DI bellowed. "Tenn-hut." The corporal paused
his lecture while Dorland bellowed at a lanky recruit for endangering
every life in the platoon by failing to learn vital military procedures, for
being the weakest link in a chain of steel, for insulting the Corps by
joining it. "Give me fifty, you miserable shithead."

Richard Austen dropped to the asphalt and began his straight-
backed push-ups, chanting, "One for the Corps, sir, two for the Corps,
sir, three for the Corps, sir."

Dorland signaled the instructor to continue. With a fist screwed
into each hip, he half-watched Austen while scanning for other signs
of insurrection. Of unremarkable height, Dorland was thicker around
the waist than Marine standard, his face marred by a bulbous drinking
nose and pocked skin.

"I can't hear you." The sergeant prodded his polished boot into
Austen's side.

Austen finished and sprang to his feet. Dorland resumed his
prowling, muttering about the impossibility of his task, of turning
the druts of 198 into men, fighting men who could think and act as
a unit.

A DOZEN BOYS WERE IN the steamy barracks shower room, their best
opportunity for sneaking forbidden talk. As usual, Harris held court.

"About time you gave the man fifty. About time he kicked some
white butt for a change," Harris snapped. Someone muttered "right
on," while Austen regarded the comedian for a moment, wiped his
fogged glasses, then turned away.

"You miserable shithead," Harris barked, imitating their DI's tobac-coed gravel voice to near perfection. The boys laughed. "Give me another fifty, you worthless turd. Son, you know what a turd is?" He paused to let his soapy audience savor what was coming, his dead-on rendering of Dorland's favorite speech. "A turd is a Trainee under Rigid Discipline, son, and that's what you are: my turd. One misstep and I'll flush your sorry ass down the can."

Austen blinked at Harris, managing a small smile, apparently nei-ther offended nor amused. No one was surprised by Austen's silence; he'd said scarcely a hundred words since stepping off the sweltering South Carolina bus. Harris grabbed him by the arm. "I'm talking to you, four-eyes. Give me fifty."

Austen shrugged his arm free.

"I'm talking to you, Mr. My-Shit-Don't-Stink. Maybe it's time for some ass-kicking," said Harris, raising his fists.

"Leave him alone, Tweeter," growled Shoer, clamping onto Harris's neck.

"Ow, ow, ow. Let go, man," cried Harris. "Come on, O. We buds."

"You want to fuck with somebody, it's going to be me," Shoer said. "You want to fuck with me, I'll stuff your head upside your black ass." With only a towel around his slender waist, Shoer looked as though he modeled gym equipment. Harris's cronies melted away. From an educated family, Shoer's everyday speech had no trace of the street or New Jersey, but he had a good ear and a gift for adapting his speech to his surroundings.

"OK, O. OK, you the man. Let me go. Forgot you two was qu— OK, OK."

Shoer pushed him without enthusiasm and returned to his shaving. Austen walked out.

"Who this?" Harris asked after recovering some of his dignity. Mimicking Austen, he stood as straight as he could and assumed a faraway look. "Scout this, motherfucker," he said, grabbing his crotch.

In his mockery, Harris was putting a different spin on the night the platoon was on maneuvers, sleeping in the field in two-man tents when an Atlantic storm roared in, blasting rain, collapsing one tent after another. Each time Harris's tent blew apart, he looked at Austen's with envy. He crawled over to learn the secret. "Pay attention," Austen had said. "Use a loop knot on the tent's eyelet. Then take the stake and wrap the line round it once like this and put a couple half hitches in it." Harris got it right after several misfires. "Set the stake at a forty-five-degree angle from the tent and counterweight it with something heavy."

"I'll use my dick. Where'd you learn this shit?"

"Scouts."

"Used to buy their cookies." Harris scuttled off.

When the bleary-eyed boys had returned to barracks and were showering off mud and crushed mosquitoes, Harris proclaimed *Boy Scout* as his main man. "BS knows more knots than Houdini." Everyone laughed with Harris, whom many would remember as the funniest man they ever met.

SHOER LAY AWAKE IN HIS upper bunk in 198's squad bay, a long, narrow white room with two rows of metal bunk beds on either side of a center aisle. The 198's quarters were on the second floor of a two-story wood-frame building that formed a part of First Battalion's barracks, a series of "H" shaped buildings on the grinder's north side. The bay was bare and immaculate. The recruits' few possessions were arranged in a precise, identical pattern in their foot lockers in front of their bunks.

Ignoring the cacophony of snores, moans, and night moves, Shoer was thinking about girls, about the locals he wanted to meet in Beaufort, about the ones he'd impress with his uniform back in Jersey. From the moment he'd discovered girls—not long after they discovered him—he'd been addicted to love. He was fondling one dream girl when Austen sneezed.

"Hey, Aus," Shoer leaned over and whispered to his bunkmate below, "you asleep?"

"No."

"Why'd dickbrain jump you? What'd you do?"

"Don't know." Austen did know. He'd been rocked by the news that the next and final phase of their Marine education—advanced infantry training—would occur in Southern California. Had he known earlier, he would have enlisted in the Army. He would never have voluntarily returned to California. "Did you know we were going to Pendleton?"

"Not till this morning. Isn't that wild? Beach chicks, endless summer, Hollywood. No more dickbrain Dorland."

"It's near San Diego, not LA," Austen whispered, his words sour.

"Wish they all could be California girls. Hey, how'd you know that?"

"Freshman geography." A geography that had terrorized Austen all day. Camp Pendleton lay forty-five minutes north of San Diego. Positive he was the most wanted man in that city's history, his heart had raced all day as he agonized over his new odds of capture. What if there were "Wanted" posters everywhere in San Diego County? What if a fellow Marine happened to see his picture in the Oceanside post office? Was his comic book disguise—crewcut and horn-rimmed glasses—worth a tinker's damn? What if the *Union* were still running articles about the crime of the century? Grasping for hope, he'd comforted himself with the bitter knowledge that no one had bothered taking his picture for years. The police had only his fuzzy driver's license photo—a picture in which his then pimpled face was overwhelmed by wild hair. He'd dismissed going AWOL in the same breath he considered it, knowing it would only set another government arm clawing after him, one that had his fingerprints and excellent photographs. After a day of misery, he had no plan save not stepping a foot off base for the duration.

"My ass. Like they teach base locations in geography." In those few moments when he was neither sleeping nor sweating, Shoer had become curious about his preternaturally silent bunkmate. When Austen uttered even a few words beyond "yes, sir," Shoer could hear he was middle class and not, as he'd first suspected, another cracker bent on upholding his family's martial record.

"Tell me how you got nailed," Austen asked, deflecting Shoer. He had overheard others repeating the sad tale about the all-state running back who'd ended up in the Corps and not the Ivy League. "Is that stuff about the white girl and her racist father true?"

Warming to his favorite subject—himself—Shoer whispered that he had grown up color-blind, the teacher's pet, and perennial brightest student, the star of every game, the beloved baby of a prosperous family, only to discover he was black the night a Middletown cop caught him with his jeans down with a fourteen-year-old with her skirt up.

"If I was white, those cops would've laughed and I'd be at Harvard—I'd already committed. But Debbie tells the cop she's fourteen—she told me sixteen—and the pig cuffs me. Cuffs me. Blew my mind. Wouldn't do that to a white halfback. See, the only blacks I ever knew were my own family. From kindergarten on, I was the only one in the class. But I wasn't black or white, just me. Get it? You don't, do you?"

"Maybe not. But how did you get here?" Austen asked.

"Easy, your boy parked with the wrong freshman. Her old man was a lawyer. He was at the jail demanding they hang me before my parents even got a call."

"Whoa."

"This Debbie's so afraid, she tells her old man she's a virgin and she didn't know what was happening—shit, she nearly broke my zipper yanking on it—and he makes her repeat that to the cops."

"But... but you're here?"

"The prick was old Corps—a top—and must have known Debbie was a slut, because everybody else sure did. So he does some private deal with the judge and they give my dad the choice. Jail or the Corps. Know what's funny?"

"What?"

"My old man had to think about it."

"ONE MORE WEEK," AUSTEN WHISPERED to Shoer, as the platoon lay panting against their thirty-five-pound packs, seven miles into a ten-mile march—incentive physical training Dorland had deemed restorative after deciding his boys were drilling like Italians. Splattered with pluff mud, the boys lay strung along a trail that wound through a forest of replanted pine. They swatted at the flying teeth, the sand fleas that bedeviled them. Sweat-thinned mud painted their exhausted faces and so balled up their boots that each step was a struggle.

Drenched with sweat as though river-baptized, Shoer said, "Six and a half days."

"I'd like that, you know, what you were talking about."

"What? Oh, coming home to visit my folks? Cool." Shoer had written home about Austen, bragging on him as the only recruit who could outshoot him. He charmed his family by detailing one breakfast when the S.O.S. was truly inedible, the recruits in the mess hall amusing one another with gagging gestures, only to spy Austen shoveling it in, cleaning his plate. Mrs. Shoer had urged him to bring his new friend home.

"Saddle up, girls." Dorland flicked his cigarette into the mud. "Beauty rest's over. Don't gulp that goddamn water. Move out."

Every boy chugged what he could while throwing on his pack. They slipped into step in two long columns and marched toward their waiting sergeant, passing him in silence, the mud sucking at their boots the only sound. Dorland hung back, observing his platoon with a measure of satisfaction.

A mile from barracks and the platoon was on an asphalt access road, scuffing their left heels every other stride to mark time. Harris sang out in rhythm with their scuffing:

> Hey, Laudie, Laudie, Laudie
> Hey Laudie, Laudie Low
> I know a girl named Buffalo Bill
> She won't do it, but her buffalo will

Sixty-five voices answered him with a chorus of "Hey Laudie, Laudie, Laudie." Another recruit sang:

> I know a girl from ol' Kentuck
> She sure can't dance but
> She sure can fuck.

A third sang and then another. The boys seemed to know girls of doubtful virtue from Timbuktu to gay Paree. With a nod, Shoer urged Austen to try a verse. Austen shook his head, a gap-toothed smile. Shrugging, Shoer lifted his chin and sang in a pleasing tenor:

> I know a gal in Tia-wanna
> Hey, Laudie, Laudie, Low
> She know how but
> She don't wanna

Pleased with his platoon's spirits, a grinning Dorland ordered, "OK, ladies. Dub-time, harch." Like horses smelling the barn, the boys broke into a trot.

CHAPTER 19

POKER

THE SUN FLICKERED BEHIND GRAY clouds billowing across the winter sky. Gulls swirled above Camp Pendleton in search of scraps. Two hundred fifty fresh Marines sat in an open amphitheater, shivering, huddling against the Pacific's wet wind, listening to yet another instructor.

With a prosthesis below the knee, the lieutenant stood awkwardly in front of the rapt boys, embroidering on his lecture notes. Behind him stood his assistant, a black corporal clasping a flame thrower, its scuba tanks on his back. The corporal pointed the hissing weapon away from the grunts, toward the scorched hillside. The flamethrower fascinated the boys far more than guns, perhaps because fire was a primeval fear while bullets took learning to respect.

"Finally, gentlemen, if your CO suspects Charlie's in a tunnel, do you want to do the recon or ask Corporal Henderson here for a light?" The lieutenant, a platoon commander whose combat tour ended on the surgeon's table after two weeks in the field, enjoyed dressing up his presentation with this flourish. On his cue, the somber corporal blasted a whooshing jet of fire toward the hillside—even the boys in the last row felt they were too close to a bonfire, the blast sucking their breath away. The corporal shut it off, and the grinning lieutenant let a moment pass as the acrid, ugly smell hung in the air.

After elaborating on the weapon's tactical uses, the lieutenant scratched out safety rules on his chalkboard as the Marines murmured among themselves. "That sucker is bad," Harris the clown whispered, fingering the barrel of his M-14. "Feature the brothers with that badass back in the hood." Harris, Shoer, Austen, and a handful from 198 had been consigned to the infantry and were now grunts, completing their training with Staging Battalion at Pendleton. Like so many spare parts, they would be rotated into the field to the rifle companies that were depleted daily by casualties.

"I'm getting me one of those."

Shoer glanced back at Austen, who was staring at his boots, ignoring the idle chatter and the chalkboard. He shook his head and turned back to the instructor.

The company double-timed it back to the grinder, the boys warming themselves against the chill. Some replayed the fire show in their minds, while others brooded over more pressing business—Saturday night's liberty—whether to settle for beers and the remote chance of luck at a bar in nearby Oceanside or venture down to San Diego or Tijuana. A few gentler souls pined after Disneyland, a long bus ride away.

"Let's saddle up, Aus, the bus is pulling out at 1800," Shoer said, eager for his night out, hoping to meet a girl, any girl. "You got to get ready. Out of the rack."

"I'm skipping it, Parse."

"Bro, you promised you'd go, you haven't been off base since we got here. Let me tell you something, you don't want the guys thinking you're any weirder."

"Yeah," said Austen after a moment's reflection, at a loss for words. He knew the squad thought him strange, an oddball, perhaps even a little slow, for he almost never spoke. But Austen lived in terror of saying something, anything, that would tip his identity. He had no gift for mendacity and knew that if he started opening up, creating a history, he would trip himself up with contradictory details and mis-remembered lies in short order. With no better solution than silence, he'd had to bury his charm, his banter and sense of humor—his very self—along with the cocaine in that forgotten bomb shelter.

"What's that?" asked Shoer, pointing to a book on Austen's bunk. "Sure as hell don't look like porno."

"Yeah, no one's going to steal it," answered Austen, chuckling, handing it to his friend.

"*Principles of Real Estate Investing*? Man, you are killing me. Absolutely killing me. And what the hell's that?" demanded Shoer, reaching for a torn newspaper article that had lain beneath the book.

"Nothing," cried Austen, snatching the article away, balling it into his fist. It was a piece from the *Tribune*, a follow-up on the infamous cocaine cop killings. As ritualistic as daily prayer, Austen had read the local papers whenever he'd had a chance and had found this article the day before. According to the newspaper, the police were calling off the search for Edward Kawadsky, presuming him the victim of foul play. Warier than ever, Austen couldn't let himself believe it; he knew it had to be a ruse. But he so ached to step off base, to catch even a glimpse of Jonnie. She was only forty-five minutes away. He longed to see her, to hear her throaty cigarette laughs, her wicked remarks, and even her scandalous gossip. Her beauty. If only he could see her sweep into the coffee shop once more, with her grand gestures, kind words for the hungry, and salacious patter for the worldly—a queen with her adoring court. If only he could let her know he was alive. Despite their last moments together, Austen knew she was more than passing fond of him, would mourn him for years, and sadly reminisce over her favorite boy until her dying day. If he could just explain how he'd been trapped, Jonnie would listen, she would understand. She would find him guilty of nothing more than teenage stupidity, of intending to smuggle a couple pounds of harmless pot. Unlike that asshole priest, she would judge him neither criminal nor sinner. She would say there's nothing to forgive. Austen broke off this reverie—one he'd had dozens of times since returning to California—with the certain knowledge that Jonnie had never kept a secret in her life and that fugitives were invariably caught when they went home. "It's nothing. I'm going to play poker."

"Who's left who will still play with you? Least the brothers are smart enough to party with their money instead of throwing it away on you. What the hell you doing with all those Benjamins anyway?"

"I told you ten times already… I'm saving up to buy a house, to get into real estate."

"What good's money if something happens in Nam?"

Austen scratched his crewcut, wondering what to say. Vietnam held no fear for him, in part because he considered himself already dead, on an extended stay of execution until he was caught, in part—incongruously—because he'd survived his first shoot-out. "You want it if something happens to me?"

"Shit, no. I'm going to Harvard, remember? Don't need your damn money. What I need is you to come hang out with me."

"We can go to the beach tomorrow. OK?" Austen smiled, his big, gap-toothed smile, the one Shoer cherished because he had yet to see anyone else favored with it.

"Later, man. I give up." Shoer strode toward the far end of the squad bay and joined the milling grunts with pocket money and unbridled optimism.

Once they departed, Austen stashed the book in his footlocker, shredded the article, and picked up a letter he had been writing. He wrote:

"Dear Mrs. Shoer: The oatmeal cookies were great, all the guys said so. Parson was happy to hear everybody talk about what a good cook you are. Me too. And thanks for the green t-shirts. I guess Parse told you what the NCOs said about white t-shirts making us sitting ducks in Nam and the Corps being crazy not to issue us green ones. You would laugh if you saw the platoon dyeing their undershirts in trash cans. But don't worry about us over there. We'll be careful, we'll take care of each other. Thanks again for the Bible. Well, I've got to go now. Goodbye. Your friend, Richard. P. S. How's Mr. Shoer doing on his boat?"

Later, the only sober one in the game, Austen played to win, folding often, shrugging off the jibes of cowardice hurled his way, seldom bluffing, and chasing pots less often, lying in wait when he held a winner, keeping the others in with low bets until the final round, never showing his cards unless someone paid to see them.

AUSTEN AND SHOER WALKED ALONG Pendleton's beach in t-shirts and rolled up utility trousers, enjoying the last few hours of their liberty on a gentle winter afternoon. They wore their boots like necklaces, tied together and slung around their necks. Both young men carried a beer, with more in their pockets. Austen wore clip-on, dark plastic lenses over his steel-frame glasses, while Shoer's aviator sunglasses cost a month's salary. They ambled in a zig-zag pattern, along the wet, packed sand until their feet were too chilled and then above the tide line, drinking fast, bumping into one another like circus clowns.

"You ought to drink more, son," declared Shoer. "Loosens you up. How many beers you got left?"

"Two," replied Austen.

"Hey, let me ask you something," said Shoer, a grin blossoming. "Serious. You think I'm getting too tan out here?"

"What?" Austen hesitated, studying his friend's complexion. Speechless, he shook his head awkwardly. "I don't know…"

Shoer crooked his forefinger like a fishhook and popped his cheek. "Hooked your ass, you big, dumb tuna." He stepped nearer Austen, snuck a leg behind him, sprawling his lanky friend onto the sand. "Surprise is the key to Semper Fi's success, boy."

"And the Corps never retreats." He whipped a leg across Shoer's ankles, knocking him down.

They stood and dusted themselves, laughing, Austen watching the waves from the corner of his eye. "Outside," he murmured to himself as a decent wave formed. The ocean was blue-green, sparkling, glittering in the wan sunlight. Shoer picked up a flat rock, cocked it between his thumb and forefinger to skip, then let it slip away. "How come you never went off base, Aus? Don't bullshit me."

"Why don't you have a New Jersey accent like DeMatteo?" Expecting it for weeks, Austen still had no answer, nothing that would wash. He couldn't lie to his only friend.

"That answer-a-question-with-a-question routine is some tired bullshit," said Shoer. "What's off base that's scaring you? Something going on here."

"That's classified information, private."

Shoer dropped his head to the side, then laughed. "OK. OK by me. I understand, classified information, chain of command. No hard feelings. Shake?" He thrust out a hand. As Austen reached forward, Shoer grabbed his arm and judo-flipped him over his shoulder. Austen landed on his back on the wet sand, laughing as the sea water soaked him. He yanked out a beer, shook it, shouted *incoming* and popped the can toward Shoer, spewing him with beer. Shoer retaliated, emptying a can on his head.

"Cease fire. We have to maintain fire discipline, private. We're down to our last round."

"You're right. Can't surrender our ammo to the enemy. Chug it."

As drunk as they were sandy, the boys trudged back to the enlisted men's club, the old Victorian where Austen had spent his liberties working at poker. As they mounted the club's worn steps, Shoer asked a couple departing privates for the time. The pair glanced at the boys, smirked at each other, and continued on their way.

"Fucking college boy reservists. Assholes," Shoer snapped, the pair pretending not to hear. The college graduates, who had joined the reserves to avoid the draft, were years older than the Nam-bound grunts. The two groups had little trouble recognizing one another.

"It's no big deal, Parse."

"That should be us. We should be in after college, as lieutenants."

"We're lucky to be grunts," said Austen. "Remember what Top said about Charlie shooting lieutenants as fast as the Corps puts the bars on them."

"The assholes don't have to treat us like shit."

"Forget it. In twenty years, we can say we won the war while those jerks were clerks at the PX."

"Yeah, except we'll be working for those jerks."

"No, we won't. We won't." Flushed with the happy beer, Austen was sanguine about his future, his past set aside for the moment. "We're both going to make it. I know it."

CHAPTER 20

ROSY FINGERED DAWN

The Annamese mountains were blackening in the dusk, the range's jagged peaks backlit by the fading sun. The day's steamy, wet, enervating heat was easing at last. The monsoon rains had fallen without pause for six days and then stopped, the clouds parting to reveal a sky shimmering in humidity, trees dropping water-logged branches like dead leaves, jumper creeks roaring mustard brown, cresting their beds.

The fifty-five men in Bravo Company's reinforced 1st Platoon were drenched. A couple replacements remembered it was Thanksgiving, but everyone else had long since ceased caring. Lt. Thomas Cook, the 1st's just-arrived commander, was regretting his tactical decision not to request a better meal for the platoon for fear it would be denied, wondering how he could demonstrate his leadership to a platoon he suspected ran itself.

After another day of flinching at sporadic sniper fire, 1st Platoon was digging in among the foothills east of the Annamese. The men were atop a saddle between sharp mountains above and the emerald chessboard of rice paddies far below. The jungle tree line, a green wall, rose about one hundred fifty yards north of their clearing.

Cook had first asked Sgt. Chris Bartlett for his opinion and then decided any attack that night would likely come from the mountains to the west. A shallow, bamboo-choked ravine fifty yards away would be the enemy's best approach. Cook ordered their two machine guns set up to face the ravine.

"City boy, if you can piss out of it, it ain't deep enough," Shoer said to his latest replacement. "You ain't gonna be in my book if you can't dig a fuckin' hole." His novel had begun as a joke, but now he could comically use it to banish anyone who displeased him. If the transgression were grave, he would threaten to write the miscreant in as a coward, or worse, as Army. After two tours and the better part of three years in the Corps, he had more than enough material, but he was stumped. Bestsellers started with catchy titles and he was convinced all the good ones had been taken. "City boy, I dig it when you dig, dig?" pattered Shoer as he dug his own foxhole with economical strokes, amusing himself and the others.

One Marine shoveled while the other stood guard, studying the elephant grass, the bamboo, the tree line, and the infinite ridges, looking for Charlie. Even the city boy knew the platoon was vulnerable while digging; completing the perimeter circle of foxholes was each evening's first order of business.

Shoer's squad had the northerly arc of the circle, facing the impenetrable jungle. "Dig, baby, dig. You don't dig deep enough, we're burying your sorry ass in it." While his squad chuckled, Shoer tossed out more shovelfuls. "You got to be KIA to get your miserable carcass flown home. Getting shot in a gopher hole ain't killed in action." He spoke in rhythm as he dug. "You lean on that tool again, son, I'm going to waste you myself and tell your mama you got boomed-boomed dead by some Danang ho." Shoer had changed, the coddled boy in him a distant memory, a battle-scarred man in his place. His laughter still rang out, but it was seldom unalloyed. And his once white-bread speech was now pure Watts, so profanity-laced that his refined parents would have been aghast. Fortunately, they would never hear about his girlfriends in Saigon—Rosy and Dawn—a pair of cheerful prostitutes who sometimes gave it away to the handsome corporal.

"You the man, O," the city boy said. Shoer tipped his helmet back and laughed.

Austen's squad was on the perimeter's west side, supporting the machine guns. Unlike Shoer, he led his own squad almost wordlessly, by example, by working harder than everyone else. His chrysalis over the preceding three years was more remarkable than his only friend's. From the numbed, terrified teenager rolling east in rusted freight cars, to the silent recruit, to a hardened leader of men. Having buried his youthful exuberance in that Lemon Grove bomb shelter, Austen seldom spoke more than a sentence at a time, as if he were reluctantly breaking a monastic vow of silence. When he did speak, his audience listened.

"I'll take over, Scout," the new replacement Palowski said at last. He should have known Austen would shovel the foxhole by himself if uninterrupted.

Austen climbed out of the hole and tucked his palms in the small of his back. He leaned back. His weight was now below 160, sinew and muscle stretched like racket strings over his long frame. The vacant stare he had before joining the Corps was gone, replaced by a darting, calculating look of animal alertness. Also gone were the steel frame glasses, useless in the steam, sweat, and rain. After a year of bottoming despair, he'd righted himself in Vietnam. He didn't give a damn about the war's politics, focusing instead on leading—and caring for—his fellow grunts. He'd talked Shoer into a second tour and would have tried for a third if Shoer hadn't been so adamant about getting on with their lives.

After slicing the clay from his canvas boots with his knife, Austen hefted his rifle and wiped away the beads of water along the M-16's barrel with a muddy hand, reconning their position, studying the water-carved ravine that concerned Bartlett.

"That's where they'll come from tonight, guys," Austen said in a low voice to his squad. "If they come at all." It had been weeks since they had fought more than the monsoon's chill, the occasional lone sniper's fire.

The foxholes were a foot short of what the lieutenant deemed prudent. Satisfied, however, the grunts sucked on a last cigarette before stand-to. Later, Cook chided himself for failing to have his men on fifty percent alert, but it was that gray between light and dark, before hunter and hunted exchanged positions, the time no one owned. The Americans had yet to retire for the night. The nocturnal Vietnamese, secreted away in some lair, would emerge only at night.

"Carlson, give me a smoke."

"Negative, ruin your health."

"Aw, fuck me. Fuckin' ham and lima beans," a tall Marine bitched when he opened a can of cees. "They feed us this shit so dying won't scare us."

"You dink-dicks all going to die if you don't get your sorry asses down." Shoer's tone conveyed more concern than reprimand. "Bunch of fuckin' sheep."

At that moment, Charlie ripped open from the tree line, a hail of bullets that might have erased his squad had it been less well trained, but the opening salvo was high, and the men dove into their holes. Bullets whizzed past, indifferent death-song hornets—thup, thup, phwat—slapping into soft mud or splintering an empty canteen with a metallic clack, flattening with a dull thud against a mahogany tree, tracers lacing yellow lines between the combatants.

Charlie's advantage, his surprise, was lost as the platoon got down. Pressed against their foxholes, the Marines listened to the same sounds, but heard different things. A few prayed. Some heard the chance to rev it up after chasing shadows for too long. Austen listened hard and heard the soft popping of three or four carbines and the chain sawing of two AK-47s. Was it a small patrol that had chanced upon the platoon or a misdirection play, a diversion from the attack that would come down the ravine? Either way, he loved it. With the electric chair his household furniture, combat was a release—a blessing—for Austen: it let him live in the moment, escape himself, shove his past into his mental attic's farthest corner. And shepherding his squad, protecting them like school children, was, if not his penance, his mea culpa.

New to the game, the lieutenant was certain it was a full company of NVA, and he radioed for artillery, the battery of six 105 howitzers idly waiting a couple miles away at the battalion's fire base. Shoer inched his head up and saw the muzzle flash in the green wall. He squeezed off a burst from his M-16 and crossed his fingers for luck. After a few shots, his squad went silent for lack of targets, maintaining fire discipline, knowing the enemy's hope was to entice a platoon into running out of ammo.

"Corpsman," Ham and Beans yelled. "I'm hit. I'm hit. Get your ass over here." The Marine examined his wound. "That was no carbine, man. Did you see that, Dwight, that fucker spun me around like a puppet. This is a goddamn AK hole." He pointed with pride to his left shoulder, just under his collar bone. "Earned my goddamn heart, just like that."

"Shut the fuck up."

"Ohhhhhh shit, listen," Ham and Beans said. A whistling in the distance grew louder, overwhelming the tinny small arms fire. "Incoming," Bartlett bellowed. The shell's awful, air-splitting sound silenced the gunfire as both sides shimmied into the mud.

Kaboom. The shell landed in no man's land, but closer to Charlie than 1st Platoon, pelting Marines with clods and chunks of falling mud.

"75 up, 50 left. 75 up, 50 left." Cook's voice wobbled as he fine-tuned his coordinates, for the moment a little boy playing with outsized fireworks. He belly-crawled to Shoer's hole for a better look, his radio man crawling after him, cursing under his breath.

With mud still falling, Austen sat up and searched for his friend, nodding when he recognized the helmet with the cigarette packs tucked into its band. "Too goddamn bad Mancini's gone," Austen muttered. "He wouldn't be wasting 105 shells against rabbits who're halfway to Hanoi by now." He reassumed his alert position, rifle outboard, peering over the lip of his hole into the gray. "Don't worry, kid, they won't get any closer. And as long as the LT wants to blow up trees, Charlie'll stay out of sight. Shake it off. No one's hurt bad. All that hollering means a glorified scratch."

Another shell whistled, then screamed toward them, and again the platoon became one with the earth. Those on the southern end of their perimeter counted their blessings while Shoer's squad cursed the perils of friendly fire.

"Man, I need to get high. I'm going to pound some of this," Palowski said, pulling a Thai-stick from his pocket. Austen shot out his hand and flung the stick into the gathering darkness. Grabbing Palowski's collar with one hand, he cocked a fist. "You do anything besides aspirin out here, I'll shoot you myself. If you're not alert, we're dead. Nobody gets high on patrol. You got that, Palowski?"

"Yeah, sure, Scout. Sure. Sorry, man." He spoke with respect, obeisance. Palowski already knew that Austen had been considered the finest point man in his battalion on his first tour; that his assignment to 1st Platoon on his second was hailed as a stroke of great fortune. Had he survived, Harris would have laughed upon hearing his denigrating nickname *Scout* had metamorphosed into a higher rank than colonel.

"You got anything else?" demanded Austen.

"That was it, man. Just that stick."

"Goddamn shelling. Cheaper to buy the little bastards houses in Arizona." The November evening would soon chill. Austen slipped on his sleep shirt and rain poncho and let himself drift as the shelling fell into its pattern of 1-2-3-4-5-6, pause, 1-2-3-4-5-6, pause. With his back against the foxhole's forward wall and his chin on his chest, he slept.

The shelling had ceased, the lingering smoke cleared, and in the still night, Palowski's imagination magnified every sound, turning a bird scuttling among the wet bushes into an assassin, field rats into a VC patrol. At last Austen raised his head and called out to his squad in the starry darkness, confirming fifty percent alert, each of the other five pairs checking in on his command.

"You should rack out, Palowski. Button your collar and your sleeves, keeps the leeches out." Smelling the boy's fear, Austen directed him to sit still for about ten minutes to give the nearby leeches a chance to attack, explaining that their warmth-sensing ability had a radius of only a yard; with a preemptive counter-offensive, he might wake leech-free. After a few minutes, a dozen thin, inch-long leeches had arrived.

"Watch." The black lines shriveled on contact when he bug-juiced them. "There, your sector's cleaned out. If one gets through, burn it off with a cigarette."

A few minutes passed while the replacement looked at the stars and the squad leader stared at the shadows. "Can I ask you something?" He took Austen's silence for consent. "This is your second tour, right? You did a year of this shit and volunteered to come back for another. Why, man?"

"The money's better."

"What? You'd risk getting wasted for a few bucks more? Bullshit, man. I wouldn't do this for a million." Palowski, a draftee assigned to the Corps, considered himself the intellectual superior of those who had volunteered to eat, sleep, and shit in the mud.

"Get some sleep."

"That's really it? The money?"

"Go to sleep," said Austen. On R&R in Honolulu after their first tour apart, Austen and Shoer had drunkenly decided they wanted to do their last year together, and not march up and down LeJeune's grinder like toy soldiers. Neither man regretted the decision.

Palowski was snoring when Austen, standing to stretch away his stiffness, pondered his newest squad member's question. Returning for a second tour had nothing to do with the money. Or his conclusion that he was less likely to be killed in Vietnam than caught in America. No. He had volunteered for the second tour because it was the right thing to do. His dead father had to be proud of him, to forgive him his follies, to know he had served with honor.

"It's 0200. You're on, Palowski. Ah, shit." Austen grumbled at hearing Billy Andrews's swearing twenty yards away. "I'll be back in a few minutes. Stay sharp." Andrews had lost his sleep shirt on the trail and was too cold to sleep. With neither tents nor sleeping bags in the field, the ratty green undergarment, worn with the poncho, provided the only warmth.

"What haven't you lost? Goddamn good thing you're not in the artillery. Losing a fucking howitzer would be hard to explain." Austen pulled off his poncho and began unbuttoning his shirt, but then stopped. "Screw it, Billy. If I give you mine, you'll lose something else. Lose your ammo and somebody dies. Tough it out."

An explosion in their midst slapped 1st Platoon awake.

One of the twilight snipers had crawled to within ten yards of the perimeter and hurled a handmade grenade, a Bangalore torpedo. A few of its packed stones and nails hit Palowski, doing little more than breaking his skin, but he was blinded by its smoke. He panicked and fired his M-16 at the sky to cover himself and ran. Confused, he stumbled west, toward the ravine, toward the snipers. They sawed away at his muzzle flash. Palowski crumpled fifteen yards outside the perimeter as the platoon's two machine guns roared to life.

"Help me, help me." He was screaming, bleeding out from more holes than he had years. Austen weighed Charlie's yellow tracers and the Marines' red ones lasering at one another and, covered by the machine guns, crawled forward.

"Help me." Only a moan now.

The sticky blood pulsed from Palowski's wounds as Austen whispered encouragement. He reached about for the boy's hands and gentled him onto his back like a knapsack.

A sniper, sensing rather than seeing the rescue, waited for the lull in the platoon's cover and then sprayed the area where Palowski fell. Austen thought the fusillade had missed them, but crawling with the grunt on his back, he felt wetness along his left thigh, and wondered how Palowski's blood was getting inside his trousers—until his leg began to twitch.

"DON'T DIE, JUST FUCKIN' HANG on. We'll get you fuckin' evacked in a few minutes. Don't die, you dumb Polack. You better be listening to me." Despite his obscenities, the corpsman's tone was as mild as his touch, daubing at one of the boy's ragged holes. "You have to fight, man. Keep fighting. The docs will fix you up good as new."

The corpsman wiped Palowski's blood from his own brow then asked, "How you doing, Scout? Real sorry I can't stop that bleeding. That fucker just took out your artery. Where the fuck is the Huey?" he shouted, glancing up at the night sky for a helicopter that should have arrived. "Get me that goddamn bird."

"Get me that goddamn bird now," the lieutenant shouted into his radio phone.

A few feet away, Austen sat with his back against the foxhole and his head bowed, both hands pressed hard against his inner thigh. Blood trickled from two small holes a couple of inches apart, the exit larger than the entry wound. The wound didn't hurt yet. Shoer squatted in front of his best friend and tucked his cigarettes behind the strap on Austen's muddy helmet. "Shit, Aus, you'll be fine, seen worse mosquito bites."

"My third heart and you don't have one." Austen grinned, then frowned at the blood trickling between his fingers.

"He'll get a purple hard-on instead for all those doses he gets," the corpsman said. As a man of medicine, he felt entitled to comment on Shoer's exaggerated exploits.

"Band-Aids," Shoer said to the corpsman, "I'm giving Charlie one week—no, three days to snipe your sorry ass. If he doesn't, you're waking up to the pineapple surprise." He pantomimed pulling the pin from a grenade and bowling it into a foxhole.

"Thanks for the smokes," said Austen.

"Best to ruin your health while they're fixing it, yin and yang thing."

"Shit, shit, shit, shit," the corpsman intoned, prayer-like. He stopped working on Palowski, his chin drooping to his chest. "The patient has expired." He was accustomed to ugly wounds from land mines and booby traps, but only one other boy had died in his arms. "Poor sonofabitch. Ah, shit. What do I have to do? Yeah, got to tell the LT. You OK, Scout?"

"Yeah." The two young men glanced at the body a yard away. Neither said anything. Fire forbidden, Shoer shook loose a cigarette and broke it in two, tossed both pieces in his mouth and chewed.

"Put him in your book, Parse," said Austen, his voice struggling slightly. He loved his moments alone with Shoer, moments when he could relax, when he could speak without fear, freely—except about his past—sometimes even joke. "Say something nice about Palowski."

"Fuck my book. I can't think of a title and you know what? I can't think of anything except this shit, and who wants to read about that?"

Shoer watched Austen's blood pooling between his legs, black in the moonlight. "That's looking like the Red Sea. Cut that bleeding shit out."

"I'll be back in a week, tops," Austen said. "If the LT tries to make anyone other than Spiese squad leader, talk to Bartlett."

"Spiese. Got it." Shoer spat out the foul taste the cigarette had left behind.

"You ought to write the book." Austen gazed at the dead boy, neither envious of his peace nor terrified by it. "Write that he'd be alive if Andrews hadn't lost his goddamn sleep shirt." Austen hung his head, exhaustion closing on him. "Nah, it's not Billy's fault, it's mine. I should have known that—"

"Maybe I will," Shoer broke in. "Yeah, I'll write it when I'm supposed to be studying at that college where the chicks major in fellatio. Not playing football—unless they let me use Baby M." He patted his rifle. "So I'll have plenty of time. Hey, you can be the hero. Need some facts for your bio, and from the looks of you, I best get them fast. Where you say you're from, Corporal Austen?"

"Nowhere."

"Not good. Mysterious heroes went out with the Brontë sisters. Maybe we can make up for it with a happy family?"

"None surviving." Austen's smile flattened as a small arc of blood spurted from his thigh. Shoer pursed his lips at the sight.

"Shit, this is sounding like that white mother—what's his name? —Dickens. Yeah, right, and nobody reads his shit anymore. And I do have great expectations for my book." He had long since given up on his friend's past, but still swatted at the mystery like a ball of yarn. "My readers need something they can sink their teeth into, not some mystery— they need porn. How's it hanging down there?"

"Two inches shorter than it used to be."

Shoer laughed, flashing moonlit teeth. "Wait a second. I've got it. The book opens in Saigon, our hero in bed with a couple hookers, my hookers."

"Just two? I thought you wanted a best seller."

He laughed again, then grimaced, contemplating Austen's pooling blood. "I'll make sure the LT puts you up for a Cross. They hand them out like candy to dopes like you. If I said, here's ten thousand bucks if you'll get yourself shot rescuing some kid you never saw before, you'd laugh at me. But for a five-cent ribbon and a piece of worthless metal?"

"You're the one with the Bronze Star. Besides, the only cross I'll ever get is the one they bury me under," Austen said, repeating a line they'd heard a hundred times. He raised his head, studying Shoer, wanting to beg him to stay safe, wishing he could hold him in his arms. He made a loose, trembling fist and bumped Shoer's hand.

"I've got to go." Shoer gently brushed Austen's cheek, rose, his rifle a part of his body, and disappeared in the darkness.

"Stay well, Parse."

"WE'RE GOING TO PUT YOU under, Corporal. Count down backward from ten," the field hospital's doctor said. Outside, the first wisps of pale pink dawn reached across the eastern horizon, soft edging the gathering storm clouds with a rosy hue.

CHAPTER 21

NO TENGO NADA

"You say, *NO TENGO NADA*. I ain't got nothing. Got it?" Roy Cross blew perfect smoke rings toward the low ceiling. "Say it, man."

"No tengo nada," the worried Stanford kid repeated, his arms crossed against his fleshy chest, hands jammed in his armpits, his shoulder-length hair greasy after two days' incarceration. "No tengo nada."

"Look them in the eye when you say it. You're screwed if the malandros think you're scared. Get it down and you'll be OK. But never go in the yard by yourself."

"Thanks, King. Thanks a lot," said Marty Thompson, grateful. He'd been robbed of his money, his tennis shoes, and his hope the moment he'd arrived at La Mesa.

"*No te preocupes*, don't worry, dude." The fabled drug princeling held court in the prison's restaurant almost daily. They sat at one of the tables in the small room, farthest from the open kitchen which smelled of fried tortillas, onions, oil, and old grease. Yellowed, peeling bull-fight posters tacked to its yellowed, peeling walls. Two small windows, frosted with grime, faced the narrow street outside where Emilio the bodyguard chose to warm himself in the teasing morning sun.

"How long you been in?" Thompson took another gulp of El Globito's coffee.

"Four years, man." Telling his story to the Americans who drifted through the prison—expanding it with every other telling—was perhaps Roy's favorite pastime, his one sure escape from monotony.

"What did you do? I mean, what did they bust you for?"

"Huge fucking drug deal. Two hundred kilos of blow." Roy dropped his voice after glancing around the empty room and repeated the fantasy that sustained him like the promise of heaven. "We pulled it off. My bud, Wad, got across the border, sold the shit in Los Angeles and stashed the cash. As soon as I'm out of here, I'll be totally rich."

Thompson eyed the pretty blond hippie. He looked less a drug smuggler than one of those untethered free spirits that floated through life, the type the university elite dismissed to mask their envy. "Why don't you bribe your way out then? You said I could."

"You can. My congressman's busting me out pronto." That his congressman was more likely to vote his conscience than return another of his mother's begging phone calls had yet to dispel this particular fantasy. Roy would abandon it one day, however, just as he had been forced to part with his other early release dreams. Wad alone was his Gibraltar, his unshakeable belief. Depending on his mood and how stoned he was—Roy was always high—Wad was either his dutiful sidekick awaiting their reunion or a Judas Iscariot who'd left him to die in Mexico. Either way, Wad had to be not only alive and well, but rich, luxuriating atop a mountain of cocaine money like Scrooge McDuck. Roy had correctly reasoned that, had the Colombians found Wad, they would have left his eviscerated carcass on the street, his bloodied remains yet another cautionary tale. He had also decided—incorrectly—that the Colombians would have pardoned him had they recovered their shipment. Thus, Wad had to be both alive and rich. Back at K-39, Wad had said he'd hide out in New York City. How hard would it be to find him there? When he did, his loyal retainer would either gladly hand over Roy's ninety percent share (right was right) or his personal Judas would learn that *cuchillo* was Spanish for knife.

"But why didn't you bribe your way out four years ago?" Thompson had every reason to doubt the drug-running tale. He had yet to see

Roy's splendid carraca or learn that the fearsome Emilio lived to serve and protect the drug prince.

"It's complicated." Roy lit another cigarette with the butt he was smoking. "Buy you another coffee, tell you a—no, give you some tips. OK, this afternoon when you go to *lista*, the check-in, wait till the crowd thins out. Don't get surrounded, stay in the back, think escape route." Roy tapped his forehead with a finger. "You got any money?"

"No. I had—"

"They rolled you. I'll loan you ten bucks. You need to grease the head guard on the telacha patrol. Unless you buy your way out, you're stuck on garbage for forty-five days. Sucks. Hardest part is figuring out who to grease. Oh yeah, watch." He scanned the empty room from habit and rolled a shirt sleeve down to reveal a few hidden bills. "Get a long-sleeved shirt and keep your money in the sleeves like this and never let change jingle in your pockets. Got it?"

Thompson got it.

Roy considered showing the kid his wicked switchblade, but decided it would only frighten him. "You really want to hear how I got busted?"

"Sure, King. Be great."

Roy called for another round of coffee, undid the top button of his pinching jeans, leaned back and launched into his epic, meandering from his world-class surfing, the clamor for him in Hollywood, his picaresque border-running, how he duped one and all. He bragged of smuggling vast fortunes of cocaine and partying away his profits on endless Arabian nights. He explained how he'd created a diversion to save Wad's life, hinting at the trail of dead cops on the wrong side of the border, describing the manhunt that, even four years later, had kept Wad and their millions underground. He said nothing about Juan Sierra or his arrangement with Rudy Schmidt. Nor did he mention the San Diego police department's announcement several years back that

Edward Kawadsky had been the victim of foul play. Roy knew that had to be a feint, a buckshot to flush a wily fugitive.

"But what exactly did you do?"

Roy tossed his thinning hair. He always waited for that question. "I shot a federale."

Thompson stared into his coffee mug.

Roy stood and used his body to bob and weave his truth into his listener. In this telling, Wad had been his loyal compadre. He sketched Wad in the distant van, he jogged in place to show how he ran up the beach when he saw the lone federale. He'd shouted his getaway warning before the gun battle.

"Wow. That's cool, really cool." Thompson swallowed the last of his coffee, licking the grinds from his teeth. "Hey, do you think they'll let me call my girlfriend?"

"You don't believe me, do you?" He barked for his bodyguard. "'Melio, 'Melio, vengas."

Emilio was famous throughout La Mesa for his frightening visage, his scarred face with its broken-tomahawk nose. He intimidated with a scowl. A small-time car thief, Emilio had accidentally killed the owner of a Buick when its owner surprised him in the act. At heart, Emilio was a gentle soul, devoted to Roy; each night he'd drag his foam mattress into the hall of their carraca and sleep outside Roy's door. Yet because of Roy's stature and the comandante's protective orders, Emilio had little more to do than shoo away junkies, a chore at which Roy and his flashing blade had become adept. Rather than a bodyguard, Emilio was Roy's factotum, from cooking to buying his marijuana and pills to exchanging money with Caesar, the middleman between the Americans and their consulate.

In passable street Spanish, Roy told Emilio to confirm the floating scrotum story, first asking Thompson, "You know what cojones means in Spanish?"

There was a sudden commotion outside. A jostling crowd of prisoners had appeared, yelling at guards farther up the street. Thompson rose, peered out the window and saw the mob part. Four guards, each holding one limb, carried a body face down. He shivered and stepped toward the door.

"Don't go outside, Marty."

"What'd that guy do?"

"Maybe he cheated some dude in a drug deal or cards, maybe nothing. Maybe nothing. Oh, yeah, the guards. Treat them with respect. It's always *con permiso*—with your permission. You want to go through the gate—you want to do anything—it's con permiso. Got it?"

"Con permiso."

"How old you guess I am?"

"I don't know, man." He stared at Roy's handsome face, focusing on his red-rimmed eyes and the web of fine wrinkles spun by smoke and sun. "Thirty?"

Roy recoiled as if slapped.

"Twenty-eight, twenty-six, twenty-four?" asked Thompson quickly, bargaining down his mistake.

"Dude, I gotta split, got some business. We'll walk you over to 'Z' and get you a spot in Don's cell. He's cool." He tossed a coin on the table.

"PAY HIM, 'MELIO," SAID ROY, admiring the miniature cowboy boot keychains, tap dancing a brown and gold pair across the coffee table. The carver, a slight man imprisoned for stealing because he had no other way to feed his family, dared not look at the drug prince. He'd learned woodcarving in La Mesa and now made charming keychains—

some with cowboy boots, others with sombreros or miniature tequila bottles—that Roy's mother sold at the Sav-On where she clerked.

"Here," Roy said, tossing a pack of Marlboros to the woodcarver. "Vaya con Dios."

Emilio glowered at the carver, mumbling against this extravagance. It was Saturday night, Roy's weekly nadir, but Emilio had little cause to share in his gloom. He lived better inside La Mesa than he ever had in Ensenada. And his sex life was unchanged because, unless he paid, women crossed the plaza to avoid him. The prison's regulars—the Sunday prostitutes who smelled of rose water—were as pretty as Ensenada's.

Had he shared his bodyguard's gift for contemplation, Roy might have realized that he, too, was better off in La Mesa. He put aside the little boots. "That dickhead thought I was how old? Twenty-six?"

"YOU CAN DO IT, KING. You're a big shot here," Marilyn Beck said. A high-school dropout who worked as a receptionist at a medical supplies company, she'd longed for the dreamy Roy back in the eighth grade. When Mrs. Cross lamented her son's loneliness in prison one day at the five-and-dime, Marilyn had volunteered to come along on a visit. Now, the freckled strawberry blonde with the traffic-stopping figure came twice a month, insisting to her suspicious husband it was the Christian thing to do. "Emilio's got to have ten cousins in Tijuana who'd do it for me. I'll do whatever you want."

"You'd do it anyway." Roy lifted an end of the stained fabric couch and felt along its seam. "Got to find my stash. Hope to Christ Mom didn't throw it out again." He shoved his fingers into the side of an upholstered chair, retrieving candy wrappers and a brown apple core. He frowned.

"What about me, Roy? About my feelings?"

"*You?* How about me? My feelings. Stuck in this goddamn prison, having to listen to you two yap about God when I'm sober. Why doesn't God get me the hell out of here? Or at least help me find my stash. Yeah, like with a belt of lightning. Hey, what's this? Score." He inspected a half-inch long butt. He tore off the top half of a matchbook, rolled it tight and, using it as a cigarette holder, lit the roach. "Yeow, that's harsh."

"God's all your mom wants to talk about, and you're not saying nothing. What am I supposed to do?" She waved away the acrid smoke and hugged him. "If you really loved me, you'd do it."

"Let's get this off of you." He toyed with the oversized buttons on her denim sundress.

"Here." Marilyn slipped a torn sheet of notebook paper from a pocket. "Wheeler lives in National City. Nobody has to hurt him, just scare him. You know, get him to leave me alone."

"So I just go to one of my guys, 'scare this dude, slap him around a little, show the blade.' Like this?" In a practiced motion, he whipped out his switchblade, shooting it open with a press of his thumb, carving his initials into a foe.

"Oh, King. Will you? Please, please, please?" A perpetual innocent, Marilyn believed his stories about snuffing rivals before breakfast—his life sentence was proof—and envisioned him dispatching her boss with a snap of his fingers. "He really deserves it. That old bastard follows me into the mail room every time, tries to corner me. What are you laughing at? I hate it when you do that." She covered her chest. "If you don't care about me, maybe you ought to find another girlfriend."

He laughed harder, pulling down her arms, cradling a breast in one hand, fingering her nipple, unbuttoning his jeans with the other.

"I'm going to punch you if you don't quit it. I mean it."

Still laughing, he kissed each breast. "Maybe the old dude just can't help himself. Look at you, Mare. I couldn't either and if they busted me, I'd go, Judge, check her out, I had to do it."

"Do you really think I'm pretty?"

"Not pretty, Mare, awesome." He eased down her dress, slipping a homing pigeon finger under her panties.

"But I'm too fat."

"You're fat like I'm fucking Geronimo. These are perfect. If I was out of here, all I'd do is sell your pictures to *Playboy* and that new one *Hustler* and kick back on the beach all day."

"Talk to me some more. I like it when you talk to me. You really going to marry me when you get out?"

"You want to know—how's Mom say it—the Lord's Truth?"

"Uh-huh."

"The first goddamn day I'm out of here, me and you are getting totally wired and flying to Vegas and doing it right in one of those love chapels. That cool? Or maybe you'd like it fancy, with the white dress, honor guard—"

"Maids of honor," she said, her eyes shining. She rolled her panties down, pulled his jeans off and took him in her hand.

"Yeah, maids, church, flowers, like, the works. Mom would dig it. Can you see me in a suit?"

"A powder-blue tuxedo, King. Tell me more about it," she whispered in his ear, pumping him hard.

VISITING HOURS WERE OVER. MARILYN dressed and brushed out her matted hair. He'd still promised nothing about Willard Wheeler. "You going to help me with that old creep?"

"What? Oh, yeah." Roy sought the right phrasing. "Just go, 'soon as my boyfriend gets out of La Mesa, he's kicking your ass, old man'. Go—"

"My *boyfriend*? Wheeler'd have a cow. Remember I'm still married, I can't have a boyfriend in jail. Jesus." She rolled on her cherry lipstick. "Then he'd really think I'm easy. Maybe I should ask one of my brothers; they'd be more help than—"

"No. It's cool. Give me, oh, ten days and it's done."

"You mean it? I love you, King." She hugged him, hesitated for the sake of her fresh lipstick, then kissed him on the lips, playfully squeezing his crotch.

"De nada," he said, smiling over her shoulder at his found stash, the baggie of marijuana buds. He wanted to be alone, to smoke a joint, to imagine a scene where one of his gang roughed up the lecherous geezer, untroubled by the fact that he knew no one, save his mother, who would deliver a pizza for him, let alone a threat.

He kissed her one last time, inhaled her perfume, clenching his groin muscles to remind himself of how exquisitely Marilyn worked his cock. He rolled a joint seconds after shutting the door behind her, took a hit, picked up his Martin guitar and began strumming. He wasn't half bad.

As it happened, Roy's native optimism and perpetual high were his two best friends in La Mesa. Together, they kept him from realizing that Comandante Garcia would never release him, that only after Garcia's successor had himself been succeeded—and the Trujillo interdict long forgotten—would he have a chance of bribing his way out. That day would be years off.

CHAPTER 22

BANKING HOPES

"Maybe Irving Trust," said the bored loan officer, casually doodling on a yellow notepad. The young banker sat behind a shoddy desk, one of many, in an open area across from the elaborate wrought-iron tellers' windows. Customers trundled along velvet cordons inside the financial cathedral, scuffing the polished white marble floor. Murmured exchanges and the sounds of shuffling papers—of money counted—rose toward the quatrefoiled ceiling thirty feet above.

"Tried them, sir," said Austen. He sat straight, shoulders thrown back, his mouth set against this latest disappointment. Although scrubbed clean, his hands revealed traces of inveterate paint and grease. With his clip-on tie and new polyester suit, he might have been a day laborer paying respects at his master's funeral.

"You don't have to call me *sir*. What about Bank of New York? Have you tried—"

"Them, too. Think I've tried every bank in New York. Could you please explain something for me, sir?" Austen asked, his voice authoritative despite his disappointment, timbered from battle command. "If I have three hundred thousand in equity in these apartment buildings, why does every bank treat me like a panhandler? Is it how I look, or that I didn't go to college?"

"No," the smug banker replied, remembering his training, avoiding the personal. He almost felt sorry for Austen, knowing the hayseed simply didn't belong at J. P. Morgan. "It's not how you look, and college would only matter if you wanted a job here, not a loan. It's money.

What you consider equity in your little buildings isn't cash as far as the bank is concerned. Good luck."

"I'm back, ma'am. Remember me? I promised you I'd try every other bank before I bothered you again." Austen grinned, his gap-toothed smile buried beneath a walrus mustache. He'd stopped shaving the day the Corps discharged him four years earlier, but—enhanced disguise or no—he'd hated the beard, and gradually pared it down to the flamboyant mustache. Wearing his only suit, he stood at parade rest before the assistant manager's walnut desk.

"Yes, Mr. Austen. Of course, I remember. Please do sit down. You're so tall as it is," she replied. "And please don't call me ma'am, I'm scarcely older than you." Rather than an office, Ann Koch had a small area partitioned from the bank's central lobby by oriental screens and a row of brass-potted ficuses. A dark, thin, attractive woman in her early thirties, Ann volleyed his smile, but knew she could only turn him down again. Yet she was intrigued by her awkward supplicant. She had vaguely remembered him from seven years earlier, the day the youth with the unusual cash deposit had bounded into the Swiss Bank Corporation's Manhattan branch. "If persistence were all that a loan required, you'd have more money than the Federal Reserve."

"Thank you. Well, I didn't have any luck."

She glanced about for eavesdroppers. "You offered to move your SBC account to these other banks?"

He nodded. "Picked up lots of free bank pens. Hell, I could make a living selling pens and bank calendars in Times Square," he joked. "But while I was hitting everybody but the pawnshops—they're next—I kept thinking SBC is my best bet. I've brought my last three years' tax returns, starting with 1973. Here, this is for you." He set a red delicious apple on her desk. "Of everyone who said no, you've been the nicest."

"Why, thank you. I hope you're not thinking of bribing me," she joshed, blushing, feeling as much as hearing Austen's resonating voice.

"I sure as hell would if I thought it would work." He laughed.

"Now tell me please, how on earth did you happen to pick SBC in the first place?" Ann was curious. She'd been impressed by his resume— he was a true war hero—but it listed no education. She studied him. She found his intensity, his palpable hunger, fascinating, found herself wishing she could help him, thinking this ambitious young man, unlike the bank's pampered trust-fund clients, was on his way.

"Let's see," Austen said, gathering himself for a plausible answer. With no gift for deception, he avoided personal questions by never asking any himself, by politely changing the topic, sometimes through a stiff silence. Mostly by not making friends. Now he had to answer. He blinked, recalling in fragmented images his fevered race through Manhattan on his way to enlist, his certainty that Roy's cash had to be deposited overseas, instinct telling him he would one day flee the country. "Sounds silly, but remember I was only nineteen. I thought a Swiss bank would be kind of cool, like in a James Bond movie. Come to think of it, your guys weren't all that crazy about taking my money. A nice old cashier suggested I tell the new accounts officer I was planning to attend school in Geneva."

"But how did you get started in real estate?"

"I bought a dump on 221st Street in Queens right after I was discharged. Fixed it up and sold it. Used the money I'd saved from the Corps. I've become pretty good at pinching pennies," said Austen, rueful.

"You spend all your time on your buildings? You have no free time?"

"Sixteen hours a day. That's how I've managed to buy these three buildings," he said, tapping his financial statement. "But now, I'm stuck, my cash is fully invested, and I can't buy anything else without bank loans, without leverage." He slipped off his glasses, rubbed his twisted nose. "Do banks ever loan to people who really need the money?"

She covered her embarrassment with a small laugh. "Well, we certainly don't." Apologetic, she offered an introduction to her SBC counterpart in Basel by way of a small consolation prize. Should Mr. Austen ever find himself in Switzerland, he could take her letter of introduction to Herr Hans Peter and if the two of them got on together, and if Austen were interested in making a substantial deposit, Peter might set up a private account for him.

"They're not really numbered, you know," Ann said. "You can use initials, anything you want. Your birth date or maybe your girlfriend's birth date."

"Don't have one."

"Oh."

"The bank doesn't have to report my deposit?" he asked, paying attention.

"No, but that law's bound to change soon. The IRS hates it." She glanced up from her desk and looked him in the eyes, holding his gaze. "You know what? I think you'll get your loan somehow. In the meantime, I get off for lunch in an hour. If you're still downtown, I'll loan you enough to buy us both a sandwich."

"You don't have to do that, Ms. Koch." Confused, reddening, Austen glanced from her to the emerald-green carpet. He had always been shy with girls, bantering beyond him, flirting impossible, his everyday glibness flustered in the face of beauty. He'd been convinced that girls found him ugly long before his nose had been crushed in that fight. The fight that had shattered his world. Eddie had shown up for water polo practice two weeks after his father's death in Vietnam. Certain the boy was still bereft, his sympathetic coach had sent him home early. So early Eddie had walked in on his mother in the kitchen—her panties around her ankles—kneeling in front of his father's best friend. He froze, horrified by the blind sensuality in her glazed eyes, and then, screaming at them both, swung wildly at the commander, getting in two good punches before the bigger man decked him. The officer zipped up his khakis, pinned the dazed, bleeding boy to the floor with his boot. His poor mother was trembling so she could scarcely pull up her skirt while Eddie screamed whore whore whore. The commander retreated, Mary Kawadsky tried to explain her loneliness over her son's shouting, his father's open infidelities—their doomed marriage frozen in hell—but Eddie heard none of it. He raised his fist, but caught himself, slamming the wall instead. Crying. As self-righteous as a false messiah, he stormed from the house, swearing he never wanted to see her again. He never did. He hid from her for weeks, living in his van, until at last the weak, broken-hearted woman gave up hope. Months later, Mrs. Cross told him his mother had left the state, perhaps to Las Vegas. Maybe Albuquerque.

"You've been too nice already," Austen added, biting his lip, hating himself, knowing no woman could ever love him. Yet this woman was kind.

"It's only a sandwich."

"Thanks, but I wouldn't, I mean, I've got to fix a leak." He shook his head imperceptibly. Ann Koch was everything he'd dreamed of in his loneliest hours—smart, caring, and lovely—but starting a relationship with her, or any woman, was impossible. It would either be built on sand, on lies repeated more often than daily prayers or tantamount to signing a murder confession. No woman could ever love him if she knew the truth.

"Yes, of course." She rose to shake his hand, reassuming her professional distance. "I do think you will get that loan somehow."

CHAPTER 23

WHITE CHRISTMAS

WITH ITS NEW PAINT AND freshly cleaned windows, the midblock apartment building stood apart from its dowager neighbors. Austen had been disappointed by his tenants' reaction—more accurately, their lack of one—to the royal blue, white-trimmed paint job he had given the building's careworn façade. A few at least had conceded his new carpeting was an improvement to the creaking four-story walk-up.

Austen stood high atop a chancy ladder in the second-floor hallway, sawing away at a yellowed wet spot in the ceiling, plaster dust snowing on him. He pulled at the stained section. As it broke free, two fistfuls of plump maggots and a rat carcass tumbled onto him. "Oh, Jesus Christ, goddamn it." He swatted at the grey maggots cork-screwing in his hair, swinging about as if hornet-swarmed, flinging the desiccated rat against the wall. "Goddamn it."

He raced up to his studio—his home, office, and workshop—on the fourth floor to scrub away his revulsion. The worst apartment in the building, its window offered little light and less air, opening onto a mildewed light well. A spent mattress lay in the corner beneath the window. A reading lamp perched atop a half-dozen books on investing. A scarred work bench, as long as the bed, stood against the opposite wall, two sheets of pegboard hung with tools above it. A large walk-in closet had a small high window that glimpsed the sky, and it was here Austen set his desk. He kept his few clothes in a wooden bureau abandoned by previous tenants, its many nicks revealing geologic layers of paint. The monkish studio suggested the whitewashed squad bay in

South Carolina that he recalled with such pleasure, every object in its place, every angle squared.

He scoured his face, his hands, even his hair with granular soap. Grabbing rubber gloves, a plastic bag, and an asthmatic vacuum, he dashed downstairs, cleared the wriggling mess, then returned to the leaking cast-iron pipe. He sawed out its cracked section, cut its replacement, and spliced it in with rubber hips and clamps. A glance at the corroded pipe showed mineral deposits had narrowed its opening to a pencil-width diameter.

The hall floor squeaked. A tenant was tiptoeing past with exaggerated stealth. Austen couldn't recall her name but knew half of her rent was past due. She was stooped over her door, drunkenly fumbling through her handbag, when he called hello from his perch. She snapped up like a vaudeville burglar hearing an offstage noise.

"Oh, hello, Mr. Austen, I didn't see you there. Merry Christmas." Mrs. Harridan had left her bookkeeping job at noon for the holiday, stopping at her favorite pub on her way home. A small, roundish woman nearing sixty, she had found favor with her wit and gentle sensibility in better times, but hard years and loneliness had embittered her. Now she was feared.

"Christmas?" Austen glanced at his cracked Timex. "Oh, damn. Merry Christmas to you, ma'am." He scrambled down the ladder to clean up. "Your rent?"

"I paid my rent," she mumbled to her warped door.

"You paid your old rent, ma'am. Remember it went up on November first."

"I paid what was fair. Does he think a lousy coat of paint lets him double my rent?"

"I only raised your rent ten percent. That's more than fair, you hadn't had an increase in eleven years." Folding his drop cloth like a flag at a military funeral, he sighed. His real estate handbooks had said nothing about recalcitrant tenants, about the human cost of their cold calculations of returns on investment.

"Does he think this paper-thin carpeting turns this dump into the Plaza?" She looked beyond Austen to an imagined jury of her peers. "Maybe if His Majesty hired real workers, union boys who knew what the hell they were doing, instead of doing a half-assed job himself, maybe this dump wouldn't be falling apart. Maybe there'd be jobs around here for the men. Maybe husbands would still be here if there was work for them. He's lucky I'm paying any rent. Goddamn slumlord."

Later, Austen stepped into his trickling shower and scrubbed himself anew, washing away Mrs. Harridan more than the maggots. He told himself a man was measured by his own labors, recalling with pleasure his grandfather, the dignified Polish plumber who had never stopped working. His smile faded when a fresher image—Jonnie lecturing him about working smart—chased away the smells of his grandfather's pouch tobacco and solder. Jonnie. He still thought of her often, sanctifying her as his memories loosened over time, missing her, longing for her, wondering whether she missed him, whether she'd changed, whether seeing her again would ever be possible.

THE SILVER RAILCAR WAS FESTIVE, office workers juggling Christmas gifts, laughter ringing out. Austen offered a middle-aged woman his seat and then stood, clutching a splendid bouquet of Penn Station roses and a bottle of '71 Chateau Haut-Brion. Unwilling—no, unable—to spend money on himself, he lavished gifts on his second family. Outside, the temperature fell with the fading afternoon while the crowded coach warmed. He slipped off his suit jacket and loosened his tie. Ignoring the bleak industrial trackside, he pondered what he had to do to ready Mrs. Harridan's building for sale.

The train emptied as it rolled south into the Jersey suburbs. He found a seat next to a stout woman who smelled of peppermint. Checking the Middletown stop on the railcar's wall map, he closed his eyes and conjured Jonnie's musky perfume, remembering his guilty longings for her. Then he drifted to Ann Koch, her smile, her throat's lovely hollow. Maybe they could just be friends. No. What decent woman would accept a man so weighted down by secrets that three personal questions would sink him? But a bright woman would surely realize it was self-defense. That he was a victim. Perhaps. But that bright woman would also know that, if he were ever caught, even an innocent Austen would be imprisoned for life: he had killed two policemen and fled. At length, he shook away thoughts of women.

The rambling, one-story brick house with the gabled entry was set on an acre of leafless winter trees, its front yard studded by dwarf pines and a weathered, fiberglass mailbox on which a wooden quail herded her chicks. Flicking a mantle of snowflakes from his shoulders, Austen entered the house through the back door like one of the family. He stepped inside the big kitchen, its windows steamed, its rich smells redolent of Christmas.

Alba Shoer embraced her prodigal son. A broad-boned, strong woman in her mid-fifties, Mrs. Shoer held him tight, then examined him at arms' length with a cocked eyebrow. "Honestly, Richard, I can't decide which looks worse. Parson's beard or your mustache." She laughed and squeezed him again. "Merry Christmas, young man. Has it been six months already? Seems that 4th of July barbecue was last week. But what's different about you? You can't be taller? What is it? Come here." She took his face in her hands, turning it side to side, staring intently. "Richard Austen, I declare. You had your poor nose fixed. You are so handsome."

"I was having trouble breathing, my sinuses—"

"Trouble breathing, my ass," Parson chimed in, laughing. "You're working on your game."

"It is a wonderful improvement, Richard. You are one fine-looking young man," Mrs. Shoer proclaimed.

"Thank you, ma'am. I brought you these." He offered his gifts with a shy, hopeful smile.

"Whoa, Scout, this is one kick-ass Bordeaux. I knew you were making too much money," said Parson, admiring the bottle.

"Thank you, dear boy. I would show you Parson's Christmas present for me—two suitcases of dirty laundry—but it's all been washed and put away." As a young woman she had never turned heads, but Alba was now a handsome woman, at the height of her career as a school administrator and proud of her family's success. She'd be remembered more for her kindness than the flashing humor she'd passed on to Parson. "I'll put these gorgeous roses in a vase before they dry out. They must be nearly as thirsty as you are after that long train ride. Would you like a glass of this lovely wine? Parson, please open the bottle for my third son."

Alba had adopted Austen the morning she read Parson's letter from boot camp about the quirky silent boy who had become his only friend. She'd fretted about Austen, imagining a wretched childhood, abusive foster parents, and apathetic authorities. After she met him at the boys' graduation from Parris Island, Alba had encouraged his correspondence, writing to him as often as she wrote Parson.

Austen followed Parson into the book-lined den where his father and brother were watching the evening news. A local celebrity was standing in a soup kitchen, preening behind an aluminum pot from which he ladled minestrone into plastic bowls, keeping his good side to the camera.

"Five bucks says he beats the TV crew out the back door," said Parson. Stashing the wine for later, he handed Austen a Budweiser.

"You should feel honored, Aus. Dad would still be out working on the boat if you weren't here. Mind if I show him your progress since summer?" Parson knew little would please his father more.

The young men tramped out into the freezing air, their breath stirring the drifting snowflakes. Parson lit a Camel. They walked into the detached shed that had become the shrine to the *Alba*, the fiberglass boat Frank Shoer was building, the boat its namesake called his other woman, the boat in which he dreamed of fishing away his retirement.

"I'm clerking in the city again this summer," said Parson.

"With Ascott Swanne again?"

"I thought I'd try someplace new. You heard of Porter & Benedict?"

Austen shook his head. With neither time nor interest in anything save his own real estate, what little he'd heard of the city's storied upper crust had come through his high-living friend.

"They thought they should hire someone descended from a real porter." Parson laughed, stepped over the gunwale. "Watch your step."

"This teak looks great." Austen knelt, rubbing the smooth deck. "I have to ask your dad what kind of varnish he used. How's Eileen?"

"She's fine. She wanted me to come to her parents' place at Lake Tahoe for Christmas. Couldn't do it." Parson sighed over his formidable girlfriend. He had tried moving out once, but failed. He did like her, but damned himself for liking her comfortable apartment more: her soft bed, her cooking, and the way she vacuumed without asking for help. The two young men puttered about the boat until Parson finished his cigarette. "We better get back inside."

Alba had softened her traditional colonial dining room with cut flowers, using Austen's extravagant bouquet as her centerpiece, her marble-topped sideboard awash with poinsettias and garlands. Candles had the room glowing with golden warmth.

Austen bowed his head while Frank Shoer meandered through a prayer-full maze of thanks for the family's many blessings. Rather than counting his own—few as they seemed—Austen inhaled Christmas's rich smells: the wreaths and the tree, the scented candles, sugar cookies, yams, turkey, and steaming potatoes.

"How much did you make when you sold that Queens fourplex?" asked Parson's older brother, Francis.

Austen stalled, hiding behind a mouthful of potatoes. "I came out OK on that one."

"*OK*? He made a fortune," said Parson, announcing the profit he'd sworn to keep secret, laughing when Austen winced. His family had to be proud of his best friend. "Bro, you spent ten years going to school, I'm doing my seven and my boy here is kicking our butts."

"That's it?" Francis asked. "You buy a building and sell it ten months later for more than I'll make practicing medicine in five years? I'm in the wrong business."

"No. You're not," countered Austen. Two unaccustomed beers and Mrs. Harridan's tongue-lashing had his words tumbling out bitter hot. "I'm a janitor who happens to own the crappy building. I patch the plumbing, rewire the electrical, haul the garbage when there's a strike. I repair wrecked apartments when the courts finally allow me to evict deadbeats. Yesterday, I carried a new toilet up four flights of stairs to replace one a tenant cherry-bombed as a going-away present. I—." He shook his head, softened his tone. "I'm sorry, I shouldn't have gone off like that."

"Maybe I'll stay in school," Parson joked.

"You should be proud of yourself," Alba said. "You're wisely reinvesting your capital. A practice foreign to every member of this household. Mr. S. invests in leaky boats and my boys invest in… what do you invest in, dear ones?"

"Free love and night baseball."

Alba peered over her glasses at Parson, bundling her affection with a stern look. "Free love. We never should have let you attend Berkeley—

you should have stayed east. They have too many earthquakes in California for us, don't they, Richard?" she asked, repeating Austen's standing excuse for avoiding the golden state.

The conversation drifted to current events, and soon they were discussing the evening news soup kitchen story, Francis dismissing the celebrity's generosity as cheap publicity.

"Motive is important when dealing with evil or crime," Alba said. "Yes, my almost lawyer? But with good acts, with charity, we should be more tolerant of motives, more charitable toward charity—"

"Well put, Mom."

"But seeing that line makes me feel so for those children. All that welfare money spent on drugs, and the poor babies at a soup kitchen."

"As long as the courts mollycoddle drug dealers, you'll have bread lines a mile long," Mr. Shoer declared. "Throw the book at crime and you could close half those handout places."

"No, Dad." Parson seldom argued with his father, but he'd wrapped up a criminal justice class days earlier and was sure the old man was misguided. "Seventy percent of all crime is drug-related. Either people getting busted buying or selling it, or users selling their bodies or robbing people to get their next high. We need to decriminalize drugs— not legalize them, decriminalize them. Besides, it's the practical thing to do: If drugs aren't available, addicts will just be drunks instead. Right, Aus?"

Frank Shoer waved a hand to spare their guest and said, "Son, a society that openly tolerates vice has its moral fiber fray like a halyard rubbing against the mast." He pulled out his empty meerschaum pipe, his signal the topic was closed.

"YOU A MILLIONAIRE YET, SCOUT?" Past midnight, the two young men were sprawled in the den, draining the Haut-Brion Parson had squirreled away. In his father's red leather chair, stocking feet crossed on the ottoman, he looked to the manner born.

"I told you what I am—I'm a building super. I fix sinks, I've yanked enough hair out of shower drains to go into the wig business," said Austen, distracted, his friend's comments about decriminalizing drugs nipping at him, taking him back to Mexico.

"You got to be a millionaire. Putting that in my book. Scout goes bucks up."

"I'm not a millionaire," insisted Austen. He hadn't had a drink since he'd last seen Parson over Labor Day, but now he was drunk, his habitual reticence faltering. "OK, OK, maybe half. Maybe a little more than half."

"Did you say a little more? Of course, old boy. Delighted." Parson splashed a couple inches into Austen's wine glass, poured himself another. "No BS, you're rich—"

"Screw rich."

"You net more out of those buildings while you sleep than I'll make in a year. That's a fact. Baby, I'm quitting school, buying a plunger, kicking your skinny white ass, and getting rich."

"I read something about rich," said Austen. "Only three ways of getting there: You can be born with it, marry it, or borrow it."

"So maybe with that pretty new nose, you can marry it. Get your teeth fixed, hell, get contact lenses too, and you'd be spanking tail. That is, if you just tried—tried being pleasant, talking. You've heard of talking? Only woman I've ever seen you talk to is my mother. Besides, why you got to be rich anyway?"

Uncorked by the wine, Austen's ambition bubbled over, words he'd never spoken aloud spilling out. "I want... I want the respect that I had in Nam."

"You were the man," enthused Shoer. "The *Scout.*"

"I need to be somebody. Really succeed. What have I got? Nothing. A couple buildings that'd fall down if they weren't midblock. Somebody told me once never to work with my hands," Austen said, rueful. "Hell, that's all I do, fix toilets, trap rats. Without fancy degrees like yours, all I can do is shit work. Eventually, maybe I can develop something good, be a for real developer, but now what I've got? Nothing."

"You're on your way, you'll get there."

"No. I'm going nowhere. Right back." Austen staggered to his feet, tiptoed to the bathroom, trying not to wake the sleeping household. He splashed his face with cold water, nodded at the nose Mrs. Shoer so admired and sat on the toilet, lost in the unfamiliar alcohol. He hung his head. Was his financial roadblock truly insuperable? Maybe if he had a dozen third-rate tenements the banks would listen to him.

"Hey, did you mean that stuff about legalizing drugs?" he asked, rejoining Parson a minute later.

"Decriminalizing them? Why not? Everyone's getting high anyway. May as well be cheaper. Speaking of which, maybe we do New Year's together, kick off next year in style. I'll score a little blow—"

"Blow?"

"C'mon, Aus, it's the best party drug in the world. Perfectly harmless if you don't count the two-day hangovers. We'll do the night with a couple ladies. Get you a date. You in?"

Austen had little enthusiasm for a blind date, less for getting high, but warmed to the prospect of a long evening with his one friend. "OK, I'm in." He emptied his glass slowly, but his mind raced. "You really think it's harmless?"

"What?"

"Cocaine."

Parson laughed so loudly Austen shushed him with a finger to his lips. "In moderation, Scout, it's a boon to mankind: conversations

sparkle, dullards shine, and the sex? The sex is amazing," Parson rhap-
sodized. "But… sure, too much will kill you same as too much of anything. Hell, drinking too much water will kill you quicker."

"You ever, you know, sold a little pot or anything?"

"Who hasn't?"

Austen nodded, sobered by memories he'd tried to bury in a Lemon
Grove bomb shelter.

CHAPTER 24

JONNIE

AUSTEN HAD BEEN WANDERING THE streets for hours, muttering and gesturing, and was fumbling for change in a phone booth, oblivious of the urine smell. A pair of pigeons roosted atop its buckled roof. Despite his gift for numbers, he knew the phone numbers of only two women and had just sworn to forget one. Nearly a year after Ann Koch's sandwich offer, he had stopped by the Swiss Bank to tell her his Harridan building was in escrow at last, hoping she would reconsider his loan application. The young Swiss receptionist stumbled before she hit upon the word *moonhoney* to explain Ms. Koch's extended leave. Outside, Austen flung the bouquet of roses to the sidewalk, picked it up, tossed it in a trash bin.

He seldom drank without Parson Shoer, but he'd started that afternoon. He'd spied the bottle of drugstore gin left behind in a vacated apartment, telling himself he would toast the building's sale. Sitting in his underwear in the airless apartment, he gulped gin and tap water, assuring himself he was celebrating, that his drinking had nothing to do with the lost Ann Koch or his string of loan rejections or his solitude.

Drunk, sweating gin, scratching at his paint-splotched t-shirt, he dialed Jonnie's number, knowing she had to be home. It was ten o'clock in California. A nasal voice pronounced the toll. He was short a few quarters and surprised the operator when he politely apologized for troubling her. Two blocks uptown, he found a convenience store where he set a Schlitz and a twenty on the counter and asked the Arab clerk if he might have three dollars' worth of quarters, telling the kid to keep the change. He pulled the tab off the beer can, guzzled it like a Marine on R&R, wiped his mustache, and threw the empty at a passing bus, cursing as it sailed wide. He stumbled back to the phone booth, redialed Jonnie's number, and inserted the quarters. He hoped she still answered the phone with yes, remembering her husky cigarette voice as if they had spoken the day before.

"Hello?"

"Sorry to disturb you, ma'am. Mrs. Collins, please."

"This is she."

"Jonnie?" Austen asked, bewildered.

"Who? Oh my. Oh … Wait a second. Dear?" Muffled sounds behind a covered phone. "Just a moment."

"This is Dr. Collins. With whom am I speaking?"

Austen recognized the thin voice, recalling Jonnie's mocking descriptions of her husband. "Sir, I need to speak with Jonnie."

"Who is this?"

"Friend, a friend of hers. Where's Jonnie, Doctor? I need to talk to her. I need her advice."

"She passed away, over five years ago. Now, may I know the nature of your call?"

"She's dead?" Austen cried, his voice cracking, stunned into a momentary silence. "No… no, not dead. Five years ago?" His straight back crumpled, forehead drooping against the filthy booth.

"I'm hanging up if you don't identify yourself."

He choked back a sob, bawled, let the phone slip from his hand and swing on its metallic cord. He sank to the pavement.

"Hello? Hello?" Dr. Collins demanded. "Is anyone there? Hello? Darn it, I'm hanging up."

Austen groped for the dangling receiver. "Where's she… where's she buried? I have to visit her, her grave. Where?"

"Here, at Holy Cross cemetery. I really must insist—"

Austen flung the phone at its cradle, crept out of the phone booth, and sat at the curb, sobbing into the night. He rocked back and forth, with his face buried in his big rough hands, ignoring the stares of the wounded night people.

WEEKS BECAME MONTHS BEFORE AUSTEN convinced himself to risk California. When the chestnut leaves turned, he bought a one-way ticket with cash and a phony name and flew to Los Angeles. He found a used car in the *Times* classifieds, and a few hours later paid a grieving Armenian woman cash for her dead daughter's Toyota. She asked for eight hundred dollars, but he countered with a thousand when he glimpsed the candled shrine with its fresh mourning lilies in the woman's living room.

He drove to the Holy Cross cemetery that evening and vaulted its black steel fence. Despite the full moon and his half-trotting gait, it took him hours to find Jonnie. He'd started his search among the carved mausoleums, moved on to the elegant marble and granite tombs, then the grandest of tombstones. He cursed when at last he spied her tarnished metal plate—one of thousands—in the cemetery's working-class neighborhood along Hilltop Drive. The square marker contained only her name, her life bracketed by dates and the words "Loving Wife and Mother."

"Goddamn it." Outraged at Dr. Collins's miserliness, Austen kicked the damp, grassy earth and then paced, calming himself. He sat down, setting roses above where he felt her heart lay. He stayed half the night, swearing at Dr. Collins, picking at weeds, scratching his car key against her plate's tarnish, chewing blades of grass. Asking Jonnie whether she would do it. Whether he should do it.

"I've been trying to work smarter, Jonnie, but I don't have any credit, I can't borrow shit and, instead of looking for new deals, I'm spending all my time keeping my dumps from falling down. I need that money to really get started. That stuff belongs to me more than anyone else, doesn't it?" When the moon set, he leaned over and kissed the cool plate.

Then he drove to Lemon Grove.

CHAPTER 25

THE HOUSE THAT CRIME BUILT

THE DUFFEL BAGS LAY UNDISTURBED in the abandoned bomb shelter, but seeping moisture had rotted their canvas. He'd carried the first bag no more than five steps before its contents burst through the bottom. But the kilos, waterproof in their shells, were intact. Telling himself to stay calm, he picked up an armful, climbed out of the shelter, climbed the pink block wall, and dropped his first load in the trunk. A half dozen trips later, he checked his count. Forty-eight. Breathing deep, he threaded his way back and forth across the yard, scuffling, kicking the purple bougainvillea, hand-checking the backside of the wall, hunting for two kilos he had long since forgotten had been seized by the police.

Austen drove cross-country in his Marine uniform, sporting a fresh crew cut, having decided an annual stint with the reserves was a good story for any cop who happened to pull him over. He argued with the cocaine, but drove on, insisting his cargo was little more than a day's worth for the moneyed elite who saw through him and his preposterous ambitions. He drove on, coffee for sleep, resting a few hours in the back seat when his neck snapped from dozing.

"It's mine," he said aloud to Denver. "They ruined my life. I would have gone to the Academy, been a pilot. I could have become an admiral. I'm owed—a lot more than this." At length, he realized he would never convince himself, that his rationalizations were no more than that, and forced himself to stop thinking about the trunk's contents.

UPON HIS RETURN TO THE Swiss Bank Corporation, Austen found everything as it had been on his last visit, save Ann Koch's nameplate. It now read Ann Sampson. He waved an unimpressive cashier's check before her and asked for that letter of introduction she'd mentioned the prior year. Amused, Ann said it would be ready forthwith, congratulating herself for predicting his success. Austen flew to Switzerland three days later. Herr Hans Peter was most cordial in his willingness to bank Mr. Austen. Over excellent coffee, Peter chuckled at the romantic notion Americans had of cloak-and-dagger Swiss accounts.

"What do you say in New York? No big deal?" He asked, pleased to display his fluency to the young American in the rumpled suit.

"Yes, sir. No big deal. That's it."

Back in New York, Austen sawed a kilo in two, sealed both halves and paid a kid five bucks to hand-deliver one to the Upper East Side brownstone the *New York Post* dubbed "The House That Crime Built". It was home to the offices of Louis La Fortune, a mob lawyer in the papers as frequently as his favorite client, Jimmy "The Bone" Carbone. Austen had addressed a respectful letter to Mr. Carbone—care of his attorney—suggesting that he could either view the pound of pure cocaine as a gift or, should he wish to do business, he could wire-transfer its wholesale value to an account in Switzerland. And should he wish to continue doing business, Mr. Carbone need only place an ad in the *Post* seeking his lost corgi. A Grand Central Station locker key would then be delivered to his lawyer, La Fortune. He wrote that as long as Mr. Carbone's wire transfer arrived in Switzerland within seventy-two hours of key delivery, he could be assured of a limitless supply. Austen politely blamed their lack of acquaintanceship for his inability to advance more than two kilograms at a time.

Almost overnight, he had difficulty keeping up with the gangster's demand.

In a series of phone conversations that began when his deposits reached a million dollars, Herr Peter suggested his bank's investment group might manage Austen's money for him in a prudent manner. Peter boasted how his managers distrusted spectacular results, how they viewed extraordinary returns with a suspicion inbred over hundreds of years. Their mission, as he described it, was to preserve capital and only secondarily to achieve a solid, consistent return. The next day Austen executed the documentation providing the bank authority to invest his funds as it deemed appropriate.

Later, when the last kilogram had been sold and his account substantial even by Swiss reckoning, Austen told Peter he was thinking of buying more New York real estate and asked whether the bank's Manhattan branch could provide him with a line of credit equal to, say, eighty percent of his Swiss holdings.

"Certainly, Mr. Austen."

Austen hung up, tried to rejoice in the fortune that was now his, but felt neither elation nor relief.

CHAPTER 26

THE JOB

"WHERE WAS I?" PARSON ASKED Austen. He'd lost his thread to a passing skirt. He popped his French cuffs, smoothed his navy blazer's pocket square, and smiled at himself in the mirror above the Oak Room's magnificent bar. He tossed a peanut into his mouth. "Oh, yeah. The surprise party. Picture this: It's the day before her birthday, so Eileen's off her guard. She walks into the restaurant for our intimate dinner and sees all her friends laughing and drinking, ignoring us. She does the jungle freeze, crushed that everyone is partying without her. I say, 'Maybe we ought to go somewhere else,' and just before her heart breaks, they all yell, 'Surprise! Happy birthday!' and the future chief justice bursts into tears. I really fooled her."

"Into thinking you love her enough to marry her?" asked Austen, not expecting an answer. As much as he loved Parson, he hated the way his friend had strung Eileen along.

Parson's smile faded, then he caught a flash of red in the beveled mirror and swiveled to sigh at a spike-heeled woman sauntering past, outside the glamorous oak-paneled bar. "Check that." He pointed through the extravagant window that overlooked Central Park.

Austen frowned. Long troubled by Parson's easy way with women and agnosticism over fidelity, he knew anything he had to say would only hurt his one friend.

"Right. Let's talk about something else." Parson tossed another peanut in the air. It bounced off his front tooth. "Let's hear about your money. Tell me about Scout's millions." Like the howitzers they'd cowered from in Vietnam, Parson barraged Austen with questions until he finally crumbled, admitting he had all four of his borough apartment buildings in escrow ready to be traded into a building on Fifth Avenue.

"Whoa. How much that cost? Nothing cheap on Fifth. Come on."

"The price isn't important."

"It is to me. Come on, spill it." Again, he fired away until Austen admitted to a broad range. Playing at cross-examination, Parson pinned his friend down to within fifty thousand dollars of the price. "Now, where did you get that kind of money?"

"I told you, I'm selling all my other buildings, and I borrowed the rest. Getting out of the flea-trap business."

"Son, I know what you paid for those dogs, and I remember what you said they were worth. They ain't buying Fifth Avenue. And your credit sucks. So what changed? Maybe you struck oil while you were sweeping out the basement?"

"I'm converting this new building into co-ops. Serious money in that."

"You're going to need a good lawyer to do the paperwork, get the city approvals—that conversion shit isn't easy. That smart guy I told you about last summer, Brendan O'Keefe at Ascott Swanne? He'd be perfect."

"They're too expensive. Wouldn't take me as a client anyway." He sighed at the grime seemingly tattooed on his hands. "Hell, you laugh at me every time I put on my suit."

"Everybody laughs when you put that suit on." Parson looked perplexed, as if stumped by a riddle. He caught the bartender's eye, raised two fingers. "One more drink, then we burn it."

"Do you want to know what my problem is now?" Austen asked.

"Nah."

"Yes, you do, you jerk. Here it is: Nobody takes a twenty-seven-year-old seriously. I call about some building, and it's OK until I show up to look at it. Then the broker asks if we should wait for my dad."

Parson caught another peanut in his mouth, said, "Long as you promise to buy us all the rounds, dinner, the works, Parson *Shoe-in* will handle it for you."

"How?"

"First clue, you're about to hire a very fancy, very expensive law firm. Nothing says big league like throwing money away on lawyers. But first we really have to burn this suit—hell, probably need a special permit, this shit's so flammable."

"It's not that bad. Is it?" asked Austen.

"Worse. Tomorrow we're going shopping. You can afford some swank building where my people can't be janitors, you can afford three new suits and a dozen shirts. And new glasses, gold frames."

"Gold?" Austen wondered if two suits would do, appalled at the thought of spending money on himself. He'd told himself he felt no guilt over selling the cocaine, that he was owed, but that was a lie. His foray into dealing was bleeding his conscience, one drop at a time. The only thing he could treat himself to was hard work.

"You want to borrow money, you can't look like you need it," Parson barreled ahead, missing Austen's tone. "A billionaire can look poor; you can't. Another thing: If you want to look like an adult, more respectable, get your front teeth capped. Don't give me that, I'm not trying to hurt your feelings. That gap makes you look like a kid."

As drinks drifted into dinner at a trattoria on 65th, Austen realized an unforeseen cost to his new fortune. He could no longer explain his financial exploits—detail his success to his audience of one—for Parson was too bright to accept fairy tales about overly accommodating sellers or one-hundred-percent financing. He wondered how many deals he would need to do before his money was fumigated. Where was the joy in success if you couldn't share it with your only friend?

The trattoria was littered with tacky Italian travel posters and empty wine bottles hanging from the ceiling, the flocking locals willing to sacrifice ambience for pasta served by the pound. Parson thought the owner a genius because his prices were reasonable and he hired only large-breasted young women as waiters. They all wore undersized T-shirts that bore his caricatured likeness, a potbellied Italian smiling over his stove. Parson lit a cigarette and glanced around, wondering how profitable the restaurant was. "Maybe another carafe of Vino Tavolo instead? That Tavolo has to be the biggest winery in Italy. You listening to me, Scout? Something wrong? You're way too quiet. Sorry if I pushed you too hard."

"No, no." Austen waved his hand, a weak smile fixed. He knew the only way out. "Sure, get another bottle. Stuff's not bad."

"Not bad? You ever thought of becoming a wine critic?" He beamed at a particularly busty blonde waitress across the room.

"Want to know something?" Austen fanned away Parson's smoke and then dropped his head, a defendant awaiting a jury's verdict. Now was the time to tell him everything, to seek understanding—perhaps, compassion—for his crimes. Parson would understand. "How I'm really buying that building? How it all began when I was nineteen?"

"What? Nineteen? You were with me then, bro. Yeah, absolutely, but just a sec." He glanced back at the bustling waitress. "Look at me, please, baby, just look at me once. All right, play it that way. Mohammed's going to that pair of mountains."

Austen sipped from an indestructible water glass, observing his friend's prowl through the bunched tables. His secrets had chafed his soul raw for years. They were his alone to bear, but, until his return to Lemon Grove, he'd had self-defense as a thin comforter. But that had unraveled when he'd begun selling to Jimmy the Bone. Now, he was a narcotraficante. Would confessing to Parson offer any relief? Was he entitled to any? He chewed his lip while Parson engaged the young woman with a smile, resting a hand on her shoulder as though they were related. She laughed at something he said.

Austen could not have been more alone in the crowded room. He lowered his head and folded his arms across his chest. The truth was simple—no one would ever understand or forgive. He was a killer and a drug dealer.

Parson circled back a moment later, eyes bright, exulting. "Got her number. She's going to bring us the better stuff. Where were we? Oh, yeah. Your building, let's hear how you're really buying it... Hey, you OK?"

Austen leaned back and tightened his grip on his chest. "Yeah, fine. Tell me about your plan. How you're going to make me respectable."

"There you go again. Dodging with a question. You really don't look good—you sure you're alright?"

"Fine, just tired. I'll bore you with that story later. So, how are you going to help me?" asked Austen.

"As you like to say, here it is: You're going to work for a swanky French investment bank, one we're going to dream up right now."

"What?" cried Austen, not understanding.

Parson laughed. "Rather than Richard Austen, boy developer, you're now the regional vice president of, oh, let's call it, 'duPlessis Freres', a fabulously wealthy firm so secretive no one's ever heard of it."

CHAPTER 27

VIVE LA FRANCE

THE WINDOWLESS ROOM WAS LONG and narrow, its walnut paneling and group of foxhunting prints suggesting a men's club rather than a thirty-eighth-floor conference room. The lighting was so low that the wags of Miller, Taylor, and Taylor said it was intended to prevent close readings of documents. At its center was an elliptical conference table surrounded by swiveling brown leather chairs.

Unnoticed in the corner, a heavy-set woman in a black dress trimmed with a white lace collar and apron tidied the silver coffee and tea service. Earlier, she had set stacks of fresh legal pads and marble holders filled with new No. 2 pencils around the polished table. An annoyed Schuyler Van Linge sat at its head, drumming his long, thin fingers against his chair. He was supposed to be signing a clutch of documents, shaking hands, and getting to his squash match by eleven. No one had said anything about negotiating last-minute items. He'd lingered at a wickedly debauched Halloween party until three the night before and felt cotton-headed, desperate for exercise.

"Sky?" Perry Whistler, the lawyer, interrupted Van Linge's pique. "Sky. We need to come to a resolution on this business point. I need your help." Whistler had charged Van Linge a minor fortune for bringing the transaction—the sale of a stunning pre-war apartment building on Central Park West—thus far. Were the deal to fall apart, he knew Van Linge would be outraged and, worse, unlikely to pay his bill. The lawyer could only hope that the young vice president of duPlessis America Properties would relinquish his company's ridiculous demand for a last-minute price cut.

"Let's get on with it, shall we? The dollar amount. How much is it?" demanded Van Linge, frowning at the stacks of documents left to sign before closing. With his height, trim physique, silvery hair, and permanent sneer, Van Linge looked—and acted—the part of a feared CEO. Those with whom he was not well acquainted listened closely when he spoke.

"Seven hundred fifty thousand dollars, sir," Austen answered, his first words in some minutes. In marked contrast to his own fidgeting, disheveled lawyer, Austen sat straight, leaning forward from his hips, oblivious, it seemed, to the stakes involved in his eleventh-hour brinksmanship.

Van Linge peered at the young man across the table as if seeing him for the first time. Trying to recall his name, he grasped why the clever French had sent such a young man to the closing. Because he had no authority, the youth could give away nothing, leaving him to negotiate with a Maginot Line. "What authority do you have this morning, Mr. ah—"

"Austen. To close the deal, sir." He wore a gray flannel suit, a starched, button-down white shirt and a conservative tie, a particular combination he'd memorized from Parson's sartorial instructions.

"Let's stop this nonsense, here and now," Van Linge said. "We both know your superiors want this deal closed without delay."

"Perhaps, there's a middle ground," said Brendan O'Keefe, Austen's garrulous lawyer.

"No, there's not. I have my instructions," said Austen, glaring at his lawyer, recalling Parson's description of O'Keefe as a brilliant man, but a want-to-be dealmaker who talked too much.

"Can you reach your superiors, Mr. Austen?" Whistler the other lawyer asked.

"Yes sir, if we hurry. It's now four-thirty in Paris. The director will be leaving for the weekend any minute."

"A two hundred fifty thousand dollar credit. That's it, my final offer. Take it or leave it." Pointing to a clerk, Van Linge added, "Hand me those documents. I will sign everything now. The French may close with this goodwill gesture or forfeit their million-dollar deposit. C'est la vie."

The clerk, actually Whistler's junior partner, jumped up from his back-row seat, handed Van Linge a six-inch stack, and glanced toward Whistler, wondering if he would correct his client's legal conclusion about the buyer's loss of deposit.

"Thank you, sir," said Austen. "I understand that's a very generous offer. May I use that phone in the corner to call?"

The complaisant title officer suggested to Van Linge that he might consider signing the deed first; the messenger could rush it to the recorder's office, then stand by and await further instructions. Van Linge signed the deed with élan and attacked his first stack of documents while the others pretended they had tasks apart from eavesdropping on Austen's conversation. Nodding, they watched him side-eyed as he gestured and listened, then responded with a string of quick *yesses* and no sirs.

"Yes, sir, I've explained that." Austen had edged as near Van Linge and the lawyers as the phone cord would allow. "I believe him, sir. He says it's their final offer." Austen yanked the receiver from his ear as if it were aflame, tinny screams coming from the receiver. The group froze until the Gallic tirade subsided, a long thirty seconds. "I'm sorry, sir. No, I won't disturb you again. Thank you." He hung up. "He forgets his English when he's really mad. Good thing I don't speak French."

The senior attorneys had grayed during the shouting, O'Keefe's queasy stomach tightened as Whistler silently rehearsed a boilerplate speech about the law's appalling lack of certainty on the subject of retaining deposits.

"I'm very sorry, Mr. Van Linge, but my director views it as a point of honor. You know the French. They lost their honor on the field of battle, and now they insist on recapturing it over and over in business."

Van Linge scrutinized the courteous young man who stood at parade rest. He inclined his patrician head and pondered his next move. He knew the money they were haggling over was of little consequence to the family trust because it would first be taxed and then divided among seven already-wealthy beneficiaries, but he feared appearing weak. "Were you in the military, Mr. Austen?"

"Yes, sir. The Marine Corps."

"You're looking at a war hero," Brendan O'Keefe said. Shoer had described Austen to him as a battlefield god.

"No, I was only following orders. Like I'm doing now."

Unable to serve because of a back condition that gave him little trouble on the squash court, Van Linge was impressed. "Were you awarded any medals?"

"Sir, please. I'd rather—"

"Tell him about the Bronze Star you got for—"

"Mr. Van Linge, believe me," said Austen. "I understand your position as completely as I hope you understand my company's. And please remember this seven-hundred-fifty-thousand-dollar credit amounts to a very small, very legitimate price reduction."

"Young man, my wife's family is already beside itself over the price I've agreed to—they and their so-called advisers ought to manage these damn assets themselves. If we didn't have a deal, I would take it back to the market for five million more."

Austen slipped into the adjacent chair and began signing the stacks Van Linge had finished. "I think I'm stuck with the amount, sir. But," Austen paused, flashing his gap-toothed smile, waiting until all eyes were on him, then a guilty-little-boy look. "I forgot to ask whether the credit had to be in cash."

"A credit against the note is the same as a cash credit. That's no compromise," Whistler said.

"No, Mr. Whistler," said Austen, "it is a compromise. Here it is: What if the cash credit is only the two hundred fifty thousand Mr. Van Linge so kindly offered, and the remaining five hundred thousand is credited against our note to the trust? I can explain I thought the note credit was just as good." He grinned as he continued to sign documents. "Monsieur Director can kick himself for not being here to make sure everything went just right."

O'Keefe eyed his adversaries like a dog guarding meat and caught Van Linge's look as his lawyer nodded toward the door.

"Excuse us a minute, gentlemen," Van Linge said, standing, grateful for the opportunity to move. He strode to the door, Whistler and his two adjuncts close behind.

"Wow. He really sounded angry. Was that DuPlessis himself?" O'Keefe asked, unmindful of the title officer and paralegal across the table. O'Keefe had grown disenchanted with his new client almost overnight, putting up with Austen only because he hoped to be assigned the company's investment banking work. He resented how Austen called him into deals at the last minute, the way he played lawyer and how he challenged nearly every legal bill.

"No." Austen shut his eyes and leaned back in his chair for the first time that morning. He breathed deep and held it for a thirty count. A seven-hundred-fifty-thousand-dollar discount turned a great deal into a near brilliant one. He would make many millions converting the stately apartment building into co-ops. Learning business the way he learned to lead in Vietnam—one hill at a time—Austen had grown more battle-hardened with each encounter, learning when to stand his ground, when to retreat… when to say no. And when to bluff.

Moments earlier, Parson Shoer had been trying to explain to a bemused senior partner why he had been bellowing gibberish French over the phone. He should have closed his door, but the San Francisco offices of McCall Sutro were empty when he'd arrived at seven a.m. He chuckled at the thought of the fictitious DuPlessis America Properties—DAP—remembering its wine-stained baptism at the trattoria. As Parson had imagined it, DAP would be the American real estate division of DuPlessis Freres, a family-held French investment bank that guarded its privacy. Since the company existed only in his fancy, he would tout it—and Austen, its American vice president—to his old mentor O'Keefe as known only in the most rarefied circles.

CHAPTER 28

BILLY CUTTER

BILLY CUTTER WORE AN ARMANI silk suit tailored to accentuate his deep chest and broad back while concealing his soft stomach. His black hair was cut in a flattop, resembling nothing so much as a boar-bristle brush. He hunched forward from the waist, head outthrust, a human battering ram. He'd been pacing DAP's waiting room all day in the hope of seeing the notoriously reclusive Richard Austen. The first hour he'd skimmed the *Wall Street Journal,* then he'd tried little mind games, closing his eyes and picturing the lackluster room: straw-colored sisal wall covering, nicked wainscoting, high ceiling, flimsy Danish furniture, and an oil painting depicting a turn-of-the-century restaurant scene.

"Perhaps another cup of coffee, Mr. Cutter?" asked MJ Watershed as she stepped from the company's inner offices. It had been four years since Austen had hired her to run DAP for him. "Actually, I should think you have had enough. Rather a spot of tea?" Mrs. Watershed had a fondness for titles, especially her own: Chief of Staff. Notable for her kindness and her English-rose complexion, it was she who had first suggested that Austen consider sharing his great fortune with charity.

"No. You said you thought he'd see me today. It's almost four. He owes me."

"I shall try again for you, Mr. Cutter. Chin up." With two sullen teenage sons, she was fazed neither by the young man's aggression nor his frustration. She'd also seen his three unanswered letters to Austen and thought his claim had at least passing merit. Yet despite her near-omniscient knowledge of all things DAP, her relationship with Austen was

based upon the fiction that she was aware only of matters he brought
to her attention. While this protocol suited them both, it occasionally
left her unable to voice an opinion. She sometimes bridged this gap,
however, by placing her husband Nigel in analogous, if imaginary, sit-
uations and lamenting his missteps. With one notable exception (from
which she decided that Mr. A.'s social life was his own concern), Austen
often drew the proper inference and did as she knew best.

"I AM PLEASED TO REPORT your appointment has arrived," Mrs.
Watershed said, a note of triumph in her voice. Smoothing her hands on
her skirt, she was reminded again of a young bull when Billy stood. He
straightened his gold cufflinks, picked up his attaché case, and followed
her into the inner offices, ignoring the once-elegant surroundings.

"In here, please," she said, indicating a door with her own name
stenciled in gold leaf across a frosted pane. She crossed to a door against
her office's far wall and, knocking twice, whispered, "Good luck."

"Wait a minute," Billy said. "Wait a goddamn minute. I haven't
waited all day to see some flunky. I'm here to see Mr. Austen."

"That is Mr. Austen," said Mrs. Watershed, stifling her grin.

"Then I want to see his father. The guy who makes the decisions."

"My father is deceased. Sit down, Mr. Cutter." Austen neither rose
from his desk chair nor extended a hand. He wore a crisp blue suit, a
white Oxford shirt and a red tie. His brown curly hair was flecked with
hints of gray, but his lean build and erect posture suggested youth. The
change in Austen's appearance over the years since he'd founded DAP
had more to do with wealth than aging. He now spoke in measured
sentences, his gaze direct, his deep voice assured, his boyish desire to
please lost or locked away. He had grown unaccustomed to being challenged. "You have five minutes."

"You're the guy I talked to on the phone? You bought the Klondike building?" Billy was in shock—he was facing a multimillionaire no older than his bum brother. Before sitting, he looked about the dark paneled office. It had a somber, almost medieval quality, with motes drifting across shafts of May sunlight. The office appeared as if it had been untouched for decades, a capitalist's lair from the thirties. It would never have occurred to Billy that a guilt-ridden Austen was unable to spend money on himself.

"Yes, sir. How may I help you?" Austen appraised the heavyset young man, reminding himself of how he had justified his earlier decision, the broker's worthless listing and the unethical firm for which he worked.

"You owe me a commission for the Klondike. I sent you the package last fall. I silver-plattered that deal for you, and you bought it out from under me."

"Your sales package was a joke; the seller had no equity left in the building and nothing to sell. We bought the loan from a lender you didn't represent."

"You never would have heard about the Klondike if it wasn't for me. Getting it by foreclosure is the same as buying it. It's got to be worth at least fifteen million more today than what you paid."

"It's empty and returning nothing on our investment."

"What's the cheapest finder's fee you've ever heard of? One percent? Right? Pay me that, and we'll call it even." Seeing Austen's hesitation, Billy urged with a broker's smile, "Come on, that's a day's interest for a hitter like you."

"Even if we wanted to pay you anything, it would take weeks getting approval from Paris because—"

"You can drop that French crap. Everybody knows it's you. I checked the records in Delaware—you're DAP's sole shareholder."

Austen closed his eyes, fighting the impulse to laugh aloud. So much for his brilliant subterfuge. If this kid knew, the whole world did. He pressed the intercom, glanced at Billy's thin resume. "Here it is. I'll have Mrs. Watershed cut you a check for twenty-five thousand. You can go get your MBA at Harvard."

"No, *here it is*, Mr. Austen," Billy mimicked. "For the first thing, I hated school. Second, I'm supporting my parents so I have to work, and finally, twenty-five thousand isn't right and you know it."

"Your father an invalid?"

"My father's a bum. He's a waiter," said Billy.

"A waiter?"

"Yeah. He's waiting for some pie-in-the-sky settlement from my grandfather's estate. He's a loser. He's been nothing but a sponge his entire life." Billy shook away his anguish, wondering if his father would ever stop plaguing him.

"He didn't put you through school?"

"Hell, no. I've been supporting myself since high school. I went to Brown on a wrestling scholarship. Listen, Mr. Austen—you know, I feel weird calling you mister. I have a brother your age—another waiter."

"You can call me sir, if you like." Austen smiled.

"Screw it. Here's the deal. I figure you owe me a couple hundred thousand. Pay me ten thou a month for twenty months. I'll work for you full time, night and day, looking for more deals like the Klondike. Then pay me twenty percent of everything I bring in. I'll work my ass off. Scout's honor."

Austen laughed out loud, shaking his head. "For a kid with no job and mouths to feed, you've got balls. Don't BS me, were you really a scout?"

"Eagle."

"Really?" asked Austen, incredulous. With his fashionable suit and tasseled loafers, the cocky broker looked incapable of Scouting his way across Central Park. Then he decided the kid was too clever to lie about something so easily checked. He uncrossed his arms, gazed out the window, musing. "Don't meet many in our world. Scouts. I really loved it. All right, come back Monday morning. I'll think about it over the weekend. On your way out, ask Mrs. Watershed for an employee questionnaire."

Billy was outside DAP's offices at eight-twenty a.m. Ten minutes later, a smiling Mrs. Watershed escorted him back to see Mr. A.

"What time does he usually get in?"

Billy was puzzled by her laugh, but would soon learn that Austen lived in the offices and, morning five-mile run aside, seldom ventured out for anything other than building inspections and high-level meetings. Everyone—from bankers to tradesmen—came to Austen.

"Read it." He handed Billy a sheet of paper. The windows were open, ushering in cool air and traffic noise from five floors below.

"What about my profit share?" asked Billy.

"That salary is twice what any MBA your age makes."

Billy glanced down at the faded carpet, searching to hook a few thousand more. "If I take the cash, how about five percent?"

"How about zero? You'd be starting out on Hearthstone. I suppose you know all about that deal, too?" asked Austen.

"The big warehouse you bought over on the Hudson, right? You're converting it into apartments? That had to be the buy of the year."

"Three big warehouses. Loft co-ops. The project's due to start construction in a couple weeks. If you take the job, you'll be in a job trailer until the last unit's sold, and you're going to bust your ass studying construction nights and weekends so my contractors can't completely bullshit you." Austen had decided Billy might serve him well as his on-site whip; if the kid were this obnoxious with a potential employer, he'd have no qualms about screaming at every new construction change order.

"That's great. But what about finding new deals? Getting a piece of the action?"

"You work for me a year, Mr. Cutter. Learn teamwork, loyalty, and the chain of command. Then we'll talk. If you hump it—if you're half as good as you think you are—you won't be sorry you camped in my lobby." He stood and extended his hand. "Do we have a deal?"

"Yes, sir." Street smart, Billy grasped that Austen was through negotiating. "I'd like to start right now."

CHAPTER 29

A SHATTERED LENS

"You're killing me. You're absolutely killing me," Stan Diamond said, clutching his chest, feigning an operatic death. "No groundbreaking ceremony? No splashy ad campaign? So do you tell the contractor to forget the cement? The carpenters to skip the nails? No. But the fat schmuck with the bad heart? Screw him. Take his cement, take his nails, let him do a worthless press release when the project's finished. When it won't do any goddamn good. No, we've got to do what's right for the project. Right?" With a mischievous grin, the rotund public relations man glanced from Billy to Austen, nodding, anxious for agreement.

"Forget it. Groundbreaking ceremonies are a waste of time," Billy said, chilled and miserable with flu. He was desperate for Austen to bend his commandment against publicity to aid their snake-bitten project.

"The front page of the *Times*." With his penchant for name-dropping luminaries—some of whom he had actually met—Diamond gave the impression of consummate insider. "People, I mean serious people, owe Stan Diamond, and I'm talking the front page of the real estate section. You can't buy publicity like that."

"So you'd work for free?" Billy snapped.

"I love this kid, Mr. Austen. If he had a neck, he'd be dangerous. Pow." Diamond swung his leg from the knee in a dainty, doll-like kick, laughing, sweeping Billy into a wet-nosed grin.

"Sir, isn't it worth it if we're on the front page?" asked Billy, hopeful.

Austen looked up from his desk to face Billy and Diamond. While he had agreed to the meeting to mollify Billy, he'd privately acknowledged the need to advertise, knowing his lofts would struggle in the down market. The public relations man was right, he had to hedge his bet this time. If the three hundred units sold out quickly, the project might still turn a profit. If they languished, more than his investment was at risk.

"We get a sexy floor plan, the architect's spiel about the project's priceless quality. A rooftop view shot, broads in bikinis at the pool, sell the sizzle." Diamond knew even a small picture in the *Times* was impossible, but he was selling hard to overcome Austen's resistance. He added, "Maybe a picture of you, smiling in front of the building."

"No. No pictures and no mention of my name. Do you read me? If we do any publicity, it's only about the project."

"So we'll run my picture instead," Diamond said, smoothing the thinning curly brown hair he parted just above his left ear. Laughing, he took a sip of his diet soda, his pinkie finger pointed. "What if we turn all this sitting around on our tushes into an asset? We pitch Hearthstone like a fine wine that was years in the making. What an idea. I like it. No, I love it."

Billy flinched at the allusion to the project's many delays—a sore that wouldn't heal. From the day he'd started at DAP two years earlier, he'd done everything short of ritual suicide to push the project forward, but he'd been buried beneath one city-planning setback after another, each display of bureaucratic indifference enraging him.

"Put it in writing, Mr. Diamond," said Austen. "But I don't like the idea of comparing my project to wine—"

"You're right. Absolutely right. Terrible idea. I would have seen it myself in another—"

"I don't like ass-kissing, either."

"Oy. There goes my ace in the hole." Diamond laughed, a jiggling belly laugh so genuine that Billy and Austen had to laugh along with him.

Unseen by Billy and Diamond, MJ Watershed had slipped inside the office and tapped on her wristwatch. Austen stood and extended his hand across his horseshoe desk. "What I want is a detailed, written proposal with an explicit scope of work. I hope you can do what you say, Mr. Diamond."

Struggling up against his chair, Diamond rose, catching Austen's hand. "Remember, it's diamond, not zircon. Give me the work, and Hearthstone will be on the lips of every buyer from here to Atlantic City. But about you?" In a cartoon gesture, he zipped his lips shut.

AN ELDERLY VOLUNTEER FOR THE blood drive sat behind a table outside Ascott Swanne's largest conference room, closed her eyes, wishing her break would arrive. How lovely it would be if only she could perform her charitable work among pleasant, civilized people.

"Lady, hello? Talk to me, lady, how much longer? Fifteen minutes? Half an hour? I give up my lunch to donate blood and I got to wait an hour? Do you know what my hourly rate is?"

"Mr. Garay," the volunteer said, reading his name from the sign-in sheet, "If you would care to come back later, perhaps about four, they could probably slip you right in."

"And lose another hour? Are you crazy? You need more nurses. Can't you people organize anything right?"

"Go ahead of me," Austen said. Once outside the isolation of his office, he was often in no hurry to return. Roaming the streets, he could imagine away the years, pretend he was still an innocent from Lemon Grove and drop Richard Austen's heavy mantle, if only for a while.

"I can wait, too. You can go next," said a young woman with a cascade of rich chestnut hair. She was highlighting sentences in a brief with a yellow marker. Austen glanced from his contract to study her, wondering whether she was a lawyer or paralegal. She wore glasses and was dressed in a navy suit and beige silk blouse. He shook his head and returned to his purchase contract, puzzling over his lawyer O'Keefe's

ornate jargon. A paragraph later, he stole another glance at her, and
then another and another, admiring her legs.

"Hey, Margaret, right on, it didn't hurt that much," said a pony-
tailed mail room clerk to the young woman, rolling down his sleeve as
he walked through the reception area. "And, oh," he added, lowering
his voice, "thanks again for saving my dumb brother. He'd still be in
jail if it wasn't for you."

"I'm just delighted it worked out so well for him, Dana," she said.

Watching their interchange, wondering what she'd done to help, guessing it had to be pro bono, Austen took in her large hazel eyes and gentle
smile, white teeth framed by full lips, and faintly olive skin. Mesmerized,
he froze when she turned an inquisitive gaze in his direction. They stared
at one another until he blushed, and, with a slight nod, she smiled and
returned to her brief. Had she been the owner of a building he coveted,
he would have known what to do: He would have dashed to her side,
summoning that seldom used boyish charm. Instead, he sat, pretending
to read, wondering about a lawyer who donated time and blood, certain
a woman so beautiful had to be married. But her fingers were ringless.
He drew up a heroic plan: He would smile when her name was called
and say hello. But when the moment came, his courage failed him. His
eyes remained downcast as she disappeared into the conference room.

"Hold your arm straight up, lovey. Press against the gauze like this,"
the aide instructed Austen. "That's it. Not so bad, was it?"

He lay on a padded table with his arms aloft, his left index finger
firm against the hollow of his right forearm. With its nurses and donors
buzzing about, the conference room reminded him of a field hospital.
The young woman he'd admired was holding up a wobbly arm, pressing the bandage with her forefinger, her other fingers clutching her
glasses. Her pallor reminded him of a terrible day when a grunt stepped
on a booby trap, his face draining of color. Her full lips were pursed,
troubled. He felt a sadness, perhaps a vulnerability.

The moment passed when she opened her eyes, slipped on her glasses, buttoned her silk sleeve and, not waiting for the aide, swung her long legs down from the table and stood. She stepped toward the finished donors who were sipping orange juice. Without a word, she fluttered a hand to her face in surprise and, tottering a moment, keeled backward. Austen caught her, her flailing arm knocking him across the cheek, flinging his glasses against a waste can, shattering a lens.

He held her in his arms, standing still, inhaling her scent, trembling at the sensation of her breasts against his chest. He knew he should set her down, yet stood motionless, looking at her lower lip, feeling her warmth in his hands.

A second ticked by, then another.

"Let's get her back on the table," the head nurse ordered.

Austen stepped back, watching her ministrations, ignoring a request that he sit down with a cup of juice.

"What's her name?" asked the nurse, holding a vial under the young woman's nose, patting her forehead with a damp cloth.

"Margaret Downs," drawled a self-assured, fortyish lawyer who'd hurried into the conference room. "What happened? Did she pass out? Is she all right?"

"She's fine. Excuse me, I need some room here. You mind stepping back?" the nurse said.

"Are you sure she's all right? Should she visit with a doctor?" the lawyer asked, his honeyed Southern accent as incongruous as a bagel in Alabama. Accustomed to deference, he persisted. "Can y'all really take care of her, do everything for her?"

She glared from his face to his wedding ring. "So, you're her husband? Or maybe her uncle?"

"Why, no, we work together." A brilliant litigator, a man jurors swooned over, Wilson Hubbard had a simple way with people: He actually listened, he paid close attention in conversations, making it seem that he cared deeply about others' opinions. He'd been after the firm's newest associate from the day she started.

"She doesn't need a doctor, she needs rest, liquids, and food. Maybe she didn't get enough sleep last night," the nurse said, fixing him with a stare. "Excuse me."

An aide—a volunteer charged with giving snacks to the donors, turned to Austen. "Lucky you was there to catch her, dearie, might have fractured her skull. Shame about your glasses—do something nice, and it costs you good money. Is it orange or apple juice for you?"

"What?" said Austen, staring at the couple across the room, the tall young woman evoking shallow-buried images of his lost Jonnie. "Oh, orange, please. Thank you, ma'am."

"Better eat a few of these cookies. Take some more, go on."

The lawyer was murmuring to Margaret, stroking her wrist, gentle as a country doctor. Austen saw the gleam in her luminous, sad eyes and her wan smile for the lawyer, and he cursed beneath his breath. If only he could talk like that. A few minutes later, when he heard her melodic laugh at some cleverness from the Southerner, he rose and marched out, chin held high, eyes forward. Margaret studied him.

In the men's room, Austen tapped the shards from his broken lens and shoved his glasses in his pocket. He splashed his face, wondering if he could ever charm a woman like that, whether he should follow Mrs. Shoer's advice about gaining weight. He stared into the mirror, as always failing to see what others saw in him—the striking, assured business prince—instead seeing a criminal who had gone unpunished, a drug trafficker who'd skated free. He contemplated the young lawyer. Could he ever appeal to such a woman? Afraid he might see her again, then that he wouldn't, he decided to skip his meeting with O'Keefe and walk instead. He took the cloth cap from his raincoat, left the building, welcoming the cleansing storm.

CHAPTER 30

CONFETTI

As HE CHUGGED HIS THIRD mug of coffee, Billy rolled his head side to side, pondering his dilemma in the quiet of his office. He had slept little since the baby's arrival, a few months after his abrupt marriage. He'd demanded his share of the Hearthstone profits in cash. An amused Austen suggested Billy think it over a bit longer, another day or two; he might wish to reinvest his share in their next big deal. A day later, Billy still wanted the money, enough to purchase an elegant home in Greenwich. Debating a new home versus a bigger interest in DAP's next deal, he jotted notes on a pad: He was smarter than Austen, they knew nothing about shopping malls, and even if they could buy County Commons, they would have to overpay. At the bottom of the page, he wrote *Greenwich-Stephanie?* Would a flight to the suburbs curtail his young wife's partying, force her to take motherhood seriously?

"Let's call Westmont," Austen said over the intercom.

Despite his ambivalence over the new deal, Billy was raring for this call to his old college acquaintance. In his view, Rogers Hyatt represented the worst of Wall Street: a glib sycophant with superiors, an arrogant overlord to everyone else. Westmont's rising star, Hyatt had been tasked with selling the County Commons mall for its owner, Seaboard Realty Investors.

Austen drew a few circles in the air, Billy turned on the tape recorder and dialed the number.

"What can I do for you?" Hyatt said, his tone belying his offer. He was in the midst of preparing a strategic divestiture presentation for

Sumitomo Bank and had no time for bush leaguers, particularly those with a reputation for bare knuckle negotiating.

"Mr. Hyatt, this is Richard Austen. Did you confirm my finances with Swiss Bank?"

"Yeah, they said you were good for it."

"So does that mean we're an approved bidder?" Billy asked after Hyatt's annoying pause.

"Nope," Hyatt said.

"Would you mind if I talk to someone else about this, Mr. Hyatt?" Austen asked.

Crumpling a sheet of paper near his speaker phone, Hyatt laced his voice with pique. "No problem. You want our managing director's number? Better yet, call Seaboard's president, Boyd Fisher."

"That won't be necessary," Austen said, nodding, the conversation unfolding as he'd anticipated. Over time, he'd learned to read business the way he'd earlier learned the bush. Both were littered with land mines, but business was easier—the trail was always marked by money. He sometimes longed for Vietnam.

"No, I'll get it for you," Hyatt said. "He'll tell you—just like I've explained to fat boy three times—the price is one hundred thirty million, and we're not negotiating off that one dime."

"*Fat boy*," cried Billy. "Why—"

"I'd like to make this clear to you, Mr. Hyatt," Austen interjected. "I'm prepared to pay one hundred twenty million in cash today for County Commons."

"Gentlemen," Hyatt said, stripping the word of its deference. "The Commons is a blue-chip, short-list institutional deal. We're not talking to shoe clerks who'll start chiseling on the price the moment we're in escrow. Are we finished here?"

"Shoe clerks," spat Billy. "You sonofabitch, you'd better hope you told SRI about Mr. Austen because we're calling them next, Roger."

"It's *Rogers*. When you talk to Boyd, tell him how much I enjoyed his wedding. I was one of his ushers."

"You could have been his fucking maid of honor, you twat," Billy barked, flashing on the sweater-knotted-over-the-shoulders Roger Hyatt from Brown, wondering when the pompous dick had added the "s" to his first name.

"There's no need for that, Billy," Austen said. "I'm sure Mr. Hyatt will reconsider our fair offer."

"Fuck you, assholes," Hyatt said and hung up.

In the silence, Billy dropped his head, waiting for his employer to say something, anything. He clicked off the Sony tape recorder. "Boss, I mean sir, I'm sorry. Shouldn't have called him a twat."

"It's OK."

"No, really. I blew it."

"You did exactly what I wanted." Austen's grin broadened into a big smile, displaying a row of perfect white teeth, his boyish gap gone. He laughed. "You're a terrible actor, right?"

"I don't know, maybe," said Billy.

"If I'd told you, you never would have pulled it off… Shoe clerks." He laughed again.

"What's going on?" Billy asked, chuckling, suddenly dog-happy over Austen's good humor.

"Our money isn't at Swiss Bank. We've been buying Seaboard stock. With 4.9 percent of its stock, we're now Seaboard's second largest shareholder. You've heard of Colwell Hyman?"

"The takeover guys?" Billy's mouth hung open, his jaw slack. "You want to do a hostile takeover of SRI? Fuck me. We can't do that. It's way too big." He stopped, ground a fist into his open palm, then slashed the air with his forefinger. "Wait, wait, wait, I get it. You don't want the company; you want to scare them into selling us the Commons."

"No, into *giving* it to us. I walk into SRI's offices next week and toss the president a copy of our stock holdings, the Colwell commitment, and Hyatt's tape. I express my outrage over this treatment and announce my first official act as chairman will be firing him."

"Goddamn, that's perfect." Billy cracked his neck, pumped his fist.

"I'll tell him I've always wanted to run my own public company," said Austen, crackling with the thrill of the hunt.

"That's fucking brilliant. Then the president will get together with his twat maid of honor and buy us off with the Commons. That's perfect." Billy marveled at the strategy, then caught himself and sighed. Expressing gratitude scarcely made his list of social skills. He scratched his bristling head, looked down, took a deep breath. "Hey, sir, uh, thanks, you know, thanks for not cashing me out."

"Forget it," Austen said, delighted with his chess moves, pleased with his generosity toward Billy. "If you've got every nickel you own invested in the Commons, it will have your full attention."

Mrs. Watershed entered with a queer little smile. "A rather important call, Mr. A. Shall I put him on your speaker phone?" Without waiting for a reply, she pressed the button.

"Walk over to the window and look down," growled a familiar voice.

Billy lumbered to the window and laughed, followed by Austen and a chuckling Mrs. Watershed. Five floors below, Parson was standing through the open sunroof of a double-parked stretch Cadillac limousine. He wore a shearling coat and a white Stetson cowboy hat, a shoebox-sized portable phone to one ear and a fist extended upward, middle finger standing alone.

"Happy birthday to you, happy birthday to you," Parson sang while snow feathered around him. "Come on, MJ. You too, kid. Sing along. OK, Scout, now get your bony white ass down here double-time. We're going to Atlantic City, and we're going to be drunk before we hit Newark."

"The Colwell meeting this afternoon?" asked Austen.

"I took the liberty of resetting that for Monday morning," Mrs. Watershed replied.

"I made her do it, it's my fault," said Parson. "Now get down here, snow's filling up this damn hog."

"Guess I'm going to Atlantic City," said Austen.

Billy sighed, wishing he could call him Scout or even Richard, then grinned as he thought about Rogers Hyatt's pending job search. Then a question arose, one which he would never answer. What would Austen have done if Hyatt had treated them with respect, if he had registered them as buyers? Would his quirky employer have walked away from his takeover ploy?

TRUMP PLAZA WAS PACKED. THE elderly, the timid, and the under-aged played the slot machines in the garish, brass-bound casino, heavyset men who fancied themselves gamblers hunched over the craps tables, women played roulette, while others cupped their blackjack cards, sipping weak drinks, frowning or gloating at their cards. More frowning. As midnight approached, the nor'easter outside might have been a heat wave as far as the patrons cared.

"Parse, nobody doubles down on seven," Austen said, chuckling.

Parson sat beneath the shadow of his Stetson, discoursing on his Montana mosquito ranch. Despite the maddening crowd, he and Austen had the green felt table to themselves, more because of the dealer's icy cards than its twenty-five-dollar minimum. Austen was tipping extravagantly, Parson calling for drinks every twenty minutes.

"14, 16, 21. Sorry, guys. Next hand will be yours." The sincere young dealer's nametag said Jerry. His sincerity may have been buoyed by the pile of chips in his tips stack.

"If it wasn't for bad luck, I wouldn't have no luck at all," Shoer sang out in a sweet tenor that carried above the din. "Wouldn't have no luck, wouldn't have no luck at all." Dealers and players glanced over, a few smiling, some wondering if the black man might be somebody.

"Wow, pretty far out. You a professional singer?" asked a cocktail waitress.

"Told you, darling. 'Squito rancher. Now, this black boy ain't singin' again till he gets a winner. An Afro-American Jack."

"Have you been taking lessons?" Austen asked, laughing. Parson's amusement in the moment was exhilarating, but, like drinking, it came with a price. The next day Austen would feel even more isolated—lonelier—the close friends saw one another only a few times a year.

"Just fooling around at the restaurant. You know, the singer takes a break, owner wants to sing, who's telling me no?" Parson lit a Camel. He had begun smoking again.

Austen felt a gentle tap on his shoulder. Turning, he saw her, his eyes widening in near panic as his mouth fell open.

"I know you won't remember me, but several years ago, my office had a blood drive and I—"

"I, I do." He leaped off the stool. "I do."

Parson glanced backward and, catching sight of her, swiveled on his stool to check out the young woman standing behind them. She was too tall, her nose a trifle long and her glasses regrettable, yet her skin glowed and her smile enchanted. She was focused on Austen, her eyes warm.

"I fainted, and you caught me," Margaret Downs said in her boarding-school voice. "I might have been seriously hurt. I would have thanked you right away, but I thought someone else—I mean, I didn't learn until later that it was you who saved me and I didn't know your name."

"It's OK," stammered Austen.

"My friend told me I broke your glasses."

In shock, Austen murmured something unintelligible. For the last two and a half years, he'd been drumming up reasons to meet with O'Keefe at his offices in the hope of merely glimpsing her.

"Are you sure you remember me?" asked Margaret. "My hair was longer and I don't think I was wearing my glasses."

"Those glasses. You were wearing those," Austen managed. She was more beautiful than he remembered. Unconsciously, he stood at parade rest, wincing at Parson's stupid cowboy hat.

Margaret felt a twinge. Austen was wearing sneakers, faded blue jeans, a pullover jersey, and a down vest: a high school biology teacher on a field trip. He must be poor. "Yes. Glasses, I know how expensive they are. Please let me reimburse you for the pair I broke."

"You don't need to pay me, it's—"

Parson whooped before she could reach into her purse. "As much as Scout wants presidents, he's definitely not taking your money. What he needs is a change of luck. Sit with us, Lady Luck." Parson removed his Stetson and, with a sweep of his arm, invited her to join them. "Come on, sit down. We won't bite you… Yet."

"Parse…" Austen flushed, embarrassed by Parson's vulgarity, envious over his easy charm.

"My new friends call me Bad-Ass Brown," Parson said. "He's Scout. Or you can call us the Lone Ranger and Tonto, long as it's understood who gets the white horse."

"I'm Margaret. Margaret Downs." She shook hands and sat between them. "*Scout*? Does your mother call you Scout?"

"She's… no, my name's Richard Austen." His heart pounding, Austen tucked his trembling hands under his legs. Here she was, the woman he'd dreamed about for years. Where were his words? What could he tell her? He couldn't answer her first question without lying. He bit his lip.

Parson charged into the gap. Knowing he had to set the hook for his reticent friend, he embroidered on their gallantry together in the Corps.

"You two weren't *really* in Vietnam," she exclaimed, certain the handsome black man was joshing her. Nobody one actually knew went to Vietnam. If they couldn't get around it with student deferments or exaggerated medical conditions, her friends and acquaintances had joined the National Guard.

"Jerry, Lincoln freed my people, not yours. Deal the cards," Parson said. He took a few hundreds from Austen's pile, placing them as a bet for Margaret.

"Blackjack," Margaret cried, clapping her hands. Jerry busted and paid the table. Her money doubled again when he turned up an eighteen against her twenty and redoubled on the next hand.

"You've changed our luck," Austen said, happiness radiating from him.

"Oh dear. Sixteen," Margaret said, turning over her new cards. "Should I hit it against an ace?"

"No, split the eights. Wait," Austen ordered the dealer. With the flick of a finger, he caught the pit boss's attention. "Five thousand."

"Yes, sir, Mr. Austen, right away. Give the gentleman five thousand. Would hundreds be acceptable, Mr. Austen?"

Surprised by his blunt command and the pit boss's obsequity, Margaret studied Austen. From his rumpled attire and mustache, she'd concluded Austen was quietly bookish, guessing he was some sort of middling bureaucrat. If anything, he'd been timid with her. Now this lordly assurance? Her hazel eyes widened as Jerry stacked hundreds in front of Austen on the green felt table. She pursed her lips, certain a small fortune was about to be thrown away.

"I'm not playing another hand," Margaret declared. "That is too much money. Please take it."

"It's yours," Austen said. "If you don't take it, we'll just lose it later."

She hesitated, then shook her head. "I know. Give it to charity. Give it to your favorite charity."

"What's yours?"

"Mine? That group that feeds the homeless, One Square."

"I'll donate it to One Square," said Austen.

"But might it not be put to better use?" Margaret knew too well how deep broken promises cut, she couldn't accept his. Nothing about him—other than his reckless gambling and that jangling moment of authority with the pit boss—suggested he should be tossing money around. She asked, "Pardon me for being terribly rude, but may I ask what you do? You've gathered I'm a lawyer with Ascott Swanne. Do you live in town?"

"Yes."

"We're in the restaurant business in San Francisco." Parson handed her his card from an elegant alligator billfold.

"The *Parsonage*," she read. "Fine dining, live nightly jazz. Is it by Fisherman's Wharf?"

"Not far, it's in the financial district, off Montgomery Street. My place is wall-to-wall every night. Good burgers, great chops, and the best jazz."

"But you live here, Scout. Yet you're involved with the Parsonage, too?"

Austen recalled the happy day he'd handed Parson the start-up capital. "Not really. I do a little real estate in New York."

"Best damn busboy we ever had," Parson said.

"Oh." Now she understood. War buddies reunited for the weekend, their shared time in the trenches spanning—for the weekend at least—the economic chasm between them. She supposed Austen scraped by selling row houses in Queens.

"Oh, *there* you are, Margaret. We've simply been looking everywhere for you." Anne Papadakos called, her quiet fiancée and Margaret's blind date following in her wake. "Scott has been absolutely pining away."

Margaret rose and introduced them. Despite their binge drinking, her tony friends showed little appreciation for a flashy black cowboy named Bad-Ass or a man who appeared as though he checked tickets on a ski lift.

"Margaret, the last revue starts in just ten minutes."

"Join us? Please." Margaret asked Austen and Parson.

A delighted Austen would have accepted on the spot, but Parson, correctly reading Margaret's entourage, nudged his friend's knee beneath the table and said, "Can't leave Jerry, he's one of the family."

"It would be such fun to have you join us," Anne Papadakos said, with less jaw movement than a ventriloquist, "but the tables are the size of Easter bonnets. I simply don't know how they'll squeeze even the four of us in. But let's get together in town sometime. Let's."

Flushed with anger, Margaret thought hard before deciding against a scene. "Would you please let me pay for your glasses, Scout? Here's my card. Or let me take you to lunch to thank you properly?"

"JERRY, AIN'T *NOTHING* SAYS LUCK goes home with the pretty women." Parson gave it a try, but the cards had frozen up, it was late, the party balloon deflated. "Let's get out of this dump. Mom's leaving the door open for us…What's wrong, Aus?"

"Nothing."

"Nothing, my ass. You've got her card. Call her Monday, tell her who you are. Nothing impresses the upper east side more than long green."

"You see her boyfriend?"

"For such a smart bastard, you're a dope about women. If she was in love with that guy, why'd she stay with us until they dragged her away? At least tell her who you really are. That way she'll stop feeling sorry for you."

"Maybe I will call her," Austen said. But what could he say? How could he explain his life?

Moments later, they were turning from the cashier's cage, jamming their little remaining cash in their pockets, heading for the kitschy entrance. Parson spied a trio of tarty-looking women wobbling toward them on spike heels. They were drunk. Instinctively, he flashed his toothy smile and said, "Good evening, ladies."

The attractive woman in the middle—an overripe strawberry blonde—smiled at him, then glanced at Austen, stopped, then gawked at him open-mouthed. Setting her hands on her hips, she leaned forward, staring hard as if peering through a haze. "Oh my god. Eddie?" Marilyn Beck squealed. "Eddie Kawadsky? Is that you?"

Austen froze, his eyes flashing dread, his heart pounding. The chance discovery that had obsessed him had at last arrived. Had Parson not been preoccupied calculating the trio's possibilities, he would have seen Austen's horror in a glance. As it was, Austen shut his eyes, breathed deep, and reset his Easter Island stone face. Although he'd rehearsed it a thousand times, he stumbled over his one line. "You have me confused with someone else."

"Hell," Parson cackled, "his friends call him Austen, but if you ladies are looking to party, you can call him anything you like. Eddie, Edie, hell, Edgar Allan Poe."

"Sorry, handsome," Marilyn said, flirting, rolling her shoulders back to accentuate her bust. "Thought I saw a ghost. You reminded me of someone I kind of knew back in San Diego."

Austen nodded curtly, grabbed Parson by the arm and propelled him toward the exit. Had it been a couple hours earlier, Parson would have insisted they have a go at the women. But the long day's drinking had him on his back foot and he contented himself with marveling over the dramatic turn in Austen's luck.

On the drive to Middletown, Parson slept, head thrown back in a snore, cowboy hat in his lap. Austen sat upright, drinking to no effect, adrenaline counteracting his guzzling of the Cadillac's miniature Smirnoff bottles. He kept telling himself not to worry, but fretted into the night. Was her name Marsha? Or maybe Madeline? He half-remembered a junior high girl that resembled her chasing after Roy. Was she in Roy's class at Mt. Miguel? Austen told himself she believed his denial, that she too lived a continent from San Diego, and that it would never occur to her to call the police. Even if she did, would the police follow up a muzzy tip on a twenty-year-old cold case? How could they? The drunken tart had no idea who he was or where he might be found.

Fortunately for Austen's equanimity—if not his vigilance—it would never have occured to him that the tart would soon regale her lover with stories of her wild time on the east coast, of how she'd been so potted she thought she'd seen a ghost from their Lemon Grove childhood. Or that her lover would remember Eddie's long ago beach advice about disappearing into New York City. Did she get the stranger's name? Austen something.

As it always does, the vodka won at last and he slumped against the limousine's cracked upholstery. He thumbed Margaret's business card, studying it, smelling it. He tried to recall their every moment together, sifting through her words. Perhaps her handsome date had been nothing more than a casual escort, but it didn't matter. The Lemon Grove woman had rung the fire alarm—he could be burned at any time. He could never tell Margaret Downs—or anyone else—who he really was.

He ripped the card into tiny bits, cracked the window and let the confetti fly. Parson stirred at the icy wind's bite, Austen yearning for his friend to awaken. He was desperate to know if anyone could forgive him.

CHAPTER 31

A WORLD OF SIGHS

MARGARET FROWNED AT THE FADING roses, thinking them short-lived, sipped the last of her tea. Although the bouquet had arrived without a card, neither she nor her motherly secretary had any doubt Wilson Hubbard had sent them. She was picking at a chicken sandwich while scanning the *Times'* city section, rolling past the dreary headlines until she saw one with appeal. She had been a reporter for several years before tiring of journalism, and still enjoyed guessing with a finger jab where the inevitable opposing view began. She was scanning a piece about her favorite charity's new campaign—thanks to a major anonymous donation—when her secretary buzzed her.

"It's a Mr. Shoer. He says he met you a month ago in Atlantic City."

"Margaret Downs," she answered. A junior associate in her firm's environmental compliance group, her career was far from what she'd imagined. Courtroom intrigue, tense negotiations with rivals, and glamorous clients hanging on her every word were all a fiction. Her reality was a daily grind of Sisyphean research, of scouring byzantine regulations in the hope of finding elusive answers for her demanding bosses. Two layers removed from the firm's clients, she was grateful for every phone call save those from Hubbard and her father.

"Hi, this is Parson Shoer. Remember, Bad-Ass?"

"Oh, yes, yes, of course. How are you? Are you here in town?"

"No. I'm in Fog City." He sat in his tiny alcove at the Parsonage. His desk was a wobbly dining table adorned with invoices, menu ideas, the names of fill-in musicians and singers, cryptic phone numbers, an adding machine, photographs of his mother, wife, and children, and a combat photograph with Austen. "You have a few minutes? I'd like to tell you a story. May I call you Margaret?"

"Please do. And you prefer Parson?

"Yes, I should apologize about that night."

"No need." She chuckled at the one bright memory from a disappointing weekend.

"It's my friend, Austen."

"Yes, Scout," she said.

"He hasn't called you, has he?"

"No."

"I thought so. I've been meaning to call you for a few weeks, but I couldn't figure out where to begin. Still can't. OK, here goes. Margaret, once upon a time I was a summer associate at Ascott Swanne and—"

"What?" She burst out laughing. "Was this before or after the mosquito ranch?"

"Guess I did have a bucketful that night." He giggled, but sounded embarrassed. "I'm serious. Brendan O'Keefe will confirm this, I clerked at Ascott a million years ago."

"You're a lawyer?"

"Everybody in San Francisco's a lawyer. But this isn't about me, it's about Austen. He's a client of your firm. Brendan O'Keefe's client. I introduced them. His full name is Richard Austen…" Silence on her end. "Hello? Hello?"

"Wilson Hubbard put you up to this, didn't he?" she demanded, exasperated at the thought, wondering how her former lover could possibly hope to win her back with this ridiculous story.

"Who?"

"Stop right there. Tell him the flowers won't work. These pointless jokes won't work. This is so not funny. It's over."

"I'm sorry. This is my fault for teasing you so much. Wait, I've got an idea. Put me on hold and call Brendan. Ask him to describe Austen, ask if he remembers Parson."

"Just to end this nonsense here and now, I will." Hubbard had tried everything—short of leaving his wife—to rekindle her love. She failed to see the humor in this latest gambit: a black cowboy parading as an Ascott associate. She put Shoer on hold and dialed O'Keefe's office.

Shoer lit a cigarette, drumming his fingers on his blotter-sized calendar, a handful of empty bookings staring at him. He made a mental note to call every acquaintance among the legal community to seek out their Christmas parties.

After her call, Margaret blanched and stood, plucking a drooping rose. She shut her door. Brendan had been out, but his secretary fondly remembered the handsome young clerk with the quick laugh and her offhand description of Richard Austen fit the poor realtor like a wanted poster. Sighing, she took Shoer off hold.

"This is so embarrassing. Please forgive me for doubting you," Margaret said.

"We should have told you who we were. But that's why I'm calling. Aus came to your blood drive because Brendan invited him."

"Oh. Oh, God," she said, remembering her condescending concern. She lay her forehead against the cool wood of her desk. Brendan's out-of-school tales about his beyond wealthy, secretive client had circulated throughout the firm. She giggled, pondering her snobby friend Anne's coming anguish. She who equated net worth with character had snubbed one of the richest men in Manhattan. "But why was he giving blood?"

"Maybe because he can." Shoer began his tale nineteen years earlier at boot camp. He told her the story of Austen's life as he knew it, the battles, sieges, and fortunes that he passed through. He told her of the day Austen had saved him, of the wounds he had suffered, the medals,

ribbons, and respect he had earned. He told her what he guessed of
Austen's childhood, of the distressful strokes his youth suffered, of his
penniless abandonment. Of how he had created an empire of buildings
with no more than his war savings and his cunning. And yet there was
more: Austen's loneliness, his crippling shyness, his fear of women, his
nineteen loveless years.

"Strange," she sighed, pitying Austen, wishing she had not heard it.

"You know why I've told you his story?"

"No." Then she blushed, recalling Austen's naked stare. She knew.
"Maybe."

"The man is in love with you."

"We've hardly spoken. How can that be?" Agitated, she bit her
thumb.

"You fell into his arms, you refused his money, you're charming as
hell, and you're beautiful. I'm in love with you, too."

"I have no idea what to say."

In fairness, he touched on Austen's oddities and what the Shoer family saw as his gradual withdrawal. Parson sided with his mother, claiming that loneliness, not success, was Austen's demon. He mentioned
Austen's solitary habits, his running, his weekends sailing the *Alba*, his
indifference to food. If she liked, he could let her know when next
Austen visited O'Keefe. She could happen to wander past his office.

Margaret sighed, ambivalent, knowing she had no one else in her life
nor any prospects beyond pleasant company. Then her father's image
came to mind. "It's probably not a good idea."

"Don't say yes or no. Just say, Bad-Ass, I'll take your next call."

She promised she would speak with Parson whenever he called. She
hung up and straightened the piles on her desk, thinking about Austen,
then her father, cataloguing the differences between them, deciding therein might lie Austen's appeal. How unlike her father he was.
Harold Gamble Downs was a man of countless words—none counting

for anything—and Austen possessed of few. She pulled a compact from her desk drawer and examined her prominent nose, her eyes, frowning at her contact lenses' nearly invisible circles. Did they really think she was beautiful? She knew better. Men would say anything. Hubbard had said he loved her mane of chestnut hair. How had she ever believed he would leave his wife?

She did not need an odd-duck millionaire, nor even a man over six feet tall. At thirty-three, she was through with aging boys, other women's men and those for whom the term "committed" conjured mental hospitals. She'd decided that, once Hubbard's ashes had grown cold, she would seek a man unburdened by furious ambition, a simple professional like herself. Someone who read but deemed authors of no particular interest, someone who exercised without fanaticism, someone who called his mother on Sundays yet had not lived at home since high school. Someone who could count his weekly drinks on one hand and who was neither threatened by nor obsessed with children.

Sighing, she rose to freshen her tea. She would thank Parson Shoer when he called, but decline. Or perhaps—just to be polite—she would thank Austen personally when he next visited the firm.

CHAPTER 32

WORDS

"Sin, should I wear that one—he's seen it before—or this? Sin, Sinner, Cyn-thi-a. You're not paying attention, you wicked cat." Margaret draped the party dress across a chair, wondering when in a new relationship an outfit could be worn a second time. The short-haired black cat purred.

She scrinched at the oval mirror inset in her bedroom door and returned to her closet, searching for a dress that bespoke simplicity and elegance. And passion. "This one?" she asked the cat, picking a dress few men might distinguish from the first. She inherited season-old ensembles from her chic spendthrift mother, but she was as likely to wear those—redolent as they were of moneyed leisure—as a sarong. After a brief purgatory in her closet, she delivered her mother's hand-me-downs to the posh thrift shop run by her middle school.

"Should I invite him up tonight? About time he invited himself. Maybe this one." She fingered a slinky, sequined dress, slit up mid-thigh. It showcased her legs.

"Meeeow" said the cat.

"He's not that bad. He's a better listener than you are."

The cat yawned, stretched, jumped down from the antique dresser, and padded away.

Margaret puzzled again over whether the polite, restrained Austen cared for her as much as Parson had sworn. "So what if he doesn't like me?" she asked aloud, "Mystery Man's no catch of the day. When he finally does talk, it's always about real estate." She picked a dress as flattering as the others, stepped into three-inch heels—a luxury his height permitted—daubed on a wicked ruby lipstick, more eye shadow than usual, and donned her antique pearl necklace. More talisman than heirloom, the pearls had been a special gift on her quinceanera. Her fifteenth birthday. The lovely woman in the mirror smiled back, pleased with how her page-boy haircut was at last growing out.

Her doorbell rang as it always did with Austen, upon the appointed minute. Just as he had with so many buildings, he had vastly upgraded his appearance. His tailored suit was Armani, his silk tie Hermes, and his thick hair coiffed by Vidal Sassoon. At long last, he dressed the part.

"I'm so glad you shaved your mustache, Aus," she said, clasping his hand, drawing in his cheek for a kiss. She smoothed his lapels. "You should consider wearing double-breasted suits more often. They hang so well on tall men. Oh, listen to me: I sound just like my mother, giving fashion advice. Dress how you please."

"You, you look great," he said, fumbling as he so often did when first in her presence. "I'll get another, two. Gray?"

"Oh, puhleeze." She laughed. "I have to be careful what I say around you. You're lucky I have good taste—darn, there I go again—now I sound like my father. Get me to the restaurant before I ruin the evening."

"That's not possible." He escorted her to the black Lincoln Town Car he'd leased after her off-hand remark about the scarcity of cabs. Stepping inside, she beamed when she caught him looking at her legs. She reminded herself of a high-rise tower sale she'd read about in the *Times*, and asked him to explain the deal.

Had it occurred to Austen that Margaret had no interest in business, that her questions about real estate were meant as a kindness, to get him talking about *something*, he would not have gone into such numbing detail about why the buyer had overpaid for the trophy asset. But for that to have occurred to him, he had to first believe that she was truly interested.

"That's it, on the next block, on the right." She interrupted his lecture with a measure of relief. The fashionable Italian restaurant was owned by a promoter who gulled B-list celebrities into becoming his partners through airy promises of free food, the best tables and big profits. For the moment the crowds were following. A small knot of perhaps six couples stood outside in the cool evening, awaiting a table.

"I'll park down there, Mr. Austen." The limo driver pointed to an alley a couple blocks away as he slowed to a stop.

Austen adjusted his new glasses, jumped out to open Margaret's door, his amused driver having abdicated the task six weeks back. She took his arm, and they strolled past the waiting diners to the restaurant's glass double doors.

"Why don't I wait out here?" Margaret said. "Unless you own this place too, I think our reservation means a forty-five-minute wait."

"I'll see what I can do." Austen grinned, palming a hundred-dollar bill on his way inside.

She ambled, admiring the Belle Époque lamps that cast a soft glow over the restaurant's windows and examined the daffodils blooming in the polished copper planters. Meandering, she came to the planter at the far end of the building, picked a bottle top from it to properly throw it away, glanced back and then stole a look at her compact. She noticed two couples laughing near the entrance and smiled when one man's laughter caused him to double over, bending to his waist, hands on his knees.

"One fucking sound out of you, lady, and you're on page one. This ain't no fucking toy. Turn around and give me the purse."

"Oh, oh… OK, OK," Margaret pleaded, instantly terrified, feeling steel jammed in her back. The mugger's outsized reflection in the window showed he had little need of a gun. Even in her heels, the massive thug towered over her. She unzipped her shoulder bag, reached in and trembling, handed over the wallet.

"The whole goddamn bag, bitch."

"I'm sorry. Here." She shivered as though freezing.

"That." He pointed at her necklace.

"This? Oh, please no," she pleaded. "It was my grandmo—"

He smacked her hard across the face with the back of his hand. Stunned, she screamed in pain, staggered, collapsed onto the pavement. The waiting patrons turned as one to see her fall. The mugger grunted. Sobbing, she raised her hands to unclasp the pearls before he hit her again. Shifting the .38 Special to his left hand, he bent to tear the necklace from her throat.

His fingers were fumbling for a grasp when Austen's flying fist smashed into his temple, pitching him onto the sidewalk a few feet beyond Margaret. The mugger heaved his broad chest from the pavement, intent on killing his assailant. Before he could raise his gun, Austen lashed his heel into the mugger's nose, flattening it against his face. The mugger groaned, struggled to his knees, and pawed at the blood gushing from his crushed nose, waving his gun. Austen kicked his larynx, and the thug choked, firing into the sidewalk. The bullet ricocheted past Margaret, flattening against the restaurant's brick wall.

Still kneeling, the gasping mugger shook his head, rubbed his throat with one hand and raised the .38 with the other. Austen dove onto him, wrenching his arm, twisting the gun away. Someone in the crowd cheered. He grabbed a fistful of the mugger's oily hair, yanked his head back, smashed his face against the sidewalk. The thud ran through Margaret like a tremor.

The mugger lay still, his blood fouling the dirty sidewalk. Austen rushed to Margaret.

"Are you alright?" he asked, breathless.

"I'm, I'm… Oh, Richard, hold me, please. That was so terrible—he was going to kill me, kill you. Is he dead?"

"No, he'll be all right. No one will ever hurt you again. Ever."

The crowd stood open-mouthed, buzzing.

"We're not pressing charges," Austen said to the pasty maitre'd who had dashed outside. "She's been through too much and we're not wasting time with police reports when that animal would beat us out of the courthouse. Call him an ambulance. If the police ever do show up, here's my lawyer's card." He placed two fingers at the corners of his mouth and whistled, a blast that could be heard blocks away. His Lincoln whipped a U-turn.

"Aus, I don't need to see a doctor, I'll be fine," said Margaret. "I just want to go home. Hold me please."

The car raced uptown.

"Will you come upstairs? I really can't be alone now." They stepped from the car, her bloody face tear streaked. The concerned Irish doorman swept open the lobby door and hurried to the elevator.

"I don't know what to do first, fix us a drink, take a shower, or simply cry. Oh, look at your hand," she said, catching sight of him cradling his right hand with his left. "I'll get you some ice. Is it broken? Maybe you should have gone to the hospital."

"I don't think so." He guessed something was broken, but thought a doctor could do little other than bandage it and suggest aspirin.

Despite her pain, Margaret felt a sense of relief that she'd straightened the stylish one-bedroom apartment that afternoon, the snug living room with its oversized French armoire, books, and framed photographs. She slipped into the galley kitchen and reappeared a moment later with an ice tray and a dish towel. Emptying the tray into the towel, she wrapped it around his swollen hand. "Is single-malt all right?" she asked, reaching for a bottle of Lagavulin. "I must look an absolute wreck."

"No, never. Let me see your hands."

"They do hurt a bit." She placed her palms in his, experiencing that reassuring tingle she sometimes had when examined by a doctor.

Examining them closely, he said, "Wash them with soap and water and put Mercurochrome on the cuts. Better to let them air out overnight and bandage them in the morning."

"I'll go take a hot shower—look at me, I'm still trembling like a leaf." She emptied her scotch.

She left him in her small living room that overlooked a row of budding plane trees. His hand began to throb and, remembering the mugger, he dialed O'Keefe's home number. With the ice wrapped about one hand and his drink in the other, Austen inspected the room, seeking Margaret through her objects, framed photographs occupying almost every flat surface. Antique, silver-framed photographs of wealthy Hispanic men and women that he supposed were her mother's family, pictures of her own family on vacations around the world, skiing in Austria, sport-fishing in the Caribbean, a photo safari in Kenya. Older pictures of a small, skinny Margaret on a Shetland pony, a preteen Margaret and an old woman standing in front of a large, pink building, one of her six-year-old brother's toothless grin.

From the little she had told him of her family, he had thought her more middle class than the photographs suggested. He shuddered. Perhaps his money meant nothing to her. Although he had long feared its gravitational pull on others, it seemed a cruel joke that his money might be no advantage at all. He gulped his drink and poured himself another.

"I'm sorry I took so long, but I just had to keep scrubbing." Margaret had donned a heavy white cotton bathrobe, her wet hair combed back. She had Band-Aids on her hands, but the thin gash on her cheek was exposed, her face flushed from the shower. "I'm still shaking too much to put my makeup back on."

"You don't need any."

"Hope you like candlelight." She lit a pair of candles and flicked off the lamps. "I can't stop thinking about it. You could have been killed. As much as I detest nicknames, I should call you Galahad."

"No," he said. "Maybe, maybe Odysseus." Aboard the *Alba*, he sometimes daydreamed of getting lost—of disappearing over the horizon—leaving his past, his money, everything behind, purging himself sailing.

"So, you do read more than the business section." Recalling the hero's faithful wife Penelope and her trick for stalling suitors, she smiled. "Aus, do you really care about me?"

"More than that."

"*More than that?* You do have such a way with words." Giggling, she set her drink down and kissed him, slipping her tongue inside his mouth. He kissed her hard, struggling with his arousal within seconds, trying to elbow it in line with his zipper.

"Give me that," Margaret whispered. She set his scotch on the table, guided his hand inside her bathrobe. He cupped first one moist breast, then the other. She kissed him deeper and, clutching his hair, pulled his head back and stared into his eyes. Scouring his face with her gaze, all of the talk, the rich bantering, the overeducated prattle she had long endured rang so false. No other man would have died to save her.

"No, leave it there." She pulled her bathrobe open to the waist, unwrapped the icy towel from his broken hand and placed it on her other breast. "Kiss me."

He kissed her, his hands marveling over her breasts. Sitting across from Margaret during their two months of dating, one elegant restaurant after another, desperate to be interesting, Austen had so often focused on her full lips. Now he was kissing them. "I'm not much of a lover."

"Have you ever loved anyone?" She removed his glasses and started with his shirt buttons. She had one left before he replied.

"No. I mean…" He gazed at her without blinking. "I mean…"

"What do you mean?"

"I mean that day you fainted. I smelled you—you smelled so great—and I felt these against me. I couldn't let you go."

She lifted his head to her face. "Then why didn't you—Oh, Hubbard. Hubbard was there when I awoke."

"The older guy."

"He's married." She disguised her hesitation behind another kiss. "I had an affair with him."

They kissed without words for some time, pausing only to sip scotch and smile at one another.

"Is it over?" asked Austen.

"Yes, dead. It's been a year. Kiss me."

With his good hand, Austen traced from her hairline to the tip of her nose. He swallowed hard. "Do you still love him?"

"I stopped hating him months ago. So, no. Do you think I'm pretty?" Feeling his hand in her short hair, she remembered Hubbard's fulsome praise and how she'd cut her lustrous mane to spite him. "My hair will grow back, I promise."

He rained kisses on her face in reply.

She wondered whether the jagged scar on his shoulder was a war wound. "I don't think I can love you," she whispered, kissing him, his body stiffening at her words. She looked into his eyes, kissed them both and then clutched him as she had on the bloody pavement. With his maddening refusal to discuss his past, she had every right to withhold affection.

He had no response, burying his face in her breasts. He pleaded, "Please. Please be with me."

"You don't want freedom?" she asked.

"I want you. I wish I had the words to tell you how—"

"Forget words." She opened her bathrobe. Drawing his hand between her legs, she unzipped his trousers, closing her eyes, clasping his heat in her hands.

"Oh," he cried.

"If we go to the bedroom, you have to spend the night," she said, her voice husky.

"I won't leave."

Later, Austen lay awake while she dozed. It should have been the happiest moment of his life, gazing upon her beautiful back, watching it rise and fall with her breathing. Instead, he fretted over his great lie, knowing she would vanish the moment she heard the truth. He wondered if he could keep it from her, or whether she could forgive him if she learned his past. Easing his conscience, he promised his sleeping lover he'd tell her one day.

Much later, Margaret slept on, Austen swallowed four more aspirin, scribbled a loving note to her, and raced down Fifth Avenue to Harry Winston. He paced the block, waiting for the jewelry store to open and, once inside, asked to see their most expensive engagement ring. A principled young woman, the sales clerk said no, telling him any decent fiancée would be embarrassed by so large a ring. They gently sparred until Austen capitulated, finally agreeing that a flawless five-carat diamond would do.

CHAPTER 33

A KEEPER

Margaret Austen sallied across the gilded ballroom, glancing from the wall paintings of Louis XIV's court at play to the crystal chandeliers to the sequins and diamonds sparkling in the audience. She imagined the bejeweled dowagers exhuming their emeralds and rubies from their safety deposit boxes earlier that afternoon. In the moneyed glow, the women were beautiful and the men elegant, the Oncology Ball's timeless scene as reminiscent of the nineteenth century as the present. She heard a laugh rising above the music-crested chatter: Her father stood in the center of the room, his hands resting on the shoulders of two sitting men, his laughter directed at a table of smiling revelers. Harold Downs was at his best in a dinner jacket.

"Margaret, Margaret," Downs called, clutching her by the arm. One might have supposed Downs a patrician beyond financial care, the picture of unruffled self-assurance. A closer inspection might have raised doubts. "Have I told you how lovely you look tonight? In those heels, you do wonders for an old man's posture." He waited in vain for an off-setting compliment. "I remember when your mother wore those pearls, it's a shame you won't wear more—"

"No, she didn't, these were Abuela's," Margaret snipped, tensing at her father's touch. "We're in the way, I'm going back to the table."

"Dear, is there anything you can do with that husband of yours?" asked Downs. "Richard's sitting there like a cigar store Indian. Could he possibly be civil to Jeff? It's a wonder I invited him at all."

She, flushed with anger, walked away.

"Wait, please, I didn't mean that," he said. On stage before a shrewd audience, he buried his vexation, and smiled—the picture of benevolence—at his daughter's overwrought sensitivity. Few among the gentry either knew him or cared what sort of ass Downs made of himself, but many paused to remark the beautiful woman threading her way between the round tables, arranged like so many chrysanthemums on a flower girl's tray.

Margaret took in the festooned stage, the pier-like runway thrust into a sea of whitecapped tables. Two plank-thin women in black evening gowns were nattering beneath an elegant banner ten yards long, one jabbing at the runway like a feeding shorebird. A bored hotel technician, his headset in his hands, stood by, ignoring the raucous mariachi band.

Austen rose as she approached, stepped around Connie Downs and Jeff Sproul and pulled out her chair. Margaret shot him an apologetic glance. They could slip away during dessert. Smiling at Billy Cutter and his wife, she tapped her father's empty chair. "Someone please tell me what office he's running for."

"He's taking care of business, dear heart," said her mother. "He'll return shortly, I assure you." Connie Downs was a socialite in her late fifties who, rather than abandoning the vices of her youth, had added to them over the years. She dosed herself with vitamins that required a prescription and, as an excuse to drink, played contract bridge three afternoons a week. Born Constanza Vandershoot, Connie was the youngest child of a union between the scion of a New York Dutch family and the daughter of the Argentine Consul. She sat between her son-in-law and Jeff Sproul, bantering with the young man her husband so needed to impress.

"And how did you survive your first winter with us?" Connie purred.

"Not so bad," said Sproul, laughing. "But when can I take off the long underwear? I've been wearing two pairs since Halloween."

Curious, Margaret observed Sproul as he launched another anecdote. If she squinted, she could see the resemblance her father had insisted upon when he mentioned his new friendship with the dashing investment banker. Tall, fair-haired, and handsome, Sproul did look a bit like the photographs of her father in his thirties. Yet within minutes of meeting him, Margaret decided the two had little in common; Sproul laughed harder at his own jokes than anyone else. Unlike her father, he had no need for approval.

Margaret pursed her lips. Sproul was playing his story—one in which he brilliantly saved the financial day—to Austen. Her father had done it again: He'd touted his son-in-law's fabulous wealth and their gilt-edged relationship to his new acquaintance. Downs could hardly take a taxi two blocks without bragging about his connection to Austen's money. Sighing, she turned to Billy Cutter. "Is this going to be the Yankees' year?"

"Yeah, sure. Well, maybe." Billy brightened at the attention. "If someone runs over Steinbrenner with a truck. Twice. A team starts with the owner, and I don't care how much money that asshole has."

"A big truck." She laughed, a warm rich laugh, her pretty teeth flashing. "The man's a menace to baseball. Don't you think so, Aus?"

"Money's overrated. If all it took was money, the Yankees would never lose." Austen had edged his chair away from his mother-in-law's chain smoking. He appeared uncomfortable.

"Money's like sex," Sproul announced, pausing to let the others shift attention to him. "It's only important if you're not getting any. But once you reach a certain age, it's more like hair. You're happy if you're only losing a little."

"Did someone say money?" Downs asked, rejoining the table. He stopped behind Sproul, rubbed his shoulders affectionately. He smiled at his guests, then frowned at the two empty seats. "Remind me to disown Trey and Darcy. A thousand dollars a ticket, and the rascal cancels with a last-minute cold. Say, there's my dear friend Senator O'Riley."

Margaret winced and cast a beseeching look at Austen. He smiled back, amused. Reassured, she chuckled inwardly, imagining her father's mortification if she were to mention whose money it actually was her unreliable brother had wasted.

Downs stole a glance over his shoulder. He'd seen his winning lottery ticket minutes earlier and grabbed it. He had the slightest acquaintanceship with the notorious Ivan Bullion, a self-proclaimed billionaire who loved publicity more than money. Knowing Sproul would be wildly impressed, Downs had begged Bullion to stop by their table, promising to introduce him to his reclusive son-in-law. Bullion was slowly working the room, stopping at every other table to shake hands, pose for pictures and acknowledge well-wishers.

"Jeff, an old friend of mine wants to meet you," Downs said as Bullion approached at last. On the train east for his first year of college, Downs had dropped Albert in favor of Gamble, insisted he be called *Gam,* added the II, and written off his father, an embittered, impoverished, widower living alone on a farm that had defeated him. Downs was an excellent salesman, but his recurring mistake was in thinking he could run a company, in failing to recognize he had no patience for detail, his weakness for fawners, and a dread of making hard decisions. Remarkable about his career were not his failures, but his comebacks. Twice, he had erased his debts through personal bankruptcy and crawled back, so debasing himself others might have preferred pumping gas.

"Who is that?"

"Just an old friend. You've never heard of him." Downs winked at the rest of the table. "Here he is. I'd like you to meet Ivan Bullion."

Looking up, Sproul sprang from his chair.

Bullion, a tall pudgy man with a cantilevered blond comb-over, was still a table away, clasping each hand flung at him. Watching the businessmen flutter about him, Margaret wondered if her father had ever exchanged a hundred words with the darling of Wall Street.

Downs and Sproul stood with their hands extended. "Ivan, I'd like you to meet Jeff Sproul. He's just taken over as CEO for Wellbourne Masterson. He's practically family, too. His wife Hillary is our daughter-in-law's sister."

"Who? Yeah, sure, pleased to meet you," Bullion said absently, searching for bigger game about the vast room, waving toward the middle distance.

"You ought to talk to Jeff about your next financing," said Downs.

"Sure, whatever, call my people. Where's Austen?" asked Bullion. "I thought you said Richard Austen was at your table."

"Dick's right here," replied Downs.

Seemingly intent upon his soup, Austen bit into a roll.

"Dick, Ivan would like to meet you. Please," said Downs.

"You're Richard Austen? I don't believe it. Then I want to talk to your father, yeah, the real decision-maker," Bullion said, a master at interweaving compliments and insults.

Austen chewed and looked up at Bullion, not unkindly, a blank, incurious stare.

"Dick," Downs pleaded.

A moment ticked by and Margaret saw panic flushing her father's face. He'd broken her heart time and again with unstrung promises, he deserved to be exposed, and yet she wordlessly implored her husband. Nodding, Austen rose, extended a hand, and said, "Yes, sir. We spoke on the phone several years ago."

"The beating you gave Seaboard Financial was classic," said Bullion. "I couldn't have done it much better myself. Actually I would have knocked them out, taken over the whole company."

"Gentlemen," shouted the photographer from the *Post*. "Smile." Bullion posed, Downs and Sproul beamed, Austen froze. "Great shot.

Thank you, Ivan. Guys, can I get your names? Ivan, can we get a quick one of you with Dr. Watson?"

Downs hesitated until Bullion was beyond hearing, then blurted, "Ivan and I go way back. Hell, I knew him when his name was still Blutarsky. We were really close."

Catching Austen's hard stare at the photographer, Billy Cutter rose and followed him across the ballroom, hoping he preferred money over fame, determined to buy the picture and protect Austen's privacy.

"I read Bullion's damn autobiography cover to cover, waiting for him to mention me," Downs said, glowing with his victory, emptying his wine glass. "Of course, Ivan barely mentions his father's money. It's a hell of a lot easier making a billion if you start with a hundred million than making ten million from scratch. Don't you think so, Dick?"

"How would you know about either, Dad?" Margaret asked, her voice flat.

"But how does anyone earn that much money honestly?" asked Sproul, as if pondering a vexing conundrum. A poor listener, the self-absorbed banker had missed Margaret's fury. "Answer: You don't. Some French philosopher once said, 'Behind every great fortune is a great crime.'"

"That must mean your crimes are all misdemeanors," said Hillary Sproul to her husband, nodding apologetically to Austen.

"Richard," Sproul stammered, "I was making a joke about Bullion. I didn't mean—"

"It's OK," said Austen, indifferent. "You're right, crime pays."

The others laughed, but Downs thought he heard something beyond a party quip in his son-in-law's remark and wondered again about his shadowy past. A grand thief himself—Downs stole with a Tiffany pen instead of a gun—he had little faith in the goodness of man, supposing only the over-fed and lazy to be remotely honest. From the day Margaret had announced that her new beau never discussed his past,

Downs had been half-convinced of his son-in-law's criminality. If he only he had proof, he could bring the haughty Austen into his schemes.

The lights went down, the ballroom turned theater-dark and spot-lights dazzled the podium and runway. Coffee cups and dessert forks clinked, and conversations buzzed over the chairwoman's introductions of her nervous models—society wives—trying their best to strut down the intimidating runway.

"Our next swimsuit is simply too divine to wear. Just wave it in front of your husband like a matador. It's a one-piece Chanel modeled by the lovely Janice Evers. Doesn't Janice look delicious?" The speaker, a kind-hearted woman years past modeling herself, complimented each of her volunteers. In the darkness, Sproul catalogued the evening, smiling over his own stories, recalling who he'd met and what useful things they'd said, his slight reevaluation of Downs. He considered himself blameless for his Austen faux pas; it would have never happened if the man had said five words to him. Sproul wondered if Austen was as rich as widely reported. If he was, why was his wife still grinding it out as a junior lawyer? He gazed at Margaret: the line of her jaw, her large breasts, and her toned arms. She was beautiful. When she reached for her glass, he noticed she wasn't wearing a wedding ring. He drew a titillating conclusion.

No, he told himself. It could interfere with business, the one shabby intersection where his moral code had the right of way over his libido. If he were to arrange the financing for Downs's floundering ice cream company—the old bastard's coy efforts at nonchalance were a joke—an affair could cause problems.

He pushed back from the table, feeling magnanimous, a fisherman tossing a keeper back into a stream. In the darkness, an ugly grin disfigured his face—a glimpse into his soul—a look that flash-froze when he saw Austen measuring him.

CHAPTER 34

THE FRESHMAN TEAM

BILLY CUTTER CONSIDERED HIMSELF TEN pounds overweight—he was closer to thirty—and somehow believed he could lose weight in saunas. He rejoiced on Monday mornings when his weight held steady. He pumped iron twice a week, allowing him to attribute more of his bulk to muscle. This week he was happy.

"Morning, Billy. You see Mr. A's picture? A shame he was frowning," said the receptionist, handing him the *Post* as he arrived. The picture was of just Bullion and Austen.

"Oh, shit," he growled, scanning the page. "'Publicity shy multi-millionaire, Richard Austen.' He's not here yet, is he?" Billy regretted not breaking the damn camera when the hippie photographer refused to sell the picture. "Shit, shit, shit." He barreled into his paper-strewn office and tossed his jacket on a wooden hanger he'd swiped from Claridge's. Sweat beaded on his forehead. How much would Austen blame him? The receptionist's voice floated over the intercom. "It's your father. Should I tell him you're in a conference?"

"No. Tell him not another goddamn dime. No. Tell him to fuck off. No, tell him—"

"I'll say you're not in yet."

SAM MEERLIE AND HIS SON Jordan waited in DAP's lobby. A burly longshoreman who'd spent years on the waterfront, Sam considered himself a working man, a democrat, one who owed much in return.

Retired, he retained a veto power in his business to prevent Jordan
from blundering too often. If his son only lost a million or so a year,
Sam would still have a fortune left over for his favorite charities.

"They spent some big bucks redoing these offices," said Jordan.

Sam glanced down at the extravagant wool carpeting. "Crazy, what
with all the muddy messengers and delivery boys."

Jordan nodded as he surveyed the room. With its brocaded ivory
wall coverings and soft indirect lighting, it looked more like a grand
hotel suite than a reception area. There were copies of the *New York
Times* and the *Wall Street Journal* on the granite coffee table, a bouquet of hydrangeas, and a cut-crystal bowl brimming with exotic fruit.
Jordan glanced at his diamond-encrusted Rolex. "Miss, how long have
we been waiting?"

"Five minutes, sir. I'll—"

"Wrong, it's been twenty. Tell Cutter we're out of here in five."
Jordan straightened his narrow shoulders and gazed at himself in the
federalist mirror, adjusted his ten-dollar gold piece cuff links, fiddled
with the knot of his Brioni tie. Jordan Meerlie was a small man with
small views who had attended law school for six months before dropping out, deciding they were only teaching what he already knew: the
whole world would fake a neck injury for a quick buck. "Six million,
tops. Right, dad?"

Sam glanced toward the receptionist, said nothing.

A tall, bespectacled man in a trench coat rushed from the elevators
into the lobby. "Mr. Meerlie? I'm Richard Austen. Please forgive me for
being late. I'm sorry."

"You didn't have to run all the way. The yellow cars, they're called
cabs," said Sam.

"You're right, sir." Austen grinned, wrestling off his coat to reveal
a double-breasted Armani suit. Billy joined them and the four men
moved into the leather-paneled conference room. After offering his

guests coffee and inviting them to sit, Austen sat at the head of the glossy rose-colored granite conference table.

"Boss?" Billy inquired after a long quiet moment.

"Sorry," Austen said. He was distracted; he'd bought the *Post* on his walk down Fifth Avenue to the office. What were the chances anyone would recognize him? Who cared anymore? Hadn't the police closed the case? Yet was New York safe? With a brisk nod, he shook off the creeping vines, brought himself into the moment, remembering with small satisfaction that this meeting would be a cakewalk—it involved a little bit of money, a desperate buyer, and a building about which he cared not at all. Telling himself to have fun, he skimmed his notes and said, "Let's cut right to it. You offered five million. Billy countered at eight. I think our board would approve a sale at seven and a half. If that's acceptable, our lawyers can hammer out the details."

"Richard, that's a ridiculous number," Jordan cried. His father stood near the window, hands clasped behind his back, gently rocking, chewing an unlit cigar, occasionally dabbing at his mouth with a worn handkerchief.

"I prefer *Mr. Austen*," Austen said, more to irritate Jordan than insist upon decorum. Rattled buyers made mistakes.

"We know you paid four million, and values have tanked the past couple years," Jordan said. "Four's a great price for the building today. Five million, you should be arrested. We'll pay five if it's absolutely confidential." He appeared calm, but his heel was tapping Morse code.

Mrs. Watershed slipped inside and said, "It's Margaret, sir, she's on the line. Should I inform her of your momentary unavailability?"

"No, I'll take it," replied Austen. He had never refused to take one of his wife's calls. He could mention the idea he'd hatched after seeing the morning's *Post*: a Hawaii vacation. "Gentlemen, please excuse me."

"Maybe we could see how far apart we really are while Mr. Austen's out," Billy said.

"Kid, we're here to talk about two things," snapped Jordan. "Money and money. And we're not talking money with the freshman team. Tell me something: What's with this *mister* crap?"

"Mr. Austen is just formal, very polite."

"If my name was *Dick,* I'd just change it—drop the manners shit," said Jordan.

"Tell me something please, Billy," said Sam, glaring at his son. "It says on this fancy card you're a vice president. Mr. Austen's card says senior vice president. So, where's the boss? Who runs the company?"

"Dad, everybody knows Austen's the own—"

"Jordie, I'm trying to learn something here. What am I going to learn from you? What? Gossip?"

"Mr. Austen has full authority to negotiate on the company's behalf," said Billy. Not for the first time did he wish Austen would simply promote himself to president.

Austen reentered, obviously pleased with the way his conversation had gone. Back to the game. "Billy, how many parcels on our block have been optioned or sold to dummy corporations in the last eighteen months?"

"All but three, including ours. Look." Billy slid a parcel map from his monogrammed leather folder. It showed sold parcels in red, those with recorded options in yellow. "See how our building is right in the middle." With feigned innocence, Billy handed Jordan the large map.

"Here it is, Mr. Meerlie," said Austen. "We're guessing one company is behind all these shell corporations and is buying up the whole block to put up a high-rise."

Jordan studied the map as if this were news to him, his face a touch too blank.

"That's yours to keep," said Austen. "I suggest you take it back to your office and evaluate it. Unless the title company is wrong, DAP could easily command eight million from whoever this residential builder is. But close now and the company will sell to you for seven and a half."

"Seven," Jordan said, wiping his sweaty palms on his trousers.

Austen looked from son to father. "You'll pay seven million? Is that right, sir?"

The older man pursed his lips as if to say something, thought the better of it, and shrugged his shoulders in resignation.

"So, we're half a million apart? We can both afford half a million, right?" asked Austen, amused, enjoying himself. "Billy, do you have a dime?"

Billy fished a coin from his pocket, then shuddered as he realized what Austen was about to do, calculating a half million's loss on his year-end bonus.

"Write down your favorite charity on that slip and I'll do the same." Austen tossed the coin to Jordan. "You flip it and your father calls it. If you win, give the money to your favorite charity before closing and we'll sell for seven million. If I win, give the half million to my favorite charity in your name. Either way, you keep the deduction, you take the glory, do the ribbon-cutting."

Neither Meerlie understood, each wondering how Austen could win this odd bet. Jordan struggled for Austen's angle. "We get all the credit either way?"

"All the credit. My name stays out."

Sam cocked his head to the side. "Jordie, maybe we should talk. Seven and a half million? That's real money."

"Yes sir, it certainly is," said Austen, smiling broadly. Nothing like having the upper hand. "But I think those other developers—the fellows assembling this block—will make it worth far more than that."

"Pick a charity, Dad. Let's wrap this up."

"Heads," Sam said. Jordan thumbed the dime into the air and watched it bounce, spinning on the table. For a moment, the men were transfixed by the coin, small boys staring at a whirring top.

"You won," said Austen, reining in his good humor. Jordan Meerlie had been right—no one else would have paid even four million, Austen had decided not to redevelop the property himself and the extra half million meant nothing to him. He would have given it to charity anyway. Margaret would laugh when he recounted the meeting that evening at dinner, readily seconding the big charitable donation.

"Did I?" Sam asked dryly. "We'll see in five years."

"What charity did you pick?" Austen asked.

"Helping Hands, the one that helps the poor crack babies—the sad little ones with the addict mothers."

"Oh." Austen winced as if he'd struck a finger with a hammer, glanced away, suddenly crestfallen. He forced himself to smile. "That's a good one."

"What did you put down?" Jordan flipped over Austen's paper and read it aloud with a mixture of cynicism and wonder. "The Boy Scouts?"

BILLY HUNCHED IN AUSTEN'S OFFICE, waiting with a hard-learned patience. The two men were supposed to be discussing the Meerlie sale details, but Austen's attention had drifted offshore. They faced one other from damask silk couches flanking the coffee table. Neither had mentioned the Bullion picture, yet the *Post* lay open next to a brass-framed photograph, a sepia picture of two young Marines in a jungle clearing, M-16s yoking their shoulders. One, a black youth, so good-looking he was pretty, a cigarette dangling from his smiling lips, the other a dirty, somber Austen. The only picture of Austen Billy had ever seen.

"Boss?"

"That Jordan's an idiot," Austen said, shaking his head. "He's done ninety percent of the work, but he's missing three critical properties.

Any of us could block him forever. Here's what you do. Call everybody who's already sold to him and see if they carried paper. If so, ask if they'll discount their notes. That way, if—"

"Meerlie screws up, we foreclose and build the high-rise ourselves," cried Billy, gleeful as a six-year-old on Santa's lap. "Wiping that little shit out would be so cool. I'm on it."

"Let me know before you spend any money." Austen drifted off again, picked up the war photograph and, staring at it, wandered to the window behind his desk, gazing across the bustling avenue below to Central Park. So much had happened since Vietnam. If only Jonnie hadn't died, if only he hadn't gone back to Lemon Grove. If only he could have made his fortune without the drug money. He would never know.

An energized Billy scribbled quick numbers: calculations of interest and discount rates. He glanced up, saw that Austen was as still as a museum tableau, and shrugged. Billy was content just to be sitting in his inner sanctum, the room on which Margaret's decorator had labored the hardest. She'd insisted that the palatial office be stripped to the raw wood and plaster. The bright corner suite was now awash in tyrannical shades of beige, a socialite's vision of a wealthy entrepreneur's throne room.

"You upset about your bonus?" Austen asked, yanking himself back to the present, reading Billy like a stop sign.

"Huh? My bonus? No, no way. Didn't even think about it. Never occurred to me."

Austen laughed. Billy was a terrible liar. "We'll figure your bonus on the five hundred I gave away."

"Hey-no-way-you-don't-have-to-do-that-thanks-a-lot."

"Might see this guy soon," Austen said, tapping on the war picture. "I'm thinking of taking Margaret to Hawaii, stop in San Francisco on the way back." He had thought of little besides leaving New York since Billy had returned empty-handed from the *Post* photographer. Wondering whether his exile had to be permanent, whether it would make any difference, whether anyone from his prior life would see the picture or, even if they did, whether they would recognize Eddie Kawadsky.

"Great." His bonus restored, Billy was magnanimous, momentarily setting aside his permanent envy of Parson Shoer.

"Do you think he's changed much?" Austen asked.

Billy fingered the brass frame, worrying his honesty might offend his boss. The sleek restaurateur who radiated charm and worldly joy bore a faint resemblance to the thin Marine. "Guess I'd still recognize him."

"Yeah."

"But you haven't changed, Boss. You look the same, I mean, you know, cleaned up, a little heavier, but your face is the same. You're in great shape."

"Not true, but thanks." Austen pursed his lips, wincing at the answer to his real question. Billy was right: He was recognizable.

"OK if I ask you something? Kind of personal? All that money, the five hundred thousand, why'd you kiss it off?"

Austen closed his eyes, knowing the half-million was only a number on a bank statement, that it mattered not at all, that he would never spend it. He decided upon the truth. "I'm trying to buy my way into heaven."

CHAPTER 35

BINGO

"BINGO, BING-FUCKING-GO. GODDAMN IT, I knew it. Marilyn, you dumb bitch, maybe I shouldn't have dumped you after all. I'm so fucking rich," shouted Roy Cross, staring at the grainy photocopy of the *Post* article. 'This your guy? "Details for $500" was scrawled across a paper-thin business card stapled to the piece. Roy plucked a Marlboro from his lip, kissed the picture, kissed it again, and, in his excitement, drummed his ersatz letter opener—a satin-wood buck knife—against the scarred kitchenette table. The investigator's envelope lay atop a litter of bills and flyers touting everything from strip clubs to herbal medicines to gambling strategies. "I'm a fucking genius," he cried, his voice heard halfway across the crumbling apartment building. Years back, he had written a dozen private detectives in Manhattan after Marilyn's mention of her chance encounter, promising them a fortune if only they could find a rich guy named Austen.

A mile off the Strip, Roy's worn-out studio baked in the summer and froze in the winter. Its second-story view was of cracking asphalt, neon signs, and a billboard promising the best odds in town. Compared with his regal carraca, his Vegas apartment was a cardboard lean-to. Had he been given to introspection, Roy might have considered himself better off at La Mesa. The prison's mythology had anointed him a great lord, he'd had the status of a Hollywood star, his manservant Emilio, alcohol and drugs whenever he wished, and sex with a remarkable succession of pliant women on Sunday afternoons. When, after seventeen years, La Mesa's new warden suddenly needed Roy's carraca to accommodate the temporarily incarcerated head of the Sinaloa cartel, the comandante had had no time for the bribery waltz. Requiring the apartment that day, he'd had a sargento drive a stunned Roy to San Ysidro. Emilio was heartbroken.

True, Roy was free in Las Vegas. He was free to scrape by dealing blackjack at the Four Queens. Free to swallow aspirin like M&Ms to ease his back pain from standing all day. Free to do his wash at a fly-blown laundromat that reeked of bleach and sometimes urine. Free to eat boiled potatoes in the final days before his next paycheck arrived, free to work on his pathetic Corvair himself because he couldn't afford a mechanic, free to do push-ups because gyms cost money, free to talk women into going back to their places because his dump would belie every tale he told.

But Roy had dealt himself a blackjack. Tapping his four-inch blade against the picture, he knew this tuxedo-clad Eddie had to be worth millions—hell, he was pals with the most famous billionaire in the country. Once Roy explained how sorry he'd be if he were forced to call the San Diego PD, Wad's generosity would be boundless. Once Roy reminded him about the special chair reserved for cop killers, Wad would fly him back to Vegas in a private jet. A big one. If he refused to listen—if the rich bastard thought himself beyond the law's reach—Roy would show him what he'd learned in La Mesa, how ugly he could make his blade sing.

Despite the early hour, he poured himself a celebratory vodka, his hands shaking as he raised the grimy glass to his lips. A car door slamming in the lot below scattered his thoughts like startled black birds. Which drug was it that had so rusted his concentration? Ah yes, New York. Screw paying five hundred bucks—he would go to Manhattan and find Wad himself.

CHAPTER 36

WAR STORIES

Margaret sat at a bamboo and glass table on the blue-tiled lanai in the Halekulani's presidential suite. She was working on a brief, struggling to focus while staring at the azure sea darkening in the distance. The postcard view—waders, swimmers, and sailboats crowding the water—delighted her, yet had her wondering how anyone ever worked in Hawaii. Closing her eyes, inhaling the fragrant plumeria lei, Margaret saw papaya, steaming white fish, and umbrella-topped rum drinks. She glanced back into the living room and shook her head at Austen's extravagance. Among her husband's quirks was how he spent money. He spent nothing on himself, his indifference to worldly possessions practically Buddhist. But occasionally his extravagance was so wild as to suggest a contempt for his fortune. Margaret had been less surprised than troubled at his booking of the rambling suite—did they really need the extra space? Was a single room with her too confining?

She frowned at the black piano in the corner of the living room. Before ordering her juice and coffee, she'd opened the suite's colonial shutters and glass doors. Now she fretted that the salt air might warp the piano, stealing its tune. Her lifelong tendency to blame herself had its roots in defending her father. When she was eight, Margaret was sure her theft of two dollars from her mother's purse had led to the family's downfall and first exile from New York City. It was her fault again when Downs filed his second bankruptcy in her fourteenth year. She'd endured the cruelty of her schoolmates—some of whose parents had lost fortunes with Downs—certain that if her father only had the money he'd lavished on her schooling, on her clothes, and riding and tennis lessons, he would have remained solvent. Even her close friends had called her a beggar, a liar, and a thief's daughter. She'd retreated into books, dreaming of romance, of finding a pot of gold to repay her father's investors.

In her schoolgirl isolation, she had seized upon her Argentine abuela, her grandmother, a kindred and comforting spirit. She wrote lengthy heartfelt—and heartwarming—letters to Abuela. In reply, Anna Maria Vandershoot spun fanciful stories about her great wealth and warned against handsome men, shopping at retail, becoming familiar with servants, and trusting girlfriends. She advised her religious granddaughter to listen to her own morality rather than priests, declaring that the greatest sins were of omission—failures of generosity and compassion. And, with visions of her first husband and son-in-law weighing upon her, Abuela wrote often of a woman's need for independence.

"I'm calling to wish Dad a happy birthday. Is he home yet?" Margaret asked her mother.

"All day, I assure you, dear."

Margaret heard the care with which her mother enunciated her words and wondered if she were already drunk. She glanced at her watch, added five hours for the time in New York. Ill at ease in any conversation with her, Margaret spoke of the flight and the weather.

"Is this purely a business trip or are you celebrating anything special?" her mother asked.

"We're going sightseeing this afternoon, and we may take the plane over to Maui tomorrow. May I speak with Dad?"

"For my birthday?" Downs asked a moment later. "A one-hundred-dred-million-dollar line of credit, baby girl. Put a blue ribbon around it and have it here by noon tomorrow, I'm having a big lunch." He laughed with the ease of the cocktail hour.

"Be serious." The joy in his voice reminded Margaret of how deeply he cared for her, softening her for a moment. "You have everything. I bet you're still getting every new tie the Hermes shop gets in stock."

"The moment they arrive in town, a standing order. You know, dear heart, you might have spoken with your mother a little longer."

"Please don't start that. Isn't there anything I can get you?" Margaret was in some ways her father's daughter. She, too, loved shopping, but like a casual drinker horrified by a stumbling drunk, his spending sprees revolted her. She stifled her own spending by paying cash, her own cash, for everything.

"I know. A family dinner at your place," said Downs.

"Do you mean just the six of us?"

"Margaret Downs Austen. A dinner party of six? Really. Your mother was thinking it might be pleasant to see the Sprouls again. After all, Hillary is Darcy's sister. I know, invite Cutter and his wife. She's attractive and he has a touch for the amusingly vulgar. Ten would make it a real birthday party."

"I can't promise any—"

"Not a word, not a breath of business. As your mother says, I assure you."

She promised to think it over, jotting down Sproul's number on a sheet of hotel stationery. Now it was neither the fragrances nor the view that jostled her thoughts, but her father's un-whispered needs. She pondered his finances, certain another bankruptcy would surprise no one. She wondered how badly off his Greek ice-cream company was, recalling Austen's amusement when Downs had explained why the failing company was a great bargain: With Yankee know-how and cheap Greek labor, he would modernize the plant, import his ice cream to America, and undercut the competition.

Margaret knew her parents would somehow get by if the company failed, yet she still felt they were her responsibility. She also knew

Austen would lend Downs whatever sum he needed—considering it a gift—if she would only lift her embargo against aiding her father. But that she would never do. Giving money to her father was handing matches to a pyromaniac.

And she feared falling further into Austen's debt. Two years before, a scared, hesitant Margaret had married a near stranger because Austen wanted her desperately, because he loved her with an exhilarating intensity, because he seemed honest and decent, because he was neither showy nor glib nor reminiscent of the few men who had preceded him. Because he had a good heart. While still an enigma, she guessed his sins were venial and that one day they would laugh over his need to hide them. Yet two years on she was still waiting to hear of his childhood, the years before a self-described street orphan had run away to enlist in the Marines. And in her darker moments, she wondered whether he had decided her unworthy of knowing his story.

JET ROWAN'S CIGARETTES WERE BROWN. So were his silk shirt, trousers, and snakeskin cowboy boots. His few wisps of hair were dyed brown, his rheumy eyes brown. Everything about the man, from his leathery skin to the color of his ink, was brown and whenever anyone asked, he claimed it his living tribute to West Texas. Brown had been Jet's lucky color for nearly thirty years, from the purchase of his first gas station through the day the Bank of America foreclosed on his empire—the largest private collection of office buildings in Houston. His penthouse with the lap pool, his Gulfstream, his Bell Ranger, and his Nighthawk cigarette boat were gone—all of his possessions were gone, except his cowboy-millionaire clothes, for which the bank had no use. These days, neither did Jet. His hand-stitched suits flapped scarecrow loose because he had lost his appetite along with his chef and now sustained himself on sugary coffee and bourbon. His girlfriend, the last pearl in a long string, had left him when she realized his newfound love of romantic evenings at home meant he was broke.

He tapped another packet of sugar into the coffee and, not bothering to stir, slurped it, a habit calcified during the time when his legion of vice presidents, assistants, secretaries, and pilots neither heard nor saw any of his peccadilloes. He wanted this Austen to quit asking questions and start talking. Frowning at him with a Texas smile, he wondered why his good-for-manure broker had bothered introducing him to yet another East Coast grinder.

"Well, son, you've been loading all morning. You going to take a shot at the old lazy 'K'? Best damn project I ever built." Back to the ocean, sunglasses propped on his leathery forehead, Jet drummed his fingers, staring at the man opposite him.

"Mr. Rowan. What's it worth as apartments, assuming the condos can't be sold?" asked Austen. He had brought Margaret to Hawaii to get away from New York for a couple weeks—to escape the Bullion photo and stories of anguished crack babies—to consider a new home. Not that once found in New York he couldn't be tracked to Honolulu, but the island somehow seemed safer. And then there was the desperate Jet Rowan and his Kahala Diamond, an intriguing busted condo project—a first-class architectural gem that would sparkle again once the recession subsided.

"About half what we got in it," sighed Jet. "If you don't believe in the condo market, this dog won't hunt."

"But even if condo prices recover, the bank's loan is still more than the Diamond's worth. By the way, can I buy you a drink?" asked Austen, rolling up the sleeves of his white dress shirt. He wore the shirt open and blue gabardine trousers, an elegant businessman in the tropics.

"I don't usually... Aw, what the hell." Jet understood the younger man's gambit; he'd used it himself when Austen was in diapers, but he didn't care. Even drunk, he could out-negotiate a Mormon. He raised his arms, stunned the waitress with a prairie whistle, and then waved the laughing woman toward them as if he were parking a 747. "Anyway, son, this recession's just about over. Remember? 'Stay alive till '95.' Six months and things'll start getting rosier."

"I hope so, sir."

Halfway into his drink, Jet began telling Austen how to cut a deal with his Japanese lender, swearing he would put the project into bankruptcy before he would let them take it back. He said, "Shit, my unit was shooting those bastards five years before I joined it."

"Were you in the Army?"

"Corps, son. Got this in Korea, at a picnic spot called Chosin." Jet pointed to a scar, a twisted bolt of smooth skin near his elbow.

"You were at Chosin?"

"1st Battalion, 3rd Marines. Look it up. I only lie about business and fishing." Jet banged his empty glass on the table. For a moment, he thought he had actually been there. "Yup. Frozen Chosin. What do you know about Korea? You one of them history buffs?"

"No, sir, I was in the Corps, did two tours in Vietnam."

"The hell you say. Doing what?" Jet had scant interest in talking war with a true combat veteran.

"Rifle platoon."

"You were in a line company? A lieutenant?"

"No, corporal. Look." Austen rolled up his sleeve and touched a faded blue Semper Fi on his forearm. Beneath it a small rococo letter "J".

"Another goddamn grunt. Shit, son, I'll buy the drinks." He ordered himself another double and, skipping past his war, guided the conversation to common memories of Parris Island. He was soon so overcome by comradeship that lying required extra effort. "I can't bullshit the old Semper Fi, son. I've got another buyer, a Jap named Shibata, flying in tonight with a pile of money. He says he's ready to domo-arigato the deal, but you know how the Japahenos are. Takes them a week to get a hard-on. If you could do something for me, you could win big."

"If fifty thousand would make you happy, we might be able to work something out."

"Come on," Jet wheedled. "Leave me a bone I can chew on, son."

"Think it over and get back to me. By the way, do you like living here?" Austen asked, relaxing back into his chair. He glanced about his surroundings, the graceful open-air restaurant, the strollers on the beach path, the sparkling blue water to infinity's edge. Was this far enough away? Wouldn't they find him anywhere?

"What?" asked Jet.

"Living in Honolulu. Do you like it?"

"Oh, hell yes. God's own paradise. Weather like this, gals like that," Jet said, dipping his head toward a strolling bikini on the boardwalk.

"Is crime a problem? Drugs, drug dealing?"

"These people don't have the ambition to take drugs. 'Cept pot, of course. Half the damn island's stoned."

Austen nodded at the thought of an unspoiled paradise.

CHAPTER 37

THE OUTRIGGER CLUB

THEY WAITED ON THEIR SECOND round of Mai Tais at the terrace bar, gazing across the glittering water toward Waikiki, the hotels crowding its sunset-gilded beach. Famous for its swimmers and sportsmen, the Outrigger Club had its own snug beach in Diamond Head's lee, a sandy volleyball court atop its parking garage, and a practice of cheerfully overcharging mainland visitors.

Margaret looked smashing. Her hours outside had deepened her tan, she seemed relaxed. Fit, she had swum in the ocean about half a mile, paralleling the beach a couple hundred yards offshore. For this evening, she had piled her thick hair in a braid, left a couple buttons on her white blouse undone and rolled up its sleeves, leaving her toned arms bare. She wore her grandmother's antique necklace.

Glancing at his runner's physique, his cheap plastic diver's watch, and aloha shirt, a club member might have dismissed Austen as just another naval officer. Despite his beautiful wife, the rum drinks, swaying palms, and stunning sunset, he was far away, as remote as New York. He seemed to be watching the club's swimmers who, in knots of twos and threes, were wading out into the jeweled waters. They followed the same course, navigating off the moored sailboats and buoys, their thick-shouldered bodies chopping through the warm water. A rower with a sense of flamboyance beached his kayak with a burst of speed.

Margaret smiled at the weathered couples around them, white-haired men in school ties and seersucker suits and their wives in climate-defying winter dresses. She felt an odd sympathy for these well-to-do locals, hearing in their lock-jawed remarks echoes from a thousand conversations among her parents' set, inwardly smiling at the thought that flaunting one's wealth required effort in a society dressed in t-shirts and flip-flops.

"I'm parched, Aussie." Her drink down to melting ice, she bit into its pineapple wedge. "I think Mother might approve of this place—everything but the service. She would be demanding the manager's head by now." Austen was silent. "Are you listening?"

"Sorry… Guess I'm a little distracted, the condos," he said too late, grasping for his line like a mediocre actor. He forced himself into the moment, to consider her remarks about the restaurant. Remembering his Inn days when he lived for fifty-cent tips, when a five-dollar tip was an indelible joy, he smiled broadly. "Service is always bad where the tip's included—no incentive for hustle."

"Do you suppose our waiter's name is Godot?" she asked, laughing, her teeth flashing white against her tan.

Now engaged, Austen smiled again, pleased with his wife's high spirits. Maybe this was the moment to pitch his idea. "Do you like it here?"

"It's a little smug. I mean all those trophies on the wall, and this has to be the whitest—"

"Not this club. Hawaii, Honolulu."

"Oh." She considered her husband. "It's gorgeous, I love those sharp green mountains, the flowers, the air, the impression one has of seeing the whole sky. The blue sea," she said, trailing off. "You don't do small talk, Aus. What are you driving at?"

He removed his glasses and ran his fingers through his curly hair. "Could you live here?"

"What? You're joking. You're serious? You can't be serious." Her stare bent his gaze to the concrete deck.

"This project, the Kahala Diamond, is big, might take a lot of management for a few years. It might make sense to have a place here. Move here."

"We've been here two days and you're asking me to emigrate?" She realized her voice was too loud when the dowagers around them hushed to eavesdrop.

"To think about it," said Austen.

"You are serious, aren't you?" Her dread of public spectacles reduced her to a whisper. "What about my, my job, our friends, my family— don't you need to stay close to your business? Anyway, until—look at me—until I know everything, until I know this is going to work, until… until we have a family, I am keeping my job." After six years at Ascott Swanne, Margaret had neither love for her practice nor any illusions about finding fulfillment as a lawyer. It was independence.

"I'm not talking about leaving New York," he said, unconsciously nego- tiating, compromising on the spot. "We'd keep the townhouse, do spring and fall in Manhattan, winter here and so on. We could get a place on the beach, you could swim every day. I'd bring the *Alba* over, sail more."

She sat back in the rattan chair, waving him off, shutting her eyes, biting her lip over how little she knew this man, remembering her hon- eymoon vision of unstrapping his armor like a dutiful squire. Could marrying Austen have been a mistake? "Stop, please stop." She opened her eyes, a tear streaming down her cheek. "The picture."

"What?"

"The picture, Aus. I want to know about the picture with Bullion. Why you sent Billy to buy that picture, why you *never* let yourself be photographed. And when you finish explaining that, you need to tell me your story." She recalled her questions the night he proposed. She'd pressed him. He'd admitted a criminal past, acts he still regretted and would tell her about one day. But he'd pleaded for time before he detailed his failings—begging her to truly know him before she ren- dered judgment.

"My story?" He twisted a stained menu into a tube and worried it in his hands.

"You're asking me to move halfway across the world. It's time for me to know where you grew up, exactly what happened to your parents, what you did, why you ran away and joined the Marines thirty years ago."

"Twenty-five. 1969."

"What did you do that was so terrible? Tell me now."

"I love you, Margaret, I wish I had the words to tell you how much I love you."

She calmed his manic hands with her own. "If you love me so much, then trust me, I know you're a good man. Everybody's ashamed of something. It's not like you're a murderer."

"Excuse me, I need to—sorry, be right back."

Forgetting his glasses, Austen splashed cold water on his face, muttering, swearing. How had he intended to handle this conversation? He'd prayed for her pregnancy, a child's bond, before having to confess. His youthful absolutes had long since been stripped away, but he'd retained one certainty: Margaret would leave him if she knew. Maybe he could justify everything else, but not his wretched decision to return to Lemon Grove. He would have been successful without the drug money. If only he'd left the damn cocaine alone. He glanced at his trembling fingers, splayed his hands against the tiled wall and hung his head. He couldn't lie to Margaret. He needed time.

"I will tell you, but not here, not on vacation," Austen said, sitting down. "All right? I can't do it now."

"Ah, an extension." Disappointment and perhaps relief floating in the pause. "This is absolutely critical to me. It's been two years. When?"

"This summer, OK?"

"No. You realize I'm thirty-three, with a ticking biological clock. I need to know before we…"

Austen blinked. Never before had she connected the two events. He had to tell her soon. "Just give me a month. All right?"

"I don't see what another month will do, but yes, all right as long as you promise. Look at me," demanded Margaret.

"I promise." He reached took her hand. "I swear. You want another drink?"

"No thanks... well, maybe... all right." His promise in hand, she sat back, contemplating her distraught husband. He was a good man. Could he possibly have done anything so terrible as to extinguish her love? No. She had to comfort him. "Lean over and give me a kiss."

THEY LAY ENTWINED ON THE rumpled bed, listening to the sea spend itself on the sand, the lanai doors open to the tropics. Austen clung to that flash of eternity, the one moment when—inside her—he could believe Margaret was really his. He nuzzled her hair and kissed her ear. He had no idea whether he was a good lover; he'd had so little experience and whatever physical confidence he possessed was offset by his certainty that he was unworthy of love. Had his mother truly loved him, she never would have gone away without a fight, she would have found him, forced him home. He kissed the back of Margaret's neck, held her tight.

"You can't be ready again," Margaret said.

"Mmmmm."

"Remember, this was supposed to be a vacation." She giggled. His mysterious past aside, she understood a great deal about her husband. She grasped his crushing need for intimacy and rarely denied him. Or herself. His lovemaking was sometimes so frenzied she fancied it sinful.

"Mmmmm."

"Oh, all right, mmmmm."

CHAPTER 38

THE ROADHOUSE

"YOU WANT TO DRIVE?" ASKED Parson, tossed Austen the keys as he emerged from the United terminal into a night of nomadic fog. Parked curbside, Parson was leaning against a red Ferrari—a 348 Spider—a car that hijacked attention.

"What the hell's that?" asked Austen, grinning.

"This? This, my friend, is an aphrodisiac so powerful the FDA is about to ban its import." Parson laughed, then added ruefully, "It's also a lifetime pass to the mechanic's shop. Hey, you really got that island tan—hell, you're darker than I am."

"Are we seeing Claire and the kids?" asked Austen, ignoring the old jest. Never fond of Eileen, Austen had been delighted when his friend had fallen hard for another lawyer, Claire Threatt, and married her within months. The couple had had three children within their first five years of marriage.

"You're spending the night, remember? You can play uncle in the morning, because tonight, my boy, we have a pass. We just need to swing down to PA, fire the assistant manager, and then we're off to the city."

"*PA?*"

"Palo Alto."

"Of course," Austen said, recalling the smug university town south of San Francisco where Parson had opened his second Parsonage. "How's number two doing?"

"Great. You'll have your whole investment back in two years. Just got some staff problems to work out. Have to can my damn manager— he's been banging the hostess," said Parson.

"Oh," said Austen, marking his friend's annoyance, idly wondering whether Parson might have any interest in the hostess himself. Parson may have been the one exception to Austen's ironclad rule of never asking personal questions, but he still changed the topic. "MJ showed me Herb Caen's column about dinners being half-off on the nights you sing." He glanced back as a jet roared skyward. Too soon to be Margaret's red-eye to JFK. He missed her already, but her decision to return early gave him a chance to talk things over with Parson—perhaps to rehearse his confession.

"I banned that freeloading horse's ass," said Parson, chuckling. "As usual, he was dead wrong. It's stone free when they have to listen to me. I guess I am getting kind of famous. Did I tell you what we're doing tomorrow morning? We're driving up to Marin County to look at a site for our next Parsonage." With two successful restaurants, he hungered for a chain, sure his simple formula—comfort food in a swinging atmosphere—was a winner.

The old friends had so much to talk about. Each was tormented, wrenched by hidden undercurrents, emotional whirlpools, edging toward decisions more important than money. Yet neither could unburden himself, even to a mirror. Between his restauranteur's hours and his wife's devotion to their toddlers, Parson's marriage had bottomed out. It was as if they lived three time zones—and a world— apart. Other than using its disintegration to justify his chance forays, Parson refused to contemplate his marriage. Or attempt to fix it. This burden, however, was a paperweight compared to the field pack Austen had strapped on in Lemon Grove.

The men had so much to talk about, yet when they were at last alone with a bottle of Hennessey X.O. in Parson's emptying restaurant, they spoke of everything else—a campfire conversation—unimportant cheery manly comforting words forgotten as they were uttered. Parson regaled his friend with jokes, recaps of funny shows he had seen, wicked tales of San Francisco's elite, the city's woeful Giants and his dreams of a Parsonage in every major city. Austen spoke of sailing the *Alba*, his newfound interest in Hawaii, the projects he and Billy were working on.

But like actors with a single Broadway hit between them, the pair soon circled back to their favorite topic. They abused Dorland as if their old drill sergeant had tormented them yesterday, fondly recalled even the least worthy of their fallen comrades, and shook their heads over the benighted policies that doomed the Corps in a war it could have won. If anyone had asked what they discussed when together, they would have answered family, business, politics, and sports, neither stopping to think how much they delighted in reminiscing about events that happened decades earlier, how they indulged themselves in a time when they were innocent, when the wrongs were perpetrated by others. And when at last the brandy bottle was fumes, neither had come a step closer to the confessional.

DRIVING TO MARIN, THE HUNGOVER men were quiet, frowzy, a generation older than they had been the night before, gulping the coffee Claire insisted they take with them. Parson pulled off the freeway at the Rodeo exit in Sausalito. "There it is." He pointed out a shuttered, weed-choked restaurant that sat just above 101. "Wait till we get to the other side—it'll jump right out at you. It's got parking, great access, and so much freeway visibility I'd never need to advertise."

They glided into the parking lot. Austen gratefully stretched his back—he was too tall for the cramped Ferrari—and gazed from the crackling, weedy asphalt to the low wooden building, a New England clapboard with a mossy shingled roof and a raftered gable above its front doors. Its few windows were multi-paned. The building seemed to lean away from the freeway.

"Is this the next Parsonage or what?" Parson exclaimed, stretching his arms to encompass his latest dream. "This is a one hundred percent, main and main location. Isn't she beautiful?" While Parson harbored fewer delusions about himself than most, he did believe he was an astute businessman. He lit a Cohiba with a lordly flourish. "My architect thinks he could turn this into a rocking 30s-style roadhouse, sexy, mysterious, dark paneling, a blazing fireplace, buckets of martinis on ice. He's doing all kinds of drawings—he's really excited about it."

"They always are." Austen could tell in a glance it would be cheaper to knock the poor building down than to renovate it, but kept his opinion to himself. As they stepped around pools of standing water in the dank-smelling, peeling-plaster interior, he pointed out pinholes of light in the ceiling and failing posts that would need replacement. "How much will the landlord give you to fix it up?"

"Landlord?" Parson struck a rich man's pose, twirling his cigar. "Aus, we're buying it. I'm tired of making landlords rich. Think how much we'd be coining if we weren't paying all that rent in the City and PA. We're buying this—"

"Wait, Parse. Think about it: We did those deals with shell corporations. If the restaurants failed—if they fail today—you walk away free, you can start over. If you buy this and pour all your own money into it, you go down with the ship."

"You got rich by taking risks, it's my turn now," declared Parson. "Let me show you the back, even has employee parking behind the building. Come on." Fumbling with the broker's keys, he shouldered open the rusted door.

"Oh," Austen murmured. A Mercedes and a BMW were parked side by side. The Mercedes was empty. The BMW held a pair of lovers, the man disheveled, the woman's sheer bra riding atop her breasts.

"Ooooh-weee," Parson exclaimed.

Austen about-faced and strode back across the gloomy restaurant, listening to Parson's howling laughter and the slamming of two car doors.

"I told you this place was lucky. Shut down, but still cooking," Parson cackled, a pleased voyeur.

AUSTEN WAS QUIET—PREOCCUPIED—DURING THEIR DRIVE back to SFO, answering Parson's desultory questions with an economy of words, a mile sometimes passing between question and answer. So quiet that Parson inferred a rejection of his Sausalito project. "If you don't want in, I can get other investors, hell, I could get it oversubscribed in a week. It's just that I owe you, Aus. Shit, you're my best friend, you practically gave me the seed money."

"It's not that," Austen replied at length. Parson's plea had cut through his visions of the parking lot couple, his baseless concerns over Margaret and Sproul, his persistent fears she would seek solace elsewhere because he'd closed off so much of his life. Why was she inviting Sproul to a dinner party for her father? "Look, if I put up the money to buy it, you'd never worry about getting wiped out, but that's not reality."

"What's reality?"

"That business is a craps game. If you're smart and work hard, the odds are in your favor *most* of the time, but sooner or later you're going to lose on a deal. If I put up the money and your restaurant flops, you'll learn nothing because I won't foreclose. Who takes care of you when I'm not here? When I go down?"

"Whoa," Parson said, shivering off Austen's iron conviction. "Let me think about it, OK? The seller would probably lease it to us." Then he too went quiet.

The silence lingered until they saw the airport's exit. Austen checked his watch, examined his glasses, and cleared his throat. "Don't take this the wrong way. You know I think Claire is absolutely the best, but what we saw back there—I know she'd never do something like that, but what if she were having an affair? Maybe if she decided you weren't giving her what she needed?"

"She'd be doing me a favor."

"Goddamn it, that's not true," Austen snapped.

"Hey, man, I was kidding, only kidding." Parson had been annoyed by Austen's reaction to his Sausalito project, and said the first words that sprang to mind, attempting humor rather than candor. Then he realized Austen wasn't asking about Claire. "Sorry, Aus, that's something neither of us will ever have to worry about. We both have incredible wives." In Parson's view, women were better than men, seldom straying except in retaliation for neglect or infidelity, and he knew God had yet to create a man more attentive or faithful than Austen.

CHAPTER 39

THE DINNER PARTY

A QUIET STREET OF NARROW-SHOULDERED brick townhouses softened by ginkgoes and plane trees. It ends at the Metropolitan Museum of Art. A six-story mansion—as anonymous as a bearer bond—stands mid-block on the south side, its stone cladding blanched in sunshine. Its French windows are white-trimmed and its glistening ebony doors are flanked by small boxwood planters, each bordered by an elfin wrought-iron fence capped in gleaming brass.

Twenty minutes before their dinner guests were to arrive, Margaret was dashing upstairs from the kitchen, her chocolate cake frosted, when she paused on the landing, glanced outside. She saw a dog walking an old man and a well-dressed couple bustling along, the young man a hurried step ahead of the woman.

"Billy? Oh my," she said, laughing aloud. She found Austen shaving. "Good, you're not dressed. You missed a spot right *there*. Smile, please, we're having a party. Guess who I just saw yanking his poor wife along outside like a little red wagon? Guess who's wearing a dinner jacket?"

"Billy's in a tux?"

"Yes, and I'm sure he'll be ringing the bell in, oh, nineteen minutes. He'll be mortified if he's the only one dressed. Would you please? You could wear your Saint Laurent with the paisley cummerbund."

"Hey there, Billy, Stephanie, good to see you. Aus, glad to see I rate East Coast formality," joshed Parson as he and Claire joined the foursome in the library, shaking hands and hugging all around.

"Parson Shoer, have you lost weight? You look great," said Margaret. She hugged him again, feeling his back. "You have lost weight."

"Breaks my tailor's heart, thirteen pounds in two months. Since I last saw this guy, I gave up drinking, gave up smoking—for about a day—I'm keeping better hours, and Claire and I have been walking forty-five minutes every morning. He visits again, I'll become a Carmelite." His puffiness gone, Parson looked elegant in a blue blazer and gray slacks.

"Aus should visit every month to help keep this guy in line," said Claire Shoer, smiling. "It's even gotten worse since the *Chronicle's* poll. San Francisco's Favorite Restaurateur—can you believe it?" She whispered a thank-you as she kissed Austen on the cheek. A pretty woman, Claire was of middling height, a couple shades darker and, at the same time, brighter than her husband. She wore her clothing understated and her hair short. According to Parson's mother, Claire was the only proof her wayward son had ever made a right decision. His law school classmate at Stanford, she possessed more common sense than her husband and an ability that eluded him— that of managing money.

"Who does a guy have to blackmail to get a drink around here?" asked Parson, laughing. He followed Margaret to the marble-topped bar in the corner near the French window. "This really is an incredible place, great ceilings. What do you call that flooring?"

"Parquet de Versailles," Margaret said, then lowered her voice. "Parse, be a dear and try to cheer up Aus. Something really upset him. Of course, he's not talking. That man. MJ thought it might have something to do with an odd character who stopped by the office, but that can't be it. Talk to him please, tell him war stories or do whatever it is you two do."

"Happy to, what about helping your dreaded father with his Greek scheme?"

Margaret blushed, her laugh bringing looks from across the room. "Did I say that? Please don't quote me."

Gam Downs bent to retie his shoes before he entered the fashionable townhouse. Straightening, he adjusted his cufflinks, then gave his wife Connie a moment to finish her cigarette. He was full of dread. Not that he was a racist himself—he loved blacks—but one never knew how others would handle the situation, whether their mere presence would stifle an evening's conviviality. And the exuberant Parson Shoer was not the refined society type who knew just how far he might impose. Would Jeff Sproul take Shoer the wrong way? But this concern was a trifle compared to the guaranty. Cornered by Sproul's vicious underling, Downs had executed a loan commitment that promised his son-in-law's guaranty, a promise Austen knew nothing about. Somehow, they had to get through the evening without discussing business. With magical thinking, Downs was convinced Sproul would override his credit committee and drop the guaranty after an evening of observing how close Downs was to his rich son-in-law. A Town Car stopped as Downs tweaked his tie for a third time.

"Jeff, what timing, great minds *arrive* alike, too," Down said, shaking hands like a competitive lumberjack. "Hillary, you are looking particularly lovely. You both remember Connie, of course."

"This is some location," said Sproul, awed.

"Wait until you see the inside. Richard stole this place—the man should be arrested—from a bankrupt Kansas savings and loan, fully furnished, the antiques, the artwork, the linens, all the way down to the napkins and silverware and the two thousand bottles of Bordeaux in the cellar. The S&L's executives would fly in on their private jet, use it as a weekend pied-à-terre... those were the days." He sighed, as if he'd been a player in that deregulated era. "He bought it the week

Margaret agreed to marry him. See this sidewalk? It's heated by coils underneath, melts snow instantly."

"Really? A heated sidewalk. No shoveling, great," said Sproul said.

"You know who also thinks it's grand? Every mutt from here to the Plaza—just think heated toilet seats—my dear Richard finally had to turn it off. True story." As they entered the home, Downs murmured, "Did I tell you about Richard's old war buddy? They were best friends in Vietnam, saved each other's life and so on, the kind of friend one sees—one *has* to see—whenever he's in town."

Downs had meant to better prepare the Sprouls, but had been unable to utter the word black, and then they were in the library. Despite his urbanity, Sproul was surprised, but he smiled, shook Shoer's hand, looked him in the eye, and introduced himself to Claire before Margaret could.

Downs was rattled. Connie had neglected to mention the evening's attire was formal. Her angry whispered denial flustered him even more. He should have worn his dinner jacket. Few things upset him as much as being underdressed. Even Sproul's identical faux pas was small comfort. After all, he was from California.

"You don't mind if I smoke." Connie's remark was not so much a question as a shot across her daughter's bow, leaving Margaret glowering into her wine glass. The pair had been estranged since her first day of eighth grade, when she rebelled against being her mother's fashion accessory, the day she threw the gold bracelet and earrings down the toilet.

"What about you, Mr. Shoer?" asked Hillary Sproul, when the small talk inevitably turned to the fading flu season.

"Call me Parson. I have a gig at my place where we do flu shots at half price during Happy Hour—Shots 'n' Shots—great for publicity. We get a picture of a couple socialites tossing back tequila while taking a shot in the arm, the *Chronicle* runs it for me every year."

"You don't mean the Parsonage?" asked Hillary, surprised.

"Show them your clipping," Margaret said, delighted at Hillary's reaction. "Behold San Francisco's 'Restaurateur of the Year.'"

"It's the hottest restaurant in San Francisco," said Hillary. "I'm dying to go—you must know it, Jeff. He's always flying to the coast on business. Haven't you tried it yet?"

"Oh," Sproul said, missing a beat. He'd been there, but not alone. "Sure, sure, for dinner. Dinner with clients. I've heard it's got after-hours music, too."

Margaret noticed Lupe by the doorway, her hands fidgeting at her side. The moment had come: She shepherded her guests downstairs into the dining room. The wainscoted room looked onto an interior, slate-paved garden with low brick walls, potted pansies, trellised ivy, and young birch trees. Margaret found it confining, a glorified light well best left to the gardener.

Clearing the first course, Lupe overheard the young blond man—so handsome and with so many words—explaining to the black man about the difference between the east and west sides of Manhattan.

"Is that it? I've always heard the east side was for those who went to plays and the west for those who wrote them," Parson replied.

Lupe saw the blond man did not think the comment as clever as everyone else did. Instead of laughing, he reached for his wine glass.

"You OK?" Parson asked Austen.

"Yeah, sure." Austen sat erect, his back away from the chair, the satin lapels of his dinner jacket gleaming, his bow tie elegantly knotted by Margaret, but something—beyond the locks of his curly hair—was out of place.

"No, I mean it." Parson dropped his voice. "Don't bullshit me, something's wrong. You want to take a walk?"

Austen regarded him kindly, pursed his lips into a semblance of a smile. His long-buried past had been unearthed the day before with a

simple pink message slip left on his desk. What would Parson think if
he knew the truth?

"I'd like to propose a toast," Sproul said, tapping a knife against his
wine glass. "Since we're about to close a loan with you two—"

"A toast's a marvelous idea," Downs rushed in, cutting off the loan
talk. "But let's make it to family and friends, shall we?"

"To family and friends," Sproul acquiesced.

"Margaret?" Downs raised and lowered his glass as if teaching a
twelve-year-old table manners.

Margaret searched her father's face. His smile was too broad, his
voice too hearty. He'd done it again, dragging Austen into his scheme.
She stared at her father until his fixed smile quivered. Wondering how
he intended to get away with it, she envisioned him on their doorstep,
crying at the last moment, begging for help. She closed an eye, touched
her cool glass to her cheek, and gazed at her father through the glass,
small, distorted. To her surprise, she pitied him.

Lupe and her sister served the lamb, and the conversation swirled
on.

Sproul was off. Ordinarily, he would have been amusing everyone
with his anecdotes, but he was misfiring, crippled by his suspicion that
the others thought Parson cleverer. His wife was annoying him, whin-
nying at Parson's absurd comments with no consideration for his feelings. Only Downs and his wife seemed to be hanging on his words.

"Thank you, dear heart," Connie said as her husband lit another
cigarette for her. "Jeff, I've been puzzling over something ever since we
met. What made you leave your Golden State for Manhattan?"

"I was tired of the mushroom treatment."

Connie looked puzzled at the old joke. "Mushroom treatment?"

"Wellbourne Masterson's home office is here. I was running its San
Francisco branch office and just like a mushroom, I was kept in the
dark and fed a lot of bullshit."

"That's so rich—great stuff," Downs said, forcing a laugh.

Sproul began a story, a tale he'd refined over the years, allowing his mind to wander to the ringless Margaret as he talked. Seemingly of its own volition, his knee pressed against hers. An affair would be bad for business and family, but at this moment she was too beautiful for words, and he knew she wanted him. What harm was there in footsie?

She had shifted away as he pressed against her, thinking the long-legged man needed room, but when she could neither move any farther nor draw any other conclusion, she daggered a look at him. He paused in his comic description of an eager life-insurance salesman. Buoyed by his wine, he hooked his leg inside hers, pulling it toward him.

Margaret slipped a fork into her hand, dropped her arm, and speared his thigh. His cry surprised everyone.

"Sorry, sorry, just a back twinge. Sitting too long, you know tall guys and their backs." He finished his wine and then his story, his timing lost, stared at the table like a child denied dessert.

Moments later, as the others were transfixed by Parson's tale of a drunken starlet dancing topless at his restaurant, Margaret whispered to Sproul, "I suggest you make that loan to my father without involving my husband. If you ever touch me again, you will deal with him."

Lupe reentered the room, her hands balled together, and said to Austen, "Señor, sorry, a man to see you."

"What?" said Austen, stunned but not surprised.

"He says he's an old friend. His name is… no, it's… no, sorry." She thought for a moment, made a sign of the cross. "Oh, si. Cruz."

"His name is Roy Cross," Austen intoned. Like a slowly falling oak, he lowered his head to the table. The others were motionless, fascinated. "Roy Cross." A whisper. "Cross, Cross, Cross," he said to no one, clenching his curly hair in tight fists, his glasses falling away, his lips forming unspoken words.

"Are you alright?" cried Margaret. "Who is he? What does he mean to you?"

"Excuse me." Austen stood, pulled himself erect and walked out, his needless glasses forgotten.

CHAPTER 40

A WALK IN THE PARK

BRIGHT AGAINST A BLUE SKY, the sun buttered the spring air. Eager crowds thronged the great park. A tall unshaven man in paint-stained jeans and a ragged sweatshirt—one might have supposed a house painter on a lunch break—strode through the Sheep Meadow, looking past the masses, seeing nothing. An hour before his reunion, Austen had told himself to stay focused, to reconnoiter. Instead, he pictured one terrible scene after another: his arrest and imprisonment paling against a vision of Margaret recoiling in horror at his confession. Yet he had to tell her. Even if Roy's lasting silence could be bought, he had to confess. She would accept nothing less than the truth. Besides, Roy could never be trusted. Austen knew of only one way to silence his boyhood friend. But he had left killing behind in Vietnam.

Vivid recollections leapt up from 1969: his drive to the border, the cop's yellow dishwashing gloves, the smell of gunpowder, the deafening .45. As if it were on film, he could replay the cop telling his partner about the gun, the moment he knew Roy had bartered his life away.

Austen approached the South Gate House, tentative, drifting off the path now and then, checking behind stouter beeches and oaks, perhaps unconsciously fearing an ambush, however nonsensical that fear. The path turned, opening to the stone building. As if confused by a mirage, Austen backpedaled. Roy was sitting on the steps beneath the black-faced Gate House clock, smiling, playing a guitar for the joggers stretching before their runs around the reservoir. Some were listening, most were chatting among themselves, oblivious to the street musician. He played surprisingly well. Relaxed, he was flirting and joking with his small audience, glancing from his fingers to the joggers, a cigarette pasted to his lip.

Beneath an electric blue sports jacket rolled to his elbows, Roy wore a silk shirt—it looked Mexican— tight across his chest. Two heavy gold necklaces, one a serpentine choker, the other a chain with a pontiff-sized crucifix, encircled his throat. His Ray-Bans perched atop a honey blond mass of curls. His tobacco-stained fingers were manicured, his nails coated with clear polish, and he wore not one but two letter K signet rings. His angelic beauty was long gone, but at Austen's distance, Roy was handsome, his tan and cascading hair suggesting youth. Closer, his face read differently. Sun lines had carved the corners of his watery eyes, ribboned his cheeks, spoked his smile.

Roy glanced back at the Gate House clock. Ten minutes left. "No preocupes," he thought, vainly trying to reassure himself. No worries. His future, the one he had obsessed over for decades, depended not only on Wad's survival, but his wealth. And Wad's home—a skinny building that looked like all of nothing—worried him. Roy knew the rich bought waterfront mansions with piers and helipads and acres of grass. That Wad might not be rich had kept him up half the night. Eventually, he noticed his old friend, strummed his last chords with a flourish, and, in the unctuous manner of a lounge singer, bowed to the small gathering.

"Looking good, Wad." Roy held out a leathery hand that went unmet, masked his frown with a drag on his cigarette. "Can you believe it's been twenty-five years?"

"Let's walk." Austen stepped over a patch of mud and strode off toward the bridle path that circled the reservoir. Roy struggled to keep pace, panting with the effort, coughing.

"Hey, man, I didn't mean to freak you out last night. I should have called first. But, you know, I'm in town, and I had to see if it was really you. Everybody thought you were dead—they had a goddamn funeral for you. My folks said your mom came from—"

"Shut up." Austen walked another thirty yards in silence, scanned the dirt path. "Take your jacket and shirt off."

"What? Oh, I ain't wearing no wire. Smart, Eddie." He set his guitar case down.

"My name's Austen."

"I'll call you Elvis if you want, man. See, not bad for a guy thirty-five," Roy said, lying about his age without thought. He flexed, showing a weightlifter's upper torso, but with a thick middle. He looked powerful, but soft. "Got a joke for you. Wait, wait, how's it go?" Roy asked himself, lost for a moment. He grasped at the air as if it were a ladder. "Oh yeah. They wrote about the first PMS in the Bible. Remember? Mary rode Joseph's ass all the way to Bethlehem."

"Where do you live?" asked Austen.

"Vegas, man. I'm in show biz. I'm really good, fact I'm this close to getting this crazy gig. You heard me play."

"How did you know I was in New York?"

"Remember the beach before our deal went down? I go, 'If you were on the run, where would you hide out?' and you go, 'Fucking New York.'"

Austen studied him, shook his head. He remembered the cocaine, hefting a kilo, pondering the money, but Roy's words, his insidious seduction, were gone. Fueled with a bottle of Oban scotch through a dark night of regret, Austen's hatred skipped a beat as he considered Roy's fragmented narrative, his reaching for words that eluded him, his voice so sandpapery one cringed. His once beautiful face a Mayan ruin.

"You look good, man," Roy said, nervously filling in Austen's silence. "You a runner? Shit, feels like we're running now. In Vegas, people drive to take a dump…. How's business, man? You must be doing great, bet you're really raking it in. You just wearing them old clothes because it's your day off?"

The elms bowered over the muddy path, moody sunlight filtering through their yellow-green leaves. An ancient couple appeared from behind a large chestnut; the old man in a baggy suit cantilevered from the waist, the woman in a jogging outfit too expensive for sweat, heavy jewelry, and up-teased violet hair. She was scolding her companion, her finger slashing the air, yet it was impossible to tell whether the old man was listening or could even hear.

The men passed the couple in silence.

"You catch the facelift on that old broad?" Roy asked. "That dimple on her chin was her fucking belly button." Again, his laugh died in a coughing fit, his battered guitar case nosing back and forth like a bloodhound. "You hear I was stuck in La Mesa—worst fucking prison in the world—for seventeen years? Every week the guards tossed out bodies like yesterday's trash. I saw more death than…" He paused, his thought lost.

"You were in prison?" Austen studied Roy's tremulous hands, wondered how long he'd been an alcoholic.

"Seventeen years, six days, and twelve hours." Roy unfolded his autobiography from the time of his arrest, panting for breath between sentences. Circling the reservoir, he dandled his story for some minutes before Austen said another word.

"You were really in prison?" Disbelief.

"I got to sit down," said Roy, wheezing. "You want a smoke?" He set his case against a weathered, initial-carved bench. "Here, read this, it was in the *Los Angeles Times.*" The clipping was dirty and rounding at the edges, its creases torn. "They did this story on La Mesa, and the reporter talked to me. See the part I marked? That's me."

Austen paced, reading the article. Stunned. His hatred had supposed an unchanged Roy frolicking on the beach all these years, still the wicked pied piper, worshipping at hedonism's altar. That the pathetic alcoholic groveling before him had endured such a terrible penance thunderstruck Austen.

"The reporter that wrote this, I nailed her."

"How did you really find me?" Austen stared at the hoof prints at his feet, lunettes stamped in pliant earth. Had he really described New York as the place to disappear all those years ago?

"My old girlfriend saw you in Atlantic City." Edging out onto spring ice, Roy added diffidently, "You know it's fucking lucky that Wad was declared dead because they have his fingerprints, the cop's blood all over his van, everything they need to fry him."

"You're threatening me."

"No, man, no way. Just shooting the shit." Cowed by Austen's glare, he fingered the four-inch buck knife in his pocket. Roy told himself he'd carve Eddie like an Easter ham if he made a false move. Or if he stiffed his old partner.

"Tell me why you did it," Austen demanded.

"Did what, man?"

"Why you set up Eddie." Austen trembled with the rage he'd buried for decades.

"I don't know what you're talking about, swear to Christ. Here, I have a letter you need to check out, man. Don't get mad." Gingerly, he handed him a scrawled note—it crudely tied the cop killings to Richard Austen—and took a long pull from a hip flask.

"You're blackmailing me."

"No, no way, man. The King just wants his share." The palsied Roy sought a cigarette from the package until he remembered the one at his lip.

"Who else is going to demand his fair share?"

"Nobody. Nobody knows a thing. Shit, even Sheila thinks I was going to San Diego to see my mom."

"Your wife?" asked Austen.

"My old lady, dude. Cocktail waitress on the strip. Killer fucking body, but dumb as a brick. Swear to God nobody knows nothing about you."

"You set me up—those cops were going to kill me, Roy." He spat his old friend's name as if it were a curse.

"Whoa." Roy slapped his hands over his ears. "Whoa, whoa, whoa. That's not how it went down, man. It was you and me together. Where's my nail?" He glanced around for his fallen cigarette. Roy had repeated his tales—of saving Wad, shooting the federale, and his imprisonment as a desperado—so many hundreds of times that they were true. He believed in nothing more fiercely than his own heroics, his innocence, his victimhood. "You have to believe me. The cops fucked us both. The cops were working for…" he paused again, trembling, losing his thread. "I didn't know those cops."

"Who were they working for?"

"How would I know? I was with you, remember? Why would I do a plan that had me rot in La Mesa? We were both fucked, man." He swigged from his flask, coughed rust, wiped his mouth with his sleeve and extended the wobbling flask. "Want a hit?"

Austen scanned the path in both directions; no one was approaching. Just as he had imagined it, he was alone with Eddie Kawadsky's killer. He could do it. No. A half hour with Roy had shown him how myopic, how bankrupt his imagination had been. Revenge would not only be demeaning, but redundant. Roy had overpaid for his crimes. But Austen had to do something. Even if he were willing to be blackmailed, this juddering alcoholic would haunt him forever. A drunken Roy would crow about his new fortune, some half-clever listener would dismiss his first improbable explanation, then his second and third until at last, tired or piqued, Roy would explain how he tripped up the cop-killing millionaire.

"How much would it take?" Austen asked.

"Two million. Like I—"

"No. Give me your bottom line."

"OK. A million and a half."

"You're not listening to me," Austen snapped, negotiating instinctively, out of habit. He had no thoughts of saving money; he simply knew that, without haggling, parties all too often regretted their deals. "I said your bottom line. Not a tooth-fairy wish."

After two more coughing fits, Roy agreed a half million would be acceptable if payment was immediate. When Austen replied it would take weeks to raise that kind of cash, Roy pleaded for a down payment, something to pay for the trip east, anything to avoid returning empty-handed. He swore secrecy with a precise sign of the cross.

Austen dropped a pile of bills onto the guitar case, turned toward the Metropolitan Museum, toward home. "I'll see you in a month."

CHAPTER 41

FATHERS

"MRS. AUSTEN? YOUR PAPA AT the door. You no home?" Lupe asked over the intercom.

Margaret glanced at her jeans and bare feet and decided her father could get over it. "No, send him up please." She set aside the environmental regulation she was trying to untangle, looked about the baronial library to confirm all was in order. Slanting sunlight played upon the oriental carpet, window panes framing diamonds on its patterned silk. She appraised herself in the Georgian mirror and piled her luxuriant hair atop her head with a clip, thinking she might have brushed it out.

"Hello, dad," she said, trying not to frown.

"No, say hello, *millionaire*. We did it, you did it, I don't know what you did, but I had to thank you in person." Downs widened his arms for a hug, one hand gripping a bottle of Cristal. Dressed in his casual attire—a striped shirt and school tie under a blue blazer—he might have been the spokesman for a tony sherry. "Where's Richard? He needs to be in on this, too."

"He's sanding something on his boat. He works on it when he wants to think."

"He should have people for that. You must have chilled glasses… oh, and ask Lupita for a hand towel, dear heart, while I pop this cork. We did it." His delight lent a spring to his step, an athleticism to his gestures.

"Did what?"

"Jeff Sproul—bless his soul—called me this morning, told me he'd had the most marvelous time at your soiree, and promised he'd make us the loan."

"Congratulations." Her voice lacked its customary warmth. "Are you going to order the new equipment for the factory now or wait until the loan closes?" Despite her antipathy to business and struggles with simple arithmetic, Margaret had closely attended to his remarks about his company, hoping to glean signs of proper management.

"In due time, but first things first. The CEO—*moi*—is entitled to a bonus for arranging this life-saving loan. He and his lovely wife are flying to Paris for a little shopping. Ha, ha. It's been ages since we redid the living room. Your mother is scarcely willing to entertain any more, can you believe it?" He popped the cork, careful not to spill a drop. "You ready for champers?"

"Don't lenders place restrictions on the use of loan proceeds?" Her eyes narrowed behind her tortoiseshell glasses.

"Suggestions, my dear. More in the line of innuendoes. Anyway, we'll get around to that boring equipment in due time, but lord, I've just been released from prison, I can breathe again, stretch my wings. Your mother and I have been living like street people, absolutely hand-to-mouth." He tossed back his drink. "God, it feels good to be rich again—maybe I'll even buy you a new outfit."

"But you're not rich. You're borrowing money you must repay. Don't buy me anything, I can't accept anything from you."

With a wave of his hand, Downs dismissed her refusal. "Of course, I'll repay the loan. I just heard about a failing ice cream company in Minnesota—how could an ice cream company fail there? Eating is Minnesota's state sport. Anyway, the plant can be bought for pennies on the dollar, *pennies*. I might just steal it and ship it all to Athens. We'd save millions over the cost of new equipment, millions we could keep in reserves for executive bonuses."

Margaret stared at her father. His handsome face clouded as she turned away. Her melancholy eyes reflected shallow-graved memories: her father's sins, his depredations against his investors, the contempt she'd endured at school, his obscene joy in buying. "Be careful with that loan. Sproul is a tough man."

"You don't understand what he's doing for me—for us—how he's overriding his minions. He's one of the family, dear heart."

"Then he wants to commit incest." She dropped onto the couch, picked up her research volume.

"What?" Then comprehension rippled across his face. "You must have misunderstood; it must have been harmless gallantry."

"He was pressing so hard against my leg, I had to spear him with my fork. Remember when he claimed his back was acting up? That's why he's giving you the damn loan."

"That's absurd. He's making El Greco Ice Cream the loan because it's a good investment, because we're family."

She paused for a moment, decided she had little choice. "He's making you the loan because he's afraid of Aus. I told him if he didn't make it, my husband would hear how I was assaulted in my own home. You can add cowardice to your pretty boy's list of glowing attributes."

Downs poured himself a third glass of champagne, sipped to keep it from spilling. Stunned, he considered his protégé and wondered how to recast this misunderstanding. "Margaret?"

"Yes?"

"I believe you without reservation, I know you're telling the truth and I'm appalled, utterly appalled." Downs drained his glass. "And you know how much I love you and please, please, this is neither a criticism of you nor an excuse for Jeff. But is it possible he misinterpreted your lack of a wedding ring? Maybe he thought that meant you and Richard have some sort of arrangement."

"Or maybe he's a pig. I can't believe you're defending him. You know I'm allergic to gold."

He recalled the fights they'd had with their teenage daughter, their certainty her allergy was mere rebellion, a biological protest against

Connie. "But how would he know that? I've never even *heard* of anyone else being allergic to gold."

"Decent men don't assault other men's wives; the ring is irrelevant."

"Then why did you force him to make me the loan?"

Her eyes downcast, she murmured, "Because I knew if Sproul didn't make it, you would raise the money somewhere else, probably from innocent investors."

"What?" he began, his mouth forming soundless words. He drifted to the French windows, lowered his forehead against a cool pane. "Margaret, I… " he paused again, smoothed his brow, seeking the comfort of his own reflection in the glass. He stared at the street below, past the blooming trees and dog walkers, past the Mercedes with their consular plates. His gaze caught a sign at the corner of Madison, a mortuary. "I have no idea what you're saying."

"Too many people have lost everything investing with you. If there were any justice, you should have…"

"I should have what? Tell me," he insisted.

"Gone to jail." Regretting her words as she spoke them.

"How dare you? If I were a criminal, how do you suppose I'd have lasted forty years? Why am I on the verge of bankruptcy? If I were a criminal, I would be rich, like your husband."

"That's it," she cried as if slapped. "Go now. Go."

"Why is it we know nothing of Richard's past? Who do you think that man was last night?"

"Get out, get out," Margaret said, her voice rising. "Get out," she shouted.

Downs had a quip about orphans only getting rich in Hollywood, but stifled it when he saw the tears rolling down her face. With one arm she gripped the environmental research volume as though it were a shield, the other outstretched, pointing to the stairs. Downs was overcome with feelings. For himself. He had spent his whole life trying to succeed, caring for his family, doing his best. And now, poised to bring his company back from the abyss, he'd been rejected by his only daughter.

THE COROMANDEL CLOCK ATOP THE fireplace mantle chimed midnight. Two large suitcases stood next to the elevator. Austen perched on the edge of a straight-backed chair, eyeing Margaret's unspoken threat. He had returned half an hour earlier, his cheeks hollowed, his gaze distant. He had spent hours sanding and varnishing the *Alba's* rails, seeking clarity in her clean teak. His hands were scraped raw, his nails filthy, his sweatshirt and knees smudged with grime. Although he reeked of sweat and varnish and sawdust sprinkled his hair, the menacing suitcases shoved aside all thoughts of a shower.

Dressed for town, Margaret rose from the couch as if conscious of being late for an appointment. "My father says you're a criminal," she said, breaking the long silence between them.

Austen stared at the carpet.

"I know you're not. But who was that man last night?"

"He lived down the block when I was a kid."

"So, you did have a childhood. What is he to you?" she asked.

"He's part of the story I promised to tell you. Remember? I have until June." His hands churned in his lap.

"That was our deal before you scared me to death last night. I don't care if your parents were Bonnie and Clyde. My father really is a criminal. Here," she said, handing him a double shot of Laphroaig.

"My father wasn't a criminal; he was a hero." Reaching into his pocket, he handed her his father's medal. "This is the Distinguished Flying Cross, one of the Navy's highest honors. They awarded it to my father posthumously after he was killed leading a bombing raid over Hanoi."

"Oh, Aus, I'm sorry," she said, wondering why he happened to be carrying a medal she'd never seen before. "Tell me about him. Was he kind to you?"

He tossed back the peaty single malt, felt its rushing warmth, and stood to pour another, her suitcases jangling his consciousness like wind chimes. After hours contemplating Roy, he still had no idea what to do and, certain she would leave him if she knew the truth, he'd agonized over what to tell her. He began with his father's life, the story of the quiet American hero, a wing commander still flying combat missions in his early forties. He weaved in his own beginnings as a Navy brat, and when he arrived at his teenage years his pauses grew more pronounced. He kept his history truthful and nearly complete, but failed to utter the name Kawadsky or mention San Diego, claiming the Navy moved them often. He described Roy as a ne'er-do-well he'd fallen in with after his mother bolted. Cross was now an alcoholic leech demanding money. Skipping past Mexico, he finished with his enlistment.

Margaret swirled her Dows port in a crystal tumbler. "Why have you insisted you never knew your mother?"

"Does it sound better to say she dumped me?" said Austen, downcast. "Which hurts more? Being orphaned at birth or having your mother run off with some jerk and never come back? I… No." He paused, trembling, staring at his glass, shocked at the words he'd spoken aloud for the first time in his life, stunned by their lack of understanding and compassion. Memories flooded his false condemnation. It had been he who'd jumped her lover, punching him furiously until the bigger man crushed his nose, knocking him to the floor. Like an Old Testament Yahweh, it had been Eddie who banished his mother from his sight.

"I'm so sorry." She stroked his varnish-stained sleeve.

"No, wait," he cried, aflame with his insight. "It wasn't her fault. I should have tried to understand what she was going through. I was such an idiot, a classic self-righteous teenager who saw everything in black and white. Hell, it was my fault." Austen let the cracked dam flood, his rushing words explaining how he'd tortured his mother, scorned her, and refused to talk to her for months—a nasty trick he'd aped from his father. She'd been a lonely housebound widow deserving compassion rather than contempt.

Now Austen sobbed from grief—the epiphany that he had driven her away, that her flight had been his fault—bleeding him. Without prompting from Margaret, he retold his story from his mother's side, describing his father's shortcomings: his escape to the garage each night after a wolfed dinner, his refusal to have a real conversation with his wife, his perpetual eagerness to rejoin the fleet. He was no longer certain of his father's rectitude or her laxity. Her weaknesses may have arisen from neglect. He recalled her single highball each day and how he'd ridiculed her for alcoholism. Perhaps atoning for his incomplete story, Austen overstated his role in his mother's unhappiness. "I guess I got what I deserved, it really was my fault."

"That's absurd, you were a child. Do you think she's still alive?" Margaret's eyes were moist over her husband's pain; she now understood his shyness with women, his reserve.

"I haven't seen her since the day I left home."

She winced at the hurt in his voice, her empathy flowing unbidden. Wanting to ease his pain, she shifted the topic and her tone, bantering, "So, your father died in a plane crash, your mother's probably still alive. Not so bad genetically. Mine on the other hand? Sheesh." She grinned at the thought of her Abuela. Was her Argentine grandmother going a little senile? Given to fanciful embellishment, Abuela had described her most recent late husband—the fourth she had buried—as a grandee with vast holdings. Since Abuela had married without warning at eighty, Margaret had neither attended the wedding nor met her new step-grandfather before he, too, passed away. She had often flagellated herself over her procrastination in visiting her grandmother, a woman now too frail to travel. But the two had kept up their lively correspondence. She knew her once wealthy grandmother hovered near poverty and suspected that this loss of position, coupled with loneliness, were the source of her escalating delusions. The two women mailed each other checks, Margaret annoyed by her grandmother's refusal to cash hers. Yet she was touched by the old woman's generosity and saved Abuela's worthless checks in her desk drawer.

"May I take those back upstairs?" He asked, pointing to the suitcases.

"Not yet, buster, I'm still asking the questions here." She laughed, relaxing back onto the couch, relieved by their progress. In a light tone that belied her inquiry, she said, "But you're still hiding something, all that Sturm und Drang last night couldn't have been over an old friend simply wanting money. Explain that please."

He selected his words with care. "Cross's mind is gone from too many drugs—he was a druggie even as a kid. He's dreamed up this crazy convoluted story about me owing him money."

"He told you all this in thirty seconds last night?"

"Ah." He closed his eyes and pursed his lips. No one had forced him to marry a lawyer. "I saw him today before I went to the boatyard."

"So rather than tell him to get lost last night, you agreed to meet this crazed drug addict to explain why you didn't owe him anything? Is that your story?"

"Margaret, please. It's late, can we continue this another day? I really need a shower. May I please take your bags upstairs?"

"All right——shouldn't be too hard, they're empty—but you're telling me the rest of the story. All those little details you glossed over, like where you went to high school, who your girlfriends were. What that little J tattoo stands for. The whole truth and nothing but the truth."

"They're *empty*?"

"Of course. You didn't really think I was going to leave you?" She leaned over and kissed him on the mouth. "That's sad about your father, Aus, but at least you have a memory you can be proud of. My father really is a criminal—I'm sorry, but I can't stand him. You can't imagine how I felt as a teenager when he went bankrupt the second time. I was so certain it was all my fault—the money he swindled from my friends' fathers bought my clothes and paid my tuition—I died every day at school." She stopped, struck by the vivid recollection, then waved it away. "Do you know he conned his secretary into putting two hundred thousand dollars—her entire life savings—into that ridiculous company?"

"You've mentioned that." His sins made her father's those of a schoolboy.

"Hug me," she said. With her arms crushed around him, her head nestled in the crook of his neck, she couldn't see the anguish on husband's face.

CHAPTER 42

PREPARATIONS

AUSTEN WALKED INTO A REGAL gun store on East 40th that sold shotguns the price of a house in Brooklyn. The clerk had heard the request so many times his eyes didn't stray from the *Times* crossword puzzle. "We don't sell handguns. Try Little Italy."

Austen found the next gun shop on Grand Street. Inspecting the racks of shotguns and rifles that lined the walls, he was flooded with memories of grinders, heat, freezing rain, bugs, and mud. The middle-aged Asian proprietor shook his head and folded his arms across his chest. "No. This honest business. No permit, no gun."

"I know about permits, but I wouldn't be keeping it in New York. Isn't there some way to buy one fast?"

"Find a gun show. Easy to buy there. Jersey or Pennsylvania."

THREE DAYS LATER, THE NEW owner of an unregistered 9-millimeter Glock, Austen stood in the drizzle outside Barney's, clenching a roll of quarters. He punched a number on a public telephone. "It's me."

"Me? Me? No way. I'm *me*. And me can't be calling me." Roy laughed, his words a rivery slur.

"Goddamn it, Roy. Remember New York?"

"New York? New York, New York is a wonderful town, the Bronx— Wad? Wad, is that you?"

"Get a pencil and paper."

"Don't need one, man."

Austen frowned at his watch. Three o'clock in Las Vegas and Roy was useless.

"Goddamn it, you're drunk. Get sober by tomorrow morning at nine." He strode down Madison—heedless of the pampered shoppers and tourists gawking at the avenue's stylish display windows—until he came to a genteel sporting goods store. He bought swimming goggles and fins.

Next morning at nine. "You sober?"

"Sorry about yesterday, dude," said Roy. "Touch of the desert flu, man. I got my pencil and paper ready."

"I'll tell you this once, then I'll repeat it while you write it down. Then you're going to read it back to me. Understood?" He spelled out his instructions as if Roy were an unpromising fourth grader.

"I got it," Roy said. "First, I make another copy of these instructions and stick them in a shoe. Then get some plain clothes, lose my jewelry, and try to look square. Maybe wear a baseball hat, hide my hair—that's no problem." He laughed, rueful. "You're not shitting me about these dudes? Can't fucking believe Wad's a big-time dealer."

"That's why we're meeting in Hawaii. I've got to get out of town. If the Colombians find out you have their money, your dental records won't ID your corpse. Go on."

Roy read off his list: He was to tell no one where he was going, catch a flight to Honolulu Thursday morning, use cash and an alias for the ticket, and check into any Waikiki motel that didn't require identification. Austen would meet him on the beach at sunset in front of the Royal Hawaiian.

"Repeat it again."

A BRILLIANT MAN WHOSE STARE alone could inspire terror, the archbishop was of middling height, soft from a long life of disdaining exercise. Despite his age, his cheeks were pink and unlined, his scalp balding, wisps of white hair nestling above his ears. The politically gifted prelate was counted by many—including himself—among New York City's top power brokers. With his driver double-parked outside on Madison Avenue, the archbishop sailed into the Carlyle Hotel with his monsignor secretary scuttling after him. He waved benevolently at the refined old women and the chic European tourists waiting for tables and glanced about for the generous donor to whom he had allotted fifteen minutes for afternoon tea. He was looking for an elderly man, one who had realized his wealth would soon go either to charity or grasping heirs. The prelate checked his favorite icon, his Patek Philippe. Four o'clock. A slight tap on his shoulder. He turned sharply, his glare fading as he beheld a tall smiling man.

"I'm Richard Austen, your Excellency," he said, enunciating the honorific with care, as if it were Greek. "Thank you for seeing me on such short notice. I have a table in the corner." Austen had arrived early, securing a booth with a twenty-dollar tip to the obliging Irish maître d'. Glancing at the two priests, he grinned awkwardly. "I thought only nuns traveled in pairs."

"What?" said the archbishop sharply. He cocked his eyebrows, then caught himself, realizing his donor was nervous. He manufactured a smile. "We can learn much from our holy sisters." He'd heard of Austen, but knew nothing about the reclusive billionaire. Instead of the ancient he'd conjured, the prelate beheld a well-proportioned man in his prime—his middle forties—graying but fit, superbly dressed. The trio settled into the booth and ordered the afternoon tea service.

"Mr. Austen, we understand that you're behind so much of the anonymous charity that has succored our downtrodden. And now this magnificent bequest—what a difference your gift will make for the archdiocese. We cannot thank you enough."

Austen pressed his fingers into the crisp tablecloth, nodded reluctantly. Then an odd, sheepish grin. "Just trying to sneak into heaven."

"*Heaven*. May we assume you're Catholic?" The archbishop was mildly puzzled. In his experience, the rich spoke portentously, as if their words were the gifts of the Magi. This man appeared modest, if not self-effacing.

Austen hesitated, glanced toward the far wall, taking in its colorful cartoon frieze. He closed his eyes for a moment. "I was raised in the Church, but stopped attending mass when I was around fourteen."

"Ah, yes," he said, masking an inward sigh with a glance about the lively room, wondering whether anyone recognized him, knowing his simple black cassock contained few hints that he was a prince of the Church. "Mr. Austen, we know your time is precious. Is there anything we might do for you?"

"Would it be possible for us to speak privately?"

"Monsignor Rogers has a number of calls to return for us." The younger priest rose, departing with a fixed nod toward his prelate. "Now, how may we help you?"

"I believe my time is running out, it may only be a matter of days before…"

"Your time?" The archbishop repeated, massaging his forehead, surprised for the first time in months. "Before what?"

"Before my past catches up with me," Austen answered quietly. "Before I'm killed. May I tell you how I made my fortune?" Fixing his gaze upon the table, he began. A half hour later, encouraged by the archbishop's occasional gentling, Austen had described coming to Manhattan twenty years earlier with nothing, swiftly amassing one of the city's largest real estate fortunes. Faltering from time to time, he'd confessed his crimes. In recounting his drug smuggling and cop killings, Austen was pitiless toward himself, ignoring circumstances all but a grand inquisitor would have viewed as extenuating. "I swear I didn't know cocaine was bad then, I swear it. In those days everyone thought it was harmless."

Grave, but with innate sympathy, the archbishop examined the troubled man opposite him, marveling how few criminals seemed to escape justice.

"If something were to happen to me and the police investigated," Austen said, "they might discover my true identity and criminality. The foundation's money—*your* bequest—might be forfeited to the state as drug money. My name would be ruined, my wife not only bereft but humiliated."

"Ah," the archbishop murmured, wishing for the thousandth time the Church's finances were not his personal cross to bear. "Are these men Catholic? Perhaps it would make a difference if they learned you've donated your fortune to us?"

"No, the dollar is their only god," Austen said. He paused, perhaps searching for prettier words. "This is awkward, your Excellency, but if I am slain, a lengthy investigation wouldn't be in the Church's best interest."

A worldly man, the archbishop nodded his understanding.

"My wife knows nothing about my past. If something were to happen to me, her innocence—her inability to think of who might want to harm me—would lead the police to suspect her. It might take them weeks to figure out Margaret inherits nothing under the terms of my will—she insisted on that as a condition to marrying me—that she had every incentive in the world to keep me alive. Knowing she wouldn't be interrogated would be a comfort."

"If this terrible event should come to pass, we will do our utmost to help Margaret."

"A botched kidnapping for ransom that led to my death would unlikely require an investigation into my past."

"We're certain it will never come to that," the archbishop said, filing away Austen's suggestion, then taking his hands into his own. "Would you like to make this a formal reconciliation, my son?"

"Thank you, your Excellency, but it wouldn't help. I'm beyond forgiveness." If only he were truly Catholic, if only he believed in confession. He knew every priest in the world could say the magic incantation, could forgive his sins in exchange for a penance of prayer. But their mumbled benedictions would be so much voodoo. And if restitution alone would salve his conscience, his burden would have been lifted years ago—he had donated millions without relief.

"Yet the penance you assign yourself, this eternal tormenting of your soul, is far worse than any we might require. You've done what you can; you've delivered your ill-gotten gains many times over to charity." The archbishop waved off his approaching assistant a third time with the mere straightening of two fingers. How extraordinary, he mused, a self-aware billionaire, one more conscious of his shortcomings than his success. He considered Austen's self-inflicted wounds, how they benefitted the Church, the vast good the Church dispensed daily, and smiled inwardly at the Lord's unfathomable ways. "Since you won't forgive yourself, would you like us to forgive these sins?"

"Thank you, Father."

"Then make the sign of the cross. Let us pray." The archbishop eschewed the modern verse in favor of the more satisfying Latin. He prayed, forgave Austen his sins, and then sighed, knowing the man would never forgive himself.

HIS NECK TURTLED INTO HIS wrestler's shoulders, Billy Cutter glanced up through his eyebrows at his employer. "What if I take a week's vacation with Stephanie and the baby and just sit in on the Rowan meetings?" He was desperate to make this Hawaii trip, to be on the team from the outset. Why was Austen smiling?

"You have to run the show here. You're in charge." Austen was browsing among his bookshelves, tugging at spines, examining one book after another before returning them to the shelves.

"But, boss, everything's running fine, construction will be done in a couple months, no need to sit on the contractor anymore."

"Call me Aus. Next trip, you're going." He set *Middlemarch* atop several others on his desk and pressed his intercom. "MJ, please have the travel people cut first-class tickets to Tahiti for Billy and his family. Hotel, too. They're taking a vacation as soon as Regency's finished."

Billy's mouth dropped open, the word *Aus* on his lips. He popped his knuckles, more thrilled at this new familiarity than the vacation. A moment later, the New Yorker in him wondered what the hell was going on, why he was being banished. He chased the thought away, blaming his paranoia on his damned liquid diet. "Tahiti? You're not kidding? Whoa, that's fucking—sorry, that's really great. Thanks a ton, Aus."

"You deserve it, Billy. You do good work. I appreciate your loyalty. You would have made a fine Marine."

Billy blushed.

"Let me ask you a question. When would you sell Regency?"

Sensing a test, Billy slowly repeated the question to himself. Why would they ever sell their latest crown jewel? "When someone offers a lot more than it's worth?"

"No. Here it is: You sell it the day the last tenant moves in."

"You kidding? This year?" Billy looked aghast.

"Sell it and start over with another big construction deal, maybe take a look at the lower West Side."

Billy dropped his bull neck to the right, reveling in its pleasing crack. "I'm in, Aus. We'll do it again."

"Good. Another thing. This may sound a little strange, but if something were to happen to me in Hawaii, the plane crashed or I was hit by a tidal wave or a bus, have Brendan call the archbishop immediately. Just to be sure, you call him, too."

"Nothing's going to happen to you. Just stay away from those big waves."

Austen walked around his desk and Billy rose. "Thinking about that reminded me of a couple things. Like I said, you've been a very good partner. You need to know I really appreciate it; I always have." He extended his large hand, surprising Billy. Austen smiled as they shook hands. "One thing you might work on, though. When you lie—yes, when you lie, don't stop me." Austen laughed. "It's OK. When you lie, you always say *huh* first to buy yourself time to think. You give it away every time. You might work on that."

CHAPTER 43

MOONLIGHT

MARGARET LAY SLEEPING, HER FACE and hands alabaster in the moonlit bedroom. Dressed for his seven-a.m. flight to San Francisco, Austen stole in to kiss her cheek, but hesitated, listening to her breathe, admiring her, marveling over how such a woman could have ever married him. He choked back a sob at the thought of losing her. She stirred, her eyes fluttered open, she sat up slowly, holding the sheet to her chest.

"Aus?"

"I'm here," he said.

"Why aren't you in bed? Oh, right, Hawaii. Be careful."

"Margaret?"

"Yes?"

"I, I really love you. You have to know that." He wiped his cheeks.

"Does that mean I get a kiss good-bye? I love you, too. You smell nice." She kissed his lips closed-mouthed, mindful of morning breath. "Please take good care of yourself."

"I will."

THE FLIGHT WAS HALF EMPTY, but first class was full. "Will you be having breakfast this morning, sir?"

"No, thank you, ma'am," Austen replied to the attendant, glancing up from the Eliot novel. "Just black coffee. Maybe toast later."

"What happened to the Ferrari?" Austen asked Parson six hours later, curbside at SFO.

"I should have torched that sucker for the insurance. It goes to the damn shop more often than Claire gets her hair done."

"Her station wagon's not so bad. It gives you a solid-citizen look."

"Good. Because I'll need it. We may be driving a wagon, but we're definitely going off it tonight. Drinking starts at four."

Neither man would have welcomed a sobriety test, but Austen might have passed. Parson had indulged himself. Blissful over his sauce-laden chops from Sam's Grill, he was enjoying a cigar—a Cohiba his London tobacconist disguised with bands from Honduras—and his own stories, apocryphal versions of their mutual past. The two were sprawled on the rough, granite steps of the Bank of America Plaza in the Financial District. Puffing away, Parson sat with his back against the chilly stone planter, his smoke trailing the fog that fingered down Nob Hill.

"You cold?" Austen asked. Clamping his hands in his armpits, his chill sprang more from fear than fog. But he had to do it.

"Cold? It's never cold in San Francisco. Am I cold? Hell, yes, but since my club has a fetish about coats and ties, we're stuck smoking these outside. You used to wear a tie in the shower, and now you've gone Oregon on me. No jacket, no tie, no shave—when was the last time you shaved?"

As if through wavering atop Acapulco's La Quebrada cliff, Austen decided it was time to dive. Ignoring his friend's banter, he asked, "Remember that day on the beach at Pendleton when we got drunk and were shooting each other with beers? I told you I would tell you my story if I thought you could help?"

"I don't remember shit one about the Corps," Parson razzed, missing Austen's somber note. He waved off a portly security guard with a ten-dollar bill. "Wait, wait, it's coming back to me: Hated the clothes, loved the guns."

"Those days you weren't always serving bullshit like hot lunches to the poor."

"Hey." Stung, Parson searched his friend's face, seeking a smile to soften the blow. "You're not OK. Fuck the 'gars." He tossed his toward a cement trash bin. It bounced off, a shower of glowing ashes. "Sorry, man, let's go to Trader Vic's. It's closing in a few weeks—it's quiet—and if we walk, I can keep smoking and sober up." Shoer retrieved his Cuban, blew on it and draped his arm around his friend's shoulder. "I'm sorry, man, you know I've always sucked as a listener. I'll shut up."

As they walked down Kearney Street, Austen stared at the pavement, as if still contemplating his plunge. "Here it is: My real name is Edward Kawadsky and I'm from—"

"What the fuck?" cried Parson.

"Parse, this is going to be hard enough. You can ask all the questions you want, but let me get it out before I lose my nerve. OK?"

"Sure, Aus, sorry."

An hour later, they were ensconced in a red leather booth in the restaurant's fabled bar, halfway through their second navy grog. Austen was still unraveling his tale, Parson sitting in profile to him, in the manner of a priest hearing confession. "If Cross fingers me, I'm cooked. I can't prove self-defense. They recovered a couple kilos of cocaine from my bloody van—my prints were all over it—and they canonized those two cops. I've been hiding for twenty-five years, and now I'm rich. Any jury in the country would fry me."

Fathoming Austen's danger, Parson nodded, searching for a way out. "Maybe you take half a dozen lie detector tests—use the FBI's top guys, no question of bias—maybe the DA would buy that, not bring charges. It's not admissible in court, but maybe that would head him off." Parson sipped his grog, swore, dismissing his own hypothesis almost as quickly as he spoke it. An ambitious DA would view Austen as his great white whale and his prosecution a sensational, career-making case. "But let's go back to something else. Maybe Cross *would* stay quiet if you pay him off. OK so he hits you up again when he burns through the money, but what's in it for him to rat you out?"

"Nothing. But he's a fall-down drunk, he loves to talk. Money needs an explanation, and someone will keep him talking till the truth spills out."

"Maybe not." Parson scratched his head.

"When Margaret finds out who I really am—what I really am—she'll leave me. Look how much she hates her father."

"You're butt-ass wrong, Aus, as always," Parson said. "You just told me and I'm still here, ain't I? I'm still your best friend, I still love you. I understand, and so will she. She'll forgive you."

"You really think so?"

"I'm positive. But her love won't keep you out of jail. You got any ideas how to handle this short of wasting a bullet on Cross?"

"Here it is." Austen laid out the plan he'd conceived in the weeks since Cross's visit, pausing only when the funereal waiter asked about another round.

When he finished, Parson whistled, "That's got more holes than my general manager's resume. And it would be hell on Margaret. Better to just off the motherfucker."

Austen winced. "I know. But that's where you come in, that's why I need your help, why you have to be there the moment the cops finish with her. It's the worst part—she may never forgive me."

"No, she will." Parson intoned, uneasy over his upcoming role. "She's a lawyer, she'll understand you had no choice. She'll probably even understand about giving away the money. I never will."

"I have to… to regain my sense of…" Austen faltered, ashamed. "It's the only way to handle Cross."

Fog had misted the half-moon when the pair stepped from under the restaurant's corrugated tin roof. For once as quiet as his friend, Parson crossed his arms against the chill and buttoned his collar. "I'll give you a ride to the airport in the morning."

Austen gripped Parson's elbow and smiled. "You're the best, Parse."

"You, too, Scout."

CHAPTER 44

ALOHA

Jᴇᴛ Rᴏᴡᴀɴ ᴡᴀs ᴡᴇᴀʀɪɴɢ ᴀ pearl-buttoned square-dancing shirt and jeans. Both were dirt brown. His left foot was in an open-toed cast he'd painted brown. With his silver and turquoise bolo tie, he might have hobbled into Duke's straight from judging a rodeo. Yet the gash on his forehead and the plaster cast somehow made him seem more energetic, more alive. He slipped on his brown glasses and read, weighing Austen's neat printing on the yellow legal pad, then feigning a frown to mask his elation. "Sumbitch." He looked across the restaurant terrace toward the gently ruffled ocean, and frowned again, exhaling his cigarette toward the lissome palms.

Austen had come straight from Honolulu International to meet Jet. Unshaven, he wore a tennis shirt and shorts. He forked a sliver of mahi mahi and, indifferent to Rowan's reaction to his proposal, wondered whether the old man intended to eat at all, the salad before him untouched. Sorrowful, he pondered the old cowboy's fate.

"Twenty per cent on the back-end and you got a deal, son."

"No sir, I'm through negotiating." Austen turned to the waitress, smiled. "The check, please."

Grumbling, Jet stifled a cuss word over Austen's air of finality. "So, when do I get the fifty grand?"

"The moment the contract is signed. The balance the day the Japanese sell your note to me."

"Deal, son." Jet extended a brown hand. "How soon can your lawyers get us something to John Hancock? My daddy always said you could tell a man by his handshake. Had a grip like a blacksmith's. Course the old fool couldn't tell a hen from a heifer." Jet laughed aloud, clutched his side. "Busted a couple ribs when my big bay threw me. Gonna shoot that horse." In fact, he'd been whiskey drunk and pitched face-forward down the circular metal staircase outside his condominium. Had he fallen elsewhere, his lawyer wryly remarked, he might have collected a few dollars, but since he was not only the owner but the designer of the Kahala Diamond, he was lacking somebody to sue.

"I'll ask Brendan to get us a draft by Thursday. Have your lawyer work out the details with him."

"I never drink while the sun's out—never have—but this here's as special as Easter in Juárez. You bring your checkbook? Last I heard, money don't fax better than a fart." Jet contemplated the feel of fifty thousand dollars and the luxurious woman who would once again be happy to see him.

"See you soon." Austen rose, dropped a couple hundred on the table, and strode out.

Billowing cumulous clouds clung to the distant horizon, obscuring the tourists' sunset. Austen shrugged his aching shoulders, rolling them back and forth, padding along the meandering high-tide line. He'd been swimming hard up and down Waikiki beach for three days—thirty minutes at a crack every three hours, each time a little farther. His sunburn was browning, his tangled curly hair matted with salt, his unshaven cheeks white-whiskered, his glasses in his hotel suite. An acquaintance might have passed him without a second glance. He was scanning the middle distance for Roy, searching for an outlandish figure among the monochrome tourists. He looked beyond a group of plump Germans drinking coffee from ceramic thermoses. Then he nearly stepped on Roy Cross.

"Whoa, whoa, it's me. Gotcha, didn't I?" asked Roy. With effort, he pushed himself up from the sand, and extended a hand.

"Jesus," Austen cried, so startled he shook Roy's hand.

Poor Roy was bald, his baby-smooth, hot-pink scalp contrasting with his withered tanned face like Neapolitan ice cream. He wore baggy Bermuda shorts and an ABC Store aloha shirt. He hadn't put on a disguise; he'd taken one off. With a shy smile, Roy rubbed his head. "Is it burned? Should have used more sunblock. Maybe I should wear this." He pulled a Dodgers baseball cap from his shorts.

"Let's walk."

"Hey, like old times. Me and you on the beach, maybe we catch a couple waves?"

"I'd sink." Austen looked Roy in the eyes, wishing to drill this point deep, wondering whether Roy was already high, then wondering at his rising sympathy. Half his age, Roy was more of a wreck than Jet Rowan. "Haven't swum since Mexico with you. You killed that along with everything else."

"These waves ain't worth a shit anyway."

"Bad news—"

"You don't have the dough?" Roy yelped.

"Sit down," Austen commanded. "No, face the hotel. You need to be on the look-out."

"What the fuck?"

"I've been followed." Austen stood over Roy, scanning, his fists on his hips, explaining he'd been trailed by the vengeful Colombians. A pair were on the beach, but he insisted they were safe because the narcotraficantes wanted him alive, to torture him before dispensing their final mercy. They couldn't snatch him in front of hundreds of witnesses. "Don't worry," Austen said, flashing the Glock under his sweatshirt, swearing he'd take a few with him.

"Whoa, whoa. Oh, shit." Roy choked, figuring he was directly in the line of fire. "Dude, this is way heavy shit. Maybe I should split and we hook up in Vegas."

"Your call, but I've got the money, and if they toe-tag me here, it's lost forever. I've got a plan."

"Be right back," Roy said, pushing himself up. He trotted over to an Australian couple, borrowed matches he didn't need, and returned, stopping a couple yards away from Austen, lying down, shimmying into the sand like a horned toad.

Austen explained they would meet at 11 the next morning, take a cab to the airport, and if the Colombians were nowhere to be seen, board a flight to Los Angeles. If followed, they would stash their bags in an airport locker and taxi back to the tourist wharf, where a chartered fishing boat would await them. Even if the Colombians tailed them, they'd be stuck on the dock. They would fish for a couple hours—killing time until the late afternoon's mainland flights—and then get dropped off five miles away at the Kahala Hilton, a resort on Diamond Head's far side. They'd be back at the airport before the Colombians realized they weren't on the returning boat.

"You got a boat?" Roy asked.

"No, you're renting one first thing tomorrow morning. Here's the cash and info on the boat I picked out."

"But what if they follow us in a boat?"

"If they do, I'll drop you off and stay with the boat. They'll follow me."

"But what about the guys running the boat? What happens if the malandros get to them later?"

Austen explained the small boat he'd picked had only a single captain, and as long as Roy never looked at him or said anything, he'd be fine. "Get bigger sunglasses—darker ones that cover more of your

face—and zinc oxide for your nose and cheeks and keep the hat on. Do
that and the captain will never be able to identify you."

"TRANKING THAT DUDE WAS A good idea. Do I still have to wear this
gun?" Roy and Austen had stowed the sedated captain in the *LuLuBelle's*
forward cabin. Roy pulled the Glock from his trunks, rubbing the soft
flesh where the gun had left its imprint. "I still don't get why that dick
had to see me with a gun."

"If the captain thinks you're a bad guy, his memory will be worse."
Austen pocketed the gun, took the wheel, glanced at the oil pressure,
and eased the boat out of neutral. He brought the bow around on a
heading southeast of Diamond Head and pulled the throttle back. The
small white craft accelerated, a gassy rainbow sheen on the water behind.

"How long's he out for?"

"This afternoon. He'll be fine. Reel in those poles." As he scanned
the horizon, Austen cursed, plagued by Roy and his own desperate
plan, certain of Margaret's loss. He buoyed himself with the thought
that with so many benefiting from his death, few would question it.
He heard the engine's knocking and, checking the tachometer, eased
off the throttle.

"Aye, aye, Admiral." Roy positioned himself for maximum sun and
closed his eyes. He was content. In the back seat of their airport-bound
taxi, Austen had handed him an aluminum attaché case packed with
rows of hundred-dollar bills. To his surprise, Austen had let him place
the briefcase in the locker and keep the key.

"You got sandwiches in there?" Roy asked a few minutes later, pointing at a Styrofoam container.

"Don't touch it."

"That's cool, man." Roy wished he had a bottle, figured the captain must like his booze and keep a little something aboard. Gingerly, he clambered through the hatch into the small, triangular cabin, high enough to sit in, capable of sheltering three in dirty weather. The old sailor lay sprawled on his stomach on a foam pad, mouth open, drooling.

Austen adjusted his course when he spied the Kahala Hilton's towers, killing the motor after a few minutes. Hearing Roy whistle as he rummaged below, Austen wondered how he could be so nonchalant in the presence of the man he had once condemned to death. He had to know.

"Look what I found." Roy thrust an arm through the hatch, waving a bottle of drug store vodka. "You want a hit, man?"

"Get up here," ordered Austen.

"Why'd you shut the engine off?" Roy's smile died at the gun pointing at his chest. "Oh, shit, shit, shit, please don't shoot me."

"Shut up."

"Take the money back. I won't say nothing." Shaking, Roy dropped to his knees. "I swear to the blessed redeemer."

Bang. The shot was swallowed by the whispering sea, silencing Roy. "Now, I want the truth."

"Anything, Wad. I swear, I'll tell you anything. God, you shot me," he screamed, shoving a hand inside his shorts. "My leg's all wet."

"You wet yourself. I want the truth about Mexico, why you set me up to die."

As the boat corked along a couple miles offshore, a frantic Roy babbled an abridged version of his favorite tale, how he'd taken a bullet holding off the federales and then gone to prison rather than betray his best friend. Unfazed by contradictions that would trouble a first-grader, he readily assented to any correction Austen made.

Bang. Austen's shot splintered the gunwale two feet from where Roy huddled small. "I want the truth. Not you parroting every goddamn word I say to save yourself." Austen closed his eyes, knowing it was all wrong, remembering the denouement he had long envisioned, a confession heroically wrought from a malevolent villain. He sat in silence—it would have been peaceful but for Roy's whimpering—eyes closed, sun warm on his face, the black metal alive in his hand. Anxiety over Margaret cutting through his anger. Austen tried again, demanding that Roy explain how he knew the dead cops.

"How do you think I knew them? Tell me, man and I'll—"

Bang. He fired the pistol again, this time aiming for silence. Beaten, he shook his head and gripped the wheel, nosing the bow toward the Kahala and its private beach. He listened to a blend of sounds: the engine's struggle, the trade winds, an occasional gull, and Roy's moans. Watching the coral reef below, he put the boat in neutral two hundred yards offshore and reached into a shoulder bag.

"Get up. Put everything in this bag. It's waterproof—make sure it's zipped tight. The bag goes on this leash and then attaches to your ankle, like a board. Swim to the left of those rocks."

"You're not shooting me?"

"Get your clothes off." Austen was defeated, his voice barely audible over the motor. "When you get to the beach, talk to no one. Take that path to the right between those lava rocks. Don't go inside the hotel, just jump in the first taxi you see. There's a flight to LA in a couple hours."

Roy shed his clothes. "I still have the key."

"Keep it."

"You're giving me the dough?" Roy tucked the key in his wallet and then sealed the waterproof bag with care. "You, like, couldn't get this boat any closer, could you?"

"No. Oh, goddamn it. Quick, get down," Austen shouted, shoving Roy to the deck, forcing his head down, firing the Glock at the horizon. "Here they come, the Colombians are in that ski boat. Keep down—down, goddamn it. Slip over the side the second I say go. Don't start swimming until I'm a couple hundred yards away. They may not see you in the water."

On command, a panicked Roy slithered over the gunwale, clutching the plastic bag, staying underwater far longer than one might expect of a man whose every breath was labored. When he surfaced, his head pounding from a lack of oxygen, he dared not look back. Instead, improvising a back stroke to allow himself to breathe, he paddled to the rich shore.

Less than an hour later, a still trembling Roy was praying that Wad had done the right thing and shot it out with the Colombians, knowing if he surrendered, they would torture Roy's name from his lips. Looking back over his shoulder every twenty paces, he half-staggered into the balmy airport, fetched his bag and Wad's briefcase from the locker. At last as wealthy as his dreams, he murmured a prayer for Wad's eternal soul when his United flight cleared Oahu's eastern shore.

The newspapers describing Richard Austen's mysterious, bloody death in Hawaii followed Roy home to Las Vegas. He dove into a drug-filled oblivion, certain Wad had given him up to the malandros, fearing he had just days to live. When—thanks to an emergency room stomach pump—he resurfaced alive and mostly sober a week later, it occurred to him that he'd outsmarted the Colombians once before. He could do it again. Leaving the AC blasting, a note for his girlfriend Sheila atop a thin stack of hundreds, he left town. Once back in Hollywood, Roy devoted himself to indulging in that city's pleasures, leading one to wonder whether his fortune or his body would fail him first.

CHAPTER 45

THE WINDOW

OUTSIDE, HAWAII'S TRADE WINDS SOFTENED the tropical sun, another perfect day in paradise. Inside police headquarters, the airless observation room was too warm, almost stifling, smelling of sweat and fear. Puzzled by the crime, the Honolulu detectives gazed into the adjoining interrogation room through the scratched two-way mirror. A female suspect was quietly crying.

"Killers cry, too." Fujikawa snapped his gum, irritated at having his theory dismissed out of hand. "Remember Dodsworth? That sick fuck cried all night." The young detective was jabbing his pencil into the yellowing soundproof wall tile, punching out a pattern that might have had some meaning to him, leaving his art to posterity, pleased that it annoyed Randolph. Fujikawa had a knack for not getting along.

"Learn something here, Fuj. Look at her. She's trying not to cry," said Sergeant Randolph. "If she had him whacked, she'd either be sitting there buffing her nails or working her ass off trying to cry." When Randolph joined the force twenty-three years earlier, he'd thought everyone guilty and, while time had done little to dim that conviction, he had gained a feel for innocence.

Margaret was pale, her face drawn, her teary eyes too tender for contact lenses, her nose a fluish pink. She sat bent at a rubber-topped metal table, her hands aflutter. Randolph watched her raise her glasses above her forehead and dab at her eyes with a tissue and then breathe to calm herself. She reached into her bag, flipped open a silver compact, and stared at its mirror until it slipped from her fingers. She took a lipstick from her purse and held it aloft, questioning her hand, gauging its reliability.

Randolph dropped his head against the mirror and said, "You watching, Fuj? You see that, Sherlock? She can't even put on her lipstick without smearing it across her face and you think she's dirty?"

She was crying aloud again. The detectives heard her sobs through the tinny loudspeaker as she wiped the bolt of lipstick from her chin.

"If she's innocent, she'll pass the polygraph. Let's strap her in." Fujikawa popped his gum and stabbed another hole in the tile.

"If the suits in the lobby aren't shitting us, nobody—least of all her—had motive one to whack this guy. She gets squat. Maybe the pope needed the dough, maybe we don't have a hit. I don't know. Maybe it was a botched kidnapping. Billionaire fights back and gets whacked." Randolph yanked his faded aloha shirt from his trousers to ease his flaring ulcer.

"Remember that movie where the wife's real smart and gets around the will so she gets all the dough?"

"Movie is right," Randolph said. "She's earning a fucking Oscar in there if she had him whacked. This doesn't add up. Maybe there's no vic, maybe Austen just skipped. Call the Coast Guard. He could be alive."

"Maybe she's Snow White, but he's definitely toast. His blood everywhere, six slugs in the boat, his bloody, broken glasses, that screaming radio call."

The phone rang.

"Fujikawa." The young detective cradled the phone between his ear and shoulder, his pencil boring into the graffiti-flecked tile. "Yeah? Tell him to blow it out his ass. She's coming out when we're finished." He hung up the phone. "Fat boy's getting antsy. Maybe he's worried she'll spill, maybe he's in this with her."

"Wish we knew a real lawyer who did this trust crap—damn city attorneys don't know shit. Her lawyer could be bullshitting us about

nobody getting rich." Randolph rubbed the bald spot above his forehead, smoothing the wrinkles. The woman's sobs made him feel tired,
too old for the job. He picked up the artist's sketch that was proba-
ble cause to detain every fourth tourist in the city. The drunk captain
had apologized, blaming his passenger's sunglasses and baseball cap,
remembering only that the missing man's companion had a gun in his
shorts, guessing he was bald. Randolph's stomach churned. "Skold and
Hassenfelt still at the airport?"

"Yeah, they'll call if they have anything."

Randolph's expression softened when he glanced at Margaret.
Keeping his eyes on her, he said, "You're right, he's history. It wasn't a
random, and as for motives, we got jack. Actually, I'm kind of liking
a botched kidnapping. Makes sense financially, and that's why they
didn't do the captain—wasn't supposed to go down that way. The vic
gets a gun in the ribs, gets on a boat that's supposed to rendezvous with
a second boat, but he fights back, gets shot, they toss him overboard,
panic, forget the captain and split."

"That's a stretch. Why not just grab him off the beach?"

"I don't know. That's why they're criminals, they're fucking stupid.
Least we know it ain't the cowboy." Randolph laughed, recalling their
interview with the inconsolable Jet Rowan. "Talk about crying. Call
the goddamn Coast Guard so I can tell her something."

The phone rang again. Fujikawa grabbed it and spat out, "Tell that fat
fuck she'll be out in a few... oh." A pause. "Sorry, Captain. No, ma'am. I
wasn't referring to... yes, ma'am." He handed the phone over. "It's Walter."

"Captain." Randolph listened, straightening his shoulders, his
thoughts on the woman who had buried her face in her arms, the back
of her neck vulnerable, vertebra pressing against pale olive skin, rich
chestnut hair plumed over the table. The paunchy sergeant nodded,
scratched his crotch, and hung up, wondering how this could ever be
kept from the widow.

"We got a motive. The chief got a call from someone who knows—not anonymous—who said Austen was a bad guy back in the day and he'd been running for years from the boys he'd burned. Long memories. Said the wife's clean."

"Bingo. Who's the source?"

"We're out of that loop. His ancient history can't be proved and the chief doesn't want any libel grief from these fucking New York lawyers. So that stays with us, you read me? We just let her go. What do you think?"

"I think we test her now. If she's clean, she's clean. Come on, it's our last chance."

"Ok. We can do her, but quick and gentle."

CHAPTER 46

AN OLD STORY

MANY OF THE HALEKULANI'S GUESTS—ESPECIALLY those for whom the romance of gritty beach sand had faded with the years—preferred the tiled pool with its blue orchid bottom to the Pacific's uncertainties. A ball toss from the beach, the pool was warm and free of jagged coral and jostling waves. Only a handful of guests were out for the early sun, yet the pool's best chaise lounges were already staked out, towels, magazines, and sunblock claiming the coveted spots. A silvery dowager, head high to protect her makeup, was swimming a stately breast stroke, a V-shaped wake behind her. A green-shirted gardener watered pots of bougainvillea while his partner gathered palm fronds that had fallen during the previous night's rain.

The outdoor bar with its island motif was deserted, a lone couple sipping coffee at one table. That the woman was beautiful and the man handsome could be seen in a glance; that she was grieving and he anxious required merely a second look. Mourning became Margaret Austen, her eyes large and sad on a thinned face, possessing an almost religious beauty, her cheekbones prominent. Dressed in white linen, Parson Shoer might have stepped from a Caribbean plantation. Despite his languorous pose, his eyes darted from side to side. He was tinkering with Austen's script, writing himself a larger role, knowing his friend could never tell his story as well as he. Austen would be too hard on himself, as he had been in San Francisco, reporting the flat facts without the leavening of circumstance and need. Parson imagined himself in a final argument to save Austen's life, moving a jury to tears as he detailed the terrible forces that brought his best friend to his knees, that forced him to crime.

"Was he really a criminal?" Margaret asked, breaking their silence.

"I'm thinking of naming my new restaurant after him. *Scout's*. What do you think?"

"Parse, please."

"Do you mind if I smoke? This tropical air is ruining my lungs." He lit his cigar and inhaled for its calming effect. "I would have done the same thing."

"What?" She was neither hurt nor surprised that the detectives considered the killing a deliberate act, a murder which must have been provoked. Yet their clumsy attempt to downplay theories about Austen's criminality had rocked her, recalling her father's words about how little she knew about her husband. "What did you say?"

Laughing, Parson patted her hand and drew on his cigar. "You're done talking to the police? They're happy with the polygraph?"

"They'd better be." A questioning look piercing through her grief.

"But they said they're finished with you?"

"Why are you asking me this?" asked Margaret.

"I want to tell you a story about Aus, true story, you already know a lot of it. How would he put it? Here it is." And with that he began the story of his friend's life, a story with the familiar peal of a village church bell. Parson expanded upon the idyllic boyhood that ended with a father's death in Vietnam: the straight A student, the Eagle Scout, the paper route, the dream of a naval career through Annapolis. He barely touched upon his abandonment by his mother.

"Was his name really Austen?" she asked, pleased that she knew more about Austen's mother than Parson. "He once told me his father's parents were Polish."

"It was Edward Kawadsky. Anyway, after his mother disappeared, he fell in with that guy who showed up at your townhouse. Cross. He was a couple years older and a total loser, a penny-ante drug dealer with a big habit. But Aus was a smart kid, and he shook him off after a few months. Despite being penniless and on his own, your boy got his shit together, got a job at a fat farm… I ought to check in, don't you think—"

"A fat farm?" She laughed. Her long fingers rested atop his hand. Enjoying his words, thinking they brought her closer to her poor husband, she hoped Parson would not tire of his plodding pace. He came to the first of the two turning points in Austen's life, slowing down, embellishing it. He knew the unadorned facts: Austen had smuggled drugs and killed two dirty cops in a shoot-out. Yet without rehearsal, almost without thought, Parson marshaled the evidence in the light most favorable to his friend. Rather than dwell on his actions—as Austen had at Trader Vic's—he emphasized the boy's loneliness, his innocence. He mixed in Cross's sophistication, his lie about bringing over only a few pounds of marijuana, Austen's shock over the cocaine. Then, teacher to pupil, he stressed the zeitgeist: the sixties considered coke harmless, almost benign.

"So, he smuggled some drugs? Just once? That's not so bad," Margaret said, sipping water, glancing about the quiet bar. She spied a pair of courting zebra doves and found herself distracted by the cock's chivalry.

"There's more," Parson said, taking her hand. With great care, choosing his words as if testing tomatoes at a market, he related the shootout, assuring her it was the textbook definition of self-defense and Austen's flight his only chance at survival.

"He killed two policemen?" she cried, gasping, unable to imagine such a scene. She drew back from Parson, hugged her sides tight, shook her head. "No, no, no. That can't be."

"It's true. Scout's never lied to either of us. He kept a hell of a lot back, but the man was honest." Parson puffed on his cigar, knowing he had to stop inhaling, but desperate for its calm.

"I need a moment. Please excuse me," Margaret said, rising. Feeling faint, she steadied herself with her hands on the table for a moment. "I'll be right back." She left the bar and, with a direction from the gardener, found the restroom adjacent to the orchid pool. She wetted a paper towel and pressed it against her forehead. Parson was right: Austen's lies were those of omission. She knew her husband—he wouldn't have killed for money. She took the long way back to the bar.

The persistent dove was still strutting when she returned. Sitting, Margaret said, "So, years later Cross finds Aus, tries to blackmail him over killing the police, and when that didn't work…." Tears once again overwhelmed her. "Have you told the detectives about him?"

"Wait, please. There's more." Gently, Parson raised his hand like a crosswalk guard, pondering how to sell the more difficult chapter of Austen's criminal career. He knew rage at a life stolen would not play like a gun in the ribs. Yet he was positive she would understand and forgive. He arrived at the point in Austen's life where his frustration had boiled over, where his missing history had pinned him down, where his hidden cocaine's allure proved irresistible.

"Stop," she said, surprising herself as much as Parson with her vehemence. Something was wrong—no one ever spoke poorly of the dead, especially not the best friend to his grieving widow. "Why are you telling me this? Why? You wouldn't be telling me this if, you wouldn't sully his memory if… oh, Parson. Is he alive? Do you know something? Tell me, please, for God's sakes, tell me."

"He's OK." Parson sighed, reluctantly dropping his script.

"Oh my God." She leaped up, hugged his neck, burying her wet face against his shoulder, then looking him in the eyes. "You're serious?"

"Yes. Please, not so tight, got to breathe."

"He's all right? He's truly safe?" She absorbed his somber nod, cried for joy, released him, ran a hand through her wild hair, pushing it away from her face. "Tell me, tell me everything, please. Tell me now.

Do you want some breakfast? I'm famished. I need to go to him, now. Where is he?"

Parson exhaled, regretting his lost speech, thinking he had failed his best friend. "I let him down, you down, that wasn't the way to tell you. You have to understand what drove him to it, that he had to erase his entire life for fear of discovery. Hell, he was a champion swimmer who had to pretend he couldn't swim. Shit, I blew it." Sucking on his cigar, he recalled how wonderful the first drink of the day tasted.

"Where is he? Is he still here in Hawaii?"

"That's it, that's all he's done bad, nothing else," he said, avoiding her question, keeping his promise to Austen about his whereabouts. "And he's given ten times that much to charity already, but the damn fool says he can't live with any of the money. Thinks it's tainted. He was giving it away before Cross ever showed up—that trust agreement is years old. All that creep did was speed him up, force him to disappear."

"Disappear," she repeated in alarm. "He's safe? You're sure? I need to see him right now. You swear he's OK? Does he still love me?" When she caught her breath, she noticed Parson's distress. "Wait, you're not all right." She hugged him again, avoiding his cigar. "Was poor Aus afraid I wouldn't love him if I found out?"

She changed her breakfast order from toast to fried eggs, Canadian bacon and hash browns. Long before it arrived, it would occur to a calmer Margaret that Austen had allowed her to suffer. He had sentenced her to a widow's anguish because he couldn't trust her.

CHAPTER 47

ACT II

THE SLEEPY FOG HAD SLINKED away from Marin's hills and Larkspur, a small town posing as a village, warmed into summer. Margaret stood under a faded blue canvas awning and peered across its main street into a coffee bar. She'd promised Parson to wait two weeks before flying to California, understanding her phones might be tapped, that bored detectives might find any sudden travel arrangements of interest. She'd used the wretched weeks to plan Austen's memorial service, ceaselessly thinking of her husband, replaying Parson's words, pondering drug trafficking, contemplating Austen's penance, in darker moments questioning whether his lack of trust was her fault, yet damning him to hell for grieving her so.

The coffee shop's windows were filmy, obscured by scraggly philodendrons, Boston ferns, and faded flyers announcing local happenings. Late-morning readers awash in a slew of newspapers sat at small tables near the storefront. A middle-aged couple lounged, ignoring one another, the bored husband intent on everyone else. An athletic-looking woman sipped a juice while reading a novel and, farther inside, a tall man awaited his coffee, his military posture at odds with the unemployed ambience.

Margaret hurried across the street and opened the door, hoping to be well inside before Austen saw her.

"Oh," she cried upon seeing him.

His hand flew to his three-week stubble. His wire-rim glasses were gone, replaced by sunglasses and a Giants baseball cap, his greying curls spilling out from underneath. Rather than his appearance, it was his expression—a hangdog she'd never seen before—that shocked her. Was he truly guilty? Was he a criminal on the run? Did he even want her back in his life? "I can't do this." Cursing the impetuosity that had propelled her from New York, she spun and walked away, tears blurring her vision.

Austen sprinted after his wife. "Margaret, wait. Please stop."

"I will not. How could you? Don't touch me. No. And take off that ridiculous hat, you look like a truck driver. Let me see your eyes."

"Oh, love, I've missed you. Are you really here? Did Parse tell you everything? Can you still, I mean, do you care—can you forgive me?"

"How could you let me suffer so?" She lanced his shoulder with a forefinger. "I can't believe you did this to me. You don't know how terrible it was, mourning your death, those greasy police thinking I killed you, everyone coming at me from all sides, my father gloating."

"I'm so sorry, I… I thought you'd never be able to pull it off if you knew the truth. I'm so, so sorry—but I couldn't think of any other way. If that idiot Cross thought I was alive, if he didn't think the Colombians were after him, I'd end up on trial for murder. I had to disappear. I'm so sorry. Did Parson really tell you what I did?"

"You should have trusted me."

"I was afraid." His deep voice high, his teeth raking the whiskers beneath his lip, his blue eyes pained. "Margaret, I was afraid. You're too good for someone who did what I did."

"You lied to me instead? Is that somehow better?"

"I did it because I wanted you so badly, because I need you, I love you." He grabbed her, pulled her into his arms and kissed her hard. She drew her elbows to her side, shutting down. He held her closer, raining kisses on her cheeks, ears and throat and then her struggling faded as the tension ebbed. "I love you, I adore you, Margaret. Did he really tell you everything? About the, you know?"

"I could have kept the secret, I—"

"But you would never have passed the lie detector test. You would have been a suspect for years. I'm sorry. I'm sorry for everything. I should have told you when we first met about selling the stuff, I tried, but I couldn't. Do you hate me now?"

"Let me go."

"I can't. Please tell me. Do you know everything?" He nuzzled her throat with his nose.

"Parson told me about the corrupt cops and the cocaine. I don't know whether I've forgiven you or I'm here to avenge the hell you put me through." She pushed him back, gripping his shoulders at arms' length, staring hard into his worn, frightened face, seeing his only fear was losing her. Then she kissed him, her mouth open and warm. She felt his hand near her breast, his body pressed against hers, his arousal. She glanced around the sidewalk, certain everyone was gawking at them, amused by her husband's state. "Does everyone do this in California?"

He stepped back but then kissed her again. "Did he explain about the money? Why I have to give it away?"

"Yes, yes he told me everything, you big jerk. That's why I'm here. I would have been here sooner, but Parson made me promise to wait." She was murmuring into his ear, kissing it between sentences. Then her fury over his deception reared again; she shimmied loose and punched his shoulder. "You trusted Parson and not me."

"Please don't go back. Please stay." He stared across the street at the tired movie theater, as if its cracked marquee bannered the words to keep her.

"If you understood me, if you truly loved me, you would have told me everything long ago. I could have refused to take their stupid tests."

"You know about the drugs?"

"Yes. That you should have told me on our first date. I might have thought you were a little more exciting. Let's face it, you're a pretty boring guy." She giggled, softening her playful indictment.

He leaned forward to kiss her, but she twisted away. He scratched his beard. "Did Parse explain how you could goose the charities for tens of millions if you forgot about me? Just by threatening them with a protracted will contest. They'd fold overnight."

"Why couldn't I get the money and then run away with you?" She lowered her head coquettishly, glancing at him, a wily smile.

Thrilled by her question, he tried to look stern, thoughtful. "There isn't anything I wouldn't do for you, but I can't have that money. I'm sorry. I need to be broke—I am broke, Parse loaned me a little to get by—I have to start over."

She shook her head, pitying him, wondering why it was that honor so often demanded imprudence. On impulse, she kissed him hard, darting her tongue inside his mouth. She broke away from his embrace and pointed at her rented convertible. "I want to be alone with you. May I assume you have a—what do they call it? —a safe house?"

"I'm sorry," said Austen. Instead of returning to his room, a converted garage behind an apartment building Parson owned, they'd driven to the Casa Madrona, a Sausalito hotel favored by honeymooners and trysters. A stewardess on the flight west had gushed about the place to Margaret, describing it as "totally romantic."

"I'm not." She slid off him, brushing his hard chest. "You're in enough trouble as it is. Damn lucky you were too fast. If you had a girlfriend on top of everything else? Pow." She examined her husband with a measure of approval, thinking he looked better, less pinched, and, with his lengthening curls, almost Byronic.

He cupped her breasts, his hands gentle against her supple skin. She lay her head against his shoulder, closed her eyes, and relaxed, knowing his penchant for silences. She gave his groin a playful tug. "Besides, if Aussie's truly been a good boy, this should be like Broadway, where one barely has time for a drink before the second act."

CHAPTER 48

MOURNING

THE PRAWNS BLANKETING THE BUFFET'S centerpiece had vanished, leaving a mountain of ice flecked with parsley and two empty pewter sauce bowls. The sushi and chicken skewers had been leveled; nothing remained of the caviar potatoes, smoked salmon, or pastry puffs. The petit-fours were long gone. White-jacketed bartenders attended the midday drinkers, diluting their private sorrows, shuttling empty champagne and chardonnay bottles to the kitchen. A brace of smokers sat outside on the limestone benches in the light-shaft patio. Other mourners floated throughout the first two floors, gathering in clusters, a few making efforts to appear downcast, others appraising their surroundings or their competition. One couple roamed throughout the townhouse with the zeal of estate auctioneers.

Of the gathering, a number had actually met Austen. A handful were friends. Margaret's family, the Cutters, the Shoers, curious neighbors, his employees, and business acquaintances had all come. Bone-certain he was alive, MJ Watershed had refused to attend the memorial service. The sleek executive directors and development officers—the fundraisers—of Austen's charities were present in force.

Earlier at Saint Patrick's, the archbishop had spoken for twenty minutes, neither more nor less, about a man he knew not at all, flogging the assembly with Austen's generosity, praising his unsung good deeds. At the reception, the archbishop consoled the widow for ten minutes, took a personal moment with each of the DAP foundation's other directors, nodded to his well-wishers, smiling at a few, and allowed Monsignor Rogers to hustle him to his waiting car.

Downs lingered in the corner of the paneled library, framed by book-shelves on one side and a French window on the other. Tanned and rested, his black double-breasted suit the picture of subdued elegance, he was determined to turn Austen's demise to his advantage. While the charitable trust was as clear as Manhattan's costliest lawyers could draft it, the circumstances surrounding Austen's death were not. Absent a body, it would be five years before the state of New York would declare him legally dead, and if his widow chose to fight, those years might stretch into decades. In the meantime, the money was hers. Only upon his official death could the foundation distribute his vast fortune to his charities. Downs would claim he was the only one who, for a prodigious consulting fee, could deliver Margaret. He alone could convince her to let the hundreds of millions flow to the charities. His plan faced just one high hurdle: He was trying to sell what she was giving away.

Speaking in hushed tones to the nonprofit's directors, Downs described his daughter's fierce, almost deranged love for her late husband, painting an obsessed woman, a woman who would conduct a search for him—a very expensive, estate-draining search—for as long as they could imagine. "Damned shame she has my bulldog tenacity. Please, excuse me for a moment, my wife—she's really quite overcome, loved him like a son—needs me. I'll be right back."

"It's Sproul. I told you he would come." Connie Downs' words hissed through a cloud of cigarette smoke.

"Damn." Downs patted his hair into place as if adjusting a helmet of war. He'd hoped Sproul would possess the decency to let him mourn in peace, but had posted Connie as a lookout.

"Jeff, there you are," said Downs heartily. "We kept missing one another—damned phones—but you got my messages. We're so pleased you could come. You're looking well."

"Messages? I'm the one who left messages, dozens of them. And you—"

"Yes, I know. I look terrible, but what with the arrangements, caring for Margaret, the details, the sadness, I'm overcome. Let's go downstairs, outside, the fresh air might revive me." He clasped Sproul's arm, marching him out. "I know you wouldn't dream of talking business at my boy's funeral, but what with our hectic schedules, this might not be a bad time to bring you up to date. I'm sure poor Dick wouldn't mind."

A mourner might have supposed Sproul Austen's closest friend, as crestfallen and sunken as he appeared. Sproul had lost so much weight his collar gapped, a faint greenish tinge beneath his eyes.

"Brisk, isn't it?" Downs said. "I love the early fall. Now, tell me, Jeff, how is everything at Wellbourne Masterson?" Downs steered him past the clutch of limo drivers smoking outside the front door.

"Goddamn it, Gam, you know how it is. You heard my messages. We've lost money the last two quarters, our new chairman wants to clean house, and the damned auditors are demanding to know the status of the loan I made to my *relative*."

"Jeff, please. That's no insult. After all, Hillary and Darcy are sisters—"

"My whole company knows that. What did you tell my disbursements people? That I was your goddamn nephew? Is that how you got them to release those bullshit draws?" Sensing his loss of control, Sproul paused, breathed deep, and began again, his voice rising with each question. "What happened with the equipment for the line? Is it installed? Is it working? Have you ramped up your production yet?"

Downs grimaced as if the memorial had been for his Greek company. "Yes, it's installed, most of it at any rate—wily Greeks—but please recall we thought it prudent to buy that used plant from Minnesota. I mentioned it to you—save on capital equipment costs, have more cash left over to handle shortfalls. You must remember."

"No. No, no, no. You never told me you were buying junk." Because his career depended on it, Sproul had hoped beyond reason that Downs would tell a different story than the one conveyed by weeks of ducked calls and unanswered letters.

"It's not *junk*, but it has yet to meet our expectations—problems with the line. It's a boring, technical conversation that frankly I'd rather not have at my boy's funeral."

"Where'd all the goddamn money go? That rusted-out crap you bought cost nothing." He was shouting, venting his boiling anger. "Where's the goddamn money?"

"Compose yourself. Those chaps can hear you."

"I don't care who hears me, you fucking fraud. Where's the money? Is this what you spent it on?" he demanded, grabbing the lapel of Down's vicuna jacket. "Did you buy a goddamn jet?"

"Let's end this conversation before you say something you might regret. Listen, I'll have my people call yours and come over tomorrow with all the back-up documentation. I can assure you we will account for every dime the company borrowed."

"I'm going to find every dime you spent, you lying sack of shit. I'm going to nail your ass—"

"That's enough. Good day." Straightening himself, Downs turned and walked away, past the highly amused, hooting drivers, toward the townhouse's glistening black doors.

"That's not enough," shouted Sproul, following him. "If I go down, you're hitting bottom, you miserable bastard. Even if I have to spend the rest of my life enforcing your personal guaranty against you." Sproul's face purple, his fists clenched, his words a blood oath.

Inured to financial threats, Downs about-faced, appraised his tormentor. Sighing with a world-weary panache, he said, "Your credit officer can readily confirm that Harold Downs has already twice endured personal bankruptcy. The second time hurt less than the first. Going after me personally would net you nothing other than more ridicule for throwing good money after bad. Now, if you will excuse me, I really must get back to my guests."

Quicker than thought, Sproul's fist smashed into Downs's face, catching the wine-red nose. His second punch, a left to the jaw, knocked the stunned man to the pavement—and then it was over, Down's blood running across his cheek, the younger man standing over him, shaking with rage, the two men cursing and damning each other to a lifetime in court, to punitive damages that would break a god. And then, with a wicked cunning look, Downs fluttered a hand toward the drivers, and—his eyes closing—went limp.

MARGARET'S ADMIRERS THOUGHT HER COMPOSED and brave, a gracious hostess despite her pain, while those few who disliked her quipped about her grief starting at the reading of the will. Neither eating nor drinking, she spent a few minutes with everyone, thanking them for coming, for honoring Austen's memory. Few would have described her enchanting smile as enigmatic.

"Billy, hug me please. Your shoulders really are enormous. Please cheer up, dear. Aus would want you to be happy." Aching to turn his grief into joy, to let him in on the secret, she settled for trying to comfort him.

Billy clung to her neck, fighting back tears, indifferent for once to breasts against his chest. He was angry at the world for letting Austen die, angry at the empty words he'd heard in church, angry at the milling insincere faces that appeared to be attending a class reunion rather than a wake. "I'm OK."

"You have to do better than that. You're in charge, you always wanted that—"

"Huh?" Then he recalled Austen's parting advice. "Never like this."

"No, of course not. You're a good man. Smile please, Billy, fool me, let me believe I've cheered you just a little."

"OK," he said, grinning at the woman he had begun to admire on their terrible trip to Hawaii. He'd held her hand during her agony in Honolulu, saw what she'd endured with the police. He had no doubts now about her love for Austen.

"I'm going away," she said at length, her tone elegiac.

"What?" A fresh hurt broke across his heavy face. He cracked his knuckles and apologized in the same instant.

"I'm sorry, but I'm leaving New York. My grandmother in Buenos Aires is very old, she's a wonderful woman, not at all like—" she stopped herself, waving a dismissive hand. "Anyway, Abuela's been pleading with me to visit for years. Besides, you don't want me hanging about DAP's offices telling you how to write leases or build buildings."

He had to nod, then lowered his great bristling head to his chest.

"But be warned, I may suddenly develop an interest in what you're doing with the foundation's money. I may start poring over the monthly reports and come up with all kinds of clever suggestions."

"Your grandmother have a fax machine at her villa?"

Her laugh drew the attention of a group swilling champagne nearby. "We better go downstairs before I thoroughly disgrace myself." Margaret lowered her voice. "There's no villa. My abuela is as poor as a church mouse."

He led her downstairs, toward a couple sitting on the stair above the first-floor landing. Seeking to impress one another, their meager efforts at keeping their conversation hushed were thwarted by the acoustics of the spiraling staircase.

"You must have heard he was a big-time crimin—"

"*Excuse* us," Billy snapped, glancing back to judge Margaret's reaction. The couple slid away from the wrought-iron banister and allowed them to pass.

They stepped into the dining room and saw Parson outside, smoking by himself in a sunny corner of the patio. "I'll be back," Billy said.

He stormed to the stairs. "You. Both of you."

"What? Is something wrong?" The man's surprise shifting to fear.

Billy leapt onto the third step and yanked the shocked man to his feet. Had he released his grip, the man would have fallen onto the harlequin marble floor below. "Get the fuck out before I break your goddamn neck. You, too, bitch. Get out. Richard Austen was a great man. A hero." The pair rushed out and he slammed the door behind them, smashing his fist into his palm. He brought it to his mouth, biting down hard on his knuckle. Tears streamed his cheeks as he sank onto the bottom step of the staircase, sobbing against the ornate molding, rubbing his eyes with his jacket sleeve.

Alone on the patio, Margaret and Parson were nevertheless murmuring, fearful of eavesdroppers. "I am calling the Marin joint *Scout's,* you know that." He twirled his Cubano in his fingers.

"Billy's so sad," she said, preoccupied, half-hearing Parson. "I have to let Billy know soon, he's so sad. He missed my hint just now."

"You hint to Billy with a club, a big one. He'll be fine, running the business, hell, he'll probably move into Aus's office on Monday. You at least going to come back for the directors' meetings?"

"Please don't sound like that. It's not that far and it's certainly not forever. My grandmother's ancient."

Parson shook his head. "Vancouver. Now, there's a city. Gorgeous. Way prettier than San Francisco, the mountains running right down to the water, opportunity everywhere with all that Asian money pouring in. That's where a white boy should start over. I could open a Parsonage there, it's only a two-hour flight. You two could manage it."

"Would you mind terribly if I asked a big favor? I'm afraid it's going to be so hard for Aus down there, not knowing the language, living in a small apartment—if only you could have convinced him to take a little of the money. Would you please visit soon? In a few months, when it's really getting to him? You're so important to him."

"Shit, woman." Delight shone through Parson's broad smile. "You really are something. I'll come, course I'll come." He puffed and then laughed aloud. "One thing I'd have to do first."

"Yes?"

"Tell Claire, too. She's an understanding woman, but she'd understand way too much if she thinks I'm flying to South America to spend a week with you."

"All right. A conspiracy's more fun than a secret anyway. As long as my damned father doesn't find out."

CHAPTER 49

LOST IN TRANSLATION

THE PLANE LINGERED ON THE icy tarmac while bundled mechanics tinkered with its silvery wing. The pilot had cut off the air conditioning to conserve fuel; the heat inside the crowded cabin was stifling. Margaret bunched her hair atop her head, hoping to cool her neck. She peered out the window and fanned herself with the American Airlines magazine. "Miss, could I trouble you for an orange juice? Any word on the delay?"

"It should just be a few more minutes, ma'am."

"Ma'am," she repeated to herself, pursing her lips. Her thoughts drifted to her parents, her last conversation with her father, his ugly certainty that his lawsuit for battery against Sproul and his firm would not only wipe away the ice cream loan but set him up forever. His genuine tears when she swore she would never speak to him again.

The air-conditioning whooshed on, whispering the hope of a departure. She took her husband's hand and studied him anew. His tanned, weathered face was framed, if not obscured, by his curling, wavy hair and salted beard. Were it not for reading glasses that at last had become a necessity rather than a disguise, he might have looked piratical. Observing him, thinking him handsome, she wondered what their children might look like. Seeing his pulse tick in the hollow of his wrist, she rejoiced at his Lazarus resurrection, that he was still with her.

"Is the Spanish troubling you?" She rubbed his brow.

"I just can't believe we're really going. That you'd give it all up to go with me."

· "All what? A job I hated, my terrible parents, and a heartless city?" She kissed his ear.

"Are you serious about this bookstore idea?" He asked, pointing to her how-to-run-a-business primer.

"It's always been a dream, but I don't know. It's much cheaper down there, but my savings may not be enough to start a newsstand, let alone a bookstore."

"Yeah."

"Don't say it like that, we'll be fine. I could work as a translator or a law clerk at one of those fancy international law firms. Besides, as soon as you master Español, you can build your second empire."

"I think that game may be rigged in Buenos Aires. Besides, it's one thing being able to order a couple beers in Spanish, another to master both the language and the business practices. I'd be lucky to run a pizza parlor." He rolled the beard beneath his lip into his mouth, reached into his pocket for his talisman. He was puzzling over why his guilt felt more permanent than his Semper Fi tattoo, why that fleeting state of grace he once enjoyed after going to confession on Saturday evenings remained so elusive. Yet hoping—praying—he might recover his honor one brick at a time in the southern hemisphere's greatest city.

"Don't worry, Señor, I'll support us while you attend language school. Afterward, too. We can live simply, there won't be any pressure on you. Look at the thousands of immigrants who succeed in Manhattan real estate, can't be that different there. And, whatever else, my poor grandmother still knows everybody, she can introduce us to the right people."

"Do you really think she can help us?" He was worried about the old woman. Despite Margaret's assurances that her mother and grandmother had not spoken in twenty years, what would prevent Abuela from sending her daughter a happy postcard?

"I hope so. But Abuela always described a pumpkin as a coach and her overblown friends as royalty. When we would remind her of the facts, she'd wave us off, saying her stories were prettier than truth. She's worse now—you should read her letters, how excited she is, the extravagant reception she plans to hold for us. We have to stay with her at least a couple nights."

"We should treat her with respect." He turned toward his wife and studied her. "Until the doors shut, I thought this was impossible, you couldn't be here. If I close my eyes, you're still not here because I can't believe it. I don't deserve you."

Blushing, she put her arm around his shoulders, and pulled him to her. They ignored the flight attendant watching them from the jump seat. She whispered in his ear and held him tight. He grinned.

"This is the captain speaking. Folks, sorry for the delay, but we're next in line for takeoff. Once we get up to our cruising altitude, I'll fill you in on our flying time and the local weather down there."

"Are you going to call her from the airport?" asked Austen.

"Yes. This is so charming. She made me promise I would call the moment we land so her driver wouldn't be late. She's such a forceful old bird, I wouldn't be surprised if she actually cajoles her neighbor into meeting us in his broken-down pig truck."

"We're going right out to her cottage? You think it has a shower?"

"I'm not sure it even has running water. Must have a cistern," she said.

Austen scratched at his beard. "It must. Didn't you say it has a couple acres?"

"I think so, how many square feet in an acre?"

"43,560."

"Two times that is about 100,000, right?" Margaret asked.

"Close enough."

"And Abuela has diez mil hectáreas or square meters. And 10,000 square meters is about 100,000 square feet, so yes, a couple acres. Enough for a pony and a swing set."

"Is hectárea Spanish for meter?" Austen asked.

"No, for hectare, of course."

"Her cottage has 10,000 hectares?" Puzzled, he scratched his beard.

"Yes, hectares—you know square meters—three feet by three feet."

"You're joking. You know, a hectare isn't a square meter. It's 10,000 square meters." He did the arithmetic. "That would mean your grandmother's place would have something like 25,000 acres—almost 40 square miles. You're sure?"

"What?" Margaret gasped. Her Spanish was flawless, but, stunned, she remembered her linguistic blind spot: She could never translate foreign numbers, could neither make sense of centigrade nor convert kilometers into miles. Her jaw fell as she recalled her abuela's boasts over her estate, what her beloved Margarita alone stood to inherit. She had not misunderstood her grandmother, Abuela had crowed about her land holdings too often. "Diez mil hectáreas."

"You OK? You are kidding, aren't you?" Austen persisted.

Margaret shook her head like an astonished little girl, squeezed his hand, and then burst into a rich, lyrical laughter that could be heard rows back. The pilot throttled the engines, the plane shook off the frozen ground and climbed into the sky, making a broad turn toward the south.

THE END

ACKNOWLEDGMENTS

For their kindness, encouragement and unfailing support, I would like to thank my readers: Christine Delsol, Mary Taylor, Coleen Ramsdale, Kay Orloff, Michael Harmon, Emma Olson, Lane Goldszer, Deirdre Kidder, George Eckrich, Lily Sandberg, Paul Gordon, Leslie Howard, Ian Paget and George Yamas. Thank you, John Geoghan, for your pitch-perfect advice, Debbie Miller for your insightful and deft editing, Robert Hunt for your wonderful cover (I truly hope people judge *Scout's* by its cover), Mel Spiese for your invaluable aid on the Marine Corps chapters and my publishing team—Julie Trelstad, Alexandra Battey and Hannah Wood—for your invaluable aid.

Last, but most, I would like to thank my principal editor, Tom Parker—my taskmaster—for making me rewrite, rewrite and rewrite again. While I may not have grown to love rewriting, I certainly learned its necessity. Thank you again, Tom.